Dead Men Cast No Shadows

Dead Men Cast No Shadows

a novel by

Sergio Ramírez

The Managua Trilogy, Volume Three

Translated from the Spanish
by Daryl R. Hague

M̄

McPherson & Company
Kingston, New York

Published by McPherson & Company
Box 1126, Kingston, NY 12402
Book and cover design by Bruce R. McPherson
Typeset in Monotype Fournier
Printed on pH neutral paper
Manufactured in the United States of America
First edition
1 3 5 7 9 10 8 6 4 2   2023 2024 2025

LIBRARY OF CONGRESS CATALOGING-IN-PUBLICATION DATA

Names: Ramírez, Sergio, 1942- author. | Hague, Daryl R. (Daryl Robert),
1963- translator.
Title: Dead men cast no shadows / a novel by Sergio Ramírez ; translated
from the Spanish by Daryl R. Hague.
Other titles: Tongolele no sabía bailar. English
Description: First edition. | Kingston, New York : McPherson & Company,
[2023] | Series: The Managua trilogy ; volume three | First published in
Spanish as Tongolele no sabía bailar.
Identifiers: LCCN 2023024556 | ISBN 9781620540619 (trade paperback)
Subjects: LCGFT: Noir fiction. | Novels.
Classification: LCC PQ7519.2.R25 T6613 2023 | DDC
863/.64—dc23/eng/20230524
LC record available at https://lccn.loc.gov/2023024556

Author's note: This work of fiction takes into consideration the events in Nicaragua that began in April 2018, when a series of public protests led to brutal government repression. The characters, however, are strictly the author's creations. This book is my tribute to the hundreds of fallen young people and to their families as they continue seeking justice. — S.R.

Translator's acknowledgements: I am grateful for Brigham Young University's support in promoting marginalized countries' literatures and for providing the time I needed to complete this publication. I am also grateful for the help of four of my translation students, who read multiple chapters of the English draft and made helpful copyediting suggestions. In alphabetical order, those students include Brigitte Morales, Washington Pearce, Emily Royal, and Brianna Stroud. I am especially thankful to Sergio Ramírez for his patience as he helped me understand unique Nicaraguan terms and cultural norms even as he confronted living in exile from his beloved home country.—Daryl R. Hague

Grateful acknowledgement to *Review: Literature and Arts of the Americas* and its editor, Daniel Shapiro, for first publishing an earlier version of the opening chapter.

FOR SALVADOR VELÁSQUEZ (CHAVA) AND ESTHER,
FOR THE MEMORABLE GOOD DAYS IN BATON ROUGE

Dead Men Cast No Shadows

Chorus:
To the square, to the square, citizens
of Mycenae! Come and see the terrible
wonders granted to our blessed rulers!

Euripides, Electra

Dolores Morales

Inspector Dolores Morales (born 18 August 1959, Managua, Nicaragua) was a former guerrilla in the fight against dictator Anastasio Somoza Debayle, who was deposed by the triumphant revolution of the Sandinista National Liberation Front ("FSLN") in July 1979. Morales also served as a line officer for the Sandinista Police Force (later the National Police Force) from the time it was founded, and since being discharged, he has worked as a private investigator.

Biography

Morales was born in the Campo Bruce barrio on Managua's east side. His father, also named Dolores Morales, worked as a cabinetmaker, and he and Morales' mother, Concepción ("Conchita") Rayo, were divorced due to his father's incorrigible behavior. Morales' mother emigrated to Costa Rica to seek her fortune, where she was never heard from or seen again. Consequently, the boy—an only child—was raised by his maternal grandmother, Catalina Rayo, who owned a grocery stall in the Mercado San Miguel in the heart of old Managua, a section of the city destroyed in the earthquake of 22 December 1972.

Still a teenager at the time, Morales joined the ranks of the FSLN under the pseudonym "Artemio," and after fighting as an urban commando in the capital city, he joined one of the guerrilla columns along the Southern Front that was battling to advance toward the country's interior from the Costa Rican border. Morales' group was commanded by a priest, Gaspar García Laviana, a Spaniard from the province of Asturias and a member of the Priests of the Sacred Heart.

In December 1978, during one of the battles to take Hill 33—a battle in which Padre García Laviana himself fell mortally wounded—a round from a Galil rifle shattered the bones in Morales' knee. To avoid the threat of gangrene, his leg was amputated, and he was then sent to Cuba, where he was fitted with a prosthetic leg.

Following the creation of the Sandinista Police Force, Morales was assigned to the Drug Investigation Unit, where he achieved the rank of inspector, and he was working at the DIU when the FSLN fell out of power in the February 1990 election, an election won by opposition presidential candidate Violeta Chamorro (1990-1997).

Submerged in anonymity, Morales continued to work at the DIU even as the police force underwent profound changes, including the changing of the force's name to the National Police Force as it was stripped of all partisan character. Devoted to modest living, Morales continued to drive his battered Russian Lada.

Morales leaped into the spotlight in 1999 when, under the administration of Arnoldo Alemán, a member of Somoza's old Liberal Party, he headed an investigation that ended with the arrest of two drug capos, Wellington Abadía Rodríguez (alias El Mancebo or "the Kid") of the Cali cartel and Sealtiel Obligado Masías (alias El Arcangel or "the Archangel") of the Sinaloa cartel. The two capos were captured at a plantation located in the hillsides around Mombacho Volcano, near the city of Granada, where the respective criminal organizations had planned a coordination meeting, and both capos were placed in the custody of the DEA, which took them as prisoners to the United States.

Given the corruption prevailing in Nicaragua at the time, high government officials took issue with Morales' actions, and under the pretext that Morales acted without authorization, the Minister of Governance ordered his retirement from service with the complicity of the National Police Force's first commissioner, César Augusto Canda, which is how Morales' police service came to an abrupt halt.

After a period of inactivity during which Morales made his tendencies toward alcoholism quite obvious, and with Comandante Daniel Ortega's newest administration in power, Morales used his retirement funds—long delayed by the government—to open a private-detective agency. To that end he leased a space in the Guanacaste Shopping Center, located in the Bolonia barrio of west-side Managua, the space having previously belonged to a children's clothing store. Armed with a camera, Morales and his assistant dedicated their time to surveilling and photographing the trysts of stealthy couples, all at the behest of angry spouses.

Morales was wrested from the foregoing routine by an unexpected request from millionaire Miguel Soto Colmenares, who offered the detective a hefty fee to investigate the disappearance of his step-daughter, Marcela Soto Contreras. The investigation exposed Soto's sordid character as well as his links to the Ortega administration; indeed, the head of the government's secret security services, Commissioner Anastasio Prado, served as Soto's intermediary and defender. The commissioner, also known as "Tongolele," preferred anonymity and maintained a ubiquitous presence, acting as a masterful but silent connecting rod in the machinery of power.

Inspector Morales followed the missing young woman's trail among the meandering lanes of Managua's Mercado Oriental, guided by an old acquaintance, Serafín ("Seraphim") Manzanares, alias "Rambo," who had served under his command in the Southern Front. During the investigation, Morales went beyond the limits of his brief—limits designed to hide a secret that his client, Miguel Soto, sought to preserve at all costs. Consequently, Soto ordered a hunt for Morales to prevent him from meddling in the case; nevertheless, Morales chose to remain involved. At Soto's request, Tongolele commanded that Morales be captured and exiled to Honduras, along with Rambo, through the border post at Las Manos.

Romantic Relationships

In the Southern Front, Morales met a combatant in the Victoriano Lozano column, a young Panamanian woman named Eterna Viciosa ("Eternally Depraved"), also known as "Cándida," whom he married in a ceremony performed by Padre García Laviana. The marriage had no chance due to Morales' continual penchant for other women's beds, a weakness even more persistent than his weakness for liquor.

Morales' most enduring relationship has been with Fanny Toruño, a call-center customer-service provider for the Enitel telecommunications company. Fanny married a topographer who works for the Department of Highways; he abandoned her after she was diagnosed with cancer. She is both Morales' lover and collaborator, freely offering opinions about ongoing investigations and frequently turning out to be right about her conclusions.

Closest Associates

In the investigations that preceded the arrest of the drug capos from the Cali and Sinaloa cartels, Sub-Inspector Bert Dixon—"Lord Dixon"—played a principal role. Lord Dixon, a native of the city of Bluefields on the Caribbean coast and a former guerilla as well, died after a machine-gun attack in Managua's Domitila Lugo barrio, when hitmen from the aforementioned cartels riddled Morales' Lada with bullets as the two policemen were riding in the car. Morales escaped unharmed, but the two friends' close relationship made Morales' recovery from Lord Dixon's death extraordinarily difficult.

One of the most significant people in Morales' life is Doña Sofía Smith, who collaborated with the FSLN during the revolution as a courier and as the mother of a rebel soldier who was killed during Managua's eastside insur-rections in 1979. Doña Sofía later worked as a cleaning lady for the Drug Investigation Unit where, given her natural talent for criminal investigations, she became a de facto advisor. A dedicated FSLN militant during the revolu-tionary era, she nevertheless remained committed to her protestant faith as a member of the Church of The Living Waters, which is located in the barrio of El Edén, the same barrio in which Inspector Morales has his home.

Unavoidable Political Events

During the time in which Inspector Morales was establishing his private-investigator business, Nicaragua underwent several transcendent political changes as Comandante Daniel Ortega, who had led the government during the revolutionary decade of the eighties, returned to power in 2006 after making a pact with Arnoldo Alemán, his old adversary. Ortega retained the presidency through successive elections, the third of which occurred in 2016 and marked the time when his wife, Rosario Murillo—First Lady and chief executive of the government—was elected vice-president of the country. As the couple has consolidated its family power, a new class of capitalists, origi-nating either from within the FSLN or its periphery, has become consolidated as well.

In 2018, the country's youth led a civil uprising supported by large swathes of the citizenry, but the National Police and paramilitary groups loyal to Orte-ga and his wife brutally repressed these protests. That repression left a toll of more than 400 dead, hundreds of people injured, and thousands of exiles.

References

Part three of Inspector Morales' story begins on the Honduran side of
the border post at Las Manos, as the inspector, accompanied by Rambo,
prepares to make a secret return to Nicaragua after Doña Sofía informs him
that Fanny has suffered a relapse with her cancer...

(https://es.wikipedia.org/wiki/Dolores_Morales)

PART ONE

Observe these miserable women who abandoned needle,
shuttle, and spindle, and became soothsayers;
they used herbs and images to create witchery.

Inferno, Canto XX

CHAPTER ONE

The Golden Cat

INTERMITTENT WIND gusts blew through the feeble trunks of pine saplings clinging to the clear-cut slopes of Mount La Campana. Inspector Morales could practically time the intervals of icy blasts slashing his face: at least two minutes between each razor-like stroke. The two men had made their hideout at the foot of the mountain beside a crushed-stone pathway. In the false dawn Rambo squatted next to Inspector Morales between two large rocks covered by a skin of velvety moss. But this refuge offered no protection at all from the tumult lacerating their napes, ears, and cheeks. When night eventually returned the two exiles planned to skirt the mountain by crossing through a field of plantains, taking the route their guide, Gato de Oro, had explained would lead them to a flat road intersecting an abandoned pasture. At the end of that road lay Dipilto Verde, a town next to the paved highway that climbed from Ocotal to the border post of Las Manos, the very same highway the two fugitives had traveled the day before in handcuffs as deportees to Honduras. And up until now everything had proceeded according to plan . . .

The previous night Destiny had provided them with their guide while still at the Honduran crossing, where the pair had been chasing sleep while propped against tandem trailer tires in a truck stop parking lot. Hammocks slung beneath the trailers cradled sleeping drivers, but the fugitives' rest was interrupted by footsteps crunching the gravel and Gato de Oro crouching down in front of them as he waved a stack of lottery tickets in their faces.

He was a kind of crude giant, and in the light of the parking lot's lamps he appeared to glow as if he were bathed in gold dust, his blue eyes striated with red, restless and mocking under the brim of his sweat-stained felt hat, his hulking body settled in his military boots. He wore a flannel shirt with red and green checks, deep blue pants, and a thick leather belt.

"What a surprise to see this gentleman selling lottery tickets to sleeping people," said Rambo, a.k.a. Serafín.

"Luck has no schedule, date, or calendar. Buy five tickets from me, because half of ten is lucky."

"Have you ever sold the grand prize?" asked Inspector Morales.

"I've been keeping them for you, so that you can see how much I respect you."

"And how did you come to look like some saint from the church?" asked Inspector Morales, looking him up and down closely.

"All of us here in Las Segovias look like this, because we're descended from the same priest that came here from Pomerania and settled in Dipilto."

"One lone priest poking his sword left and right," said Rambo.

"Better to say that he was dispensing holy water with the same sprinkler. That's probably why the bishop who made an apostolic trip from León on a mule's back ordered the people to separate themselves from each other and abandon sin."

"What sin?" Inspector Morales asked, continuing to study the man.

"Incest. Men and women together, all from the same blessed family tree. A single red-hot ancestry."

"That saintly priest must have ended up as nothing but skin and bones after such a big fiesta," said Rambo.

"It was a sad thing to see him as no more than a skeleton, completely exhausted and unable to breathe. The same bishop who ordered everyone to leave and follow their own path administered the priest his last rites."

"Serafín, if you let him keep talking, he'll soon tell you that his great-great-grandmother was a cloistered nun and that the Pomeranian priest corrupted her."

"She was an Ursuline nun who suffered from an incurable case of nymphomania, and she was probably his own daughter, or maybe his sister," the giant said, sitting down between the two men and protecting the lottery tickets under his flannel shirt.

"I have never seen anyone so inconsiderate about what comes out of his mouth, *Jefe*. He can't even forgive his own great-great-grandmother," said Serafín.

"My name is Genaro Ortez y Ortez, but people have given me a ridiculous nickname: Gato de Oro, your servant and friend. And I'm at your command to return you to Nicaragua safe and sound."

"And how do you know that we want to go back to Nicaragua?" Inspector Morales asked.

"I've been watching you since they took off your handcuffs at the border and pushed you to this side," answered Gato de Oro. "So, I thought to myself: *Genaro, if they've been sent here and they haven't made any effort to make their way to Tegucigalpa, it's because they don't accept the situation and want to go back.*"

"The lottery-ticket seller who defames his great-great-grandmother becomes a coyote after offering the grand prize to a couple of outcasts," said Rambo.

"But that's why you're here, Genaro," said Gato de Oro, gesturing as if he were addressing himself in the mirror. "Without you, these two dusky swallows will not return to hang their nests under the eaves."

"And to make things worse, *Jefe*, he knows the poem about swallows after a single summer with our poet, Rubén Darío."

"How much do your services cost?"

"Only 5000 measly pesos, with the bonus of my warm company. I'll leave you safe and sound on any stretch of the Ocotal highway you choose. I accept dollars, córdobas, or lempiras."

"Now the Angora cat exposes his claws," said Rambo, and he moved as if he were taking a swipe.

"It's a pity that we can't enjoy your warm company," Inspector Morales sighed. "But even if they stood us on our heads, not a single coin would fall out of our pockets."

"What about something of value? A watch? A fine gold necklace? A man's gold wristband?"

As if removing a luxury cigarette box from the back pocket of his pants, Inspector Morales extracted the Samsung Galaxy that Fanny had given him.

"Is this enough?"

Gato de Oro delicately took the phone and raised it before his eyes so that the light from the streetlamp high atop the post could reach it.

"Well, it's a bit used and all, but I'll get something out of it," he said, and he put it in his shirt pocket.

"I'll give it to you when we go our separate ways," said Inspector Morales, extending his hand to take the phone back. "I'm not going to remain incommunicado until then. And the SD card isn't part of the deal. I'll take it out when we say good-bye."

Gato de Oro hesitated a moment, but then returned the phone.

"Deal. Now allow me to ask a question: What did you do to have such a large escort bring you here, handcuffed and all?"

"Ah, that's a long story, and I'm not going to tell you," said Inspector Morales, adopting a bored expression.

"The truth is that my friend here, even crippled as you can see, and somewhat pot-bellied as you can see as well, managed to make his way into the bed of a woman married to a police commissioner, some very important prick. And since I was his accomplice in the whole unexpected affair, they punished me too."

"You show a lack of respect when you say all those negative things about me, Serafín."

"On the contrary, I'm giving you high praise. Even with all those things working against you, no one is better at getting into other people's beds."

"My honorable friend with the cane can be anything, except a man who jumps from bed to bed," laughed Gato de Oro. "He has a cautious look about him."

"You're not wrong. By simply taking off his underwear and shaking it, he can leave all the women pregnant within a kilometer around."

"That's what happened with our grandfather priest. That's why the bishop prohibited him from wearing underwear."

"For all I know, you and my *jefe* may well be related. It wouldn't be surprising if he himself was a descendant of that same priestly stud," said Serafín.

"Since you two don't want to tell me the truth, it's better that you get your asses off the ground. It's time to start walking."

"Right now? But it's dead midnight," complained Serafín.

"So, what are you waiting for? Do you want the *migra* clowns to grab us in the middle of the day? We're not just taking a little stroll here. And particularly with this limping ladies' man, we'll take twice as long to make it."

"Now you see, Serafín, what your disrespect gets me."

"Where do you want me to leave you?" asked Gato de Oro.

"Any place on the highway where we can catch a ride back to Managua," Inspector Morales shrugged.

"Dipilto Viejo, then. I have a brother-in-law there, Leonel Medina. He owns an Uno gas station and a mini-bus called El Gorrión, which takes the route to Ocotal."

"Maybe your brother-in-law will be more charitable than you and not charge us for the trip," said Rambo.

"Or take my cane as payment," Inspector Morales proposed.

"Walk behind me, one after the other, and act like you're looking for somewhere to take a piss."

They passed by a shed filled with goods for a duty-free store. A watchman, armed with a shotgun and protected from the condensation by a jumbled towel stuffed under his hat, kept a close eye on them.

They left a group of outhouses behind and reached a barbed-wire fence. Among the still-wet blouses and pants hanging there, they saw a pair of maroon panties with the English words NO MEANS NO written on the front in coquettish script.

Gato de Oro lifted the wire strands and passed beneath them, and the other two men did the same.

"You're in home territory now," Gato de Oro sighed. "But don't start singing the sacred notes of the national anthem because the *migras* at the command post will hear you."

Always leading the way, he constantly carried a battery-operated lantern, turning it on from time to time so that he could orient himself and follow the route through a patch of old Arabica coffee bushes that had just begun to bear their first fruits.

After half an hour, the three men arrived at the open macadam path between the slopes. The path ran parallel to the paved highway, which lay only slightly more than a kilometer to the west.

As instructed by Gato de Oro, they walked along the path's edge. They also avoided detection by hiding in the bushes whenever the headlights of passing vehicles might appear, for Gato de Oro had warned that motorized patrols regularly searched such places. The hike covered at least eight kilometers, and Inspector Morales' disability did in fact make the journey difficult: from time to time, either the tip of his cane became stuck in the mud beneath the beds of rotting leaves or his foot tripped against hidden tree roots. Consequently, Rambo had to support him by the elbow.

SERGIO RAMÍREZ

Leading the way, Gato de Oro entertained himself by using a very low voice as he obsessively sang the same traditional nonsense verse over and over again:

Al otro lado del hombre   *Away on the rider's far shore*
estaba un río parado   *Stock still stood a river full sore*
dándole agua a su capote   *His poncho lapped up what it could*
embozado en su caballo...   *While his pinto wrapped up what it should.*

Sometime before dawn they had arrived at the foot of Mount La Campana. On the other side of the path stood the hill of San Roque, where a settlement's scattered homes hugged the slope.

Between two rocks, each about the size of a man, the fugitives saw the cavity where they would wait until night fell again.

"If you have to take a piss, you can do so all you want without leaving this crack. And the same goes if you have to take a shit. You can do that right here. The smell of shit never killed anybody," Gato de Oro lectured.

When the sun came up they would have to be more careful. No one should even hear them breathe while they waited patiently for the night. If they were caught they'd be dead, because the *migras* had a hut on San Roque, and the night watchman had binoculars, and he had a radio to alert the motorized patrols about any unusual activity. The hut was located where the red light of an antenna was blinking.

"And what about you?" asked Rambo.

They could see Gato de Oro laughing once again in the shadow, as the darkness was already becoming lighter.

"Everybody in these parts knows me very well. So, I'll just go calm as you please to eat breakfast at Las Culecas, owned by the Culeca sisters, of course, a little eatery right here in the village."

"As for me, I'd love a few fertilized eggs, some refried beans, some soft white cheese, and a tortilla from a skillet," Rambo said, smacking his lips.

"I'd like my beans with cream, with the tortilla well toasted," said Inspector Morales, imitating Rambo.

"I'd be happy to bring you some food, but you can't make a web without a spider," sighed Gato de Oro. "Your phone won't give me enough money for all that food."

"So you're going to spend the rest of the day at this Culeca place?" asked Rambo.

"After breakfast I'll go to Dipilto Viejo, have lunch, take a nap, and be back here at seven on the dot for you two."

Gato de Oro was crossing the path when he suddenly turned and came back as if he had forgotten something important.

"Have you heard about the woman who was studying English? Her teacher was doing conversation exercises with her and said: 'Let's learn the U.S. national anthem. It begins like this: *Oh say can you see…*' And the woman says: 'Who's this guy *José*?'"

Eyes filled with mirth, Gato de Oro looked from one man to the other, then put his hand to his mouth to restrain a cackle and turned to walk away, laughing quietly to himself.

"You're certainly not going to kill us with laughter, buddy, but you will kill us with hunger."

The sun began to rise behind the hill of San Roque, its rays first touching the tin roofs of the houses built with unfinished boards and topped with satellite dishes. Each house was connected to a bewildering mass of electrical wires hanging from wooden poles throughout the community.

On the fugitives' side atop the summit of La Campana, heavy equipment cut into the soil, and the two men could see the profile of the fuchsia-red metallic Tree of Life that they had seen the day before from the highway. Next to that tree another one—canary-yellow—had already been bolted onto its pedestal, and a work crew was using a crane to hoist it into place. Two other trees remained to be installed: one emerald-green and the other a bluish gentian-violet. The crew had left the crane and the enormous electric-cable pulley on-site to complete their work. Once the trees were illuminated, the glow would be visible from the villages and towns nearby.

With each gust of wind, the two men huddled more tightly into the crack, Inspector Morales with his cane between his knees and his head buried in his chest.

"I'm remembering a song about the top of a mountain that my Grandmother Catalina used to sing," he coughed, spitting out a thick gob of phlegm.

His Grandmother Catalina made cigars with Nicaragua's black Chilcagre tobacco, which she sold in her stall in Managua's Mercado San Miguel. With a tabletop balanced on her knees, she used a finely-honed blade with no handle to cut the tobacco leaves. After adding a small handful of granulated tobacco, she rolled the layer up and sealed it with starch. While working, she frequently sang the "Habanera" song that was usually performed during Holy Week's Maundy Thursday on Radio Mundial from the Luciérnaga Theatre. The Radio Mundial program featured "Judea in Dramatic Scenes," and the song represented the voice of Boanerges, "the son of thunder" who was in love with Mary Magdalene:

I was born high atop a great mountain,
bright lightning struck low and above.
I grew up in the heart of a cabin.
And now I'm a man, yes.
And now I'm a man, yes,
a man who's just dying of love...

"Dying of love is a sad thing, and it's what would have happened to you with Marcela, the girl who's nothing but chicken bones and is now enjoying herself with her old boyfriend on Miami Beach," said Rambo. "But dying of hunger is far more cruel. Gato de Oro is a heartless and gutless swine."

"How did we end up in such a hopeless situation, Serafín? We don't even have a cup of coffee to drink, no matter how bitter or watered-down."

"And on top of that, we're trusting Gato de Oro not to put us back in Tongolele's hands."

"Don't assume that the same thought hasn't occurred to me too. He's most likely up at that guard post right now, sealing the deal."

"There's no question now that Tongolele will lock you up in El Chipote. And there's no question that Tuco and Tico will hold your head in the sink until water shoots out your mouth and nose."

"None of that scares me, Serafín. There are worse things for me."

"Tell me that when they take your head out with water gushing everywhere and you feel like your lungs are bursting and you're vomiting your heart out of your mouth, like what happened to me. What could be worse than that?"

"What if Fanny dies on me?"

Rambo went quiet for a moment.

"Do you have enough minutes left on your phone to leave a message with Doña Sofía and ask about Fanny's test results from the hospital?" he finally asked.

"That will take some time, Serafín. It's an MRI. They won't know until noon."

"Then call Fanny directly. Her cancer certainly hasn't left her mute."

"I'm such a dumb-ass when it comes to conversations like that. What am I going to say to her?"

"You're not a coward. You've always been a man with balls."

"But what to do? I have a cowardly heart. And hearts have nothing to do with balls."

A new gust of wind blew furiously through the cavity between the rocks, as if it were trying to force them out. Rambo looked toward the road and saw Gato de Oro walking down from the town, rubbing his belly with satisfaction. He seemed taller and fatter, even more golden under the light of the sun.

"There's the fat swine now, and he's going to walk right by us on his way to Dipilto Viejo without saying anything about all the delicious food he ate."

Inspector Morales raised his head and saw the man too, serene and content as he used a toothpick to explore his teeth. Gato de Oro then spread his legs and pushed to emit a loud fart, his hands on his waist as if he were beginning a dance step.

Because the gravel was limestone, the roadway stretched out like a sparkling white trail between the scrub on either side, crawling beneath the genízaro and guanacaste trees that rose up beyond the wire fences that marked all the coffee plantations' limits.

Gato de Oro was preparing to cross the road when a Hilux pickup appeared on a curve, moving slowly and noiselessly toward him as if the driver had turned off the motor. The tires crushed the rocks and raised a light cloud of chalky dust.

As if out of nowhere, two armed men stood up in the truck bed and pointed their guns at Gato de Oro. The big man took several steps back, hesitated, then tried to start running, attempting to rush upward again as his hat flew off his head. But when the shots rang out he went down as if he had tripped, falling first to one knee and then the other, and ended up lying on his back.

The pick-up continued its journey north toward the border, never accelerating, and the two shooters disappeared into the depths of the bed.

Rambo turned to look at Inspector Morales.

"What happened, *Jefe?*" he asked, his voice a hoarse whistle.

"They killed him."

"What do you mean that they killed him?" Rambo asked again, grabbing Inspector Morales by the arm.

"Two short bursts, one for each rifle," Inspector Morales answered, never taking his eyes off Gato de Oro, who lay with one hand forward over his head and the other at his side. A dark bloodstain began to spread across his plaid shirt.

"It was the men in the truck," Rambo said as if he were just discovering the truth at that moment.

"They were hiding under a tarp in the bed. They had their faces covered."

"Have I lost my mind, *Jefe?* It seems like I don't see anything until you tell me."

"The driver was the only one with his face exposed. The truck had no plates."

"Do you see what I mean? I don't even remember what color the truck was."

"A green Hilux. I've got everything on here," said Inspector Morales, showing Rambo his phone.

"What are you saying? Did you video the whole thing?"

"I saw the pick-up coming near and I just got a feeling and took out my phone."

The people from the village had begun to appear at their doors, but a long time passed before anyone approached the body, which now lay in an enormous puddle of blood. Eventually two women came down, one in a sweater and the other wearing a man's jacket that was too big for her. The two walked one behind the other, the woman with the sweater leading the way and carrying a tiger-striped blanket, which she used to cover Gato de Oro. Only his pant legs and boots remained visible.

The second woman, the one in the man's jacket, went to search for the dead man's hat, which the wind had blown rather far away. She placed it on the blanket, which had already begun to become saturated with blood.

"Those women have to be the Culeca sisters, *Jefe*, the ones who fed him his final breakfast."

The two women stood next to the body, their heads lowered. They appeared to be praying. Later, the one with the jacket said something to the other, and a gust of wind carried some disconnected words up to the fugitives' hiding place: "Monseñor Ortez... his uncle... tell him... Ocotal... phone... but there's no way to..."

The women then returned the way they had come, shaking their heads hopelessly.

"Serafín, we have to leave here before those men in the pick-up come back."

"Do you think they'll come back for us?"

"We're not going to stay to find out."

The first members of a squad had already appeared at the top of La Campana. Inspector Morales was the first to exit the hiding place. He remembered the route that Gato de Oro had described: cross the slope, find the banana field, and continue through the pasture until they reached Dipilto Viejo.

Explain to your ignorant associate here that the poem about the dusky swallows isn't by Darío; it's by Bécquer, said Lord Dixon.

"You show up late, and on top of that you insist on talking about poetry when a paramilitary squad has just murdered Gato de Oro and is probably coming after us as well."

What's new about that, comrade? said Lord Dixon. You're going to have to survive among paramilitary squads from here on out.

CHAPTER TWO

Cups and Clubs

THAT MONDAY AFTERNOON was already turning dark when the black-painted electric gate slid back to allow the exit of a platinum-gray Kia Morning taxi, which made its way toward the highway to Masaya. Once the gate returned to its closed position, the terracotta-tiled house—the outside of which had not received a single coat of paint for years—remained hidden once again behind a wall topped with coiled barbed wire.

Located at the end of Del Campo Avenue in the residential area of Las Colinas, the block saw little traffic, and the leafy chilamate trees planted along both sides created dark shadows like standing water on the sidewalks, where pedestrians were never seen. To all outward appearances, the house functioned as a customs agency, according to a metal plaque attached beside the gate.

Commissioner Anastasio Prado sat at the taxi's steering wheel. To his annoyance, he was known by acquaintances and strangers alike as "Tongolele" due to the white stripe in his hair, which reminded people of the exotic dancer and actress of Mexican films. Stopped in the line awaiting the light to change so that he could enter the highway, Tongolele leaned into the rear-view mirror and confirmed that a new pimple, hardened and red, had sprouted near the corner of his mouth. Not without some pleasure, he squeezed the pimple with his fingers, feeling the deep stab of pain.

His personal cross to bear was a virulent kind of teenage acne that had afflicted him his entire life; his face was pockmarked with reddish scars that he would have gladly torn off like a mask to reveal a completely different visage beneath, one with skin as smooth as those in the beauty magazines' facial-cream ads.

Even though his deeply ravaged face was not well known, Tongolele followed a rule of never attracting attention. That's the reason his car had the plates and emblems of a taxi, and the same reason he never had a motorized escort. After so many years of battling in his position, anonymity continued to be his best security measure.

Regardless, no one was ever going to hail Tongolele's taxi because he always had a passenger seated behind him: Captain Pedro Claver Salvatierra, also known as "Pedrón" or "Pedrito," his faithful protector and head of operations, valet, court jester, and confidante. Just in case of any problems, an AK-47 lay within Tongolele's reach at the foot of the back seat. The gun was set on automatic-fire and had no safety.

Pedrón barely fit in the Kia's seat. His knees were bent and his scalp rubbed against the headliner, while his huge nervous hand extended to the side, his fingers almost touching the Uzi and its two replacement magazines—again, just in case.

"Where did I find you, Pedrito?" Tongolele would sometimes ask to kill the time, as he did so now.

And the gigantic man—with tanned skin, unruly hair, and thick lips that moved as if his teeth did not fit his mouth—would respond as he did now, talking with his hands spread out:

"Commissioner, I was hiding in the kitchen pantry of the Combat Service Support Company in Campo de Marte."

At noon on 19 July 1979, the guerilla troop under Tongolele's command was searching the deserted military installations in Campo de Marte. In the corridors, sleeping quarters, bathrooms, and the yard for practicing military exercises, the troops found a trove of infantry helmets, boots, cartridge belts, short sabers or yatagans, camouflage uniforms, and assault rifles. When the soldiers reached the kitchen, Tongolele ordered them to open the pantry door with a single kick. The door had obviously been bolted from within, for there was no padlock on the outside latch. Pedrón was hunched down inside, covering his head with his hands.

"And your hand. What were you holding in your hand that was so hard to see within the shadows of your hiding place?"

"My clarinet, commissioner."

"I would have had you blown away without a second thought if I hadn't realized that it wasn't a weapon, but rather your little horn," Tongolele laughed.

A huge man, clutching his clarinet atop his head and trembling,

Pedrón was a musician in the National Guard's philharmonic band; he had tried and failed to flee with his instrument, then decided he would be better off hiding in the pantry, where all that remained was the stench of rancid cheese and onions. The clarinet was shaking in his hands—hands befitting a boxer rather than a clarinet player—and his enormous body was shuddering as if he had St. Vitus' Dance.

He had shown the clarinet to Tongolele as if offering it to him, an act that made the older man laugh, as it did now.

"'Do you know how to shoot a gun?' I asked you. 'Don't tell me that the only thing you can do is blow that piece of shit in military parades.'"

Pedrón had said nothing at first, as he now did before finally answering: "They gave me and the other bandmembers some last-minute military training, but they did the same thing for the cooks and the custodians."

"What kind of gun did they teach you to shoot?" Tongolele asked while still aiming at Pedrón.

"A Garand, sir," Pedrón answered with a low voice.

"Louder. I can't hear you," Tongolele insisted.

"A Garand," Pedrón repeated, but with an even lower voice. "And they taught us how to crawl and advance, load and unload, and use automatic fire."

"And besides playing marches for the military parades, you were always there, blowing on your little mouthpiece whenever the ass-kissing generals serenaded Somoza on his birthday," Tongolele now said.

"Affirmative, sir. They took us in a bus every December fifth to play *Las mañanitas* for General Somoza, first when he was living at El Retiro with his legal wife, Doña Hope, and later at his home in La Curva, way up on the Tiscapa hillside, when he was living with Doña Dinorah."

"His lover."

"His wife or his lover. Was it for me to say who the general wanted to keep his bed warm?"

"I adopted you either because you made me laugh or because I pitied you. Who knows? Nobody wanted you because you were in the National Guard, even if you were nothing but a sorry clarinet player."

"Then you were right to send me to Cuba for re-education," and Pedrón now laughed as well, as if the issue of his re-education had been a joke.

Six months of training with the Special Forces in Palma Soriano, a crash course in intelligence and counterintelligence in Villa Marista, plus an ideological-education seminar at the Ñico López National Command School.

"Enough to cleanse you of your sins. The Ministry of the Interior chewed you up, gulped you down, and then forgot about you."

The taxi merged into the southbound highway traffic, a slow line of taillights like red embers. It was the time of day when the city emptied toward the increasingly numerous housing developments that either line the highway to the city of Masaya or extend throughout the nearby regions—Veracruz, Esquipulas, Valle de Gothel—and onward into the neighboring municipalities scattered around the volcanic craters of Santiago, Ticuantepe, Nindirí, and Masaya, a vast porous wasteland of dark lava flows and the eternal column of poisonous gases blowing westward to the Pacific Ocean, incinerating all vegetation with their sulfurous breath.

At that moment, Tongolele was traveling to visit his mother, who lived in Aranjuez Estates in Valle de Gothel, for her birthday.

"What a huge coincidence that your name is Anastasio, commissioner," Pedrón remarked. "Just like Somoza senior."

"And just like his son, the one you used to serenade, and just like the son's son, who never got to be dictator," Tongolele answered.

"I assume your father just really liked that name," said Pedrón, affecting a look of complete innocence.

"My father was a boot-licker among boot-lickers. He named me Anastasio and sent a telegram to the dictator that said: *My newborn son will be named after Nicaragua's illustrious hero.* The telegram contained the shortest number of words possible because people had to pay by the word."

"At least he didn't name you Hero, commissioner. But I'll bet they sent some kind of gift from the Presidential Palace in Tiscapa."

"A small silver spoon. So my mother could feed me my mash."

"Speaking of your mother, how old is the great lady turning this year?"

"I asked her this morning when I called to congratulate her, but she says she's lost count."

[29]

"A triumph to arrive at this point without owing anything to my own son," she had answered that morning in a joking manner that still managed to sting.

"Your mother was widowed at a young age. Right, commissioner?"

"Forty years old."

As she had so many times in the past, she had given him a reminder: "You didn't even seem to realize that I had to shut the pharmacy down when it ended up without any inventory—the display windows and shelves were empty."

"Do you think I was just idling about, partying around?" he had responded to her again. "Sometimes I had nothing to eat; other times I didn't sleep. We finally won, and the revolution's enemies went into hiding, sometimes under the rocks themselves."

"Not even a single word for your mother," she had kept complaining. "'He's not in the office, comrade señora.' 'He's busy, comrade señora.' 'He's in a meeting, comrade señora.' 'Would you like to leave a message, comrade señora?'"

"And when did your mother become a fortuneteller?" asked Pedrón, already knowing the answer.

"It happened during the years of the Contra war, when I was neither eating nor sleeping, and she closed the pharmacy down because she didn't have even a pain pill—not a single Mejoral—to sell. She first learned how to use Spanish playing cards and how to read horoscopes."

"From what I understand, she was the granddaughter of a famous seer in León: Gregorio the Wise."

"And when Gregorio died, my mother ended up with the books from his library," Tongolele confirmed. "My father used to laugh at those massive things. Who could have known that they would be so useful to my mother in her new profession as she contacted the ethereal spirits?"

She kept the volumes locked in a glass cabinet in the pharmacy's back room, and during the hours when she had no customers, she would sometimes leaf through a volume atop the display case while leaning on her elbows. The books included Dr. Papus's *The Book of Destiny*, Madame Blavatsky's *Voice of Silence*, Allan Kardec's prophecies, and Dr. Brassier's *The Gentleman and the Sword: Secrets of Cartomancy*.

"You carry the gift in your blood. I'll bet you eventually become as famous as your great-grandfather, who could use his thoughts to heal others. People came from as far away as El Salvador and Honduras to see him."

"I've already told you that I'm going to open an office when I retire and that you'll be my assistant. You'll look great with a turban."

"And when did you learn, commissioner, that your mother had taken up the profession of divination and telling the future?

"From the very beginning. After all, my job is to know things. But I let it go. I thought that if she could distract herself that way, then I should allow it. At least she wouldn't spend all her time accusing me of abandoning her."

He listened to her complain over the phone. He listened to her complain every single time he visited her, each of them sitting in a rocking chair and swaying slowly back and forth without looking at the other's face, even as his hands held her increasingly fleshy hand, a hand that was always covered with more age spots than before, shiny and slippery like a fish fighting to return to the water.

"And your sister, Alba Rosa, yet another ingrate who disappeared from my life as well," his mother had continued on the phone, her cracking voice coming between fits of coughing. "First in the cotton-harvest brigades of the Sandinista Youth in Cosigüina, later in the women's battalion, where she was sent to the Honduran border."

"We were doing what we were doing, Mamá," Tongolele had answered again, now impatient.

"And to top things off, your farewell letter when you joined the guerrillas in El Salvador," she continued. "As if Nicaragua won. El Salvador actually won. Another war, Blessed Virgin, as if the war here hadn't been enough."

"She says that in the beginning, she predicted the future in exchange for some kind of staple item," said Pedrón. "A pound of beans, half a liter of cooking oil, a small bag of detergent."

"That's all true. She began to test her skills with the neighbor ladies. They were the first to pay her that way. No one can deny that those were hard times, Pedrito."

If a client's question was about a husband searching for a job during a time of rampant unemployment, Tongolele's mother used the clubs cards. If a son was conscripted into the Patriotic

Military Service and the question was whether he would return safe and sound from the war, she used the swords cards.

"And even jilted husbands would become clients when their wives ran off, claiming that the revolution had freed them," Pedrón laughed.

Will your ungrateful wife come back or not? The cups say that she'll come back when Venus leaves the house of Sagittarius. So, when you least expect it, sir, she'll show up at your door begging for forgiveness.

"If they ran off with another man, it's because they had loose panties," Tongolele laughed as well. "Finding a new bed is what people meant by the so-called women's liberation."

There was uncertainty. There was fear. And fear and uncertainty were the greatest allies to bring clients to Tongolele's mother. Long lines; blackouts; battle reports; vigils for recruits' bodies in the neighborhoods; the sonic boom of the Black Bird—the invisible U.S. plane that flew regular sorties punctually every day at noon, breaking the sound barrier, shaking roof tiles, and breaking windows. Would there be a U.S. invasion or not? Was the end of the world coming or not? Would the Devil himself carry us off?

"Your mother got almost every prediction right. That's why she became so famous in León."

"Has she also told you how she switched from charging eggs, oil, and beans for her predictions to charging dollars?"

"Commissioner, you have to acknowledge that our córdobas—what people called *chancheros* in the streets—had less value each morning than they did the night before."

"Inflation was a consequence of aggression," Tongolele responded with a surly expression.

Because "Prado's widow Josefa" was a poor name for a fortune-teller, Tongolele's mother adopted the name Zoraida—Professor Zoraida—and abandoned the house in the San Juan neighborhood, where she had worked from the portion of the pharmacy that gave onto the street. The San Juan house hadn't actually belonged to her, and she moved to a smaller house in the Zaragoza neighborhood where she opened her business. She did not limit her work to divining good or bad fortunes. In addition, she cast hexes or freed victims from them, and she taught people how to recite prayers for healing: the Prayer in Praise of St. Peter's Shadow, the Prayer to the Anima Sola or "Lonely Spirit," and the Great and Powerful Prayer to the Divine Garrobo:

> Oh, powerful and invincible garrobo, divine iguana that God has blessed with great privileges such as rainy and dry seasons, having armed you with the bravery to launch yourself from the highest tree and fall into any gorge and upon any rocky crag without suffering any injury... [W]hen they discovered you in that cave, you had spent forty days without eating food or drinking water, and you promised to share your secrets with anyone who trusted you as I do now with blind faith in your divine powers and privileges...

"About that garrobo prayer, commissioner, is it true that people need to fast all day, then recite the words at midnight in the nude, stretched out on the bed with their arms extended like a cross?"

"I don't know shit about garrobos. You talk with my mother more than I do, so you should ask her."

"You find out about the entire world's lives and miracles, and yet you never knew when I moved to Managua with everything I owned," his mother had scolded him.

"I knew very well, Mamá. I was aware of what was happening with you," Tongolele had answered. "This whole thing about me abandoning you is all in your head, and you keep adding details however you like."

Professor Zoraida found a wattle-and-daub house in the Campo Bruce neighborhood, a place where the Mercado Oriental's tumult lay only blocks away and continually inched forward, devouring entire blocks, always carrying a stench ever closer: the odor of burnt diesel fuel from transport trucks, the smell of cattle feed, and the bloody reek of butchered chickens. And that house was where her clients went, disguised behind huge sunglasses that could hide their entire faces. These women had heard about her fame, and they walked to the house as if forgiving the ground itself, then sat down fearfully in front of the great lady: they wanted to know when the suffering of the revolution would end.

Will my son be healed? Will we save him? All he wears nowadays is olive-green, and he's become our enemy: he never lets us say anything, and he says that we're nothing but bourgeoise scum who deserve the firing squad. Would it be better to go to Miami or wait here for the miracle that the Virgin Mary vowed would happen? In Cuapa, the Virgin appeared encircled in light to her servant Bernardo, the sacristan for the chapel, and she promised him that the Communist serpent would be crushed under her foot and that all the atheist books would be burned.

And throughout each consultation the faithful chauffeurs remained waiting, their dark gabardine trousers mended and their shoes cracked but shiny, standing beside pick-up trucks from bygone eras and Mercedes sedans, true relics that remained working thanks to parts bought from scrapyards or the black market, which the vehicles' owners patronized and then returned home to their refuges in Las Colinas, Los Robles, Bolonia, and Altos de Santo Domingo, dwellings where lightbulbs were missing from porches, slogans were painted on the walls, gardens were overgrown to a frightening degree, and the dead waters of swimming pools were covered with slime.

After Doña Violeta Barrios de Chamorro unexpectedly won the 1990 elections, the streets were busier than ever, overflowing with a parade of Suburbans, Land Cruisers, and Nissan Patrols—all with darkly tinted glass and driven by chauffeurs, now wearing impeccable long-sleeved guayaberas and smelling of Tres Coronas cologne, who conversed happily as they breathed the newly fresh air. And Professor Zoraida added new clients to her existing list, women newly arrived from Miami who posed numerous questions about the return of confiscated properties and countless other questions about reconciliations: My sister refused to even talk to me before, and now she wants us to get together on Christmas Eve, but my husband won't allow it because she's still a Sandinista.

In the same way as Professor Zoraida had done during her hard economic times, she received her clients while wearing a gingham robe with a floral pattern, giving the impression that she either had just gotten out of bed or had had no time to dress, her hair rolled up in pink plastic curlers as if she later had to arrange it for a party. Because this was her costume: no sari or turban, no curtains or shadows, just a domestic fortuneteller who walked around the house in rubber flip-flops and interrupted her sessions to check the beans boiling on the gas stove lest they burn. Her consultation room was a corner where two folding chairs faced each other, separated by a green-surfaced table for laying the cards down, a place where children could be heard playing baseball outside and street dogs came by out of curiosity but eventually lost interest and left.

"Commissioner, were the rancid old women interested only in magical prayers, or did they also ask for curses to be removed? Frogs in the stomach, for example?"

"What do I know, Pedrito? But I imagine that more than one of them wanted to hurt her husband's lover—make her lose her hair or have her teeth fall out."

"And to think that you never took advantage of her clients to find out about the bourgeoise's reactionary plots."

"It was hard enough to convince my mother to tell me anything back then. Can you imagine how she'd respond if I asked her to wheedle information from her clients now?"

"And she keeps wasting opportunities. If she has the ability to send her spirit walking through the air while her body is sleeping, which allows her to enter any house invisibly because no wall or door can stop her, imagine what we could find out."

"Don't even think about flying while you're sleeping, Pedrito. Accidents occur when the soul can't return to the body."

"Because of what your mother is, she has a great deal of experience with this kind of thing. That's how she went to India to have a meeting with the great guru Sai Baba."

"She did that using magnetic fluids, which are like radio waves. And she had the advantage of no jet lag."

"Sai Baba transmitted his wisdom to your mother. She brought it from over there. And she deposited it in a Chinese box."

"Email would be easier. Pedrón *cabrón*, my asshole friend, this conversation never leaves this car. Because if it does, I'll castrate you."

"Sai Baba is the one who commanded that she wear white from that time on, because white represents the Spiritual Luminescence."

"But she decided that regardless, she wasn't going to wear a tunic. Just a white blouse and pants. Ah, dear Mamá, poor lady, she looks like a nurse instead of a soothsayer."

"Well, commissioner, no matter how your mother looks, she's a formidable person. She closes the León pharmacy because she has no medicine to sell; she doesn't get scared; she becomes a fortune-teller; she comes to Managua; and she becomes an advisor to an unknown woman who appears one day for a consultation. And not just any unknown woman."

Wearing jeans that were unwashed from disuse, the unknown woman had waited her turn, then humbly sat on the stool across from Professor Zoraida, who dealt the cards for her. None of the beneficent clubs was standing up; instead, all appeared head down, a sign of good fortune. The cards provided clear signs of a fire that never burns out because the person's resolve and persistence keep stoking it. At the same time, all the cards' maleficent suits—the swords and the gold coins, the heralds of frustration, bad fortune, negative vibes, and the evil eye—remained hidden within the deck.

The new woman began a habit of making a visit each week, every Friday at five, always carrying a list of people's names, and Zoraida armed her with predictions and warnings about those people: this one is loquacious but hides poison; that one looks trustworthy but has excessive ambition; that one fawns upon you, but don't get too close because his words are pure hypocrisy; scorpions, you must shake the scorpions out of your shirt while the bell tolls for your return to the throne.

"Couldn't it be, commissioner, that the list contained the names of the people that the woman wanted to get rid of so that she could become the owner of their land?"

"And couldn't it be, Pedrito, that it would be better for us not to get involved in what doesn't concern us?"

"That sounds like good advice to me, commissioner."

"Regardless, always remember that the person pointing at the names on the list of undesirables is not my mother, but rather Sai Baba. Even to this day."

"Even though Sai Baba is already dead, commissioner? Because he abandoned his mortal clay years ago, and they buried him in his sanctuary—an enormous marble mausoleum."

"It's easier now that he's dead because he can attend consultations more quickly in spirit form. Wandering spirits know nothing of time or distance."

"Well, there's no spirit wiser than he is. He doesn't just identify potential troublemakers or sneaky traitors. He also knows which opposition leaders to buy; he offers positions on councils and committees; and he recommends making agreements with this group of businessmen or the other to keep them happy."

The taxi remained trapped in snarled traffic and had still not reached the Ticuantepec roundabout. Tongolele pounded the steering wheel impatiently.

"Sai Baba in spiritual things, and the two of us in material things. We couldn't be better equipped for our job."

"And you, commissioner. Don't you receive any mental communication from Sai Baba through your mother?"

"I'm flesh and bone. I have nothing to do with spirits, but I pass through walls and doors better than Sai Baba, Pedrito."

"No one would argue with that, commissioner. When it comes to earthly maneuvering, no one comes close to you."

"And I don't need some consultation with a soothsayer to do that. Like I said, that's the way things will be until we retire."

"As for a consultation, your mother already said good-bye to that, commissioner. She now has her own unique and exclusive clientele."

"When the Chinese box began to make regular visits to Campo Bruce protected by a convoy, the high-society ladies fled from there like cockroaches from an exterminator," Tongolele agreed.

The convoy secured the block by force. Police had cars make a detour into the blocks near the traffic circle, and patrol cars closed the street entrances to prevent vehicles and pedestrians from passing through.

The top of the black-lacquered Chinese box depicted a female phoenix, its wings extended as it attacked a serpent with open jaws. The box always arrived in a Mercedes Benz SUV with darkened windows, and an aide always carried it inside. Only two keys could open the box: one was in the hands of the sender, who deposited a hand-written question inside; the other resided with Professor Zoraida, who returned the box with an answer after completing her consultation.

"The residents began complaining about the street closings. People complain just because they like something to complain about, commissioner."

"That's right. It became a political problem. At first the neighbors saw it as quite the spectacle. They came out of their houses and gathered on the sidewalks. But then they started shutting their doors, angry because the interruptions sometimes happened every day, not just on Fridays at five."

"I remember that the local leaders led the uproar. They wanted to make a stink, and no matter how many groceries and supplies were sent from house to house, they kept on making a stink."

"It wasn't just that they wanted to make a stink, Pedrito. A lot of people got hurt."

"That man with the glass eye, the one with the auto shop, and that other man, the one with the belly of a pregnant lady, who owned a metalworking shop where they made cemetery gates. Both of them had their employees working in the streets, and they kept whining that every Chinese-box day was a day wasted. They even opened their big mouths on Radio Corporación, so they needed to be taught a lesson."

"The lesson went too far, Pedrito. Your men broke the metal-worker's cheekbone with brass knuckles."

Tongolele had spoken with Commissioner Arquímedes Manzano, the head of ASP, the Agency for Special Protection. The government was paying a high price, and they couldn't be threatening or arresting people every time they complained. Wouldn't it be better to send the Chinese box in a discreet way?

"The same way you receive yours, commissioner, which is just like the other one, only lacquered in red. The aide delivers the box on time, without any escort or song-and-dance."

"But Manzano claimed that he couldn't do anything about it. He said that the Chinese box's trip with a motorized escort was all done according to the ritual of some empress or another of China. He also insisted that the entire issue didn't fall within the purview of either one of us."

"Every court dwarf dances how he will. There's no rational explanation for it. How come your box doesn't follow the same delivery ritual as the other one?"

"According to the dwarf Manzano, it's different. The female phoenix on the red box attacks the serpent with her left talon, making her invisible to the eyes of the powerful demon Gong Gong. The female phoenix on the black box attacks with her right talon, so the box always remains visible."

"So why not use a red box the same as the other one and solve the problem with Gong Gong?"

Tongolele saw a gap in the line of cars beside him, then made a quick lane change.

"Do you know the purpose of the Trees of Life, Pedrito?"

"To use electricity. They use enough energy for twenty houses when they're turned on."

"That's what right-wing propaganda says. However, those trees actually provide a protective shield against the evil schemes of the enemy, because their magnetic fields negate all pernicious and destructive forces."

"Yet another way to neutralize the powers of Gong Gong, the great Chinese demon?"

"Gong Gong, Lucifer, Belial, Beelzebub. Take your pick."

"That's why they're planting those trees everywhere. On the streets, on the highways, in barracks, even in schoolyards."

"But that's all bullshit anyway, Pedrito, and you and I know it very well. I'm the one who really protects him and her from every misbegotten son-of-a-bitch."

"Didn't Sai Baba make the recommendations to plant all the Trees of Life?"

"And the idea to use the Hand of Fatima, the amulet where every fingertip has a watchful eye painted on it. Each eye represents one of the five virtues."

"Didn't Sai Baba also have the idea to pile mountains of roses on the stage during mass gatherings?"

"And during the ceremonies for presenting credentials in cabinet meetings. The flowers repel negative influences."

"What I don't like about all that is that everything smells like death, commissioner. It's as if they're holding a vigil over some dead body."

"I warned you already: If anything about this conversation comes out of your mouth, I won't just castrate you. I'll cut off your dick and wrap it around your neck like a tie."

"It's as if we just met for the first time, commissioner. My mouth is a lockbox with no key."

A gasoline-delivery truck that had been leaving a gas station had made a bad turn near the exit to Veracruz, and with its front tires stuck on the road's median, the truck was blocking the traffic flow. Car horns created an infernal howl.

"Maybe if your brother-in-law had recited the prayer to the garrobo, he wouldn't have ended up in a grave, commissioner."

"He would be in a grave regardless of anything else and any prayers to the garrobo. If a stranger chooses to screw you over, well and done. But if some asshole from my own family does something like that, it turns my stomach."

Tongolele's sister, Alba Rosa, the one who had gone to fight in El Salvador, had fallen in love with Lázaro Chicas, an FSLN guerrilla fighter and a member of the security detail for Schafik Hándal. After the peace accord was signed, the couple got married and settled in Nicaragua, but after several years Alba Rosa ran off to the U.S. with a baseball player recruited as a prospect for the Los Angeles Dodgers, a young coastal kid from Laguna de Perlas who could have easily been her son. And from that day forward, Lázaro did nothing but spend all day crying his tales of woe to his mother-in-law, who cried along with him.

Zoraida dumped him on Tongolele: the poor boy; please help him; he's an honest man; he's a hard worker. So, although Tongolele hated to do so, he allowed Lázaro to manage his businesses. He started with the Super Body gym in Managua, then the dairy farm in Chontales, and finally the fleet of trucks that transported cargo throughout Central America.

Lázaro was efficient with bookkeeping, implacable with underlings, and ferocious with debtors, although he loved to talk and boast. Furthermore, he was stylish in his own way: he always dressed like a cowboy from the Old West—Roy Rogers with a fringed shirt, a ten-gallon hat, and stamped leather boots, the kind of crap that Tongolele was willing to ignore. But Lázaro had a vice that Tongolele knew nothing about: betting on the New Zealand greyhound races streamed on the Internet.

Lázaro lost huge sums of money, and when he realized that he could no longer skim money from Tongolele's businesses, he forged a deed to the dairy farm so he could sell it to some Salvadoran cheesemakers, and he hid the fleet's trucks in Guatemala and El Salvador with the intent of transporting them to Mexico, where they could be sold under false papers. But all the money he would gain from these activities would far exceed his debts. What did he hope to do once he had obtained that pile of money? Did he think he could spend the rest of his life lying in a hammock on El Cuco Beach in El Salvador, a daquiri in his hand and a little Japanese *kasa* hat on his head, with a laptop resting on his legs as he continued to make the same stupid bets on dogs on the other side of the world?

Thanks to a Supreme Court justice who lived in the closet and knew that Tongolele had proof of his indiscretions, Tongolele managed to annul the sale documents for the dairy farm, and the justice also helped the farm's buyers soil themselves with fear when they learned the identity of the injured party. As for the trucks, they were discovered at the last minute and were now making their way back to Nicaragua.

During the morning of the previous day, Lázaro had fallen off a cliff into the crater of Asososca Lagoon while driving his Toyota Corolla from his house in Bosques de Jiloá, and the police had reported the victim as unidentified. At the dead man's house, Pedrón had found a briefcase hidden behind a closed door. The briefcase contained the stacks of money paid for the dairy farm, so the Salvadoran cheesemakers ended up with absolutely nothing: they didn't get the pretty girl or even her picture.

"My mother has no idea what happened to her son-in-law."

"What do you mean that she has no idea? She sees and knows all."

"Don't believe that for a second. There are things in this world that go far beyond her powers."

"Don't tell me that she would feel sorry for a loser like him."

"He was her favorite. Everything he did to take my money just looked like mischief to her."

"How do you plan to explain his disappearance to her?"

"He went back to El Salvador and shacked up there with a new woman—any story she'll accept."

"Lázaro is never going to return from the grave. In order to push him into the drop, we shoved a ten-ton truck on top of him."

"Remember that we have to take his body from the morgue and bury it in an unmarked grave."

"Already done last night. No noise, no trouble."

"Well, Pedrito, you can certainly be efficient when you want to be. And what about the message we planned to send to that priest in Ocotal, the one that makes so much trouble with his subversive sermons?"

"The message has already been sent. We ordered his nephew killed. Those boys that Doña Fabiola loaned us turned out to be first-rate."

"I hope La Chaparra rewards them properly when they get back to Managua."

"How much will their reward be?"

"All the weed they can fit in their backpacks. But they need to sell it far away from the schools. Disobey, and they'll pay the price."

"You should give me a reward like that, commissioner. Not for making money, but for recreational purposes."

"You're no minor leaguer, if I know you at all. I doubt that even angel dust would affect you."

"If you add a bit of that dust like salsa to your weed, the effects are much more delicious—it's like floating around in starry space."

"One of these days you'll get lost in those heights, and then it's *Adiós*, Pedrito. Gluttony will leave you stuck there."

"If I meet Sai Baba in the great abyss of the firmament, I'll say hello to him for you."

"And tell him not a single new Tree of Life, please."

"Do you know what else? The tourists that you sent on vacation across the border have already made a secret return to the country."

"Who are you talking about? The King of the Vultures?"

"He wouldn't dare. It's that cripple who was such a pain in the ass for Miguel Soto, your millionaire friend. And that drunk from the Mercado Oriental, the one we held under the sink to teach him a lesson."

"How did they make it back?"

"The priest's nephew, the one we shot to hell, served as their guide. When they saw he was dead, they ran off."

"That cripple certainly has some stones. Have they been apprehended?"

"We're giving the cripple a little bit of rope. We're allowing them to return to Managua, and then you give the order."

"Leave them alone for now. Let's see what I come up with. I don't have any desire to bill him for services rendered—sending him on vacation to Honduras was a favor I did for Soto."

"I hope Soto thanked you properly."

"These rich types are stingy, Pedrito. Do you know what he gave me?"

"A small herd of Swiss dairy cows and a house along the sea in San Juan del Sur, at the very least."

"Two first-class tickets to Cancún. He can shove those up his ass."

CHAPTER THREE

Monseñor Bienvenido

IN OCOTAL, CAPITAL of the state or department of Nueva Segovia, Monseñor Bienvenido Ortez O.P. served as a friar of the Dominican Order and parish priest for the Church of Nuestra Señora de la Asunción. He had graduated *cum laude* from Rome's Pontifical Gregorian University, where he had received a doctorate in biblical studies.

Nearly sixty years old, brown-skinned, thin and of medium height, his sideburns already turning gray, he ensured that the barber's scissors kept his hair quite short. Despite his efforts to be affable and maintain a cheerful disposition, tension pressed his lips together so hard that it had sketched two highly pronounced lines from the wings of his nose down toward his mouth. And whenever he spoke he tended to hurry his words, requiring him to work to avoid having one word trip over the other.

He owed his name—Monseñor Bienvenido—to the kindly bishop from *Les Miserables,* because his mother, an elementary-school teacher who had graduated from the Women's Normal School in San Marcos, had been a devoted reader of Victor Hugo, although she never imagined that her own son would become a monseñor as well.

His name was always crossed off the lists of candidates to fill open dioceses that the Apostolic Nunciature sent to Rome. He was unpopular because he constantly insisted that the Church needed to be less diplomatic and more prophetic, less concerned about grand halls and more about the streets. He was especially disliked now for his unvarnished denunciations of the government. Many years before, the Church had granted him a consolation prize, an honorific and useless title: "Domestic Prelate of His Holiness." The Roman Curia's directive included the words *Ut sive sollicite,* authorizing him to be called "Monseñor" and wear a button-down cassock with purple trim, along with a waist band of the same color, none of which he ever wore except for his required official portrait.

On this particular Monday, lunch having been cleared from the table, the monseñor was wearing a short-sleeved gray shirt with a clerical collar, his pectoral cross hanging from a thick chain, and he was serving coffee to his two secret guests, who were seated on either side of him. He held a small glass flask in his hand.

"Here's an entire pound of Dipilto coffee, distilled for hours," he said, pouring a few drops into the mugs full of boiling water, which instantly turned black. "Anybody who drinks the essence of this container all at once will either have permanent insomnia or go crazy."

The parsonage dining room's arched windows opened onto a humid yard filled with acacias, cypresses, and lemongrass plants that broke up the one o'clock sun. On the other side of the room, on the wall that gave onto the street, a plaster image of Jesus' Sacred Heart sat upon a plinth, illuminated by an electric votive candle. A few Christmas decorations that no one had bothered to remove extended along the same wall.

Having eaten a heavy meal, the group felt the weight of drowsiness fill the air of the after-lunch conversation. After offering a blessing on the food, the monseñor himself had used a ladle to serve the soup from the steaming tureen, his finely-made eyeglasses clouded with vapor, while Rambo had hungrily eyed the wicker basket in the middle of the table where, along with roast beef dripping with fat, flank steak, brisket, and ribs, there had been cabbage, ripe and unripe plantains, yucca, cocoyam or malanga root, corn on the cob, and baby corn. In addition, another platter contained a salad, another had avocado slices, and yet another was filled with rice.

"We ate like starved street kids," Rambo panted.

"Don't think that this happens all the time. The collection plate doesn't usually cover something like this," laughed the monseñor.

Inspector, the other Monseñor Bienvenido invited Jean Valjean to sit at his table, and the extremely ungrateful guest stole the silver utensils, said Lord Dixon. Don't let your own traveling companion pay his meal back the same way.

"My niece says to tell you hello, inspector," the monseñor said jokingly, then lowered his nose to the cup of coffee that he had previously sweetened with saccharine.

"I feel terrible about the deception, but there was nothing else we could do. We couldn't tell her that Genaro had been killed, because we might well have been accused of the crime ourselves."

Anxious to reach the banana plantation, Inspector Morales had repeatedly planted his cane as far forward as possible, as if doing so would help him to increase his pace. With each passing moment he feared hearing the pick-up truck behind him and then the bursts of gunfire.

From the plantation, the two fugitives had been able to hear the ongoing construction work at the top of the slope—the sound of a chainsaw cutting metal, the echo of hammer blows. As they entered the old pasture, they ran into a solitary cow dragging the end of a rope as if it had become lost. They followed the few houses and huge plots of land along the settlement's pathway, always staying close to the route of the nearly-dry river—a river that had become a dumping area for trash—that made pools among the rocks. By an apparent miracle, they did not encounter a single living soul during their journey, and eventually they arrived at the highway and saw the gas station.

"She picks things up very well, so don't worry. Her name is Edelmira, a wonderful girl."

Edelmira had been sitting alone, examining invoices at a small desk alongside a stack of old tires. Concerned about his appearance, Inspector Morales sniffed his armpits, flexed his muscles, and held his cane elegantly. He said "Good morning" to her and asked about Leonel. Because she was near-sighted, she furrowed her brow to look him over. Pale and pretty, she wore eyeglasses with sky-blue frames, and her short hair was still wet from a recent wash. Leonel wasn't there. He had left early that morning for Managua to address some issue with the Uno oil company. *How could she be of service?* They had come on behalf of her brother. *Her brother?* Yes, her brother was in great difficulty, and he had asked Inspector Morales to introduce himself to Leonel. *Her husband?* Yes, he wanted Leonel to take them in his minibus to Ocotal, because they had an urgent message for Monseñor Ortez. *Her uncle?*

My uncle? She had said. *What difficulties are you talking about? Is there something I can do? Money, perhaps?* It's not a question of money, but he asked me to tell no one but the monseñor himself, a thousand pardons. *And where is Genaro?* Please forgive me for not being allowed to tell you, even though you're his sister. And then she smiled: *It has to have something to do with skirts, because Genaro still thinks he's a young man, and he's always getting into trouble with women, whether they're single or married. For him, every woman is a target of opportunity.* She shook her head as she laughed, displaying the dimples in her rosy cheeks and her tongue-tied mouth—the frenum attached to her teeth as if she were still an adolescent. At that moment all was well, and she could even joke around without the least degree of suspicion. *The mini-bus, El Gorrión, travels throughout Ocotal leaving passengers but he'll return soon, so wait a while and soon the driver will take you to my uncle. Would you like some coffee? I have some rosquilla bread too.* No, señora, thank you, but we already ate breakfast. That lie made Rambo glare at Inspector Morales with a barely supressible urge to wring his neck.

So, before noon they had found themselves at the parsonage doors. The doorbell's chime resounded around the block, and the housekeeper opened the door to them. Surly and distrustful, she examined them top to bottom, and they could see the monseñor in his office doorway saying good-bye to a couple that any observer would conclude was preparing for their First Communion if not for the newborn baby cradled in the woman's arms and swathed in a small embroidered sheet. This Sunday. I'll look for you this Sunday, then, during morning mass at eight o'clock in the morning. And right there, in the entryway guarded by a photo of Pope Francis, without receiving an invitation to enter the office, Inspector Morales explained the whole situation in a rush: who he was, "his friend" Serafín, the entanglement with Tongolele, the millionaire Soto, Soto's stepdaughter Marcela, the deportation, and their secret return to Nicaragua.

Monseñor Ortez had taken the detective by the hands: For the love of God, Inspector Morales in the flesh; what a pleasure to meet you; what a surprise. But the monseñor was not pleased: the pathway taken at midnight; the lottery-ticket salesman who in reality was a guide. My nephew, Genaro? Tall, blonde, and strong? No news until they had arrived in San Roque; the hiding place in the rocks of Cuapes; and the pick-up bed with masked men. Holy Virgin! The monseñor raised his hands together to his mouth, lowered his head, closed his eyes, offered a prayer, opened his eyes again, and heaved a great sigh. Did he know las Culecas? Very well: good women both. The one who wears a man's jacket said a few words that we caught in the wind, and that's why we came to see you. That one is Herlinda, the older sister. The younger one is Eufrasia. From what we could hear that Herlinda said, they had no way to warn you. Well, they don't have a cell phone. They're old school. And no one else in the area would lend them a phone for fear of the terrible things happening every day, all of the killings. There's no one here who doesn't have "Dear Jesus" on their lips.

The monseñor thought for a moment as he gripped his pectoral cross, then called out to the housekeeper and introduced her to the two visitors. Her name was Rita Boniche. He asked her to make a place for them in the back room, prepare bedding for the two cots there, and give the men something to eat. The monseñor would head immediately to San Roque, and then he added a warning: The fugitives must not go out to the street for any reason.

At that moment, Felipe de Jesús appeared with quiet steps. Felipe, the parish's sacristan, also served as the monseñor's driver, not to mention serving as the electrician and the carpenter who repaired pews and altars. He left to start the Land Rover SUV parked in the hallway. The motor thundered in the parsonage, and Rita Boniche opened the gate to allow the car to exit. After shutting the handles and closing the latch, she returned to escort the visitors to their room in silence—a hostile silence.

She pounded on the door with her palm to let them know it was time to eat, and she did not allow them to go to the kitchen. Instead, she served them right there: a plate with rice and beans together, a piece of cheese, and either a tortilla or half of an unripe cooked plantain on top, accompanied by a drink made with chia seeds or tamarind fruit. All three meals were the same, and the men had to eat standing up, treating them as if they were fieldhands.

Rita Boniche was a diminutive elderly woman, gaunt and very dark. She walked with an agile gait, her feet shoeless like the talons of a bird of prey, and her disproportionately large head appeared as if it had been attached to the wrong body. She watched the two men warily from the corner of her eye as if hoping for a fight, and although Rambo tried to comb his hair well, put on his best face, and behave submissively in her presence, nothing helped. Most likely he carried the mark of the beast branded on his forehead.

Despite the housekeeper's animosity, after numerous requests Inspector Morales eventually convinced her to find him a phone charger, which she brought from the monseñor's office, delivering it along with a thousand warnings that he return it as soon as he was finished.

Doña Sofía's reports about Fanny contained no imminent alarms: the MRI had shown nothing in the bones, and the metastasis of the lungs—if it even existed—was at an incipient stage, so Fanny would begin new chemotherapy sessions, but not for another two weeks. And yes, she would lose her hair again.

The two men washed their shirts, underwear, and socks, and they passed the time in their enclosed space speculating about the possible motives behind Gato de Oro's death. If the killing had nothing to do with them and if Tongolele was not involved, who was behind it? The narcos? Some group of smugglers? An angry husband? But what kind of jealous husband had an army of killers at his disposal? Could Gato de Oro have been murdered by mistake?

Over and over again, Inspector Morales watched his phone screen, studying the 40 seconds of video he had recorded. One of the masked shooters sported a baseball cap and was wearing a balaclava. The other was wearing a palm-leaf hat and had covered his face from the nose down with an indigenous bandana. The bandana, red with a black-print design, was the type that campesinos typically used. The guns were AK-47s. No matter how much Inspector Morales zoomed onto the unmasked driver's face, the image told him nothing. Slanted eyes, thick lips, and a moustache with mismatched tips. A face like so many others.

On the morning of their second day they heard the SUV as it entered the hallway, and when they went to the door of their room, they saw an exhausted Monseñor Ortez walk into his own room. They also watched Felipe de Jesús as he disappeared, walking silently as always. But Felipe's footsteps were not his only silent characteristic: the two fugitives never heard him utter a single word. The monseñor explained that Felipe's stuttering inhibited him from speaking and that he preferred to communicate with signs.

Later the two heard an argument between the monseñor and Rita Boniche—the man's voice consistently calm and persuasive even as hers became increasingly irate, her anger underscored by the shocking sound of dishes crashing in the kitchen. The negotiations were difficult but successful, because the housekeeper had gone to the market shortly thereafter to buy the food necessary for the generous lunch that had just been lavished on them.

After depositing his cup in a bowl, the monseñor carefully removed his glasses and cleaned them with a handkerchief soaked in vetiver water. He then gave his report:

When he arrived in San Roque, the police had already picked up Genaro's body, which they took to the Ocotal state hospital's morgue for an autopsy. Two officers remained in the area, and they went from house to house questioning the neighbors, but of course no one had seen anything, and people shut their doors as soon as the officers walked away. Because of his pastoral work, the monseñor knew everyone in these border towns quite well, but they refused to tell him anything either, even after the police had abandoned the area. Not even the Culeca sisters would talk. They embraced him and wept, but that had been all.

He had gone to Dipilto Viejo to look for his niece. Consoling her was difficult. While Genaro had been her older brother and they had a substantial difference in age, she had always considered him an overgrown child, a boy who needed to be spoiled and wanted someone to laugh at his frequently terrible jokes. Because he was a confirmed bachelor, she and her husband allowed him to stay in a back room of their house. They took care of his clothes; the three of them usually ate together; and they would watch TV together at night. Genaro never told them when he was heading for the border, and they never knew he was gone until they saw the lock on his door.

She called her husband in Managua to report the bad news and asked him to hurry back, then went to put on a black mourning dress at the house, which was next to the gas station. She left the young pump attendant in charge of everything, and then she and her uncle went to Ocotal to claim the body at the morgue. They retrieved the body at about eight o'clock that night, and they still had time to take it back to Dipilto Viejo. Leonel had been busy preparing for a wake. Few people attended, and those who did—women, for the most part—left early.

"When fear runs free, it's worse than a rabid dog, and people think they're better off behind closed doors," the monseñor sighed.

Genaro's body was buried the following afternoon, a deserted Sunday, after a mass that the monseñor officiated before a bier erected in the house's back hallway. Later the next morning, he had traveled to Ocotal to request the autopsy report and find out how the investigation was progressing. But at the police station they told him that Commissioner Vílchez, the state's chief of police, was not there and would not be coming that day.

"It's the same old story," said the monseñor, sighing again. "They'll drag their feet day after day, and in the end nobody will know anything."

Lacking his usual school-notebook, Inspector Morales wrote details in a notebook he found on a shelf in the room. Many different hands had used the notebook to copy hymns to the Virgin and record English-learning exercises, but the last few pages remained blank.

"Your nephew told us that everyone in this area is a descendant of a rather naughty priest from who-knows-where, and that's why his family all appeared so similar: good-looking and shining. Right, *Jefe?*"

This is exactly what worried me about your traveling companion, inspector. The man has no shame, said Lord Dixon. This is passive racism, the kind that comes from an inferiority complex.

"Well then, I must have gotten too much sunburn from the time I was a boy," the monseñor smiled.

"That's exactly what I was going to tell you: You're olive-skinned, like us. But is the story about the bed-hopping priest true?"

"I never knew anyone in my life with more imagination than my nephew. That libertine priest from Pomerania came straight from his head."

Interrupt this dumb-ass right now, inspector, and show him who's boss, said Lord Dixon.

"Monseñor, I haven't talked with you about the most important thing," said Inspector Morales, moving his head close. "I made a video with my phone when they killed your nephew."

The monseñor made cautious signals telling them to follow him to his office.

The frosted and yellow-tinted glass of the windows that gave onto the street reflected a pale glow that seemed to tremble on the walls of the office, which were unadorned save for a lithograph hanging behind the desk. The Virgin of the Ascension, patron saint of Ocotal, was rising into heaven among azure clouds from which cherubs' heads stood out in abundance. From somewhere behind the furniture where baptismal and marriage certificates were stored, the sound of rats rummaging around could be heard.

The monseñor went to his desk, where he sat down in an easy chair that had stuffing poking through a tear in the headrest. Inspector Morales moved behind him and extended the cell phone to him. They watched the video time and time again, while Rambo, who had a clear memory of the crime's sequence of events, entertained himself by perusing the dates on the spines of the registry books, which went back to 1878.

At the monseñor's request, Inspector Morales froze and enlarged the pick-up driver's image.

"That man was with the police officers that I saw when I went to the station today."

"Was he wearing a uniform?"

"No. Dressed like a civilian. He was wearing the same shirt."

"What was he doing there?"

"Nothing in particular. He was talking to the duty officer about Zidane's return as the coach of Real Madrid."

"So they were a paramilitary unit. They were following the two of us, but they found your nephew instead."

Rambo moved closer. "If it's true that they were following us, that means they were watching us from the border, which means they probably figured out where we were hiding," he said. "And if that were true, we'd be a couple of stiffs."

Never underestimate a fool, for he can surprise you with a lesson in wisdom. An astute maxim from Confucius, said Lord Dixon.

"Let's assume that they weren't following us and that the killing had nothing to do with us. Why make such an effort to murder a coyote? Unless he owed them a huge debt."

"What could such a simple soul possibly owe such criminals, inspector? We can't even be sure that my nephew actually worked as a guide. His real job was selling lottery tickets, and he did it more as an excuse to talk with people than to make money."

"But he knew how to find the shortcuts very well at night, even with a crippled man like my *jefe*."

"The path he showed you is no shortcut. It's the same one he used every time he crossed the border. People on both sides of the border knew him well and considered him harmless. So they never stopped him."

"So what could possibly motivate him to take the risk of helping us cross back?" asked Rambo.

"Five-thousand pesos, Don Serafín. And when he found out that you didn't have the money, he accepted a phone as payment."

"But to kill him at that time and place, they must have had him under close surveillance," Inspector Morales interrupted.

"Inspector, someone in town had instructions to notify them when my nephew appeared. Seeing him there wouldn't have been an unusual thing."

"Someone from the guard post on the summit spotted him when he went for breakfast at Las Culecas," said Rambo.

Your protégé here continues to earn my respect with his perspicacity, inspector, said Lord Dixon.

The monseñor opened a desk drawer and passed a loose sheet of paper to Inspector Morales.

"They killed him because of me. They shed the blood of an innocent to silence me."

The top of the sheet contained an emblem depicting two crossed AK-47s.

Inspector Morales read the sheet aloud:

COMMANDOS IN DEFENSE OF LIGHT
AND REDEMPTION ("CLR")

The imperialists, oligarchs, bourgeoise, demons in cassocks, etc., built their kingdom of unrighteousness upon the dead bodies of thousands of people and numberless outrageous lies before the arrival of LIGHT AND REDEMPTION.
One of these cassock-wearing demons, a faithful lackey

of his imperial masters and back-stabbing traitors, is as despicable as other priests and bishops like him, and he uses his church's pulpit to spread his venom.

But the five true elements known as earth, wind, fire, water, and ether, that is, the transcendent spirit, have created a pact of love and balance that will never allow our people to be robbed again of their revolutionary dream, the dream of a vibrant, passionate, and proud people who can use their right hand to offer either the sword of war or the branch of peace.

By word and deed, the only thing these priests and monseñors know how to do is spread lies while protected behind their luxurious robes. They seek to fog the minds of their believers and usurp their churches on behalf of their false god. In their search to create formulas for extermination, they devote all their power to poison souls with their psychological terrorism (an alternate mythology of death).

As servants of the demon-king Asmodeus, they use their sermons to report false information and close the ears of church members, seeking to confuse them with merciless acts of manipulation.

As has occurred in the past, the time has now come to return everything to harmony, to a peace represented by the balance of the elements.

We warn you now, Monseñor UNWELCOME, that you either shut your mouth or we will shut it for you. Our patience is running out. AND YOU BETTER SHUT DOWN your radio station too, or we will shut it down for you.

Remember that bullets can penetrate priestly robes.

But before they do,

WE WILL GIVE YOU AN INITIAL WARNING.

Watch for it.

AND IF YOU DON'T HEED IT, THE SECOND ONE WILL COME FOR YOU.

The Light of Truth is the precept of Love.

"The psycho who wrote this has so many rocks in his head that he's absolutely bat-shit, *Jefe.*"

The crazier they are, the more dangerous they are, said Lord Dixon. There's nothing worse than a lunatic with a gun.

[53]

"Beyond the word-salad here, what exactly are they accusing you of, monseñor?" Inspector Morales asked, returning the letter.

"The Church is prophetic, inspector, and when facing corrupt and deceitful power, the Church cannot be silent. That's why I don't mince words in my sermons, or take half-measures in my apostolic work with the people."

"What radio station are they referring to?"

"A station called 'Madre y Maestra,' which does its broadcasts from beside the parsonage here. The station always gives a platform to people who want to expose crimes and injustice."

"And this little piece of trash. When did you get it?"

"A week ago. They distributed it during Sunday mass, and one of the members brought it to me in the sacristy."

"Is this the only threat you've received?"

"They paint the church's walls with graffiti that I stopped trying to erase some time ago. And they add comments to all my social-media posts: vulgarity and constant death threats."

That's what Doña Sofía, who's an expert in this kind of thing, would call a professional troll, said Lord Dixon.

"I still don't see how your nephew fits into this picture. Why do you think the threat refers to him?"

Your powers of logical reasoning are beginning to fail you, inspector, said Lord Dixon. Even your associate Serafín can figure out that one.

The monseñor searched his phone, and after finding one of the last messages he had posted to his Twitter account, he gave the phone to Inspector Morales:

> The blood of Celedonio Rivera, a campesino murdered by a military patrol after he was falsely accused of possessing firearms, cries out to the heavens. His family has been harassed for denouncing this crime. A country without justice is like a tree felled by axe blows.

Someone with the user name MAMA CHANCHONA, who had no followers, had written the following response beneath the Monseñor's post:

> We're going to cut your tree down with a freshly sharpened axe, priest and son of a thousand whores, but we'll start first by pruning your branches.

"You interpret *branches* to mean any of your nieces or nephews?"

Inspector, your neurons are drowning in alcohol, said Lord Dixon.

"Can't you see, *Jefe*, that their little manifesto talks about two warnings? They've already given one."

"A short response posted on Friday, and they killed my nephew on Saturday."

"They kill Gato de Oro, who is a branch, and the message they send with that murder is this: If you keep hammering away at the tiger's balls, we'll go after your niece, who is the other branch, and we'll leave the tree without branches at all," declared Rambo, absolutely convinced.

"But that's not the way I do things, Don Serafín. I won't allow them to twist my arm. Inspector, can you send me the video on WhatsApp? I'll post it on social media and expose the crime."

"I'd advise against that. The video shows some masked men shooting guns on a country road, but the victim doesn't appear at all. That doesn't prove anything. And as for the pick-up driver, they hide him as soon as the video starts."

The monseñor thought for a moment, his hand on his pectoral cross.

"Regardless, they won't silence me."

"Don't be so pig-headed. Listen to the *jefe*, or at least tell your niece to find a deep cave where she can hide."

"As for the two of us, it's better if we continue to Managua. There are too many dangerous eggs in the same basket here."

"What kind of crazy idea is that, inspector? You have nowhere to go, and it will be more dangerous for you in Managua than here."

"We're safe right here, Jefe. As long as we don't go out on the street, we'll be fine."

This one's already enjoying la dolce vita, said Lord Dixon. Get out of bed, have something to eat, and then go back to bed.

"In cases like this, staying in the same place is the most dangerous thing to do. We'll find a way to arrange things in Managua."

"Why not try the parsonage for the Divine Mercy Church? Padre Pancho is a friend of mine, and he would be more than happy to let you stay there."

You'll meet the old sacristan there, the prefect for the Padre Pío guild. She's the one you heard about before, inspector, said Lord Dixon.

"We can try that," Inspector Morales agreed.

"Tomorrow is Tuesday, which means Padre Pupiro has a trip to make," said the monseñor, standing up. "You'll leave with him very early."

CHAPTER FOUR

An Ill-Fated Birthday Party

I N ARANJUEZ ESTATES, people can buy any house with a twenty-year mortgage. All the houses are the same size and have the same façade, repeated block after block, and the real-estate developers baptized all the streets with attractive Mediterranean names: Málaga, Torremolinos, Ibiza, Alicante, Marbella, Formentor. The neighborhood includes a carefully mowed lawn along the walk-ways, a playground for children, a clubhouse with a pool, and outdoor grills for Sunday barbeques, all done with modest proportions, plus a gated entry manned by uniformed guards to make the illusion of exclusiveness complete

Professor Zoraida abandoned her old house in the Campo Bruce neighborhood after receiving nothing less than the Aranjuez Estates' model home as a reward for her work as a spiritual adviser. A copy of the transfer deed, photos of the house's interior and exterior, and blueprints (which helped guide the installation of hidden microphones) all appeared in the security file that Tongolele opened on his own mother.

Tongolele learned about security files from the start when he underwent a training course at the State Security School in Plovdiv, Bulgaria. Such files cannot omit anything, beginning with donations like the one his mother received, along with other favors and gifts, the value of which can later be collected in case of some misstep. And no one is free of missteps.

When Professor Zoraida received the key to her house, the furniture and decor came with it—all from El Gallo Más Gallo home furnishings, as listed on the copy of an invoice that also appeared in the security file:

> 1 Automatic Washing Machine with 30-Pound Capacity
> 1 Side-by-Side Refrigerator

1 Stove with 6 Burners

1 Microwave Oven, plus 1 Toaster and 1 Blender

1 Bedroom Set comprised of 1 King-Size Bed, along with a Headboard
and Footboard

1 Living Room Set comprised of 4 Pieces, 2 Easy Chairs, and 1 Sofa with
Seating for 4, upholstered with a raffia-fabric print

1 Colonial-Type Bar with 3 Stools

1 Sound System

1 Dining-Room Set comprised of a Table, 6 Chairs, and 1 Hutch

In addition, a Nissan Patrol had been parked in the garage, with a red-silk bow on the hood—photo included in the security file.

A Chinese box began to arrive regularly in Aranjuez Estates. Whenever the box's convoy approached, an Air Force helicopter patrolled the area. In addition, the guards manning the gate were disarmed, and the neighbors were forced to form a long line of stopped vehicles, prohibited from going to their own houses, regardless of whether they were returning from work or bringing their children home from school.

Night had already fallen when Tongolele's taxi finally exited the highway to Masaya and entered the patched and pothole-filled road to Gothel Valley. Through the tree branches, the dim signs for various businesses could be seen: mom-and-pop stores, bars, mini-markets, open-air fried-food places, a video arcade, and an auto shop converted into an evangelical church, where the preacher's forceful imprecations against sin resounded from large box speakers located on the sidewalk. Yet another line of cars appeared, slower because people were either trying to park near the sidewalks or stopping before attempting the challenging task of entering narrow gates that someone would come to open after repeated honks from car horns.

Laura León's voice began singing "Suavecito"—the ring tone from the phone in Pedrón's shirt pocket.

"It's Fabiola, commissioner," Pedrón said, lowering his voice and covering the microphone.

"I can't talk. I'm driving. Can't you see that?"

"He's driving, Doña Fabiola. Just give me a message for him and he'll call you back." Pedrón's voice was courteous as he held the phone close to his ear, agreeing respectfully between pauses.

"What did she want?"

"She's arriving from Sébaco. They have disturbances there: some students won't allow a Tree of Life to be installed on the school's grounds."

"And what about their shit-wipe police force? Why do they even exist?"

"The citizens' committees caught the student leaders and turned them over to the police. The police brought them as prisoners to Managua, but the uproar has become much worse."

"So why call me? What do we have to do with that? We don't beat people up in the streets."

"She just wanted you to know because she sees the whole thing as an ugly situation."

Fabiola Miranda, 35 years old, raised in the Las Calabazas region of the municipality of Ciudad Darío, had a high-school diploma and owned a wholesale and retail business. Despite the fact that she was Tongolele's lover, he had a security file about her as well because she fell under the category of Class A agent.

From the age of 13, Fabiola had belonged to a group of street peddlers that had also been known by several names: *weeklies*, because they reported to their distributor each week; *swatchers*, because they had begun their business by selling swatches of fabric; and *sector heads*, because each was assigned a particular territory or sector. They offered all kinds of merchandise on credit from door to door, region to region, plantation to plantation, and neighborhood to neighborhood. The merchandise included women's shoes and socks, underwear, bras, blouses, aprons, and printed bandanas, all of it sold in eternal weekly installments.

By age 15, Fabiola understood the business well enough to dispense with her distributor in Ciudad Darío, a stingy old woman who always manipulated the accounts in her favor. So, Fabiola began working directly with Abdul Mahmud, a Turkish wholesaler on Matagalpa's Comercio Street, whom she beguiled when he saw such a young girl with exceptionally sharp fangs.

And that is how Fabiola created her own network: twelve, fifteen sector heads, experienced men and women who knew all the tricks of the trade. She called them *uncle* or *aunt* and they called her *niece*, but such niceties did not deter her from controlling them with a firm hand: she brooked no games. Fishy excuses? Fired on the spot. And as to customers, the sector heads had strict orders if

[59]

anyone missed two payments in a row: repossess the merchandise, even if that meant ripping a woman's panties off while she was wearing them.

At age 19 Fabiola transferred her headquarters to Managua's Mercado Oriental. By then she had three trucks, and her net-work—growing larger by the day—covered Matagalpa, Estelí, Jinotega, and Nueva Segovia. After years of hard work, her inventory of goods for home-delivery now included school back-packs, wigs, picture frames, table decorations, saint statuettes and religious cards, saucepans, frying pans, sheets, tablecloths, bed-spreads, and duvets.

Shortly after Daniel Ortega's electoral victory in 2006, Zorai-da had talked to Tongolele one day about Fabiola: I don't want to get mixed up in the professional activities that you never tell me about, and I understand perfectly what you've said: I attend to my life, and you attend to yours. But I have a client—intelligent, sharp—who comes to me for advice about the future of her sales business, and she has become a close friend. She has a network of around 300 salespeople who carry suitcases filled with goods as they wander the streets. Some carry their suitcases by hand, while others go by horse, or motorcycle, or bike. They walk through plantation gates; they enter day laborers' camps and the most isolated settlements; they go everywhere you might look for them: to Puerto Morazán in the west, to Wiwilí in the north, to El Ayote in Chontales, and even to La Fonseca in the depart-ment of Nueva Guinea—the most remote part of the Atlantic coast. And she's operating here in Managua too. These sales-people are the Devil himself: they know every neighborhood, street by street. Imagine the most godforsaken place possible, and they go there. They're all over Ciudad Sandino; they cover Los Brasiles; and they're arriving in Mateare. And I thought to myself: Surely my son will be interested in the ears of these peo-ple who hear things everywhere, and my client—more enterpris-ing than almost any other woman—can put those ears to work for him if he treats her with care and respect. Because what she wants is to keep growing, to earn respect, to continue expanding her business. Do you know what she wants, among other things? She wants everything on computer: inventories of goods, all the bookkeeping. Since she's not stupid, she hasn't wasted any time, and she's already finished a course of study. She knows all about operating systems, hard drives, and the cloud—forward and backward. And she's learning English too; she's already reached an advanced level in conversation.

My client says that in addition to needing an injection of capital to automate everything, she also needs protection and support, of course. She's afraid of scheming bandits, customs agents who demand bribes for everything, high-interest lenders, banks that drown people in seas of documents overflowing with fine-print, and lawsuit-addicted lawyers who explain everything backwards. I always show her the same card—the three of gold coins—to convince her that good fortune awaits her like a golden steed at her door, but that steed needs a hand to tame it. And I always prophesy to her that the owner of that hand will make his appearance. And that hand is yours; there's no other.

Tongolele set up a meeting with Fabiola one Monday at noon in the port of Salvador Allende, making a reservation at a restaurant owned by Mono Ponciano, a long-time collaborator and informant. The room, which contained round windows resembling the portholes of a trans-Atlantic ship and provided a view of the gray lake ruffled by small waves, never smelled like anything but a restroom, its ceiling a fishing net dotted with crystal floats and bobbers. Fabiola entered the room. She had strong dark African features, her hair dyed a somber blonde, with bunions that caused excruciating pain as she walked on rubber-soled platform shoes, and the Ferragamo purse that swayed from her shoulder was as counterfeit as counterfeit could possibly be. Her blouse revealed a piercing hanging from her exposed navel, while sequined butterflies adorned each of her pant legs.

They had barely sat down when the waiter brought two glass bowls of mixed ceviche that she had ordered before entering the room, along with two large glasses of Mexican michelada.

"I don't drink," said Tongolele, stopping the waiter before he could place the micheladas on the table.

"Leave them," Fabiola countermanded.

After a moment of uncertainty, the waiter obeyed her. And with the caution of a person who fears getting burned, Fabiola raised the glass—its great cold creating condensation—to her lips.

"Professor Zoraida has told me …," he said, trying to begin.

"Your mother," she said, stopping him. "Or is the fact that you are mother and son classified information?"

"Professor Zoraida," he persisted uncomfortably.

"Don't be ridiculous, sweetheart," she said, and advancing her fingers with blood-red painted nails, she caressed his facial scars.

He grabbed her wrist to remove her hand from his face.

"How can I help you?" he asked

"I'm not asking for help. We scratch each other's backs. I put my network of sector heads at your service, and you resolve problems for me."

"What problems do you have?"

"What your mother already told you: protection, and a bank loan that doesn't kill me with high interest. I have to modernize my company, and I need fresh money. More storehouses, a bigger trucking fleet. Desktop computers. And certain software."

"The last item: What is it?"

"It's a program that allows me to track even the very last needle in my warehouses: when an item leaves the warehouse; where it goes; when do I need to replace it. And on my computer screen, the program can show me every sector head's accounts, how much each client owes each sector head, and what the pay-off dates are for every installment plan. Plus my cash flow, and the bank balances."

"Is this program expensive?"

"I'm thinking of an Abakus XL program. It costs a bit of money, but I don't want some pirated copy. I want a new program, still in the box."

Tongolele began chewing on a soda cracker, the kind normally served with ceviche. He then inserted his fork into a piece of shrimp, followed by a chunk of pompano fish.

"The protection is free. But as for the new capital, there will be no banks. I'm going to give you my own money."

She looked at him, her lips pressed together with an expression suggesting displeasure, but her eyes smiled.

"Are you proposing a partnership, commissioner?"

"You tell me how much you need, and we split the profits 50-50."

"We'll write it all up so we don't forget," she said, and she extended her hand to touch his face again with her fingers and their blood-red painted nails.

Before that year came to a close, the agreement bestowed several Mercado Oriental crowns upon Fabiola: queen of the sector heads, with a network that eliminated all competition within the nation; queen of contraband, with no customs inspector or police chief who dared to stop the cargo trucks that entered the country's northern border from Guasaule; queen of pirated videos, which she made and distributed herself; and queen of bulk used clothing or *ropa de paca*, which she imported from the United States, laundering, ironing, disinfecting, and then selling each item—be it a blouse, a shirt, or a pair of pants—for a fixed price of two dollars. Pedrón flattered her by saying: "With all that *ropa de paca*, Doña Fabiola, you should call yourself 'Paquita.'"

Once both parties understood the agreement's basic terms well enough that the lawyers could draft a contract, the michelada had been warm in Tongolele's hand for some time, and the lettuce garnishing his ceviche had long since wilted. After the fingers with their painted blood-red nails had touched his face for the sixth time, he thought to himself: If she's such a demon in business, she must be a demon in bed. An overwhelming desire washed over him to see her undressed—or better yet to undress her himself—and he made a bald proposition, without any preamble and with a voice that was more like a bark, that they should go to his house.

Dying of curiosity to see Tongolele's lair, the demon accepted, already deep into her third michelada. And so they took a taxi there, with Pedrón following at the wheel of Fabiola's car, a mustard-colored Ford Fiesta into which he managed to stuff himself only after great difficulty. The lair stood in a hidden corner of Lomas de Motastepe, close to Asososca Lagoon, with a high wall surrounding the yard just like the customs agency in Las Colinas. The house's interior walls contained no paintings or photographs, while the living-room furniture—dark, unyielding, and made of woven cane—looked like something from an office lobby. The bedroom had only a solitary bed, lacking a headboard and fitted with lemon-yellow sheets, while the air conditioner left any occupant chilled to the bone.

Tongolele had broken the commandment about never getting involved with agents or collaborators, a commandment printed on page one of the Bulgarian code of conduct; he had also violated his own personal rule about never bringing women to his own house.

A ferocious demon in bed? To his surprise, he found that Fabiola was a woman of minimal experience, an unsalted potato that required patience and just the right touch because she insisted on maintaining the missionary position, and she never gave off any scent of passion but rather a smell like that of some wild animal's hair, while the michelada's beer fermented in her mouth. Furthermore, despite the fact that she wore blood-red, or rather, demon-red lace panties and a lace bra that matched the color of her nails, there was no way to remove the bra, and she wrapped herself in a sheet before using the bathroom to empty her bladder. She was undoubtedly one of those women who sleeps in her own bed wearing a long-sleeved nightgown that covers her ankles.

"Almost a virgin," she had breathed into his ear. "I'm almost a virgin."

"There's no such thing as almost, Mamacita," he had answered. "With this issue of in-and-out, there are no such things as half-measures, and that which is torn open can't be sewn back together."

"But you haven't understood me," she had said, bending over in the bed and leaning her head on the palm of her hand. "I'm still half a virgin, because very few men have touched me."

Meaningless sexual encounters, without consequences or commitments. If there was one rule that had served Fabiola well in life, it was keeping her sex life separate from her business—caution and prudence, no fooling around with subordinates or distributors, because otherwise she could lose everything she had worked for by rutting like some animal. Mahmoud the Turk had said that very thing after he confessed he had wanted to take her into his soul. One day, the two of them had been driving from Matagalpa to Ciudad Darío to make an inspection. Without prior warning, he pulled into a motel gate. She responded by bursting into tears, as if she was about to have her throat cut, a reaction that spurred the stunned man to beg her a thousand pardons. *That's how we're alike, Mamacita. We follow rules,* he said, although he tried and failed to add: *But we make exceptions.*

Her performance in bed continued to be ordinary in every way. No matter how much Tongolele tried to force her to try other variations, no matter how many new perversions he tried to teach her, she angrily rejected all of them no matter how modest they might be. *What do you think I am? Some whore from La Conga Roja?* She said and did such things, but she quickly forgot to take precautions about appearing naked, and she began carrying a small music player in her purse, which she played at high volume, filling the room with lively music, and every time she went to the bathroom she returned in the nude and danced to Colombian *cumbias* by Sonora Dinamita, and she would try to convince him—still naked as well—to leave the bed and join her, deliberately annoying him and dancing with abandon. Who could reconcile all her words and actions? Regardless, everyone knew that while the commissioner's nickname came from Tongolele, the panther goddess and Mexican cabaret dancer with the white stripe in her hair that matched his own, the man didn't know how to dance. He had lead feet: a broomstick moved more gracefully. *There'll be no dancing, Mamacita. If I don't dance with my clothes on, you're certainly not going to see me dance naked.*

He had became infatuated with her. Pedrón would not drop the subject: *What has that woman given you? Has she hexed you with a panty infusion, the kind where a woman steeps her panties in water and makes a man drink it?* But the couple didn't live together; Tongolele wouldn't allow that. When he wanted to see her, he would send Pedrón to look for her in the Mercado Oriental or in Bello Horizonte, where she lived. Their encounters were like trysts in a motel, although they always met in Tongolele's house in Motastepe, where signs of Fabiola's sales business became visible: a plush rug on the threshold that read WELCOME in English; a ceramic plaque depicting the Holy Family attached alongside the door, the legend beneath declaring GOD BLESS THIS HOUSE AND ALL WHO LIVE HERE. In addition, the living room, which had been so uninspiring before, now displayed myriad porcelain objects dispersed all over the place as if they were wandering about lost: a pair of ballerinas balancing on their toes; a sad clown; Snow White and the seven dwarves; a little girl moving back and forth on a swing; the Scottish terriers from Black and White Whiskey; an elephant with an oriental palanquin on its back; lambs with ribbons on their necks, a girl shepherding them along with her crook. Fabiola was the person who had given Tongolele the pencil sharpener with a Fred Flintstone figurine that he carried everywhere in his satchel.

During the moments when the two were alone within the

bedroom's four walls, after the cold air had overcome the heat, they had their best conversations about the confidential matters in their mutual areas of competence, for there is no bed that does not become a confessional. If Fabiola's sector heads, who were committed to seek out conversations, told her something containing relevant information, she passed that information along in the bedroom, although she also included it in her weekly report. Her report included military subordinates who had interactions with disaffected elements, government employees who made seditious comments, municipal officials who acted on their own, highly ranked political secretaries involved in activities they did not report, protestant pastors who resisted the Sandinista party line, and priests who took hostile stances in their sermons. All this in addition to rumors, hearsay, nonconformity, jokes, and pranks.

Not infrequently, the intelligence Fabiola gathered through her network filled gaps in the details of cases he was already investigating. So the two compared information, made connections, and summarized everything. And before saying good-bye to each other, before Pedrón drove her back home, Tongolele repeated his ritual words: *No one else knows or needs to know what you know. Remember that regarding who knows what, you and I will answer with our necks.*

The taxi was approaching the gates of Aranjuez Estates when it met the convoy headed by traffic police on motorcycles, who cleared both lanes. Behind the motorcycles came the patrol cars with their light bars flashing like Christmas decorations: the Chinese box was coming back.

The motorcycle officers raised phosphorescent batons into the air, obligating Tongolele to abandon the narrow band of pavement. He watched from the gutter as three Mercedes SUVs—all sporting the same silvery color and polarized glass—passed by, one of them containing the Chinese box. Hilux pick-ups marked the end of the convoy, all of them filled with special-forces artillerymen equipped as if for combat.

"Not even my mother's birthday can stop the arrival of the Chinese box."

"Who knows? Maybe this time the convoy was simply delivering her birthday present. The powers from on high always send her generous gifts."

Still bewildered, the gateway watchmen who had been forcibly removed from their guardhouse during the visit were returned to duty. Meanwhile, Tongolele's taxi—last in line—waited to enter, the gate rising for each vehicle in turn.

"By this time they'll have drunk all the champagne, commissioner. And they'll have eaten all the caviar."

"An Aeroflot flight-attendant once offered me caviar, Pedrito. I asked her what it was, and she said eggs, so I asked for two of them, scrambled with ham. Now you see how ignorant I am about the finer things in life."

"They all talk about how great caviar is, but it smells like pussy," Pedrón said with disgust.

Tongolele did not regret arriving late. His mother's birthday was always celebrated like a child's party: an arch of multi-colored balloons decorating the front door, garlands of crepe paper hanging from the roof, a marimba band playing in the yard. And the ASP's own Section for Banquets and Social Events provided everything, from waiters to food to liquor—even the cake and birthday candles.

To celebrate the occasion, his mother, always dressed in white, would wear a silk sari draped down over her head, and on both wrists she would display bracelets with healing stones: amethyst, pink quartz, tourmaline, and tiger eye. She would remain seated in one of the large dining-table chairs to receive congratulations from government ministers and vice-ministers, army and police commanders, and ambassadors from four allies: Cuba, Venezuela, Iran, and Russia.

In a small suitcase, Tongolele carried the gift that Fabiola had asked him to bring: a heavy pewter table clock, the dial containing Roman numerals and supported by two pudgy cherubs. A formality. He could easily have come with his hands completely empty: His mother already had more than enough living-room decorations and kitchen items, and the clock would simply add to the excess.

Pedrón remained in the taxi as Tongolele had ordered, while a man named Paquito, who held the rank of corporal within the Agency for Special Protection and had been assigned as Zoraida's

manservant, came out to welcome Tongolele. Paquito made an ob-
sequious effort to take the gift, but Tongolele refused.

The manservant's effeminate affect never sat well with Tongolele. He never knew if Paquito's obedient smile was sly or sar-
castic. The man always walked with overly cautious steps and wore
floral-print shirts with narrow-legged pants, and he constantly
chewed gum with regular jaw movements. He cried over the most
trivial things, and he consistently failed to link his stories together
because he kept on lengthening them and adding details.

No lingering visitor could be seen, nor were there any vehicles in the street or expectant chauffeurs. The doorway contained
no balloon arch. No garlands hung from the roof. And the area
showed no sign of the kind of disorderly theatre that typically in-
dicates that a party has ended: dirty plates waiting to be picked
up, glasses with melting ice, baskets with leftover food, half-empty
bottles, half of an iced cake with its candles fallen over.

Nor was there any indication of the gift from the woman who
was Zoraida's single client, a gift that was usually highly visible. Last year the gift had been a smiling pot-bellied Buddha in
chrome-plated porcelain, seated in the lotus position. Perhaps this
year's gift had been a different type. Maybe even a genuine trip to
India to visit Sathya Sai Baba's mausoleum in Puttaparthi.

"Your mother went to bed early because she has a headache,"
Paquito told Tongolele.

Tongolele walked to the bedroom carrying the gift, and pushed the
door open with his shoulder. The shadowy room received light only
from the bathroom's half-opened door, and Zoraida sat up in bed.

"Well, this is a great time to wish me a happy birthday," she
said, sounding listless.

He laid the gift on the bed and sat down gingerly next to her.
Zoraida moved one of her plump, smooth hands—hands that continually sprouted more and more spots the color of ripe cocoa—
toward his lap, and the bracelets on her wrists jingled with an echo
that sounded far away. Tongolele used both of his hands to hold
onto the hand she had proffered.

"And the party?" he asked.

"There was no party," responded Zoraida, her hand escaping
like a fish struggling to return to the water.

"What do you mean?"

"No one came."

"They most likely had an emergency cabinet meeting. There are some problems with people disturbing the peace."

"Nobody told me that the party had been canceled. The magnetic field that surrounds me has been filled with chaotic waves since yesterday."

"So many collisions between magnetic waves can create a headache," said Tongolele, testing her with the kind of facetious comment that he well knew annoyed her.

Social media contained all kinds of memes mocking magnetic waves, astral planes, Fátima's hand, and the Trees of Life, and for that reason Zoraida made regular appearances in the information and reports submitted by Fabiola's sector heads. Those reports showed Zoraida sitting nude on the floor within a five-pointed star, her thin sagging breasts hanging over her stomach, a cigar held in her mouth as she recited the prayer to the garrobo.

"One of these days, the negative waves will create a shadowy field for you, and they will hide what you hope to see."

"I have eyes everywhere that see far beyond any magnetic ones. And those eyes can see through walls."

"Once the appointed hour arrives, those eyes won't help at all. Any lightning bolt that hits me will leave you blind."

"All of this drama just because some government ministers didn't come to sing 'Hoppy Birdie' to you," Tongolele responded, attempting to laugh again.

"My client gave an express order prohibiting them to come."

"You're imagining things, Mamá. If that were true, she wouldn't have sent you a present at all."

"She didn't send me a present. The waiters didn't come; nobody brought any food, not even drinks."

Tongolele took her hand once more.

"You're tense, Mamá. You're completely tense. What did you take for your headache?"

"Ibuprofen, just in case. For the agony that's drilling into my brain, but nothing helps."

"Mamá, she's feeling tremendous tension too because of all these ridiculous protests about the Trees of Life. You have to put yourself in her shoes."

"The protests against the Trees of Life are precisely why she's angry with me. She was very clear about that in the message from the Chinese box."

"I ran into the convoy as I was arriving here."

"She doesn't want to understand that the beneficent aura that protects against the evil eye stops at the number 69."

"What does the number 69 have to do with it?"

"Once you plant more than 69 trees, the trees begin to have the opposite effect, and you enter a phase of reverse magnetic action."

Her hand tried to escape, fly away, but Tongolele held fast.

"Nothing bad can possibly happen with one more tree or one less, Mamá."

"The number 69 represents the upright and the inverted, heaven and earth, the place where the yin and the yang simultaneously complement and oppose each other. That balance is sacred."

"And that's why she's angry with you? Because you said that she shouldn't put up more than 69 of those trees?"

"I warned her at her tipping point that the number 69 might have been more than tripled. Such a thing means complete confusion of the magnetic elements."

"You should have been careful about giving her such warnings. Now she'll blame you for all the school protests."

"That's the accusation she made against me in the Chinese box. She says I provoked the conjunction of opposing elements."

"You play a political role, Mamá. Don't you realize that? Sometimes it's better not to make predictions about things that people don't want to hear."

"I'm not a fake," she responded, wrenching her hand away. "The fact that you don't believe in my science doesn't mean the arcane forces don't wield their power."

"What's the role of all counselors, no matter what kind?" Tongolele asked, trying and failing to take back her hand. "They give their opinions, which can then be accepted or ignored. And if they're ignored, that's that."

"It was wrong for me to listen to you when you told me to add or remove names from the lists for Sai Baba."

"These are questions of national security, Mamá. And the fact is that it doesn't happen all the time."

"What questions of national security could possibly be involved?

Nothing but your own plans and schemes—and all very dangerous."

"Sometimes I need to help you decide what's best. For strategic purposes."

"I'm here to protect my client, not manipulate her. The Great Powers themselves gave me that mission. You're nothing but a spy, but I see into the great beyond."

"It doesn't hurt my feelings that you call me a spy. I uncover facts so that political decisions can be made with information verified by different sources."

"And what am I to you? A charlatan. And despite what you think of me, I defend you. You can't even imagine how much I defend you."

"What can you possibly defend me from, Mamá?" Tongolele said cautiously. "No one has ever complained about me. I fulfill all my professional responsibilities."

"In the Chinese box that I just received, an entire side of one of the papers was all about you."

"I'm dying of fright!" Tongolele said as he stood up, then stretched and raised his hands as if faking a big yawn.

"*Your son laughs at me behind my back because he says I'm filling the country with trees that are either sterile or gay, the kind that can never bear fruit.* The message says things like that."

"Show me the paper."

"You know very well that every message has to be returned in the same box it came in."

"That is absolutely absurd," Tongolele said, yawning again.

He searched his memory for any occasion from which that accusation could have originated, and he remembered the wizened-child's face of the dwarf Manzano, a man who wore high-heeled boots to make himself look taller. Tongolele had broached the subject of the trees only with Manzano, and he had done so only a single time. And Manzano himself had suggested that the trees were gay, which had made them both laugh.

"Is this the first time she's talked about me?" Tongolele asked, sitting down on the bed again.

"Until now she's never mentioned you, as if we weren't mother and son."

"We're always exposed to schemes and envy. There's nothing we can do about it."

"You need to find out where this accusation came from. Don't let it go."

"Let's not pay any attention to it. Stories get more tangled as we try to disentangle them."

"But someone has attacked you with this, so the best thing to do is to be on guard. You never know what's going to happen when an enemy is lying in ambush."

"You'll tell me," answered Tongolele, his face no longer able to hide his concern.

"This time it will be the other way around," said Zoraida. "The lightning bolt that strikes you will blind me."

CHAPTER FIVE

The Dark and Fetid Mouth of the Wolf

INSPECTOR MORALES' BLACK clerical shirt stretched tightly across his belly, so much so that he felt the buttons were about to burst, while Rambo's clerical collar constantly made him feel like a turtle with its head stuck forever outside its shell.

The fugitives' disguises for the Managua trip were the brainchild of Monseñor Ortez, who had urgently requested the shirts from a woman in the guild of La Virgen de la Asunción. The woman served as a guild custodian and also owned a sewing and tailoring school in the barrio of San Nicolás de Tolentino. Felipe de Jesús had left to fetch the garments when the woman had reported that they were ready, and Rambo had opened the back room's door wearing only his underwear to accept the bag containing the painstakingly ironed shirts.

Barely after seeing the two men leave the room in their new clothes, Rita Boniche covered her mouth to contain her laughter. Failing to stifle her merriment, she fled quickly to the kitchen with giant heron leaps. But she returned with careful steps as the monseñor bade the men farewell in the parsonage hallway at the door of the car that would take them back to Managua; furthermore, she stuffed each man's shirt with a 100-córdoba bill and then ran out again, offering no opportunity for explanation or expressions of gratitude.

The two men squeezed together into the cabin of the Mahindra Scorpio pick-up, which looked for all appearances like a pull-string toy. At the wheel sat Padre Octavio Pupiro, who served as the parish's coadjutor and drove every Tuesday to Managua's Cáritas storehouses, where he collected supplies and medicine for the San Antonio de Padua Home for the Elderly.

Padre Pupiro, likewise a Dominican, was originally from Catarina and had been ordained in the seminary of San Juan de la Cruz, which was located in an indigenous village called Mixco that Guatemala City had swallowed up many years ago. A hearty eater—as evidenced by his jowls, double chin, and rotund body—and a cheerful man, he nevertheless burned like a match when he became enraged. As a legacy of his indigenous Chirotega ancestors, he also had wispy hair, which he tried to smooth down using a pomade saturated with powder.

As they all said farewell, the monseñor told Inspector Morales that his niece Edelmira and her husband were planning to move to Honduras for a time. Leonel had a cousin there in Danlí who managed a tobacco company owned by some Cubans who lived in Miami, and the cousin would hire Leonel as a transport manager. Within two days the gas station would be turned over to someone else, and the couple would be on the other side of the border. The two could arrange things fairly easily because they had no children.

The monseñor appeared serene, perhaps even content to have that burden lifted from his back, and Inspector Morales simply could not bring himself to ask: *And what about you? What's going to happen to you?* Now that the tree no longer had any branches to be shot away, all that remained was the trunk.

A great deal of naiveté resided in the monseñor's heart. That naiveté was dangerous, as Inspector Morales had argued the previous night with Lord Dixon, who had suddenly become overcome by sleeplessness.

Without what you call naiveté, there's no sanctity, inspector, declared Lord Dixon.

"Isn't a living shepherd more useful to the flock than a dead one? He gets killed; people make a statue of him; and then the bats take a dump all over the statue on his altar."

And when you were a guerrilla, didn't you believe that it was better to be alive in a woman's bed than dead on a mountain at the mercy of buzzards?

"I never stuck my neck out so that they could cut my head off, which is why I carried a gun—one that was always loaded."

The monseñor is armed with the Word. The Word is more powerful than a four-barrel machine gun, comrade.

"That's just the kind of ridiculous shit you believe. Bullets can penetrate priests' robes, just like those assholes did with our guide. No word can stop bullets."

Would you take up a gun again, inspector?

"Tongolele's gorillas took the pistol I had before sending me to Honduras. That's why I don't have a gun."

And would you shoot it if you had it?

"If necessary, I wouldn't hesitate. I can't run because of my limp, but I'm not handing myself over to them without a fight."

That's nothing but bravado on your part. You'll be shaking as your pulse is pounding, and they'll fill you with holes before you even take a shot.

"You're asking. I'm answering."

Your days as a fearless balls-out fighter are over. That's the same reason that I don't believe the monseñor should fight for what he thinks is right. With his weapon, which is the Word.

"When it comes to making convoluted statements, you're a master of convolution."

Aren't you the one who said that the monseñor suffers from dangerous naiveté? I'm sure that's exactly what the high Church dignitaries—the ones who sit around shitting their robes with fear—say about him. And what did Christ himself say? I came not to send peace, but a sword. *The monseñor fights his war from the pulpit.*

"So you're a theologian now?"

The truth is that a fat gut and a fat ass make you think more middle class, said Lord Dixon.

"Go to hell," Inspector Morales ordered before falling asleep.

As they were arriving in Totogalpa, before the junction that leads north toward Somoto and south toward Estelí—and from there to Managua—Rambo reached forward from the back seat and turned on the radio looking for music, eventually settling on the Madre y Maestra Station. The station was broadcasting the monseñor's sermon from the final Sunday mass. Rambo tried to change the station, but Inspector Morales grabbed his arm to stop him. He wanted to keep listening:

"…because there are two Nicaraguas, my dear brothers and sisters in Christ Jesus. One consists of those who profit from lavish flattery, from perpetual feasts and orgies, from the egotistical elite, from the old oligarchy that believes only in money, and this first Nicaragua has been joined by a new class of arrogant elites who live in luxury, who used to call themselves revolutionaries, and who now believe only in money as well. The second Nicaragua, the other Nicaragua, is that of the marginalized citizens, the immense majority, those who live in offensive poverty—the poverty of campesinos who eat salted bananas, the poverty of humble laborers who lack a change of clothes. And we watch all this and do nothing.

"We watched those who fought for a new world when they were young as they later committed a coup d'etat against our own people, amending the Constitution to allow them to keep power forever in the name of a dead revolution, and we said nothing. We watched as they robbed and prostituted our institutions, and we said nothing either. We watched as they commandeered the police and the army, and we kept our mouths shut. How easy it is to keep our mouths shut. And how cowardly.

"We watched as they hijacked the unions, and we didn't bat an eye—that wasn't our problem. We pretended not to see when they took over the television and radio stations, and we said nothing. We watched as they plundered the Social Security System and brazenly stole the money we had saved for a dignified retirement, and we remained silent.

"We watch as they shamelessly deforest our land right before our eyes, destroy the pine trees, and pollute and dry up our rivers, and we're all just fine with that, thank you. We watch as they change the history books and fill them with lies. And we watch how they trample on education and take control of the universities. And what is all that to us?

"And most incredibly, we remember the parable of Lazarus and watch as the rich man, dressed in purple and fine linen, a glutton for business who acts as if he can never have enough, sits at the presidential table of Caiaphas. We watch as they cackle and celebrate among themselves, one with the other, the old rich and the new rich. I've said it before and I'll say it again: They surround themselves with flowers to cover the stench of death, the stench of corruption, and we still say nothing. And we keep our mouths shut when they throw crumbs left over from the banquet—crumbs like pigs, chickens, and tin and zinc roofing sheets—all designed to pacify the poor.

"And we watch as their mobs grow, how they mercilessly use clubs to beat those who dare to raise protests, and we continue to say nothing. We watch army patrols murdering campesinos in the fields, as we just saw in the case of our brother Celedonio Rivera, who was killed nearby in Susucayán. We watch them accuse the poor of having hidden weapons, of being cattle rustlers, of growing marijuana and dealing drugs, even though the accused don't even have an extra shirt to wear. And we watch the police dedicate themselves to repression, to supporting the mobs, to throwing innocent people into jail, and we say nothing. Are we going to say nothing forever?

"More taxes to create more tin trees, more schizophrenic whims, less food in the houses of exhausted laborers, and we say nothing. But the shepherd who smells like a sheep places his ear close to the hearts of the humble people, those who are suffering... worthy people... young people... such disgrace... abuse... gnashing of teeth... two Nicaraguas... one only..."

The broadcast signal became lost after they left Yalagüina behind.

"Could they have cut the signal off?" Rambo asked.

"The FM transmitter only reaches half a kilometer; it doesn't go far," said Padre Pupiro as he drove cautiously, both hands gripping the wheel. "It's a miracle that it even reached this place."

"But whoever keeps track of the monseñor is definitely listening closely, and they're recording every word he says," declared Inspector Morales, turning off the radio.

"We're in the Lord's hands, and we commend ourselves to him."

"And you're in the hands of the paramilitary groups."

Pay attention here, said Lord Dixon. Don't get involved where they haven't asked you to preach.

"We can't be priests if we're wearing a muzzle. The cowardly shepherd who's afraid to confront the wolf loses his sheep."

"Until the shepherd earns his palm frond and dies as a saint in the wolf's jaws," responded Inspector Morales.

"Shepherds who smell like cologne become the wolf's allies, inspector. As you heard the monseñor say, we are shepherds who smell like sheep."

"Sermons like that don't even tickle the wolf's ears," Rambo interrupted.

At last some reinforcements, said Lord Dixon. Your friend here is a theologian with something important to say.

"But they warn the sheep that the wolf is stalking them," answered Padre Pupiro.

"And do you believe that the sheep actually want to listen?" Inspector Morales asked, turning to look at him. "The monseñor talked about people who say nothing. But there are poor people who say nothing because of fear, or because nobody else does, or because of apathy. And some say nothing because they actually support the wolf."

"So according to you, the remedy is to say nothing and discourage others from speaking out or protesting or becoming aware of what's happening," said Padre Pupiro, deliberately pounding the steering wheel.

"Those who dare to speak out will remain mute forever after they've taken a tour of the underground cells at El Chipote," Rambo declared. He had lain back in his seat and locked his hands behind his neck.

Padre Pupiro's neck and cheeks turned a deep red that was practically violet.

"And you two, weren't you guerrillas who fought against injustice?" he said sarcastically.

Their guns have oxidized, padre, as have their minds.

"And what was the point?" said Inspector Morales, speaking with complete calm. "We all took a ride on an action figure—a doll like Buzz Lightyear, the astronaut who shouts To Infinity and Beyond! And look what we got: Chucky, the devil doll."

"I think it's more accurate to say that we got Freddy, *Jefe,* the S.O.B. with the razor-blade hand who enters your nightmares and kills you in your sleep. Those movies scare the hell out of me."

We always have to put the doll together from the beginning again, until it comes out right, said Lord Dixon. If you take a walk around the place I live now, inspector, you'll find that time never comes to an end, so it's always incredibly stupid to be in a hurry.

"Those of us who serve as shepherds of the flock want to rebuild the country without weapons of war."

"But there are priests who have taken up arms," said Inspector Morales. "Padre Gaspar, who served as the comandante for my column on the Southern Front, was one of them."

"And if he were resurrected, he'd see the same devil doll you just described, and he'd have a difficult time believing it, inspector. And he would undoubtedly try to find another one to arm, one who would actually turn out right. And the best handbook is the Gospel."

Stop provoking the priest, inspector, said Lord Dixon. That's enough screwing around.

"I'm not screwing around!" Inspector Morales exclaimed, surprised at hearing his own voice out loud.

"I'm not screwing around either," said Padre Pupiro, growing angry.

"The *jefe* sometimes talks to himself. Don't pay any attention to him, padre," said Rambo, trying to calm the priest.

Without acting as if he had heard anything, Padre Pupiro checked the fuel gauge on the instrument panel.

"We're going to have to stop at the first gas station we find. This piece of junk guzzles gas like crazy."

Noon was approaching when they abandoned the last foothills of the Dariense Range and entered the Sébaco Valley, which the Pan-American Highway divided with a straight line. The sun glinted off the flooded rice-paddy puddles as a lemon-yellow crop-dusting bi-plane sprayed insecticide—gliding low, startling the flocks of herons, and introducing the smell of poison through the windows of the Mahindra, which lacked air conditioning. The travelers caught a glimpse of the pilot's face in the cabin during one of the plane's passes, but then the aircraft flew up high again.

As they watched the small plane over their heads, coming and going as it sprayed streams of insecticide from the mouths of the tubes installed under its wings, Padre Pupiro began to tell his companions about another morning in his childhood, when he had seen a different plane flying over the roofs of Catalina and dropping packages. Children had brazenly left school to grab every possible box of that celestial rainfall: Could it be candy? Could it be canned food? Could it be a surprise gift from some kind of business? Soon half the population was fighting for packages in the streets and in the church atrium where several boxes had broken open during the drop, and the boy Pupiro found himself atop one of the packages, battling for it with other students.

[79]

"And can you believe what was inside?" he added. "Flies. Mature fly eggs. The flies hatched and swarmed everywhere."

"Who thinks dropping flies is funny?" asked Rambo, moving forward in the back seat.

"There was nothing funny about it. They were sterilized male flies sent to end the plague of Mediterranean flies that were attacking the fruit trees. All of us felt embarrassed and went back to school. What a bunch of dumb-asses. The most ashamed person of all was the teacher, who had run outside with the rest of us to grab what he could."

"During that time, our Bulgarian comrades installed a cannery here," Inspector Morales remarked, pointing at some enormous industrial buildings alongside the highway.

"What were they canning?"

"All the tomatoes harvested in this valley, padre. Whole peeled tomatoes, tomato paste, tomato juice, tomato sauce, tomato jam, poached tomatoes in their own syrup."

"An excellent idea," Padre Pupiro agreed.

"But the soldering on the tops of the cans always went rusty. Socialist technology, so the entire investment went to shit, if you'll pardon my language. A lost dream, just like your dream with the fly packages."

"Packed flies, canned tomatoes, peeled tomatoes too… Sounds like hip-hop lyrics," said Rambo, trying to create a beat by knocking his knees together.

Padre Pupiro took his foot off the accelerator. They were arriving at the triangle where the highway to Matagalpa separated from the Pan-American Highway, but before Padre Pupiro could reach the gas pumps, several detonations boomed. One explosion followed another, and a cloud of smoke moved forward and enveloped the vehicles that were either trying to pull over or go back. Truck drivers leaped from their cabs and ran to take cover in the businesses along the sidewalks, while a group of street peddlers—people selling onions, beets, tomatoes, carrots, and radishes—stampeded from their usual spots in the triangle.

Leaning on Rambo for support to get down from the truck, Inspector Morales forgot about his cane, and as the pall of acrid tear-gas smoke overcame them, the three men managed to stumble into a small clothing store, Modas Jaqueline, where they knocked mannequins into a pile while the Mahindra remained a half-block away, its doors still open.

The storeowner rushed over to rearrange the fallen manne-quins, used a hook to lower the metal curtain, closed the glass door, and pushed the three through the aisle of stands displaying shirts, blouses, shorts, jeans, and skirts until they reached her liv-ing quarters. This way, padres, a room with a full-length mirror made of molded gold plaster and a set of velvet easy chairs protect-ed by transparent plastic covers, alongside Formica dining chairs squeezed together around the table, the center of which contained a fruit bowl filled with plastic fruit, including pears, apples, and a bunch of grapes. It looks like a furniture store, Rambo thought, noticing a crib with high handrails standing in one corner—My mother takes care of my son during the day, the woman said, as if giving an explanation—and a television with an embroidered sheet on top in another corner—Jaqueline, at your service, padres—and next to the television a refrigerator, atop of which stood a four-speed fan—Appliances section, Rambo said to himself. Please do me the honor of taking a seat, she asked them, and they sat down on the plastic covers, whereupon she went to the kitchen, which gave onto the yard, and returned with a plastic tray containing wa-ter and lemon slices, then went into a bedroom and came back with a hand towel—Wash out your eyes and chew the lemon. It helps. Baking soda helps too, but I don't have any.

"A thousand thanks, but there's no need. The tear gas didn't affect us," said Padre Pupiro, returning the towel.

Outside they heard more explosions, but more muffled. Shortly thereafter came two or three bursts of deeper gunfire.

Inspector Morales listened closely.

"That's not tear gas. Those are automatic rifles shooting rubber bullets. And the people are responding with homemade mortars."

"And the other sounds are machine-gun fire," Rambo added. "Live rounds."

"And how do these priests know so much about weapons?" Jaqueline asked curiously.

"Just as we were about to enter the seminary, they conscripted us into patriotic military service," smiled Inspector Morales.

"So if they're using real bullets, they're shooting to kill those boys," said Jaqueline, beginning to sob.

"Hopefully they're just shooting into the air, but you never can tell with savages like them," said Padre Pupiro, moving over to console her.

"Who are the boys involved in the protests?" asked Rambo.

"Students from the National Institute demanding the release of three of their friends, and some others from the San Luis Gonzaga School who support them," Jaqueline answered, using the towel to wipe her tears. "The boys were arrested yesterday for subversion, according to our corrupt police force."

"What kind of subversion?" asked Inspector Morales.

"Ah, padre, all because the students wouldn't allow a construction team from the Ministry of Public Works to enter the school and install a Tree of Life on the grounds."

"Why didn't the school's Sandinista Youth beat them up? That's what they're trained to do," Rambo said.

Inspector, your friend here sounds anxious to pick up another club, said Lord Dixon.

"They tried, but they felt like they were in the minority. But then the citizens' committees arrived to provide reinforcements, and they're the ones who beat and captured the three students— two boys and a girl—and turned them over to the police surrounding the institute."

"Those are the shock troops. There are brigades in every municipality's headquarters now," said Rambo.

So speaks the wise voice of experience, said Lord Dixon.

"Those aren't the words of a priest. Watch yourself, padre," said Padre Pupiro, warning Rambo quietly.

"How did the mobs get into the institute, señora?" asked Inspector Morales.

"The principal herself, the worst batracia of all, opened the gate for them."

"*Batracia*, señora?" Pupiro asked, confused.

"A toad, padre. A batracia is a toad—a toadie. All these people are repulsive and poisonous toadies who lick the feet of their masters..."

"Do you people know who's behind the idea of those metal trees?" Rambo interrupted. "Professor Zoraida."

"Who is Professor Zoraida?"

"Knowing the future is a simple thing for her, señora," Rambo continued. "She sees everything at once. She buzzes freely around like a dragonfly, communicating easily with other mysterious witches and wizards like her. And worst of all, as if there could be anything worse, she's Tongolele's mother."

"I've already heard about this witch. But who is Tongolele?"

"This country's number-one assassin, although he never shows his face," Rambo answered darkly.

"So in the case of the students who were arrested and taken to Managua, Tongolele himself will probably be in charge of torturing them at El Chipote. This is all horrible, padre. The girl is my niece."

Instinctively, Inspector Morales searched his pocket for his notebook, as if he wanted to write this information down.

You don't need to take notes, said Lord Dixon. What do you want to do? Accompany those students to the El Chipote Hilton as some kind of know-it-all?

"My niece's name is Yubranka Molina Arauz. She's a third-year student at the high school, and she just turned fifteen," said Jaqueline, looking at Inspector Morales and pausing as she talked, as if giving him time to take things down. "Her mother, my older sister, is Julie Arauz de Molina. Last night she left for Managua to see what she could find out, but they haven't let her pass the chain at El Chipote's entrance."

"We're going from bad to worse," said Padre Pupiro, shaking his head dejectedly. "Throwing girls in jail!"

"The youngest girls are the kind that those sex-crazed sadists like the best. They make the girls do squats in the nude in front of everybody," said Rambo, his urge to fight returning.

Inspector Morales tried to calm the woman's fears: "Don't listen to what this padre has to say, señora. He's had a reputation for exaggeration ever since we were in the seminary."

Take that cassock off this idiot right now, said Lord Dixon. Even if it's not really a cassock, just a clerical collar. His behavior is atrocious.

"Do you really believe we don't know that they're capable of doing practically anything? But if they do anything to that young girl, my niece, if they try to break her will like that, she'll give them hell."

Suddenly, as if reproaching herself for having forgotten something extremely important, she removed the sheet covering the TV and hurried to find the remote to turn it on.

The 100% News Channel was showing video clips posted from cell phones showing street protests in León, Jinotega, Masaya, Diriamba, Jinotepe, and Nandaime. The target for each protest was the same: the Trees of Life. The students were joined by pass-ers-by, office workers, bank tellers, store clerks, street peddlers, motorcyclists, taxi drivers, street-cart drivers, and people converging from local neighborhoods.

"The people of God weren't so asleep after all," said Padre Pupiro as he looked triumphantly at Inspector Morales, who kept his eyes fixed on the TV screen.

"We'll see how long they stay awake. This party will be short-lived, padre."

"The Lord has blessed Nicaragua with these students, make no mistake. Blessed be His name," said Padre Pupiro, putting his hands together.

"The other two prisoners—Berman, my niece's boyfriend, and Donald, her cousin—sometimes come here to do their homework. You should hear them talk. They sound like they were born as adults—the way they think things through logically, the way they explain things like the dictatorship, democracy, and the betrayal of the revolution."

"The seed germinates deepest in the dung heap that they've tried to make out of this country," Padre Pupiro smiled, exultant.

"Berman talked about all of those thoughts in a rap song he wrote. I hate rap music, but the lyrics are worth listening to."

Here in front of you stands a hip-hop composer who will make history, said Lord Dixon. Our flies are packed in shells, tomatoes in a can, old rope pumps run our wells, and shit still hits the fan...

The explosions became sporadic again until they finally ended, and the noise of motors reverberated as vehicles started back down the highway. Jaqueline moved to raise the metal store curtain halfway, and she returned to tell the men that their way was now clear.

"So we can go, then," said Inspector Morales, failing to find his cane.

"Yes, the catechism class is waiting for us in Managua," Rambo agreed.

"Did you hurt yourself in an accident, padre?" Jaqueline asked Inspector Morales.

"When I was playing soccer at the seminary, somebody broke my tibia with a single kick," he answered.

"It was me," said Rambo, helping the detective to his feet. "But it was an accident. He was running right at me, and I was like a defensive wall."

"Please give me your blessing before you leave," Jaqueline pleaded.

Without giving Padre Pupiro a chance to react, Rambo rushed toward her and blessed her, waving his hand above her head as she lowered it respectfully.

You're to blame if you don't stop this ridiculous farce, inspector, said Lord Dixon.

The Mahindra traveled half a block with the doors open, but the men could still sense the tear-gas smell, which tingled in their noses.

"Wouldn't we be better off going back to Ocotal?" Padre Pupiro had said hesitantly as he climbed into the truck. "The highway from here to Managua is bound to be filled with checkpoints."

"God save us from having Rita Boniche see our faces again. She only offered us an olive branch because we were already leaving. *El jefe* can swear to that."

"There will be checkpoints between here and Ocotal as well," said Inspector Morales. "We don't want to put you in a compromising position, padre. If you leave us at the bus stop, we can take a bus to Managua."

"Absolutely not. My instructions are to deliver you to Padre Pancho. Let God's will be done."

"Everything depends on whether they ask for our IDs," said Inspector Morales, and he settled himself on his seat.

"Let's pray that they don't," Padre Pupiro responded, starting the Mahindra and putting it in gear.

The Sébaco police were diverting Managua-bound traffic onto nearby streets toward the city's west side, and the Mahindra took its place in a line that stretched slowly until it reached a pothole-covered road that ran parallel to the Río Grande.

When then entered the Pan-American Highway again, a group of riot police guarded access to the bridge over the river, while government agents, their faces covered in balaclavas, authorized people to cross. Flags of the Sandinista Front waved high atop the bridge's iron framework.

Padre Pupiro concentrated on the rosary beads tangled between his fingers while pushing ceaselessly against the steering wheel, but everything turned out much simpler than the three men imagined. When their turn arrived, the masked man approached the window to study their faces, then pounded the cabin roof to signal that they could proceed. Rambo even had time to give the man his blessing.

This man already enjoys going around and making the sign of the cross, said Lord Dixon. Next time we'll find him sitting in a confessional.

Padre Pupiro floored the accelerator to move as quickly away from the bridge as possible, and then he searched the dial for Radio Corporación. The broadcaster was reporting protests in Managua. University students had gathered in the Camino de Oriente Mall, which lay near the highway to Masaya, as tear-gas bombs exploded and riot police shot at store and cafeteria windows where the protesters they were pursuing had taken refuge. Dozens of people had been taken prisoner or wounded.

"All of that for a few tin trees," Rambo complained.

"Don't let those tin trees keep you from seeing the forest," said Padre Pupiro, increasing the volume. "They're just the drops spilling over from a glass of unrighteous behavior."

On the highway's right side the three men spotted the solitary tower of the Church of San Pedro Apóstol in Ciudad Darío as it rose above the green canopy of trees. They could also see the tear-gas smoke as it dispersed through the trees, and they could hear the far-off detonations of the bombs.

"So the youth have also been protesting in the birth city of our nation's poet," said Padre Pupiro, sounding more and more pleased.

"Our nation's poet, Rubén Darío, was born in Metapa, formerly known as Chocoyos, and today as Ciudad Darío," Rambo recited.

It looks like your illustrious associate learned something from elementary school, said Lord Dixon.

"I wonder where this will all end," Inspector Morales sighed.

"If we accept what you think, this is not going to end anywhere," said Padre Pupiro, moving his eyes from the wheel for an instant and glaring at Inspector Morales.

"We know very well where we're going to end up, *Jefe*. Right in the wolf's mouth."

"Don't pay attention to some poor disillusioned guerrilla," said Inspector Morales, extending his hand to touch Padre Pupiro's shoulder.

The dark and fetid mouth of the wolf, said Lord Dixon. And his sharpened claws.

They were nearing the town of Las Maderas in the department of Managua when Padre Pupiro's phone vibrated with the buzz of a wasp. He reduced his speed so he could answer and pressed the phone to his ear. All they could hear him say was "Holy Mother of God!" three times. He returned the phone to his pocket and continued on his way.

"Someone attacked the monseñor with a piece of pipe when he was leaving the parsonage. Whoever attacked him left him unconscious with a blow to the head. They're bringing him to Managua in an ambulance."

CHAPTER SIX

The Chinese Box

T HE FAKE CUSTOMS AGENCY in Las Colinas had been the home
of a minister of Agriculture and Livestock under the last Somoza. The revolution had confiscated the home, but so much time
had passed that no one remembered who the minister was or where
he had lived.

Tongolele's office occupied the master bedroom that had belonged to the former minister and his wife, a woman who in her
youth had been named Queen of the National Agricultural Fair
that Somoza had inaugurated every year, and the room still retained its original heavy old-gold-colored curtains, which reeked
of mouse urine because they had never been taken down from their
rods for cleaning. The curtains left the room in perpetual shadow.

The metal desk had been installed where the bed had been in
order to face the picture window, while a plasma TV had been
screwed into the front wall. Within the dark mahogany closets that
covered the entire length of one wall, old secret files gathered dust
inside cardboard boxes. The enormous bathroom displayed lines
of fireproof metal cabinets, which contained the files that were cur-
rently being used; all these cabinets were secured with combina-
tion locks that were always sealed at the end of the day. Tongolele
had also ordered that a metal grille be installed on the bathroom
door. Every time he needed to do his business in that dark dun-
geon, where the ceramic toilet, bidet, and sink glowed a rosy pink,
he had to unlock the grille.

The other rooms had been converted into offices for intelligence
officers. One of the rooms had belonged to a government minister's sister, paralytic and condemned to stay in bed for life, who
had enjoyed a reputation as a saint. She never performed a single
miracle, but she had prophetic dreams that she wrote down in the

morning and later placed under her pillow, as occurred in the case of the earthquake that struck Managua in 1972. In another dream she had seen Dinorah Sampson, Somoza's lover, desperately careening along the street of a strange city, sobbing and repeatedly saying "Manora, Manora." The seer had ordered that Dinorah be warned about the danger involved with this word, which turned out to be the name of the residential area in Asunción, Paraguay, where the dictator, many years later and living in exile, was blown to pieces by a bazooka while riding in his Mercedes-Benz.

No one remembered the name of the invalid fortune-teller, who followed Somoza into exile along with the minister and the rest of his family and now lay as his neighbor—about half a row away—in a Miami cemetery known as Caballero Rivero Wood-lawn Park North. No one remembered the woman's prophecies either, nor did anyone know that the letter sent to the Nicaraguan newspaper *La Prensa* wherein she reported her vision about the Managua earthquake ended up among the rubble in the editing room, where the shift editor had used a red pencil to provide the following headline that was to be published the next day: "Strange Experience of a Reader."

The dining room with its exposed beams served as a meeting room, decorated with the same Tudor-style table and chairs that the minister's family had used for dining. And because the fake customs agency never received any visitors, the great room—its furniture long since removed—was nothing but a desolate place to walk from one area to another.

If Tongolele had ever opened the curtains of the bedroom in which he worked and taken a look through the picture window, he would have seen the pool emptied many years before, where vegetation sprouted through the tile bottom's cracks and frogs croaked in chorus within the puddles that the rain left behind shortly after sundown.

And if some visitor had managed to enter the fake customs agency's doors, that person would have seen that the offices were poorly illuminated, containing fluorescent tubes screwed into the ceiling that made a constant buzz. Above all, the visitor would have noted the incessant clicking of typewriter keyboards, the noise of paper being removed from typewriter carriages, and the bell announcing that the typist had arrived at the end of a line. A militant from the Los Ángeles barrio, who owned a typewriter repair shop that no longer had clients, was responsible for reviving the ancient and heavy Underwood machines whenever a problem arose, and he worked on Tongolele's own machine as well, a portable Remington. Aside from the TV, the most modern device in Tongolele's own office was a fax machine connected to a telephone line with a long-forgotten number; for unknown reasons, this fax machine tended to ping at ungodly times of the day.

Two security advisory groups—Cuba's G-2, who returned after Ortega's 2006 electoral triumph, and for whom Tongolele continued to feel great loyalty and respect; and Venezuela's SEBIN, who talked too much and were paid by their own country—had tried and kept trying to force Tongolele to adopt the Skorpion digital encryption system, which was linked to a satellite code. Skorpion could access computers, modems, encoders, antennas, and technical training as part of a cooperation agreement with Russia's FSB, but Tongolele was always reluctant to participate. His files—protected in his office bathroom's cabinets and kept as type-written reports with a single carbon copy—had never been compromised in any way.

Within the computer-banned world he controlled, he allowed one exception: that of his personal assistant, First Lieutenant Yasica Benavides, a.k.a. La Chaparra, who occupied the fortune-teller's bedroom next to Tongolele's office.

La Chaparra grew up among the mountains of Matagalpa in the Yasica Sur region, which explained her given name. Her parents actively collaborated with the Sandinista guerrillas, which explained why her father was thrown from a government military helicopter into the emptiness above the Diablo Mountains' dense thickets. She also had a brother who was killed in a 1988 battle with a Contra encampment during Operation Danto. And if Pedrón was Tongolele's left hand, La Chaparra was Tongolele's right. Wide at the hips, broad in the bust, and short in stature as befitted her nickname, La Chaparra had inherited blind loyalty to the Sandinistas from her parents.

Her greatest treasure was a photo taken in La Casa de los Pueblos on the night when she received—along with other mid-level members of the police and the military—the Medal for Fidelity in the Service of the Country and the Revolution. A group photo was taken, but La Chaparra was selected for special treatment because when the time came to toast them all, she was called to stand between the President and the First Lady, and after the photographer shot the photo with the ever-present mound of flowers in the background, the photographer shot another with only La Chaparra and the First Couple, which the Division of Protocol later sent to her, framed and signed by both leaders.

La Chaparra was nearly forty years old, and she did not permit wisecracks about her single status, her diminutive height, or anything else. She could stand on the soles of her feet and throw a fit, and she was perfectly capable of spitting in someone's face. On one occasion, Pedrón had whispered into her ear like a hero from some Mexican ranchero movie: *Chaparrita, it's time to seize the day. You can pleasure me and I can pleasure you, both at the same time. You'll never regret it.* She had no recourse other than to stay quiet, her eyes filled with tears, her jawbone trembling with rage, because the beast was a captain and she was only a first lieutenant, which meant she could do nothing more than swallow her bile.

She had married the revolution and was happy with her ideological union, like the nuns who marry the Holy Ghost. But Lord Dixon would have opined that even the most chaste nuns end up falling into the dark abyss of sin. La Chaparra got pregnant, and her many pleas were finally heard: it turned out that Pedrón was indeed the baby's father, although he refused to recognize the child at first. But Tongolele made him confess: It's true that we had sex one single time, commissioner, and as you can see, we had the bad luck of hitting the bullseye with one shot. You really are a swine, Tongolele had scolded him. So what are you going to do now? If you see fit, we'll get married and that will be the end of the story, Pedrón had ventured to say. But La Chaparra refused: I'll take care of the baby myself. I don't need to be smelling anybody else's farts.

Nevertheless, on some nights she allowed Pedrón through the door of her place in the multifamily buildings in the San Antonio barrio—irregular trysts, nothing more, as Tongolele well knew, because Pedrón would enter her office, rest his enormous hands on her desk, and speak four words to her, whereupon she would whisper a response, always with a stubborn attitude, and then he would leave as if nothing had happened or as if he she had rejected him again. But Tongolele understood that that they had agreed to meet.

An efficient right hand with an infallible memory, so infallible that she could recite the contents of every file locked in the fire-proof cabinets behind the bathroom grille: red for lost causes—people who would be torn apart without mercy, their punishment made obvious to all; blue for troublemakers—people who could be offered mercy in exchange for an agreement not to reveal proof of their sins, such as homosexual husbands or adulterous spouses; yellow for those who required close surveillance because of potential seditious activities; and green for the faithful, who required attention because everyone was capable of committing sin regardless of who they were. Professor Zoraida's file sat among the green files.

La Chaparra's computer, the one she alone controlled, was used in the fake customs agency for searching data on the Internet, although she had another computer at home in case Tongolele needed information outside regular office hours. After returning home from work, feeding dinner to her son—Daniel del Rosario, now eight years old—and helping him with his homework, La Chaparra never wasted time before dedicating herself to trolling any enemy of the Government of Love, Peace, and Reconciliation that crossed her path.

As about eleven on that Tuesday morning, La Chaparra interrupted Tongolele without warning—her standard practice—with her spiral notebook in hand and a mechanical pencil in her hair.

"The street is on fire, commissioner. There's a protest on Camino de Oriente even bigger than yesterday's."

"I already know, Chaparrita. I ran into the gangs and mobs everywhere on my way here."

"Most are university students. But people from the street are joining them too."

"Have the leaders been identified?"

"Our boys are working on that using photos taken by our agents on the ground. But as far as we can tell, the leaders don't appear in our files."

"Have we managed to infiltrate some of our people among the protesters?"

"We're trying, but the fact that the leaders are new faces makes it difficult to tail them."

"And the police are standing around scratching their balls, as usual."

"The riot police are already there. Some people have been wounded and some businesses have been damaged."

"Fine. Let the riot police tear into the protesters. That's what they're paid for."

"The special forces have been activated," La Chaparra continued her report. "And the local shock troops as well—they're being transported in buses."

Normally during an emergency, the Chinese box arrived suddenly and announced the time for a meeting. This time, however, no aide appeared. Whenever the divine government forces were being mobilized from within the barrios, that meant a red alert had been issued after a meeting of the Council of Security Operations. All of this without Tongolele.

"Who's giving you all this information?"

"The agents on the ground, commissioner. But everything they report is confirmed."

"And what about the police headquarters' liaison officer? What do they report?"

"Nothing. They don't answer. They always tell me that the liaison is in a meeting."

"Get the first commissioner on the phone for me," he ordered.

La Chaparra liked to wear short-sleeved guayabera shirts, the tucked style with four pockets (two on top, two below), and from one of those pockets she extracted her phone, which had a lacquered cover that made it look like some kind of cosmetics case. With a single touch she called the stored number. From his desk, Tongolele could only listen hopelessly as the phone buzzed repeatedly in the distance.

Commissioner Victorino Valdiva was known in the confidential files as Melquíades because during the revolution García Márquez's novel *One-Hundred Years of Solitude* was passed from security institution to security institution and became a source for guerrilla codenames. Valdiva never took more than ten seconds to respond to Tongolele's calls. He treated Tongolele with sickeningly sweet obsequiousness, simply because he feared him.

Ever since the previous night, Tongolele had tried to avoid thinking about the conversation with his mother, but he could not. It was a demoralizing kick to the solar plexus, one that some-times left him angry and sometimes embarrassed. If you're going to be a fool, why agonize over it? But he did agonize, and now even more. If Meliquíades—always anxious to please him—now refused to take his calls, the only possible explanation was an or-der that Tongolele be isolated. More than anyone else, Tongolele knew how these mechanisms worked. And for the first time in his life, the searing feeling of isolation ignited within him like a mute flame.

"All this over those shitty trees," he tried to say to himself, only realizing too late that he had spoken out loud.

"Jesus, commissioner!" La Chaparra exclaimed, shocked.

"I wipe my ass with those things," he said, not even caring now whether La Chaparra heard him or not.

But beneath that uncomfortable sense of exclusion crouches an-other feeling—a small creature that dares to poke its furry head out of its cave, bare its sharp teeth, and play at returning to its hid-ing place, only to reveal itself again and show its teeth once more, along with its claws, which are no less sharp. That creature is fear.

"Aside from the commotion in the streets, what else do we have?" he asked, battling to gain his composure.

"That priest from Ocotal who keeps fucking things up so much, commissioner."

"We already sent him a free sample of medicine. Didn't he get enough?"

"He actually seems to have gotten worse. We have the record-ing of his last sermon. It's nothing but a counter-revolutionary speech."

"Well, then, we have to find another way to calm him down. Remind me what's in his file. Is there any female parishioner who can alleviate his pains?"

"We recruited a girl from his catechism class to seduce him, but he turned her down flat from the start."

"I wonder if he prefers to have another man's dipstick check his oil?"

"No such inclinations either. This monseñor will be tough to bring down."

"Chaparrita, nobody in the world has a strong enough neck to withstand everything. Have someone put a ton of money in his bank account, then we can have some fake narco testify that that it was a deposit for drug trafficking."

"He has no bank accounts, commissioner."

The monseñor's case had been discussed at length in the Chinese box. Everyone was awaiting some paperwork from the Roman Curia just in case the monseñor had not been scared into silence, as he obviously had not.

"Regardless, the Church's highest levels are working to move him away from here. But we still haven't received an answer."

"The authorization from Rome has already arrived, commissioner."

"What authorization?" he asked, looking at her with surprise.

"To send him to the Vatican, where he'll serve in the Pope's lodgings. At the end of the day, he's the domestic prelate for His Holiness."

"And how do you know that?"

"A woman who's a friend of mine in the party secretary's office mentioned it to me."

"If you already knew that, why didn't you tell me at the beginning so we didn't waste time talking shit about what to do with that asshole priest?"

"Forgive me, commissioner, but I didn't dare because it's something that they should have told you first with the Chinese box."

"Look at the situation I'm in: Relying on leaks from your friends."

"Permission to enter, commissioner," said Pedrón, who had already walked in and closed the door, knowing that the question of permission was nothing but pro forma. "An emergency report is on its way."

"Don't tell me they haven't been able to control that rabble in the streets."

"A priest has been assaulted. Someone hit him on the head with a piece of pipe as he was leaving a funeral."

"Which priest? Who are you talking about? We have far too many priests in this country."

"The one in Ocotal. The one who's been stirring things up so much."

Tongolele examined the two people in his office, one after the other, studying their faces carefully.

"How can that be? No such order went out from this office."

"It must have been spontaneous," said La Chaparra, shrugging her shoulders. "Someone who acted on their own."

"I don't believe that. Everything about the attack was well co-ordinated," said Pedrón, contradicting her. "A vehicle picked the man up at the corner of a park across from the church."

Tongolele asked La Chaparra to contact Commissioner Vílchez, the Ocotal police chief, who defied all expectations by answering the call immediately. Negative. The attacker was not from Ocotal. Yes, the escape vehicle whisked him away just across from the church. The vehicle had Managua license plates. Affirmative. Vílchez had witnesses who could provide the plate number and a description of the attacker. He would send the information along momentarily.

"My superior, Commissioner Valdivia, called and ordered me not to share this information with *anybody*," Vílchez said at the end of the call. "But you're obviously not just *anybody*."

Undoubtedly, Tongolele thought to himself, Melquíades had forgotten to be specific when he had ordered his underling to keep Tongolele out of the loop. The email arrived shortly, and La Chaparra printed it off to bring it to him.

The suspect was described as athletic although obviously going to fat, about age fifty, with skin darker than lighter, bulging eyes, and thick lips. He was wearing light-blue gabardine pants and a long-sleeved white shirt. The pipe he had left behind was wrapped in pages from that day's edition of *El Nuevo Diario*, which did not normally arrive in Ocotal until twelve, a fact that strengthened the assumption that the suspect was from Managua. The vehicle was a sky-blue Hilux pick-up with a crew cab; the plate number was 204533 with an MA prefix, indicating a Managua registration.

La Chaparra returned quickly with the details about the Hilux provided by the Division of Transportation Security. According to the plate, the truck was registered to Pantera Inc., a private security company.

Tongolele knew who owned that company all too well: Melquíades and the dwarf Manzano.

"A couple of novices," he said, waving the print-out. "Why did they stick their noses in something they know nothing about? How could they be so stupid as to use a truck from their own company?"

"I know the man with the thick lips, the one described in the report," said Pedrón, picking the piece of paper off the floor.

"Don't make us laugh. Black men with thick lips are every-where," La Chaparra said with disdain.

"But it just so happens that this man tends to dress a certain way when he's not in uniform. He has a habit of dressing as if he's attending First Communion: all he lacks is a tie and a candle. He used to work for the ASP, and now he works for Pantera."

"Who is this communicant that you know?" Tongolele asked.

"Abigail. Abigail Baldelomar Cantillano."

"Do some research and find out what you can about him," he ordered La Chaparra.

"They're playing you for a fool, commissioner," Pedrón remarked as he took a few steps toward the desk after La Chaparra had left. "Melquíades used to be so loyal to you."

"If the problem was just him, I'd have already grabbed him by the neck and put him in his place, Pedrito."

"Ask for the Chinese box, commissioner, and ask them what's happening."

"No. Patience is a virtue for lice, because the nights are long."

"I wouldn't be so sure in this case. Melquíades and all of his partners are trash, absolute trash. If someone is on their way down, they'll be there helping to shove him down."

"Who told you that I'm on my way down?" Tongolele asked arrogantly.

"No one, commissioner," Pedrón answered, lowering his head. "I just feel that they can smell blood."

La Chaparra came back soon thereafter. The Public Security Division of the National Police had provided all available information about the suspect, who appeared in the registry of private-security guards, along with a photo that La Chaparra had already printed off. The man had been born in Camoapa in 1963, and his current address was recorded as a place in Managua's Memorial Stadium neighborhood across from the Bendición de Dios upholstery shop. The photo corresponded to the eyewit-nesses' descriptions.

"The Chinese box, commissioner. Don't waste time," La Chap-arra urged. "Something is obviously balls-up."

"It's almost two o'clock and the tiger's scratching my stomach," Tongolele responded, trying to smile. "Order some fried chicken, Chaparrita."

The food arrived late because the disturbances had snarled traffic in the streets. As La Chaparra returned from throwing the bones into the garbage, she heard powerful detonations coming from the direction of the highway to Masaya, and she ran to turn on the TV in Tongolele's office.

Near the Jean Paul Genie roundabout, the protesters had re-grouped from different directions after the tear-gas bombs had exploded. Now in large numbers, the protesters wore rags over their faces to protect themselves from the smoke cloud, and they had re-commenced the job of taking down one of the Trees of Life that had been erected in the highway's central median. People had tied ropes to the tree's spiral metal branches, and a shirtless young man was diligently sawing the iron trunk, surrounded by a group urging him to finish. Finally, the group pulled on the ropes, and the monstrosity collapsed with an enormous crash on the pavement within the tumult and celebration. People leaped and danced atop the fallen structure.

Followed by a sprinting group of TV camera-people, a crazed army of ants ran toward another Tree of Life that had been plant-ed in the same median. The riot police kept their ranks closed behind their shields, but they did not advance, while the neigh-borhood shock troops, armed with clubs and chains, seemed to be stuck in place.

La Chaparra, her hands in the pockets of her guayabera, watched the TV in shock, as if everything she could see was happening on an unknown planet. Pedrón, supporting himself against the wall, shook his head in disbelief. In contrast, Ton-golele leaned against his chair's back support and rested his feet on the desk, appearing to be half-asleep rather than alarmed by the televised scenes.

At that moment came a knock on the door, which was opened without hesitation, and there stood the aide, wearing white leg-gings and white gloves—with chin raised, the military cap's glossy peak sculpted to meet the eyebrows, the golden braid looped be-neath the uniform's epaulette—and carrying the Chinese box. The aide took three steps forward and offered the box to Tongolele. Pe-drón made a hasty exit from the office, while La Chaparra reached over to turn off the TV, then followed Pedrón and swiftly closed the door from outside.

Tongolele accepted the box, searched for the key, and became enraged when he noticed that he struggled to find the keyhole because his hand would not remain steady. The female phoenix with extended wings and sharp talons watched him with a fierce gaze from the lacquered cover.

Inside the box, which was lined with crimson silk, lay a lacquered envelope that contained no writing whatsoever. And within the envelope was a sheet folded in half, which was absolutely blank.

This message was one of those communications sometimes deemed so important that it was written with invisible ink and could be read only if the recipient drew a flame near it. Tongolele did not smoke, but he kept a box of matches in one of the desk drawers for just such an occasion.

Tongolele's hand trembled again when he lit the match and moved it toward the sheet of paper, fearing that he would burn it, while the aide remained standing in place, hands extended down both sides so that the middle fingers brushed the seams of the uniform's pants, as required by military regulations:

We hope that we can always count on you, comrade, the brief message began, its convent-school letters slightly slanted, the flame apparently toasting the letters into a mild sepia color. An ironic greeting, as if a hard, dry voice—but mocking as well—vibrated within the strokes of the words, followed by a definitive conclusion: *Therefore, we need you to report to Comandante Leónidas at the allotted time.* That was the entire message.

We. Yes, we. We want; we desire; we hope; we direct; we order; we command. This *we* was an inclusive *we* that eliminated any possible vacillation, doubt, or appeal, because it was an *I* that extended to everyone: we the people, we the anonymous comrades, the multitude gathered in the town squares, the rank and file, the heroes and martyrs who keep watch from their graves. The historic achievement of the revolution.

He searched the drawer for the mottled nib holder where he kept the pen, removed the inkwell, dipped the pen into the invisible ink, and wrote the following:

Orders received will be followed.
A free country or death! Country or death, we will be victorious!

He deposited the sheet into the box, closed the lid, and stood up to extend the box to the aide, who gave a click of the heels and turned around.

Alone in the office at last, Tongolele dropped back into his desk chair, which creaked under his weight.

CHAPTER SEVEN

The Gunpowder Conspiracy

THE MAHINDRA PASSED through the gate of the property enclosed by the Jesus of Divine Mercy Church in the Villa Fontana neighborhood, then parked in front of the parsonage. Padre Pancho, who had been anxiously waiting on the porch for quite some time, rushed forward to greet the travelers.

He tossed his half-smoked Ducados cigarette onto the pathway's flagstones and approached the newcomers with long strides. Behind him everyone could hear the sound of the living-room television, as the voices of reporters from 100% News provided live coverage from the Hospital Metropolitano about Monseñor Ortez. The ambulance transporting him from Ocotal had already arrived; he was now in the doctors' hands; and the reporters would soon have news about his condition.

Padre Francisco Xabier Aramburu, a Basque Jesuit who had lived in Nicaragua for twenty years, was lovingly known by his parishioners as Pancho. He was tall and bony; he bent forward as he walked as if the wind was pushing him along; and his grayish hair looked like a fox's tail, although his eyebrows remained charcoal-black. His firm jaw, shaded blue, required two shaves per day. He was probably about fifty years old, and he still played soccer on the Centroamericana School's pitch with the high-school boys, moving surely and quickly against his opponents. He wore religious dress only during official rites, customarily opting for a checked shirt, jeans, and sandals as he bought groceries at the supermarket, prepared food, or cleaned the parsonage, mop in hand.

From outside, Padre Pancho opened the truck's front door for Padre Pupiro, who stepped out and explained their delay in arrival: Traffic coming from the north had been shut down past the airport; Pupiro had had to take a detour toward the Mercado de Mayoreo;

Larreynega Road had been jammed; the government had barricaded the side streets; and riot squads filled the city along with police patrols in Hilux pick-ups, their beds manned by officers wearing bulletproof vests.

"Troy is certainly burning now," said Padre Pancho. "Protesters are tearing the Trees of Life out by the roots. And the cutting has barely begun."

"We heard it on the radio when we were coming," said Padre Pupiro. "The sterile forest of iron trees, just like Ernesto Cardenal said."

"The ambulance has already arrived. The TV people are reporting from the hospital."

"An ambulance passed by us close to Tipitapa with its siren on. It must have been that one. Is there any news about the monseñor's condition?"

"The doctors haven't come out yet."

The two passengers remained in the truck, contrite and silent. We look like freshly bought chickens, whispered Inspector Morales. Better to say homesick chickens, Rambo whispered back. Suddenly, however, Padre Pancho was looking at them through the window: Get the fuck out now, you morons!

As they walked to the parsonage, Padre Pancho enveloped them in his wings with his hairy hands on their shoulders, and they struggled to keep up with him, particularly Inspector Morales, continually searching where to place the tip of his cane among the flagstones, with Padre Pupiro following behind. Dressing like priests was fine for the trip, but here at the Managua parsonage, the sight of two extra priests might look suspicious. What are they doing here at Jesús de la Divina Misericordia? So I, Padre Pancho, will have the honor of having the celebrated Inspector Morales working as my gardener and his friend here—Don Serafín?—as my assistant gardener. But, of course, the two of you will have a room here in the parsonage, a room I've already prepared for you, and I've bought you a change of clothes according to the sizes that Monseñor Ortez estimated for you, and we'll see how they fit and whether my taste in clothes matches yours.

"You're not going to fire your current gardener to make room for us," said Inspector Morales.

"No firings at all. I'm the gardener already, and the cook and the custodian too, and I also wash and iron clothes and throw out the garbage," answered Padre Pancho. "And if the time comes when you want to help me peel vegetables, I'll happily accept your help."

On the porch stood two identical doors—one that said OFFICE and the other that led to the sitting room. Pushed against the wall sat a bench, the kind that appeared to have been rescued from an old train station, while a sign attached to the wall announced an Ultreya, a revival of sorts in the Church del Niño Dios de Praga in Chiquilistagua, kilometer 14 on the old highway to León, 200 kilometers north. The sign depicted a young couple looking toward the horizon: To Thee, Lord, I raise my soul.

Padre Pancho led them to the sitting room's door, which was open.

"Monseñor Ortez certainly has some huge balls!" he said, freeing their shoulders from his hands.

"Where did you meet each other?" asked Rambo, who felt that he should say something.

"In the spa at Casares, and neither of us was wearing anything but our underwear," Padre Pancho smiled. "We had never met before in our entire lives, and the monseñor said to me: 'May our Lord bless you, padre.' And I answered him: 'May our Lord bless you, padre.'"

"How did you each know that the other man was a priest?" asked Rambo.

"It's something imprinted on the skin itself, something like a varnish from the Holy Spirit," Padre Pancho declared.

"I was in the spa that day because we were holding some spiritual activities that weekend, and he had come on a bus trip from Ocotal with a group of parishioners."

"Two padres in their underwear. I can't imagine it," said Rambo.

"We sat there talking half-naked in water up to our knees—for hours, I believe. Because we left the spa as red as a couple of boiled lobsters."

Although no one besides Padre Pancho himself took care of the parsonage, the dwelling's tidiness and cleanliness suggested that an entire guild of devout members had taken responsibility for it: the shiny checkerboard floor smelled of kerosene; the windows were adorned with lace curtains secured with ties; the sitting room's four rocking chairs were arranged equidistantly from each other around a small table, which displayed a crocheted runner; a vase graced the hutch, and the vase bloomed with forget-me-nots, flowers that looked as if they belonged on an altar; and next to the hutch stood a four-place dining table, the center of which featured a china fruit bowl containing real fruit, including bananas, sweet limes, and mandarin oranges.

The TV showed clips of people lighting candles in the hospital parking lot, other people kneeling to pray in the dark as the camera lights illuminated them, others waving Nicaraguan flags or Catholic Church banners, and still others waving signs and sheets with messages: THE BLOOD OF THE RIGHTEOUS CRIES FROM THE EARTH. THE TRUTH WILL SET YOU FREE.

Padre Pancho offered beer to his two guests, then went to the kitchen refrigerator to fetch the drinks while the others settled down in their rocking chairs. As they did so, a photo of the monseñor suddenly appeared on the television. The photo was a studio shot with the monseñor wearing his domestic prelate's garb. His scarlet skullcap stood out, as did the buttoned scarlet cassock, the scarlet band around his waist, and the heavy pectoral cross hanging from his neck. His lips revealed a slight smile, a somewhat ironic expression on his face.

Broadcasters displayed the photo every half hour as they repeated the report recorded by 100% News in Ocotal:

> ... local priest in this city and beloved by the population in general, brutally attacked at the main door of the Church de Nuestra Señora de la Asunción about eleven o'clock this morning by an unknown assailant who fled the scene. Monseñor Ortez was struck on the head with a piece of plumbing pipe; as a result, he fell to the ground, bleeding profusely. Parishioners picked him up and put him in a pew while they waited for the ambulance to arrive.
>
> The prelate had just finished a funeral mass, and he had exited the church to say good-bye to the deceased man's relatives and others who had attended the service. As pall-bearers were carrying the coffin down the church steps, the assailant rose up from behind the prelate to strike him with the pipe, which was wrapped in a newspaper.
>
> Another man awaited the assailant at the wheel of a pick-

up with its engine running. The truck was parked in front of a restaurant-bar called Llamarada del Bosque, which is located at the northeast corner of the central park. During his escape, the suspect—described by the funeral attendees as an older man with a muscular build—dropped the pipe he had used as a weapon.

According to people close to Monseñor Ortez, he had received constant death threats during recent days, and only a short time ago, his nephew, Genaro Ortez, was killed under mysterious circumstances in the San Roque area, the victim of a shooting for which no investigation is open.

"Well, the man with the pipe is clearly not from Ocotal," declared Inspector Morales, both hands gripping his cane.

"Why do you say that?" asked Padre Pancho.

"He wouldn't have shown his face."

"They couldn't sneak a masked man into a funeral service. People would notice him before he could get close," Padre Pupiro interrupted.

"Exactly. This was a public attack, so they used a person with an uncovered face, a person who wouldn't be recognized. And as for the escape truck, I'll bet the plates aren't local, if it even had plates at all."

"Just how important is any of this?" asked Padre Pupiro.

"It means that this wasn't some local operation. They brought the attacker from outside to do what he did, and they took him out of Ocotal immediately."

"None of this helps the monseñor's chances of improving his survival."

"But it does show that the order came from very high up."

"The hunting dog, Tongolele," said Rambo.

"But they didn't anticipate such strong repercussions," Inspector Morales continued. "The coincidence of the student protests drew attention to the attack."

"So, the fact that people have come out of their houses to pray for the monseñor has nothing to do with his goodness?" said Padre Pupiro, unconvinced and moving around in his chair.

"You think it's a good thing to be assaulted with such savagery?"

"We've already discussed this, inspector. Martyrdom is an honor for a Christian."

"So, the more beatings the better, padre? The people in power are happy to spread martyrdom far and wide."

"Well, shit. I'm happy to stay far away from any beatings," laughed Padre Pancho, shaking his rib cage.

"You need to be watch yourself, padre. You're a good candidate for just such a beating," said Padre Pupiro, emptying his beer can.

"Look, we have to take some precautions. There's no reason to stick our necks out right away. Especially when we know that we're dealing with a bunch of Cro-Magnons."

"You have far too many affinities with Monseñor Bienvenido," responded Padre Pupiro, reproving him softly. "You're in the same hole that he is, and he trusts you without reservation."

"Who the hell is talking about reservations? I'm on the side that needs us, because the Church can't be neutral."

"The Church has to be on the side of the poor of the earth."

"The poor, the oppressed, the small, the weak, the defenseless. Add any other group to the list that you please."

"So what should we do?"

"Nothing. What I don't want is for someone to crush my head with a pipe and leave me for dead. But if the pipe comes it comes, and there's not a damn thing I can do about it."

There was a moment of silence. The murmur of people praying on their knees could be heard from the television. Devotees had begun to pray the rosary. More candles burned on the asphalt.

"Padre Pupiro will stay with Serafín to finish his beer, while Inspector Morales and I will take a moment alone in my room," said Padre Pancho, standing to his feet. "Bring your can along, inspector."

"If none of you minds, I'd rather go to the hospital," said Padre Pupiro, standing up as well. "Edelmira, the monseñor's niece, and her husband are waiting for me there. They were going to go to Honduras for protection, but they've postponed that trip for later. I'll tell you any news that I hear."

"Be careful, padre. Flies aren't the only things that rain down from the skies," Rambo said by way of farewell.

"Don't I know it," laughed Padre Pupiro. "A bird could take a crap on my head."

Padre Pancho walked Padre Pupiro to the truck, where they continued talking for a while. Meanwhile, Rambo, who had fetched another beer from the kitchen, sat in front of the TV, and Inspector Morales took the opportunity to call Doña Sofía and inform her that he had returned to Managua without incident.

Doña Sofía had moved to Fanny's house in Colonia Centroamérica to care for her, and she had barely said hello before passing the phone to Fanny: I'm giving her the phone because she's trying to grab it out of my hand. Inspector Morales heard Fanny sobbing on the other end of the line—very extensively, very slowly, but then, she stifled her tears and tried to laugh. What a fool I am! Crying, a full-grown woman, and anyone would think I'm crying over myself, but what can anyone do? I've accepted my fate, whatever the Holy Virgin decides. My tears are for you, my dear Papacito. I was so shocked when Doña Sofía told me that they had dragged you off to Honduras, and I was even more shocked when she told me herself that you had taken so many risks just to come back for me, and here I was unable to tell you not to worry about me, that you were better off staying where you were, and it was as if you were far off anyway because no one could possibly know when I would see you again.

And faced with her effusive words, her tears, and her questions, he responded with dry monosyllables, and he constantly reproached himself as he answered "Yes," "No," and "Yes," but he would have felt like an idiot if he had tried to comfort her, nor did he wish to sound religious or pious to her. When they said goodbye, she started wailing again to the same extent as she had in the beginning, drowning all words.

Padre Pancho was already waiting for him in his room. On the bed lay a beautiful indigenous quilt depicting Guatemala's high plateaus, and the wrought-iron headboard looked like the gate of a garden fence. Above the headboard hung an Ernesto Cardenal portrait of Christ crucified, drawn with very simple lines. Near the bed stood a reclining chair upholstered with imitation black leather, while the side wall presented a cobblestone bookcase, its shelves made with unfinished pine. The other side wall contained a tourist poster of Vitoria, the Basque Country's capital city, with the Santa María Cathedral in the foreground, and in the corner of the room was a wooden hanger that displayed a white cassock. The polished panes missing from the window had been replaced with newspaper pages.

As Padre Pancho sat down on the bed, he offered the reclining chair to Inspector Morales.

"Do you know a woman named Lastenia Robleto who has a close relationship with this church?" he asked. "She takes care of the altar dedicated to Padre Pío."

"The sacristan," answered Inspector Morales. "Doña Sofía knows her."

"That makes sense. She arranged a meeting between Doña Sofía with a parishioner in the sacristy here while I was on a trip to El Salvador."

"That was the meeting with Doña Ángela, the wife of the business tycoon, Miguel Soto."

"And she's a significant benefactor to this parish."

"Your benefactor took her husband's side after he raped her daughter."

"And they exiled you from Nicaragua for investigating the case. You have every reason to express your outrage about the whole thing."

"Are you the woman's confessor?"

"If you think I told her to appear on television and support her husband, you're very mistaken."

"I have no reason to believe anything, reverend."

"I like that word reverend. I haven't heard it for a long time."

"My Grandmother Catalina always said: 'I'm going to give you a righteous beating—a reverend's whipping—with this strap if you don't stop disobeying me.'"

"Very persuasive, your grandmother."

"But let's get back to what we were talking about. What's happening with the sacristan?"

"She had a visitor: A woman in mourning—small, middle-aged, with her head covered by a shawl—came into the church about five o'clock this afternoon and gave her an envelope addressed to you, but she said I could open it.

Padre Pancho gave Inspector Morales the sheet of paper. It contained only a few lines:

> The attack against the Monseñor from Ocotal was ordered by Anastasio Prado, a/k/a Tongolele, the government's head of spies and hitmen, and the attacker was Abigail

Baldelomar Cantillano, who lives in the Memorial Sandino barrio across from the Bendición de Dios upholstery shop. He works as a security guard for PANTERA.

"And this came in the same envelope too," said Padre Pancho, passing along a passport photo.

Inspector Morales examined the photo.

"It fits the description of the man who attacked the monseñor, according to what we just saw on TV."

"That's what I thought as well. From the first time I heard the description on the TV, I began to imagine a picture of the attacker, and all it took was the photo to leave me stunned."

"And what about this little face here at the bottom of the page?"

"It's a kind of signature. It's the mask that the character in *V for Vendetta* wears, history becoming film."

"I'm as confused as ever."

"At some time in the future, England becomes a totalitarian state. 'V' is the masked figure who leads the revolution to overthrow the dictator, Adam Sutler. I have the movie on video if you want to watch it."

"The day I sit down to watch a movie is the day my leg can no longer take me anywhere."

"That mask has become so popular that the hacker group 'Anonymous' has adopted it."

"For now, let's see what The Mask wants. To begin, he's sent us information that doesn't help much. Are we supposed to go to the police and denounce the attacker even though the police already know who he is?"

"Maybe Vendetta, The Mask, as you call him, wants us to make the information public."

"I can't imagine how. But I have a much bigger concern: The Mask knows that I was coming here to hide."

"That was the first thing that surprised me too," Padre Pancho agreed.

"And that means that it's dangerous to stay here, for you and for me."

From the nightstand, Padre Pancho picked up a seashell that served as an ashtray and placed it on his lap.

"Look at the problem from a different angle. What if 'V' is an insider who opposes the administration?"

Now, inspector, you have Father Brown on your side, said Lord Dixon. You can't complain about that.

"The wolf who repents of his killings and abuses? That kind of thing happens only in poems and sermons, reverend."

"Oh, come now. Don't dismiss me out of hand. Repentant sinners are my specialty," Padre Pancho smiled as the recently lit Ducados cigarette burned in his hand.

Inspector Morales fixed his gaze on the condensation stains that marked the smooth ceiling, as if looking for some key.

"I need to climb up on the roof and take care of those leaks," said Padre Pancho, looking up as well.

"This whole stunt may simply be the evil hand of Tongolele. His mind has all kinds of twists and turns."

"Regardless, you're staying here with me," said Padre Pancho, vigorously crushing out the cigarette.

"The truth is that I don't have many choices. If you take the risk…"

"Come on now, sir. Put up a fight," Padre Pancho laughed, which ended with a deep cough. "God doesn't help cowards."

"I'm going to need to see Doña Sofía," said Inspector Morales.

"Of course. You can meet in the sacristy. She knows the way quite well," Padre Pancho said, laughing again and restraining his cough, as he had just taken his first puff on a new cigarette.

A knock sounded at the door. Rambo came in to tell them that the TV broadcasters were about to report the monseñor's condition.

"The situation concerning Monseñor Ortez's condition is as follows: Due to a powerful blow to the parietal bone of the skull, the scalp suffered a linear fracture with no splinters or cracks, leaving no depression or distortion in the bone. CAT scans show no epidural or intradural hematoma, and therefore no compression in the brain area. The patient will remain in intensive care for the time necessary."

"I didn't understand a damn thing," said Rambo.

"There's no skull fracture, and no internal bleeding in the brain," Padre Pancho explained. "It's good news."

Reporters asked questions from within a mob, but the hospital's head of public relations told them that they would have to wait for the next public announcement, and the doctors disappeared down a hallway.

At that point, Padre Pancho received a phone call. The caller was Padre Pupiro, phoning from the hospital. The two men expressed their mutual gratitude that the monseñor was not in danger of dying. Padre Pupiro had some additional news: a delegate from the Government of Love, Peace, and Reconciliation had told the monseñor's family that the President's office would cover all expenses. Edelmira, the monseñor's niece, had politely but firmly rejected the offer.

"Those people have no problem with killing someone and attending the funeral," said Padre Pancho, gripping the phone.

"As for me, I'm going to bed," the priest heard Rambo declare.

"Wait, Don Serafín, we haven't eaten dinner yet," said Padre Pancho, trying and failing to detain his visitor. "I was planning to make some repochetas leonesas."

"You can save mine for tomorrow," Rambo answered from the corridor that led to the bedrooms. "I'm more sleepy than hungry."

"Doña Sofía is coming here," announced Inspector Morales, who had moved some distance away to talk on the cell. "She has something urgent to tell me."

"Given the circumstances, this is a bad time to be walking the streets," said Padre Pancho, checking his watch. The time was almost ten o'clock at night.

"If the police try to stop her, I've told her to tell them that she's coming here to help a dying man."

He had estimated that if Doña Sofía had no obstacles to overcome, she would need half an hour to find a taxi and make the trip from Colonia Centroamericana to Villa Fontana. So he was surprised when only a short time later he heard a car stop in the street and stay with its engine running, followed by the slam of the door as the passenger stepped out and the car started forward again and went off into the distance. He never even realized when Padre Pancho left to open the gate, and suddenly before him stood Doña Sofía, wearing phosphorescent-green running shoes.

"Nowadays you have to be ready to run," she said by way of greeting, glancing at her feet.

I wouldn't be shocked at all if she didn't premiere those psychedelic shoes by leaping atop the broken pieces of some Tree of Life, said Lord Dixon.

"Make yourself at home, Doña Sofía. I leave you in good hands," said Padre Pancho, who had met her at the door. He went into the kitchen to make some repochetas.

Repochetas were his favorite dish on solitary nights in the parsonage, where he always ate late. Preparation was easy: it was simply a question of cutting corn tortillas in half, filling them with soft white cheese, frying both sides of the tortillas in the pan, and preparing some pico de gallo with tomatoes, onions, ground spicy pequin peppers, cilantro, and a splash of vinegar.

After Doña Sofía studied the photo and read the message signed by "V," she gave Inspector Morales another sheet of paper that she removed from her skirt pocket.

> The death squad that killed Genaro Ortez with the purpose of reining in his uncle, Monseñor Ortez, was comprised of three first-cousins from Ciudad Darío known as the "Smurfs"; their true names are Josiel, Gamaliel, and Joel, and all three have the same last name: Pastora. Josiel and Gamaliel were the shooters, while Joel drove the Hilux pick-up. The three cousins work as street peddlers or "sector leaders" for Fabiola Miranda, who secretly works for Tongolele, her business partner and her lover. Señorita Miranda organized the trio for the mission, and each man's payment consisted of drugs he could sell in the sector where he works.

Someone had knocked on the door of Fanny's house. By chance, Doña Sofía had been walking through the living room on her way to the kitchen. She opened the door and saw a manila envelope addressed to Inspector Morales on the ground. She approached the envelope. A woman dressed in black, her entire head concealed by the old kind of chapel veil that women used to wear when entering a church, disappeared down a side street.

"The Mask wants me to understand that he can reach me however he wants," said Inspector Morales.

"These pictures were in the envelope too," said Doña Sofía.

The small-format photos depicted each of the Smurfs, their names written on the back. Inspector Morales recognized Joel immediately, but he checked his phone video to be sure. On film, Joel appeared in profile, his eyes on the windshield. Nothing his brothers did from the truck bed distracted him, nor did the shots startle him in any way. The photo showed a full-face view, the man's forehead wrinkling as if he had been dazzled by the sun.

Padre Pancho entered with the repochetas and asked Doña Sofía if she would like a soda, but when she spied the empty cans on the center table, she asked if she could have a beer, if it wasn't too much trouble.

All I need now is to see Doña Sofía smoking, and the signs for the end of the world will be complete, said Lord Dixon.

"Since when have you been a drinker?" asked Inspector Morales in a low but pressing voice as Padre Pancho went back to the kitchen for the beer.

"As the saying goes, comrade, 'When in Russia, do as the Russians do.' Besides, it helps me calm my nerves. Are you scolding me?"

"I'm not scolding you. I'm just surprised. What are you nervous about? Is it Fanny? Has something new come up?" he asked, his voice even lower.

"She's the same. The doctors are optimistic, under the circumstances ..."

"So, then, you're better off calming down, because you're making me nervous too."

"That's not what I'm upset about, Comrade Artemio. What worries me is how our police officers have become a savage horde that does nothing but beat up our young people."

You've found the way to drown your sorrows, Doña Sofía, said Lord Dixon. You have every reason to find comfort in alcohol. That's exactly what it's for.

Using a bartender's care and attention to detail, Padre Pancho emptied the beer can into a glass and offered it to Doña Sofía. She sipped it slowly while rocking the chair enthusiastically and listening to Inspector Morales bring the priest up to date about The Mask's second message, which he handed over to him along with the photos.

"The woman in mourning that Doña Sofía described is the same one who brought the message to Lastenia at the church," said Padre Pancho.

"Tell me about Lastenia," said Doña Sofía. "Doesn't her niece always study bones in a box in the sacristy?"

"She'll graduate soon. We're about to have a new doctor."

"What do you think about the character with the mask, Doña Sofía?" asked Inspector Morales.

"To begin, I've seen that movie on cable at least three times. Lots of people think that 'V' is an anarchist, but I think he's a hero who seeks vengeance as a very noble cause."

Seeking vengeance isn't Christian at all. It violates your own Protestant religion, Doña Sofía, but we'll let that pass, said Lord Dixon.

"I'm not talking about the movie character. I'm talking about the person signing those messages," said Inspector Morales, making a great show of taking deep interest in nibbling a repocheta's edges.

"The first thought that comes to mind is that if this other Vendetta wanted to capture you, he would have done so a long time ago."

"Now you understand, inspector," said Padre Pancho. "That's why I have to believe that it's someone who opposes the administration from within."

"We're not going to have another debate about killers with a heart of gold, reverend."

"Regardless, they must be sending these messages for only one reason: they want them to be made public," Doña Sofía concluded.

"Damn right, Doña Sofía. We're both of the same opinion, and the inspector is in the minority."

"That's certainly what they want us to do," said Inspector Morales with a negative tone. "But no one can guarantee that it's not a trap."

"What kind of trap?" asked Doña Sofía.

"I have no idea," responded Inspector Morales, contemplating

[114]

the advances he had made on his repocheta. "Maybe all that information turns out to be false."

"Regardless, we have to take the risk," said Doña Sofía, belching with great restraint. "My idea is that we create a fake Twitter account and post everything there as text images. Then we post anything our friend Vendetta sends to us afterward."

"That's like sending a message out to the ocean in a bottle," responded Inspector Morales, wiping the repocheta's grease on his pant legs. "Most likely no one would ever see it."

"That's what hashtags are for," answered Doña Sofía. "They're the compasses for navigating the web."

"You and I understand each other, Doña Sofía," said Padre Pancho. "We can be sure that these charges will go viral."

"I'm not saying that we shouldn't try," Inspector Morales conceded.

"Let me borrow your computer when you're finished eating, Padre," said Doña Sofía, who had a disconsolate look on her face after studying her glass, now empty but for a bit of foam. "The hashtag will be #freenicaragua."

You should all mark down this historic day, said Lord Dixon. The Gunpowder Society has been born in this parsonage.

CHAPTER EIGHT

Angels, Seraphim, Cherubim, Thrones, and Other Heavenly Authorities

A S TWILIGHT FELL, the same smoggy cloud was descending once again upon Managua when the sliding gate opened at the Las Colinas home that housed the fake customs agency. Pedrón was driving this time with Tongolele beside him, his head bent down, the acne pustules burning red from a sudden inflammation, the white stripe in his hair rapidly turning ashen.

The car had barely passed through the gate when Pedrón began flipping through the channels on the radio dial, and on Radio Corporación, between musical fragments from "A People United Will Not Be Defeated," the hymn from the Chilean group Inti Illimani that been revived practically overnight, the broadcasters reported a huge protest planned for the following day in Managua. The broadcasters added that due to the large number of people expected to participate, the protest had already been dubbed the "Mother of All Protest Marches."

The song's rhythm returned from the depths of the decades: "You'll march with me at the great hour; you'll watch as your flag and song flower; the red dawn will glow with new power." And the beat continued: Your sore feet shod with stinking boots, your camouflage uniform tattooed with sweat that had dried out countless times, the heavy rifle slung across your back during a march that always seemed to be going uphill, the small transistor device stuck to your ear that repeatedly played the same hymn and gave a platform to the announcer from Radio Sandino—located "somewhere in Nicaragua"—which transmitted military reports as the revolution's triumph grew closer.

Tongolele turned off the radio.

"You're wise not to want to hear the songs from those times, commissioner," said Pedrón. "The right has corrupted them."

"What would you know? At that time you were playing the tuba in the National Guard's band," said Tongolele, his eyes fixed on the windshield.

"It wasn't a tuba. It was a clarinet."

"Tuba, trombone, clarinet. They're all the same thing no matter what you say. The problem is that you sang 'Happy Birthday' to Somoza."

"I'll accept that, but there's no reason to keep beating me over the head with it. At the same time, it doesn't change the fact that the government should have stopped Radio Corporación from playing those songs a long time ago."

"We put a C4 charge on the antenna at Tipitapa and it had no effect at all. They fixed the damage and continued with the same subversive activities."

"That crime happened forever ago. Now they need another dose. Corrupting revolutionary music is enough to justify punishment."

"Everything's moving in reverse, Pedrito. If you don't believe that, just look at where I'm going. And under whose command."

Pedrón said nothing. He was not about to stick his finger in the wound that had ripped out Tongolele's heart and soul.

In the areas surrounding the Santo Domingo Mall, their drive became difficult because vehicles had to navigate the waves of protesters who seemed to move in no particular direction. In addition, branches from the iron Trees of Life cluttered the way, thrown down and tangled within a jumble of electric cables and telephone wires.

The taxi sought alternate routes, but in every direction it encountered improvised barricades made from cobblestones, the chassis of abandoned vehicles, door frames, and even transport trailers turned over on their sides. And behind the barricades, Tongolele and Pedrón saw young people armed with backpacks filled with rocks and the odd pyrotechnic mortar launcher. Protesters covered their faces with towels, blouses, camisoles, and every now and then with masks from the annual *torovenado* festival that celebrated indigenous rights, masks of a horned red devil or a sharp-fanged jaguar, and rubber hoods depicting the long-gone faces of Gorbachev or Margaret Thatcher. And a thick black cloud of burning tires penetrated everything.

Without taking his eyes from the dark scene before him, Tongolele thought to himself that soldiers could make an initial charge into this group and simply fire their rifles, and when the first protesters fell dead, all of these kids would have to run and thereby become easy to hunt down. But he didn't really care whether or not the little shits—none of whom had ever heard a real gunshot—were forced to abandon their barricades or stop tearing down Trees of Life as they chose.

The aide had barely left with the Chinese box when a man appeared, looking as if he had been waiting behind the door. He introduced himself as an army officer whom Tongolele had never before seen. The man was obese and had a cheerful face; he wore a carefully ironed uniform and brilliantly shined shoes, and he carried his military cap under his armpit. *With your permission, commissioner*, and he handed Tongolele an official Military Intelligence Directorate document from his satchel. By order of higher authorities, the jolly fat man with this document in hand, namely Colonel Jacobo Pastrana, was taking interim authority over the customs agency's departments, and all the agency's personnel were now under his command.

Those personnel necessarily included La Chaparra—Tongolele's right hand now cut off—and Pedrón, Tongolele's left hand likewise removed. Nevertheless, *assuming you would grant permission, commissioner,* the jolly fat man would allow Pedrón to accompany Tongolele to his destination on the condition that Pedrón return the fake taxi after dropping Tongolele off, *where you will find other means of transportation made available to you, commissioner. You'll receive another weapon as well, commissioner. So, be so kind as to hand me your regulation pistol.*

They exited the highway loop, which was blocked in the heights of the San Judas barrio, and by using side streets they arrived at the Sierra Maestra barrio and later the Camilo Ortega barrio, and from there they reached the Torres Molina area and eventually the southbound highway, and not until they had left the Nejapa junction in their rearview mirror and were driving on the old highway to León did Pedrón dare to speak again.

"Explain everything that's happened, commissioner, but do it slowly because I'm not very smart. The problem is that when I was playing in a kids' baseball league, I went up to bat and the pitcher threw a fastball that hit me on the head, and players didn't wear batting helmets at that time."

"What do you want me to explain to you, Pedrito?" Tongolele smiled vaguely. "I'm in a free fall and I haven't hit the ground yet. So the truth is that I have no idea exactly how screwed I actually am."

"Your mother told you last night, commissioner. They were already making the bed for you, and you didn't pay attention."

"They had me pretty well plucked by then, ready for skewering on the spit. I really didn't have much of a chance to escape."

"The truth is that they should have been grateful. After all, your messages in the Chinese box provided early warning that the disturbances we're seeing now could actually happen."

"Who knows if anyone even read my messages? Who knows if there aren't dozens of Chinese boxes stored in some warehouse, never having been opened?"

"And your mother insisted on warning that too many Trees of Life would upset the magnetic balance. And they didn't listen to her either."

"They're cutting down the Trees of Life with me and my mother on top of them."

"The thing that makes the least sense of all is that they've put you under the command of Leónidas."

"That just makes my humiliation complete, Pedrito. Nothing could be clearer than that."

"I was one of Leónidas' prisoners when he led the Sandinista commandos who took the Nejapa Country Club, right in the middle of the debutantes' ball."

"Leónidas, like the Spartan king at Thermopylae," said Tongolele. "His true name is much more laughable: Silverio Pérez, like the dancing bullfighter in an Agustín Lara song."

"When I was in the National Guard at Campo de Marte, they allowed me to play in Julio Max Blanco's orchestra, which is why I was there that night, earning a little money."

"I imagine you soiled yourself with fear."

"Who wouldn't soil themselves under a hail of bullets like that? I can't explain why, but I was so nervous that I jumped into the pool."

"Somoza soiled himself even worse because the people at the ball weren't just government ministers and ambassadors. One of the people was his nephew, a blood relative, who was escorting one of the debutantes."

"The guerrillas freed us—the musicians, the cooks, the waiters, and the young debutantes—at 2:00. But they threw all of Somoza's allies and close friends into a locked room, with the nephew at the front of the line."

"And by the next day Somoza agreed to trade them in exchange for all political prisoners. That was a powerful blow. We humiliated him."

"And that's where Leónidas took advantage of the situation. He was the last person to climb up to the plane, and once he reached the top of the mobile stairway he raised his arms with his Galil rifle in his hands, turned toward the photographers, and took off his balaclava."

"A clown. He broke anonymity to make a name for himself, which violated one of our basic rules in such cases."

"But that picture is what made him famous. The bushy Camilo Cienfuegos beard, the Galil rifle held high, the hand grenades hanging down each side of his neck on the straps of his grenade belt."

"A first-class shit-eating fake. Anyone even mildly acquainted with actual combat could see that those grenades were straight from a theater costume, copied from some war movie."

"So the revolution triumphs, and he realizes he's been left in second place."

"Vice-minister of one thing, vice-minister of another. He never climbed above that, and his ego couldn't take it. That's why he deserted to Honduras and started fighting for the Contras."

"*The Traitor*. When people talked about the Traitor, everybody knew it was him."

"He betrayed the revolution because of his egomania and his ideological ignorance. He was a man who prided himself on never having read the classics of Marxism and Leninism, and yet he still talked about the class struggle."

One afternoon around 1981, Leónidas went to the barbershop that Tongolele, then-Chief of the Agency for Special Protection, had ordered to be established in the Ministry of the Interior's basement. The barbershop, managed by master stylist Romualdo Traña, was intended for revolutionary leaders' exclusive use, yet from beneath the hot towel covering his face, Leónidas waxed poetic about how he came from a dirt-poor family and how his father, a widower, had made huge sacrifices to send him to El Colegio Centroamérica, an exclusive Jesuit boarding school in Granada attended only by the children of oligarchs and the bourgeoise, as Leónidas told the story, which explained how, without ever reading Konstantinov, Leónidas had learned there were such things as classes. A booming voice, that of Tongolele himself, had responded: "…classes at nine, at ten, at eleven…" Surrounded by general laughter, Leónidas had not even dared to remove the towel from his own face.

"Until he was forgiven," Pedrón said. "The revolution returned to power, and they even gave him a plantation. And they name him president of the Association of Historical Combatants."

"These policies of reconciling even with traitors and deserters never stop turning my stomach," Tongolele said.

After exiting the old highway to León and taking a neighboring road, they arrived at Leónidas' plantation in the Chiquilistagua region, where Tongolele had been ordered to present himself. Leónidas had baptized the place as "La Quinceañera," a name that recalled the fifteen-year-old debutantes who had been celebrating their coming-out when he had become famous.

A guard wearing rubber boots and a shotgun hanging down his back opened the gate for them, and they drove along a pathway bordered by whitewashed royal palm trees until reaching a house with pine siding and a zinc roof, its front graced by a covered veranda, while the entire building rested on pilings cured with coal tar. In front of the veranda sat a seventies-era Porsche, its hood raised and its moss-green body well-polished, as if the vehicle had just left a sports-car show.

A shed was attached alongside the house. The shed contained a tractor and barrels of diesel fuel, beyond which sat an empty chicken coop, and behind the chicken coop stood four stables, which were empty as well. At the stables' entrance a rusted horse trailer languished where it had been stuck among quarried stones, accompanied by several dovecotes atop poles.

Pedrón stepped out of the car to say good-bye and handed Tongolele the phone and the charger, while Tongolele gave the big man a powerful pat on the back and fought the urge to embrace him. Without further delay, Tongolele turned and ascended the steps to the veranda, as the sound of the retreating taxi's engine disappeared behind him.

Leónidas had undoubtedly heard his footsteps on the floor-boards because he met Tongolele at the door and offered a mischievous smile as he made an exaggerated gesture of extending his arms. Tongolele approached him and allowed an embrace without enthusiasm.

Many years had passed since the two had seen each other face-to-face. Leónidas had put on quite a few pounds, notable by his large belt, but he still retained his agility. Several weeks before, Tongolele had seen him on one of the official TV channels during an interview honoring his eightieth birthday, and when the reporter asked Leónidas about his physical condition, the man's entire response consisted of launching himself to the floor, doing fifty push-ups on camera as he counted each one out loud, and then finishing by leaping to his feet in a single bound and returning to his chair on the set.

Leónidas was wearing a polo shirt with blue stripes and cargo pants. He obviously dyed his beard, always black and bushy, which provided a sharp contrast to his advancing baldness.

The two men walked across the small sitting room, which displayed four bamboo chairs around a varnished tree trunk that lay on the floor, bark and all, which served as a table. In addition, a stuffed crocodile—two green-jasper marbles acting as its eyes—had been mounted on the main wall as if it were crawling along by using its claws to grasp the wood panels, which were connected with a tongue-and-groove technique.

The office smelled of bat guano, and its walls were covered with photos that reached the ceiling: Leónidas with Fidel Castro, who was demonstrating a rifle with a telescopic sight to him; Leónidas with General Ómar Torrijos, the two wearing swim trunks at a beach on the Bosquerón military base; Leónidas with Yasser Arafat, both wearing Palestinian keffiyehs; Leónidas on the ground inside a Bedouin tent next to Colonel Muammar Gaddafi, who had given him the solid-gold Rolex—a watch with Gaddafi's own image on the face—that Leónidas still wore on his wrist.

And on a wall set apart from the rest hung the famous photo of Leónidas climbing the plane's mobile stairway with his rifle raised high. The picture drew attention because it had been blown up so much and had been framed in golden plaster; alongside it hung another photo of the same ancient time, the same size, and the same golden frame, where the comandante appeared along with a group of guerrilla comandantes who posed like a soccer team—some standing, others kneeling—and displayed an enormous variety of guns at the ready.

Before sitting down, Tongolele examined the main wall's many photos while Leónidas observed him with a simultaneously attentive and playful attitude, and Tongolele stopped to study three pictures, bending down because they occupied the lower section of the wall. In one photo, Leónidas posed at the Palmerola military base with CIA officers dressed as if they were going on safari. In another photo, Leónidas appeared with Oliver North, who had managed the Iran-Contra Operation from the White House, each man pointing at the other and laughing. And in yet another photo, Leónidas greeted Ronald Reagan with a handshake in the White House's Oval Office; Reagan had signed and dedicated the picture himself.

"Those photos belong to my history, and I am a part of history," said Leónidas, leaning on the high-backed easy chair upholstered in red and black vinyl. "I have no reason to hide them."

Tongolele said nothing as he moved to take a seat across from Leónidas. A bald eagle with wide-spread wings had been rather crudely carved across the front of the desk.

"It's true that I was a Contra. But I was a Contra against the revolution's direction, trying to change its course," Leónidas cackled, praising his own clever turn of phrase. "I wanted to have freedom, democracy, progress for the needy, which is what we have today. Unfortunately, nobody listened to me at the time."

Tongolele did not respond to this statement either. The word *needy* carried the flavor of class hatred. Ideological nonsense. All he wanted was for this particular meeting to end as quickly as possible, then receive the orders Leónidas was supposed to give him, swallow them as if he were taking some kind of purgative, and ask how he was supposed to leave the house as night was falling, or if he would have to sleep at the plantation in his underwear because he hadn't even brought a toothbrush.

"In the end, no one from my own party wanted me, and neither did any of the Contras, because I've always had the problem of thinking for myself," Leónidas continued, now seated in his red-and-black easy chair, with his hands spread across the desk and his eyes gazing forward, as if he were being interviewed.

Distracted, Tongolele could manage only a nod.

"And later, I became nothing but a rotting corpse. The neoliberals didn't want me in power, nor did the Sandinistas like you," Leónidas said, slowly rising to his feet again. "But once the Comandante got the presidential sash across his chest again, he sent for me."

He walked back and forth with his hands clasped behind his back, and then stopped.

"What do you think he said to me?" asked Leónidas.

Tongolele shrugged his shoulders.

"The past is in the past, Leónidas. What do you want? Just tell me how I can serve you. I want nothing, I answered. I don't want a government position. That's not what I fought for. And I didn't fight for some cushy job either," said Leónidas. "I just need help getting a bank loan. Then I'll do the rest."

He had received a loan from Alba Coruna, a credit union founded thanks to funds from Nicaragua's petroleum cooperation agreement with Venezuela, signed after Comandante Chávez's first visit. Leónidas then bought La Quinceañera, a small bit of land, only seventy acres. He attempted to buy some ponies, a market that had exploded in Nicaragua: small horses with easy gaits for children. He also built a coop for guineafowl—ornamental birds used to brighten gardens—with the hope of eventually raising peacocks. In addition, he tried to breed messenger pigeons, hoping to export well-trained birds to the rest of Central America: the armies would be excellent possible clients. None of these projects required much land, so there was enough acreage to plant experimental cotton of different colors: the seeds came already modified such that the fibers grew red, green, yellow, or any other color desired for the fabric. If someone wanted a particular blue color for blue jeans, for example, the cotton eliminated the need for dyes.

"And then?" Tongolele finally said.

"And then the seven plagues of Egypt hit me," Leónidas answered, crouching down with his eyes peeled as if he were facing an enemy.

Vampire bats bit the little ponies, infecting them with rabies. Gumboro disease attacked the Guinea fowl, creating a true massacre. Bats scared away the homing pigeons, who flew off to destinations unknown carrying the capsules with the test messages in their feet; even now, the bats lived in the dovecote, as comfortable as if it were the own house. And the cotton plantation was devoured by a cloud of spiked weevils that seemed harmless because they were so small, but they had steel mandibles that never rusted.

"You would have been better off raising boxing kangaroos," said Tongolele. "They have strong resistance to disease, and you could have become rich training them as security guards."

Confused, Leónidas looked at him.

"Are you making fun of me?" he asked. "I'm not in the mood for jokes."

"And what about the multicolored Chinese fibers used for making printed fabrics. Didn't you think of those either?"

"Now I know you're making fun of me. Go ahead and indulge yourself. We need to find some way to entertain ourselves when things go wrong."

"I'm not making fun of you, and I'm not joking. I'm just trying to give you some helpful advice, although it's a bit late now to save you from bankruptcy."

"Being the comandante has always saved me."

"I'll bet Alba Coruna was ordered to eat your loan."

"You're a better seer than your mother," Leónidas smiled. "The man himself called me to his office and said: Forget about your experiments, Leónidas. I'm ordering you to write your memoirs because that's what the revolution needs. And stop worrying about your income, because from now on the Government of Love, Peace, and Reconciliation will take care of that."

And so Leónidas was now enclosed in La Quinceañera, dedicated to writing his memoirs as he wrote about many things that nobody knew: descriptions of intrigue and plots among the comrades from the time of the guerrilla war; reports about ideological and nonsensical debates, particularly the debate over whether we revolutionaries should first form a proletariat party before organizing the working class to take up arms or whether we revolutionaries should simply take up arms and hide in the mountains, eat grilled monkey, and wait for the right conditions before firing the first shot, the problem being that doing so would have left us living in the same conditions as we did then, lost in the wilderness with our

beards growing down to the ground; a chapter about how Leónidas had renounced the sweet taste of power to live in the swamps
and correct the revolution's lost course; and yet another chapter
about how the CIA had never been able to flip Leónidas and how
Langley had ended up hating him because of his rebellion.

"But then this emergency suddenly arose, and my help was requested," said Leónidas. "A single phone call, and that was enough
for Leónidas."

"And what did your help consist of?" Tongolele asked, relieved
that they were finally coming to the point of the meeting.

But Leónidas seemed not to hear him.

"Like a good soldier, Leónidas responded: I hear and obey," he
said, and to re-enact the situation he extracted his cell phone, put
it to his ear, snapped to attention, and raised his other hand to his
forehead.

Tongolele had forgotten that after Leónidas spoke for a while,
he consistently began to refer to himself in third person.

"What's my role in your plans?" Tongolele asked again.

Leónidas laughed, stroking his beard.

"I understand how much it burns you up to be under my command. Leónidas is still a traitor in your eyes because you can't stop
seeing the past through those ideological leather goggles you never
took off."

"I follow the orders they give me, and if they name Judas or
Barrabas as my leader, I don't argue about it or question it, nor do
I switch to the enemy's side."

"The great asshole of conspiracies, the great brain behind so
many schemes, dethroned. And here's your traitor, converted now
into your commander, because when they need a man who fights
with balls of steel and doesn't make them vomit, the man they call
is Leónidas," said Leónidas, pounding his chest.

"Up above they must know why I'm under your command. I
came to receive orders, not to have a dick-measuring contest."

"It's sad that they kick you in the ass without even telling
you why."

"If you're the one designated to tell me, I really have hit rock
bottom."

"You should console yourself with the thought that your reha-
bilitation period won't last long."

"A revolutionary always accepts the place he's assigned," Tongolele said.

Leónidas' eyes never ceased to watch him, and they gleamed with a spark of mockery. Then, he meticulously donned a pair of half-moon eyeglasses, removed a Managua city map from a drawer in his desk, and spread it across the desktop. The city map was divided into zones, marked by red felt-tip lines.

"They've given Leónidas command of Operation Abate, like the bug killer," he said. "We have to exterminate all these insects that have come out into the streets to try to force a coup."

"A coup? These little savages? Coups are for armies."

"The army is on our side, so be careful about misinterpreting my words. The priests, the gringos, and the bourgeoise who want to sell out the country are using these idiot students for a coup. And we're going to stop them all at once."

"And what about the SWAT teams and the riot police? Have they retreated to their barracks?"

"The police will provide tactical back-up. Our own people, armed spontaneously, will defend us against the conquistadors."

"How will they be armed?"

"Weapons from the military's stores. Leónidas is not going to send them to battle against fleas and cockroaches with little toy guns."

"Are we talking only about Managua?"

"Managua, Masaya, León, Matagalpa, Jinotepe, Estelí. Wherever we need insecticide. And the tacticians directing the defense forces will be the original historical combatants. We'll use walkie-talkies with special frequencies to communicate."

Historical combatants. A collection of ancient pot-bellied guerrilla commanders with problems like enlarged prostates, joined by others with pacemakers, diabetes, and high blood pressure, all organized into a veterans' group headed by Leónidas, the means through which they asked for cataract operations, dialysis, medications they couldn't afford, recommendation letters for family members, and economic assistance to repair their homes.

"I'm not a historical combatant. I'm on active duty," said Tongolele.

"Active? I don't think that's true anymore," responded Leónidas, the smile no longer reaching his entire face.

"Let's limit ourselves to the operation at hand. What do you specifically want me to do?"

"All of eastern Managua is yours," said Leónidas, tracing his finger along the line of one of the red circles on the city map. "The first place I want freed up is the highway to the airport."

"With two or three shots in the air, these little snots will run off to seek refuge beneath their grandmothers' skirts."

"There will be no shots in the air. We'll be locked and loaded, shooting to kill with well-oiled AK-47s. Real weapons. And the bulldozers will be following behind us, clearing out the barricades."

"There will be a lot of dead."

"And if all we do is shoot into the air, we'll be the dead ones. They'll hang us from the same Trees of Life that they haven't torn down yet."

"How many men do I have?"

"Because your zone is one of the hottest, Leónidas will grant you a force of 200 well-armed men along with enough Hilux pick-ups, all brand-new. Your operations base is the Mercado de Mayoreo. And you'll have the support of snipers shooting Dragunovs."

"Are the snipers really necessary? You'll have more than enough firepower already."

"You'll have snipers in your zone, and Leónidas will have them in his central theatre of operations. People have been announcing a huge march for tomorrow. Leónidas will allow them to reach the cathedral. And at the right time, the Dragunovs will blow their heads away, and a barrage of bullets will send the others scurrying everywhere."

"Do you want a staggered or simultaneous attack?"

"We'll all start firing at the same time, targeting the protesters themselves and the barricades in the zones. Anybody who escapes one line of fire will fall under another."

"Six red circles, six clean-up zones. And on top of that we have to break up the protest march. We're taking the risk of killing each other with friendly fire. Every unit needs some kind of identification mark."

Tongolele suddenly heard himself suggesting ideas that came to his head against his will and despite his humiliation. At the deepest level, he said to himself, what I want is a place, some reassurance. I don't want to be left on the sidelines, forced to see what might happen tomorrow and wait until the wind changes. I must survive.

"What kind of identification marks?" Leónidas asked, checking his Rolex. "The people are going to start gathering together at 5:00 this morning. There's not much time."

"T-shirts. One color of t-shirt for every zone of operations. I can get the shirts before 5:00."

"What about something like masks? Something to cover the shooters' faces."

"I think silk stockings would work. And knitted hats that can be pulled over the eyes. It's easy to cut eye-holes for them. And bandanas."

"Will all that stuff be sold or donated?"

"I'll take care of it. There'll be no problems."

"Well then, take everything to the baseball stadium. That's where the logistics center will be. And now I have to take a piss."

Tongolele examined his cell's contact list to find Fabiola's number, which he struggled to do because he was accustomed to having Pedrón pass the phone to him once the call was ready. Meanwhile, in the bathroom on the other side of the wall, Leónidas emptied his bladder with a heavy stream that would have made a horse proud.

Tongolele heard Fabiola shrieking through the phone, so he first had to calm her down. What's happening to you, my love? I call and I call, and you don't answer. I'm hearing terrible news about you, rumors that you've been arrested. Nothing's happening to me; everything's fine; you know we have an emergency here and that I have to put all my focus on that; we'll talk later.

He told her about the t-shirts: they were intended for a soccer league for poor children from different regions, and the championship was scheduled to begin very early the next morning. The shirts needed to be plain, without logos or any other markings. The colors needed to be as bright as possible so that the shirts could be seen from far away: fuchsia red, Prussian blue, canary yellow, emerald green. Like the colors for the Trees of Life, she remarked. Tongolele also gave her the details about the silk stockings, the hats, and the bandanas. Is all of this for the same soccer league? Let's say that the other things are gifts for the players' mothers, as I'm sure you take my meaning, and there's no need for further explanation. Fabiola also had game-day paraphernalia, which was commonly sold in the areas where fans gathered, including items like red-and-black scarves. She asked if such things would be helpful. Absolutely, he answered, so please add the scarves to the other things. She explained that because the clothing and other items came in different types and weights of packaging, she would need to track them down in several storehouses, and the shirts would be the bulkiest of all. He answered that if that was the case she should get started at once: she had to gather everything together and deliver it to Dennis Martínez Stadium. No later than five o'clock in the morning.

Tongolele clicked off the call and put the phone in the back pocket of his pants. As he did so, Leónidas returned closing his zipper.

"I didn't bring clothes and I don't even have a toothbrush," Tongolele said. "I'd like to go to my house for a bit. I'll be back before 4:00."

"There's no one to take you," Leónidas answered as he returned the city map to his desk drawer. "And I can't let you borrow the Porsche. It's very touchy, and I'm the only person who can get it started."

"So I'm a prisoner here then."

"A prisoner? What kind of stupidity is that? You're Leónidas' guest, which is no small thing."

"Let's stop the sham right now. They gave you orders to keep me here."

"Whatever Leónidas' orders might be, he certainly cannot discuss them with a subordinate."

"Where will I sleep then?"

"You can't sleep in my bed. I don't sleep with men."

"The chicken coop is good enough for me."

"Things aren't that bad. We'll put a mat here in the office, and until the dawn breaks you'll have more than enough time to dream about angels, seraphim, cherubim, thrones, and other heavenly authorities."

CHAPTER NINE

Bishop of Ruins

WEDNESDAY WAS DAWNING when a chicken's nervous flutter-ing awoke Inspector Morales as the bird flew down to the ground from a nearby tree, the light diffused under the window's chintz curtain. The inspector realized that he was not at home in his El Edén neighborhood because he had no chickens in his yard and no chintz curtains in his window.

He examined his room with bleary eyes: two camp cots, one of them his, were pushed against opposite walls, both cots adorned with delicate spinster's bedding, the sheets and pillowcases embroidered with a checked pattern, while a small statuette of the Immaculate Conception—a rosary around the base—stood on a table between the cots. He had perceived, or at least imagined he had perceived, a vague odor of incense or of a recently extinguished candle, or per-haps even the scent of holy water, but he knew that holy water had no scent. And at that moment he realized that although he had no idea how much time would pass, his life would be confined to par-sonages, where everything appeared to be wilting away.

He sat down on the cot, his bladder so full that it pained him. Leaning on his cane, he walked to the bathroom in his underwear, exactly as he had slept, and urinated with difficulty. Not until he returned did he notice that Rambo was absent from the cot that matched his own. He opened the room's door part-way and leaned into the hallway. The house was deserted: Padre Pancho must have been holding the first mass of the day. When he turned back to the cot, he found something pressed beneath the base of the Virgin's statuette: a kraft-paper sack that smelled of onions and had undoubtedly been removed from the kitchen garbage container. A lead-pencil message with smudged strokes had been written on both sides of the bag:

Esteemed and Respected Jefe colon
You'll come to forgive me but even though it was true that my
head was about to fall off due to lack of sleep, it's not true that I
left to go to bed, considering that I had to write you this letter so
that you could have my reasons in writing because I knew that
you wouldn't give me permission if I asked to go on a mission
since you're the type of man who makes a decision and never
changes it. I want to say in all honesty that I wasn't born to be
cooped up or to pretend to be a priest, and I'm particularly not
suited to work as a gardener for this padre while sunbathing and
knowing that you've always said that people who stay in one
place are easier to capture than people who move around freely
from one place to another. So I'm leaving to find out what I can
about all the repression that's going on and whether things are
going to get even worse. Which is what I believe. I think they're
going to grab their guns and start shooting the kids on the streets
because this rebellion is bubbling over like mad, and that means
that the tear-gas bombs, chains, and clubs won't be able to stop all
those people from knocking those trees of life to the ground until
the forest that the señora ordered to be planted is left completely
bald, and that's an offense that she won't forgive because the people are scaring off her protective spirits, the very spirits that have
been nesting like birds in those iron branches after flying here
from India and the great beyond, and her husband isn't the type
to give up power without a fight, nor are the mobs who surround
the couple going to be frightened easily and allow themselves to
be knocked off their horses, because they know that if the tortilla
gets flipped over, they'll be sent to prison as guests in El Chipote
to pay for what they've done, and so they'll say it's us or them.
And they'll say that it's better to die fighting. Jefe, I will either
send you a message as soon as possible or see you in person, and
I ask you to trust that I am still loyal, but the problem is that I am
who I am, and god willing and with luck Tongolele won't capture
me, but if he does then that's as far as I got and the only thing left
for me to say is good-bye, not just to you but to this life as well,
which means that the devil Mandinga has me now, which is the
same as saying that the devil Candanga has me. Explain to the
priest that I didn't steal the change of clothes but that I couldn't
leave wearing nothing at all. I know that you couldn't come with

me even if I asked because that stiff foot of yours won't allow
it, and I hope that your Fanny gets over her terrible sickness
sincerely yours.

He finished reading while sitting on the edge of the cot, and he
stroked the sparse bristles of his morning beard. Something like
this had been bound to happen sooner or later. Serafín could be
happy only in El Mercado Oriental's alleyways, living off other
people's leftovers, enveloped in the sweet smoke of Mary Poppins,
plus some of the sorcerer's stone if it was available: Krakatoa, a
term he himself had used. He would happily smoke a joint even
if it was practically used up, or try a little rock candy even if the
effect lasted no longer than a sigh, and all the more after so many
days of severe abstinence.

Don't be such a fucking idiot, comrade. It doesn't look good on you,
said Lord Dixon. *You know very well that your faithful squire has gone
to seek out a place among the shock troops.*

"Don't talk to me about Serafín, if you would be so kind," said
Inspector Morales.

*And even better now that they're probably paying triple the usual
rate for each beating with a chain or a club, Lord Dixon continued,
ignoring the inspector's warning. And exactly as Serafín's intuition—
the wisdom of a hired killer—tells him, the government is soon going
to hand real guns to those lepers so they can start killing the innocent.*

"You don't know Serafín like I do. That's why you're so hard
on him."

*And your Rambo of the slums will happily accept one of those rifles
and shoot down defenseless students, just as he's said in the past, Lord
Dixon went on.*

"You've always disliked him, so you don't have objective judgment here," Inspector Morales reproached.

*Are you suggesting I'm making things up, comrade? Lord Dixon
challenged. Wasn't he a member of the Mercado Oriental's shock
troops? So, it's just like people say: He was just an innocent wolf cub
among the Boy Scouts.*

"They tortured him at El Chipote; they buried him in the sink;
they water-boarded him until he nearly drowned."

Old habits die hard, said Lord Dixon.

"Fine, then. Let's say that you're right. What the hell am I supposed to do?" Inspector Morales responded angrily. "Keep him tied to the foot of the cot?"

You couldn't possibly have kept him from leaving. I understand that, said Lord Dixon. But put yourself on guard right now, because there's an immediate risk that he could tell them where you are.

"Serafín betray me? Forgive me for laughing."

You'll laugh even more when they come here to pick you up, but they won't take you back to the border; instead, they take you to the dungeons of El Chipote, said Lord Dixon. And the worst part is that they'll take Padre Pancho too, because he's given you aid and shelter.

"I would hold my hand in a fire for Serafín, no matter how it hurts you."

That hand would end up burnt to a crisp, comrade. All you'd have left is a stump, said Lord Dixon.

Padre Pancho knocked on the door and quickly stuck his head in the room, smiling and newly shaved, while Inspector Morales put on his pants as quickly as possible. The inspector was not so embarrassed to be seen undressed as he was by the fact that his vinyl prosthetic leg (more pale than his own skin) was so battered and filthy—a condition reflecting the fact that he did not consistently follow the rule of washing the device with detergent at least once per week.

Breakfast was ready, and two bits of good news came with it. The first bit was that according to Padre Pupiro's morning report, the monseñor had made excellent improvement, and the hospital would release him in three days. The second bit was that The Mask was wreaking havoc on Twitter. In fact, according to Doña Sofía's phone call, the digital editions of both *La Prensa* and *El Nuevo Diario* had published complete copies of the tweets, and many websites had been re-posting them along with extensive re-tweets and likes.

"It goes without saying, but Doña Sofía is a true genius," said Padre Pancho.

"Serafín left," Inspector Morales told him as he buttoned his new shirt, which was plaid just like Padre Pancho's. "He wasn't in his bed this morning."

"Let's get walking. Our breakfast is going cold," said Padre Pancho, using his head to signal that Inspector Morales should follow him.

On the kitchen's small, uncovered table sat two iron skillets that had been recently removed from the diminutive two-burner stove. One skillet contained fried *huevos perdidos*, eggs served with a generous amount of crushed tomatoes; the other contained black beans that were still bubbling. A loaf of sliced bread and two cups of freshly brewed coffee completed the meal.

"I have to be frank with you, padre," Inspector Morales said, taking his seat. "Serafín's running away creates a great risk."

"Are you saying your friend isn't trustworthy? He was a guerrilla fighter along with you."

"The problem isn't that he'll run directly to the police station and come back here with a bunch of officers like Judas Iscariot."

"What's the problem then? Start eating. There's nothing worse than cold eggs."

"The only thing that any wild animal wants when it's taken from the jungle is to go back home. Serafín just wants to go back to El Mercado Oriental. That's where he feels at home."

"His habitat, like the documentaries on *National Geographic*," Padre Pancho smiled.

"The problem is that Serafín is not a model of discipline. And if he's wandering around in an environment like that, there's always a risk that he could suffer a slip of the tongue."

"Your responsibility is to determine the seriousness of that risk," said Padre Pancho, and in order to say grace over the food, he closed his eyes, raised his hand to the spot between his eyebrows, and crossed himself.

"That's exactly why I don't want you involved in any way. Now more than ever."

Fork in hand, Padre Pancho raised his head from his plate.

"Frankly, I don't believe the people at the highest levels are thinking about you at all."

"You don't know Tongolele."

"They have far more serious things to worry about. All those public speeches about love and peace and reconciliation, then all of a sudden they have these young rebels crawling out from under the rocks."

"Tongolele knows I'm back because The Mask knows I'm back. Regardless of The Mask's intentions, he has to be an insider," said Inspector Morales.

Although Padre Pancho's plate was still half full, he chose to light one of his Ducados.

"The fact that a person like The Mask exists simply proves that the gangrene is beginning to spread within the administration."

"If all this isn't part of Tongolele's scheme, he must be trying to track the mole's trail within his own lair. Very few people ever have access to confidential information."

"If it's true that the mole is actually in Tongolele's lair," said Padre Pancho, taking a long drag on his cigarette.

"Where else could the mole be?" asked Inspector Morales. "It's someone filled with resentment or someone who believes that the boat is going to end up sinking."

"Or someone from a different power structure that doesn't communicate with the system. You may say I'm a fool, but the more I think about the situation, the more convinced I become that I'm right."

"I propose something halfway between our positions," said Inspector Morales, his mouth half-full. "Not the last-gasp hero who is sick of the system, and not the villain Tongolele who wants to catch me in a trap. Instead, let's assume that the mole is either an insider filled with resentment or a rat who realizes that a shipwreck is coming."

"Regardless of whether the mole is a hero, a villain, a rat, or someone resentful, The Mask is a careful person who doesn't leave clues behind. Actual letters of flesh and bone, no traceable emails.

"Or perhaps the mole is someone old-school, like me."

Padre Pancho knew how to blow smoke rings like the ones seen only in old black-and-white movies, which had a lot of smokers. But the smoke he exhaled spread the pestilential stench of his Ducados.

"I wouldn't simply jump to the conclusion that The Mask avoids using technology because he's fallen behind the times," he said. "Instead, I'll bet he probably avoids it on purpose."

Inspector Morales stood up to take his plate to the fridge.

"I know from my own experience that you can't teach an old dog new tricks, reverend."

"You knew nothing about this Vendetta character connected to the hackers. In contrast, The Mask uses Vendetta as an emblem. And if you pay attention, you'll notice that The Mask's messages are written on computer."

From the street they could hear the intermittent and persistent wail of sirens from police cars.

"So, what's happening now?" Inspector Morales asked, alarmed and standing up again.

"Calm down. It's got nothing to do with us. The students at the Universidad Nacional, which is nearby, took over the campus this morning and put barricades in the entryways."

"I came to a bad neighborhood," said Inspector Morales, laughing now and returning to his chair. "How long do you think this youthful rebellion will last, reverend?"

Padre Pancho was already extracting another cigarette from the pack as the old butts, accompanied by burnt matchsticks, swam around at the bottom of his mug.

"A new experience for this country: peaceful resistance," he said. "Maybe we're beginning our own Nicaraguan Spring, just like the Arab Spring."

"Unfortunately, we have only two seasons here: winter when it rains, and summer when it doesn't rain. Muck or dust clouds. Spring shows up only in color photo calendars."

Padre Pancho lit a match and contemplated the flame before moving it toward his cigarette.

"Inspector, Arab Spring is just a saying. Ukraine was in the middle of winter, with people up to their knees in snow, when the riot police threw their shields down in front of the crowd. That crowd contained the officers' own friends, neighbors, and relatives."

"The difference here is that if they can't control the crowd, they're going to start shooting into it. And once the riot police aren't enough, the government will send the neighborhood paramilitary units out, and they'll be armed to the teeth."

"The Islamic Republic, then, and not the Ukraine. I hope you're wrong, inspector."

"I know what kind of feed my cattle prefer," said Inspector Morales. "The fanatic death-wish and the opportunistic desire to kill are twin diseases."

"A sad turn of phrase, although it deserves to be written down."

"Here's another phrase to write down: Many of those who fought against Somoza and survived have a perverse nostalgia for using their arthritic fingers to pull a trigger—and for putting their uniforms on again, even if the olive-green can't cover their swollen bellies."

At that moment, the sacristan—tall and wide as ever, dressed in her gray wool with a rosary around the waist—appeared at the kitchen doorway. Because Inspector Morales sat directly in front of her, she greeted him with a slight bow that was not exempt from embarrassment. Her nurse's shoes, milky from white lead, slid cautiously across the floor as if she were trying to avoid crushing any of God's small creatures she might find in her way, and she handed a manila envelope to Padre Pancho.

"Another message from The Mask," he said. "Did the same woman bring it?"

The sacristan responded with an emphatic no.

"A boy," she said. "He came into the church with no respect at all, riding a bike."

And without saying another word, she left the room.

"Now you see, inspector, that your friend The Mask manages his affairs quite artfully," said Padre Pancho, handing over the envelope. "He's changed couriers."

"And is that woman trustworthy, reverend?"

"She knows who you are and why you are here. But she's not an inquisitive person, and she doesn't talk much."

"One slip-up, and I'm dead."

"If you trust your friend Rambo, then let me trust her, and we'll call it a tie."

Inspector Morales unfolded the paper and read it out loud:

> Pope Francis will call MB to Rome almost immediately after he's released from the hospital. They'll leave him there like a kite without a string after naming him as bishop of a place that doesn't exist, and they'll do all this with the purpose of preventing him from causing trouble here, although the Vatican will officially announce that the Church is acting to protect him.

"So because they couldn't stop him by killing his nephew or even by knocking him silly with a lead pipe to the head, they have him towed away," said Inspector Morales. "A great example of high diplomacy."

"Fuck that! That just can't be true," said Padre Pancho.

"What can't be true?" asked Inspector Morales.

"Well, that," answered Padre Pancho, pointing at the message. "Pope Francis isn't capable of participating in a scheme like that."

"Isn't the Pope a Jesuit?" Inspector Morales asked with false sincerity.

"So what?" Padre Pancho responded angrily. "I'm a Jesuit too. You're not going to say that you actually believe the stories about the Jesuits being two-faced, are you?"

"No, reverend. I asked because perhaps you can discover whether The Mask is telling the truth," said Inspector Morales, backing down.

Padre Pancho studied him closely, then put out the cigarette he had just lit by drowning it in his coffee cup.

"My provincial superior in San Salvador won't possibly know anything, but I have ways of investigating."

Inspector Morales listened from a distance as Padre Pancho spoke on the phone. The priest soon came back, and he seemed to be searching blindly for his chair.

"They've named him titular bishop of Forontoniana," he reported. "I just spoke with the Dominicans' provincial superior in San Salvador."

"Forontoniana? What place is that?"

"A place that doesn't exist, just like The Mask says. It's nothing but ruins. It used to be the capital of the Roman province of Byzacena, which is known today as Tunisia."

"A bishop of ruins?"

"It's an honorific responsibility, nothing more than a title. Bishop in partibus infidelium."

Bishop over a land of infidels, Lord Dixon interpreted. A phantom diocese that came to an end after a conquest by the Arabs or the Turks, who invaded the area and cut off people's heads with unsheathed scimitars. A few ruins show that a city used to be there.

"But he was already a monseñor," said Inspector Morales. "He already held a high rank in the Church."

"Domestic Prelate of His Holiness? That's nothing, inspector. Some priests get swollen heads about these empty honorific titles, but tinsel has never meant much to Monseñor Ortez."

"So, he's won the double lottery, then. Domestic prelate before, which is nothing, and now he's the bishop of a place that's nothing as well."

"Plots, nothing but plots," said Padre Pancho, shaking his head like a bull. "It's all designed to send him off to Rome and ensure that he gets lost and forgotten in a dicastery."

"That's not a word I know either, reverend."

A dicastery is like a government ministry or department, row upon row of desks, said Lord Dixon. It's nothing but a swarm of cassocks.

"They're sending him to a dicastery called the Congregation for the Causes of Saints."

"What do they do there?"

"They manage the canonization process by opening files on each candidate and investigating their miracles."

"He can at least help the Church grant an altar for Sor María Romero. She would be the first Nicaraguan saint."

Centuries could pass before they blow the dust off her file, said Lord Dixon. There are thousands of lost files like that in Rome's catacombs, where they store the records of people who never were saints and never will be.

"I don't believe that they'll give the monseñor any power like that. He'll just be a simple office worker," said Padre Pancho. "One lone man in a horde of people."

"Maybe the Pope, who's ordering him to Rome, will rescue him from that office and name him as a secretary to the Papal Household."

"The Pope doesn't even know that Monseñor Ortez exists. Everything is done in his name. Rome's an embarrassment."

It's advantageous for Francis if average Christians believe he knows nothing about what happens around him, said Lord Dixon.

"So they're forcing the monseñor to leave. They've ordered him to get on that plane."

"They've been planning this coup from on high for a long time. People don't just improvise something like this," said Padre Pancho, brooding.

"And the Vatican allows the whole thing to be disguised as removing the monseñor from danger."

So, you can believe in Sai Baba and the Eye of Fátima, and you can still receive blessings from the Holy Father, said Lord Dixon.

"This is what goes wrong when Gospel power gets involved with secular power," lamented Padre Pancho, removing the last cigarette in his pack. "That's Rome, unfortunately."

There's a short and winding road from Bethlehem to Babylon, said Lord Dixon.

"Can the monseñor refuse? Can he say I'm not moving from here, and I'm not going to Rome even if they tie me up?"

"He will have publicly disobeyed the Pope and he would be punished with the canonical penalty of suspension *a divinis*."

"He'd be defrocked?"

Padre Pancho crumpled the empty Ducados pack in his fist.

"He couldn't say mass; he couldn't administer the sacraments; he couldn't listen to confessions."

A priest who's no longer a priest, said Lord Dixon. A naked turtle outside its shell.

"A dead man living, in other words. And for a man who can't live without a cassock, it would be like having his soul torn out by the roots."

"Even worse, he would be penniless. He who serves the altar lives by the altar. What else do we priests know how to do? Neither I nor the monseñor even have a pot to piss in."

"So, what do we do with this message?"

"One thing is certain: They won't publicize the pontifical decree until the monseñor has returned to his parish."

"Then we need to move fast—the quicker, the better."

"We would gain nothing in this case. The Vatican wouldn't delay anything just because we leaked a decision that's already been made. And Monseñor Ortez doesn't even know about it anyway."

"This is war, and we have to use all our ammunition. We can't possibly know what will have an effect and what won't."

"Well, let me talk it over with Padre Pupiro."

"You can't talk it over, reverend, not even with Padre Pupiro. No one else should know that we're controlling the Twitter account."

And here I thought the Jesuits were great conspirators, said Lord Dixon.

"But let's at least give the monseñor a chance to leave the hospital."

"Regardless, he's going to find out sooner or later. The important thing here is the element of surprise."

"San Ignacio understood the value of surprise attacks," Padre Pancho agreed. "His regiment learned that in the Battle of Pamplona."

He didn't learn that lesson just in war, but in pursuing women of the court, said Lord Dixon. He was an incorrigible ladies' man in his youth.

Inspector Morales read the message over the phone to Doña Sofía so she could copy it, but Padre Pancho took the phone from him without a word, photographed the sheet of paper, and posted it on WhatsApp. He returned the phone to the inspector a few minutes later.

"Doña Sofía answered like a bolt of lightning," he said. "Her fingers are tingling from tweeting the information."

Outside, from the direction of the university campus, the sound of detonations began to echo, sporadically at first and then more regularly, each explosion louder than the last.

"Loads of tear-gas bombs at first, and those last explosions were stun grenades," said Inspector Morales.

"They're trying to prevent the students from attending the protest march planned for today," said Padre Pancho.

In the parsonage's living room, they heard some ferocious howls followed by gasping breaths, as if someone were having their throat cut. Padre Pancho ran to take a look, followed by Inspector Morales.

The sacristan had plopped into one of the rocking chairs and was leaning against the backrest, where she was muffling her wails with a fist in which she held a handkerchief.

"My niece!" she said between sobs.

They had kidnapped her niece from the university traffic circle. Some men wearing canary-yellow shirts had arrived shooting guns from the bed of a pick-up, wounding several people. They had used the butts of their guns to beat the sacristan's niece, then they had handcuffed her, thrown her into the truck bed, and carried her off to parts unknown. According to Doris, the niece's study partner who had run to the church with the news, the young woman's head had been bleeding.

"Why did she come all the way here when she's a student at a different university?" the sacristan bawled. "This is Doris's fault, a promiscuous girl who filled her head with fantasies."

"What the hell are you talking about, Lastenia?" Padre Pancho scolded her. "Promiscuous my ass. They're just girls with a talent for recruiting other girls."

"What's your niece's name?" asked Inspector Morales, ready to take notes on the manila envelope that had contained the last message from The Mask announcing Monseñor Ortez's forced exile.

"Eneida," answered the sacristan, dabbing her eyes with the handkerchief. "Eneida Robleto. I'm the only mother or father she has."

I already told you to stop this compulsion to write everything down, Lord Dixon said, reprimanding the inspector. For once and for all, you have to accept the fact that you are nothing but a fugitive.

PART TWO

FIRST WITCH:
Round about the cauldron go;
In the poison'd entrails throw.
Toad, that under cold stone
Days and nights has thirty-one
Swelter'd venom sleeping got,
Boil thou first i' the charmed pot.

MacBeth, Act IV, Scene 1

CHAPTER TEN

A Gift from Taiwan

A LONG WEDNESDAY BEGAN. Stretched out on the mat lying on the office floor, Tongolele had barely managed to sleep intermittently throughout a long blank night when he heard Leónidas, who was already on his feet, moving around. Tongolele heard him enter the bathroom and noted the noise of the toilet flushing, which was followed by the stream of the shower water hitting the floor and the gurgle of the water draining away. Shortly thereafter he sensed Leónidas' footsteps as they moved closer in the darkness along the floorboards, the smell of chlorine wafting from the frayed towel that he allowed to fall over his face. Tongolele also heard Leónidas laugh for no apparent reason as he left again.

The bathroom curtain, printed with flamingos the color of raw meat and standing on one leg, was torn from its hooks with large gaps, and the gaps became much bigger when Tongolele drew the curtain back even farther. He entered the shower, griping because the soapy water hadn't finished draining from the floor. Furthermore, since the soap dish contained only a small chunk of soap tangled with matted hair, he decided that washing himself off with a bit of water would be sufficient.

He vigorously scrubbed his head, his shoulders, and his chest, as if what had happened the day before were some kind of filth that whirlpools of water could remove. But when he donned the same sleeveless undershirt that was no longer in style, the boxers that reached his knees and were likewise out of style, the mouse-colored jeans, and the blue-striped shirt stained with sweat where the sleeves tended to stick, the thought occurred to him that sorrow and discouragement were nothing but bullshit for queers, as were all feelings of resentment. He also decided that the only way to climb back up the precipice and return to the top was to prove his value, demonstrate his worth no matter where they put him. He must show them that he was made for discipline. Humility is a weapon of war if a person knows how to use it.

Leónidas had already eaten breakfast when Tongolele left the bathroom, but atop the kitchen pantry he found a cup of coffee, which he drank black, and a cold slice of sweet bread, sticky with sugar, which he began eating apprehensively but ended up devouring without leaving a crumb.

Outside the house, Leónidas had already entered the Porsche and was revving the engine, urging Tongolele to come out. Leónidas was wearing desert camouflage pants the color of sand and pale foliage, along with a jersey from Nicaragua's national baseball team, a large "N" embroidered on the left side of the chest and a number 1 sewn on the back, the backs of the sleeves displaying logos from corporate sponsors. Leónidas explained that FENIBA, the Nicaraguan Federation of Baseball, had unanimously elected him as president of the organization, while Tongolele sat down in the seat alongside him and leaned back, willing to listen with patience and understanding: Who am I to question the decisions that come down from above? Who am I to question the directives deposited in the Chinese box? The entire national team had presented the number-1 uniform to Leónidas in a special ceremony, he said with a broad smile, inspecting the jersey's grey color closely because it was the color used for home games. And today we're playing at home on our turf.

The FENIBA presidency was a post that granted political power, and the Comandante had phoned Leónidas to ask him to run as a candidate. You're probably extremely busy with your memoirs and helping historical combatants, but please take some time off from those things because I need you. So, the asshole Leónidas comes forward, says Leónidas himself, and answers as follows: If you guarantee that I have enough votes, *Comandante*, I'll declare my candidacy. And the Comandante justifiably laughed at this answer: Fucking-A, man, if you didn't have the election in your pocket, I wouldn't have phoned you.

Leónidas talked as if Tongolele didn't know these things already, while the truth was that the Chinese box had provided strict orders for Tongolele to ensure that Leónidas won the election. The problem was that some delegates of FENIBA's general assembly opposed Leónidas even though they still belonged to the party: *He's a traitor. How can we vote for a traitor?* So Tongolele had found himself forced into placating some delegates with gifts, satisfying others by fulfilling requests, and twisting the arms of yet others in a less-than-friendly way.

The two men arrived at Dennis Martínez National Stadium, located between the university's avenue and the highway to Masaya near the Tiscapa Lagoon, close to the environs of the metropolitan cathedral, the Universidad Nacional de Ingeñería, and the Universidad Centroamericana, this last a gift from the Taiwanese government to ensure that Nicaragua continued its membership among the fistful of countries that had not deserted Taiwan by opening diplomatic relations with the People's Republic of China.

Important properties were under police control, their access points protected by metal barriers through which only certain vehicles could pass: transports carrying paramilitary units, Managua city buses as provided by the local transportation cooperatives, trucks and buses from public works, and mini-buses and pick-ups from various government ministries and entities.

Local forces had been mobilized along with the State's apparatus, transportation resources, and the police, not to mention the army, which tried to obscure its presence but could not remain behind, particularly given the appearance of military weapons that Leónidas claimed were going to be used, beginning with the Dragunov rifles. And regardless of whether Tongolele liked the decision about who was named to command the operation, be he a clown or no clown, a traitor or no traitor, the powers on high had made an express commitment to render an overwhelming response. And he represented part of that commitment, which was focused upon a single objective: taking back control of the streets. Tongolele had to hammer that objective into his head.

The orders to move the barriers and allow the Porsche to pass were quickly repeated from one controlled area to the next, and the guards offered a military salute to Leónidas at each checkpoint.

The trim that decorated the highest part of the stadium, braided in blue, black, and white, began to be visible in the shadows of the dawn. The lobby's wide picture windows were illuminated as if for a gala event, and contingents of men of all ages carrying red backpacks disembarked from their vehicles in front of the brightly lit doorways. The groups included police officers dressed as civilians, relieved from their regular units; private security guards; common criminals who had been set free; members of the neighborhood shock troops, chosen for their familiarity with firearms; youthful comrades from the party; and the most capable of El Mercado Oriental's underclass. Once these people hit the ground, they were ordered to form rows of two facing the box seats and the mezzanines.

We had a debate, Leónidas announced to Tongolele, turning off the engine and pocketing the keys in his camouflage pants. Tongolele adopted a courteous expression to listen: Part of the discipline he imposed on himself was to maintain the appearance of courtesy. A debate? Really? With whom? Leónidas raised himself up from the driver's seat, and Tongolele found himself still stuck in the depths of his own seat as Leónidas stood on the pavement, the map of Managua rolled up under his arm. We the directors of FENIBA debated whether the name was written with one "n" or two: "Denis" or "Dennis," and in the end we decided to leave his name as it appears on his ID card: "Dennis."

Now there's a transcendental debate, Tongolele thought, and he immediately forced himself to maintain control; then he opened the car door and finally managed to climb out of his hole. The solid letters that spelled DENNIS MARTINEZ NATIONAL STADIUM gleamed as well, illuminated by white bulbs on the front of the stadium along the trim.

With twenty-three seasons as a big leaguer, Martínez broke Dominican Juan Marichal's record of Major League wins by a Latin American pitcher, and if that wasn't enough, he pitched a perfect game on the historic date of July 28, 1991, nine innings of batters going down one-two-three, Dennis throwing fireballs above 90 miles per hour, and the Montreal Expos defeating the Los Angeles Dodgers 2-0. Would you like something more to chew on? Leónidas was a veritable talking encyclopedia of baseball, a fact that couldn't be denied. So, answer this question, inspector: Why isn't Dennis in Cooperstown's Hall of Fame? Tongolele, walking a bit ahead of Leónidas, shrugged his shoulders: he didn't understand baseball; he never had understood it; it was a complicated game; it bored him. The problem must be pure envy, he responded, or perhaps it's because Dennis isn't a Yankee.

Leónidas continued preaching as they passed through the main lobby: the quality and deep-green color of the grass, which was imported from Miami's best growers; the spacious VIP suites, with their exclusive sky boxes; the giant electronic videoboards; the lighting system that provided better clarity than normal daylight; the food court; the fan club; the souvenir stores, a stadium where every detail helped fans feel is if they could be inside any one of the best Major League parks. And four losers wanted to lead a coup and stop all this progress so they could return to the dark days of Somoza.

Bales of t-shirts, cinched together, along with the items that would serve as masks that had been packed in three large cardboard boxes, had arrived on time and been deposited against a wall in the stadium's lobby. The two men inspected the contents, and Leónidas handed the city map to Tongolele so that he could assign a color to each zone of operations and proceed with distributing the merchandise.

The driver who had brought the items was a wizened, hunchbacked, and gray-bearded old man who appeared incapable of handling a transport truck, much less carrying the baled t-shirts and cardboard boxes alone across the parking lot, as he had obviously done. He guarded the merchandise, attentive to Tongolele's arrival, and when he saw Leónidas walk away, he stepped forward and asked Tongolele to sign the receipt accepting delivery; he also handed Tongolele a note from Fabiola, enclosed in a company envelope and written on graph paper:

> They're going to flush our business down the shitter
> because in a tweet from The Mask, they sold out the
> Smurfs, who went to do that border job at your request,
> and the tweet contains the Smurfs' photos, and they've
> published my first name and last name and everything
> else, but that's not all I have to tell you because in anoth-
> er tweet from The Mask, and who knows who's hiding
> behind that name, they're claiming that you ordered the
> pipe attack on the monseñor and they posted the name
> and photo of the attacker, and then later I tried to contact
> you again because I'm worried about whether the tweets
> are coming from someone way high up who wants to
> hurt you, or from your own rivals, or maybe from some

insider in your own office, because the things they've
tweeted are secrets from your work that couldn't possibly come to light in any way other than the three I've
mentioned. I'm on tenterhooks here and since it's barely
midnight right now, I already know the horrible morning that's waiting for me, but I don't want to burden you
with all my fears because I know that you have more than
enough of your own. Señor Prudencio, a man who has
my complete trust and delivered this letter to you, has
to collect the merchandise from other warehouses and I
don't want to delay him. We'll see what happens when
the sun comes up.

He folded up the sheet of paper, put it in his pocket, and spoke to
Don Prudencio, who had been chewing on his mustache and keeping a wary eye on him while waiting. Tongolele told him to leave,
assuring him that he had received the message. The old man left,
hunched over as if carrying a heavy burden and moving as if he
feared that the air could whisk his paper-thin body off the ground
at any moment.

The dawn was about to break when Tongolele walked over to
the box seats; he was carrying the city map, its zones already colored. As he walked, he made an extraordinary effort to disperse
the storm clouds that increasingly billowed around his mind, because if what Fabiola reported was true, his problems were just beginning: They kicked his ass by demoting him; they kicked his face
by publishing compromising secrets; and they even accused him
of actions that had nothing to do with him. And could the kicks to
the face have come from above? Or had one of his subordinates
decided that now was a good time to take advantage and smash his
teeth? If he couldn't answer those questions, he was better off not
asking them. And he flailed his arms in front of his face, as if he
could dispel the burgeoning storm clouds that way.

All the troops were scattered around the skyboxes, and a cacophony of voices chattered as if some game was about to start.
The commotion increased as the t-shirts were distributed and
troopers snatched them away, either exposing their torsos to don
the shirts or pulling the shirts down over those they were already
wearing, and then moving on to try different masks and tie knots

in bandanas. Then they received the order to group themselves according to t-shirt color: fuchsia red, Prussian blue, sky blue, canary yellow, emerald green, and pearl gray, the number of colored shirts equal to the number of men for each zone. Satisfied with his idea, Tongolele observed how easily the men arranged themselves together and simultaneously quieted down. A contribution on his part.

Afterward, each contingent was called down to the field, and the platoons were placed along both sides of the infield, the first- and third-base lines, with the commander of each platoon at the head of the line. Among the commanders was Tongolele himself, wearing canary yellow because it made him stand out and a red bandana, which was knotted around his forearm. The red bandana was an idea that had come to him at the last minute: a means to identify the commanders.

Covered by large tarps, the rifles and ammunition boxes were spread across the infield grass, and Leónidas perched himself upon the pitcher's mound holding the megaphone to his lips: We could easily use the wireless microphones in this stadium, where everything is intelligent, and we could see ourselves on the giant videoboards, but if we did so we would warn our enemies from many kilometers away because the sound system is so powerful, and that's the reason's we've chosen this megaphone to announce that we'll be exterminating rats in El Mercado Oriental, and we're serious when we say "exterminating rats," comrades, because today we'll be applying *Abate* pesticide throughout the country. We'll begin here in Managua, but you'll have barely begun your mission here before other troops begin doing the same in other cities where we also have to battle the vermin that have come out of their lairs—rats as well as snakes, spiders, scorpions, bedbugs, lice, fleas, mosquitoes, cockroaches, ticks, and midges. You must understand and be clear: This nonsense about the Trees of Life is just a pretext cooked up in the Devil's own cauldrons to overthrow the revolution that all of us have sworn to defend with our own blood.

The megaphone distorted Leónidas' voice as it echoed among shrieks of sharp feedback, although he did not speak with the third-person approach that made him seem far away, hidden among the clouds; he spoke instead with the "royal we" that envelops everything, the "we" who sent the Chinese box's final message and kicked Tongolele to the curb.

And now Leónidas ordered that the tarps be removed to uncover the weapons: We're free to choose any *chunche*—any bauble—we like, comrades, whether it be a Russian AK-47 with a folding butt or a standard butt, or perhaps one of the gringos' M-16s, the kind we took from Somoza's genocidal army in combat, and I can guarantee that they're effective guns because they're old friends. And since we're not going to die from lack of ammunition, we can take all the magazines we can carry in our backpacks. But we won't ask for handguns because there aren't any—no little shots here or little shots there: What we need is concentrated firepower. Still, we'll give out a few handguns, and he patted the nylon holster pressed against his waist: pistols are reserved as a distinction for only very special comrades. These pistols are nothing other than Israeli-made Jerichos, and say what you will, the Jews do exquisite work when it comes to guns.

With weapons of such quality and variety, we'll have more than enough to enjoy ourselves as we keep the enemy down with constant fire for as long as necessary. There'll be a break, of course, a lunch break, and I beg your forgiveness for not arranging breakfast, but you'll get lunch for sure: half a roasted chicken, crunchy French fries, and even a Golden Delicious apple and a chocolate bar. The same goes for dinner, all courtesy of *You Know Who*. And *You Know Who* have also ordered that each meal include two cans of Heineken beer so ice-cold that they'll make your hands hurt. Finally, of course, you can't possibly believe that *You Know Who* have forgotten about your individual household needs, which explains why at the end of each encounter you'll receive fifty green *lolos*, which *You Know Who* will send with all their love.

The team leaders had to rein in the recruits' impulse to throw themselves at the weapons as if they were attending a Christmas-toy giveaway. Incredulously, the recruits walked all around the batches of arms. "So beautiful!" one recruit said, crouching down to pick up an AKM assault rifle with a 75-bullet magazine, but Leónidas' voice stopped him: comrade, the AKMs are only there to help us visualize what's going to happen today, so let's not be selfish. And there are other guns to see alongside it that you must not touch: the Remington 700, which is a hunting rifle and allows different calibers of bullets, because hunting is precisely what we'll be doing today; the Mossberg 500 shotgun, which has a sliding trigger; the PKM machine gun, which comes with a bipod for support; and a few other older and well-known items, such as the Russian RPG-7 missile launcher, which looks like a bassoon. All these weapons will be selectively assigned to each team, and they will be given to comrades who know how to use them without wasting them.

And here behind everything, between the shortstop and second base, we can admire the Belarussian Dragunovs with telescopic sights alongside their twins, the Catatumbos sent by our Bolivarian revolutionary friends in Venezuela. The Catatumbos are lighter because they are made with polymers, and we'll give a few here and a few there to comrades who are also familiar with sniper rifles. We should all know, however, simply for purposes of increasing our confidence, that these guns have a range of 1300 meters; that means more than a kilometer, so a sniper can take position high above us here, from the stadium's roof, and blow any rebel's head in half as he's running away from us to hide in the cathedral.

Leónidas now held his own gun in his hand, one of the Catatumbos, the butt displaying a small plaque engraved with Nicolás Maduro's signature, and he raised the rifle above his head just as he had after climbing up the moving stairway to the plane after the attack on the Nejapa Country Club more than forty years earlier. At the same time, he held the megaphone in his other hand: And just so this pack of fucking *pendejos* understands what they're dealing with, we're going to hold a victory march before the operation starts. They'll soil themselves when they see that, and the stench of their own shit will probably scare them off once and for all.

In the FENIBA private skybox, which had a VIP lounge behind it with a bar, a kitchenette, and a 12-person dining set, Leónidas gathered the team leaders around the table to make a final review of each zone's borders and establish the places for their respective command centers. Before dismissing the commanders, he gave them each a walkie-talkie and one for their column leaders. Leónidas would be Alpha Zero in coded communication. Tongolele, Delta Uno.

And now that the canary-yellow contingent was properly outfitted and ready to climb into the Universidad Nacional Agraria buses that would take them to their center of operations in El Mercado de Mayoreo, Tongolele asked who among them held active military rank or had tactical combat experience, and two members of the police department's SWAT team took a step forward: Sergeant Juárez and Sergeant Mendiola.

Next to them another man came forward: a slender man in his sixties, sporting an afro, heavily framed glasses, and a sparse goatee. He was wearing a long-sleeved, extremely tight, and brilliantly colored pearl-grey shirt, with the collar points sticking over his yellow t-shirt, and his pants were bell-bottoms made of Diolen fabric. He looked as if he were stepping out of a time machine after having spent the night enveloped in marijuana smoke while listening to the Bee Gees.

Neither of the sergeants gave any sign that they knew Tongolele, to his relief. But the man from the time machine never took his mocking gaze off him. Behind his thick lenses, his eyes seemed to belong to a person with a much larger face. Tongolele was intrigued to know where the man had obtained his combat experience, whether he always wore the same clothes he was wearing at the moment, and if he always handled the AK-47 with the same indifference he displayed now: holding it by the barrel, allowing the butt to hang between his legs, and permitting the strap to drag along the ground.

The older man had served as column leader for the Sócrates Sandino Battalion of Fighting Irregulars against the Contras, and he now worked as an in-house editor of news reports for Radio Comrade, he said. Also, he added in lower tones, with a smile that begged for complicity, he was a poet. A journalist and a poet. He had won a poetry competition at the Instituto Nacional de Cultura and another at Banco Central, which had been organized for the celebrations honoring Rubén Darío. His name was Armando Lira. Tongolele didn't think the man was serious when he heard the name, and he wondered if it was a literary codename. But then the man extracted his national ID card and showed it to him.

Tongolele didn't like the man's looks nor the fact that he was a poet, but only the three men had raised their hands. So, with no other choice, Tongolele gave the poet and the two sergeants the walkie-talkies, explaining the operation's frequency and assigning each man his codename: Delta Dos, Delta Tres, and Delta Cuatro.

And when Tongolele sat down in the front seat of the last bus, the poet Lira sat down next to him. His grey shirt smelled of old sweat, and his sneakers decorated with fringe along the uppers were the least appropriate shoes for a military operation. Regardless, the entire operation was nothing but target practice.

Because barricades had cut off Larreynega Road, the buses had to make a long detour to arrive at El Mercado de Mayoreo. They began by taking Solidaridad Road, then continued to El Mercado Robert Huembles, crossed the Schick area, kept moving to Las Colinas Estates, and finally arrived at the highway to Sabana Grande.

"I know you," said the poet Lira, whose breath smelled like cough syrup. "I've seen you on the stages in the plaza, always hidden in the third or fourth row."

"We'll limit ourselves to me giving you orders and you obeying my orders. That way, both of us will be happy," said Tongolele.

"To reporters, even those like us who belong to the party, you don't officially exist," the poet Lira continued as if he had just heard the rain. "And your customs agency doesn't exist either."

"Either you haven't heard me, or I haven't made myself clear," responded Tongolele more severely. "I don't want to talk to you."

For his own weapon, he had chosen an AK-47 with a foldable butt, a gun with which he had felt comfortable since his guerrilla days, and he held it across his legs.

"There are only a few people here that a man can talk to about anything even remotely interesting," said the poet Lira, grabbing his AK-47 such that the barrel pointed toward the bus's roof.

"I'm going to have to relieve you from command," Tongolele said as he tried to cut him off again. "For deafness."

"You remind me of my battalion leader, Captain Chirinos," said the poet Lira, an impertinent smile pasted across his lips. "He never wanted to talk to me, but whenever he needed me, I was always right by his side."

"It's the same with me. You stay quiet, even if you end up stuck to me permanently, and things will be fine."

"Captain Chirinos was wounded badly when the Contras got close to us in Santa María de Pantasma, and I carried him through a storm of bullets to the medical post. He ended up owing his life to me."

"Just like the movies. You're not going to have to carry anybody around here because we're just going on an outing. And regardless, you wouldn't be strong enough."

The poet Lira extracted his wallet from the back pocket of his pants, and he then removed a packet from the wallet. Between the folds of a faded blue ribbon, the packet contained a medal, which he freed from the ribbon so that he could show it to Tongolele.

"It's the gold Medal of Camilo Ortega Saavedra for valor in combat," he said, then returned it to its place without waiting for anything else.

"That's not the reason you're such a big asshole."

"That's right," answered the poet Lira, and his smile now covered his entire face as if someone had applied it with some sticky varnish. "But it would be worse to be on the side that doesn't have it. And I don't mean you, commissioner. You hold the Order of Carlos Fonseca, the party's highest recognition of all."

"Why are you talking about this?" Tongolele asked without turning his head to look at the man.

"Because the Right has to be stopped," laughed the poet Lira, shaking his head as if the situation were a joke. "This whole thing is the rich attempting a coup d'état. They receive the benefits of power, but the benefits aren't enough. They want the power for themselves."

"These kids wandering impulsively around the streets have never met a single one of those business tycoons in person," responded Tongolele, regretting what he had just said too late.

"You and I agree about that. The rich don't invite these rebels to their parties or their weddings. But that doesn't change the fact that the rebels, like all the good petite bourgeoisie, are acting as an instrument of capitalist interests."

"From what I can see, your poetry must be about the class struggle."

"The proletariat wouldn't understand my poems," the poet Lira cackled again. "I explore existential subjects. The anguish of life, the mystery of death."

"Bourgeoise poetry, then. So that you can blow the minds of the idle rich you want to reach."

"I don't think either the poor or the rich read my poetry," answered the poet Lira, continuing to laugh. "At great cost, the judges that give me my award will read it. Although I suspect that the powers on high command the judges to grant me the award."

Tongolele laughed as well. This moment marked the first time he could remember in ages that he genuinely wanted to laugh.

"You've made my day, poet."

"And you, commissioner, why are you here?"

"Someone offers you a mango and you want the whole bag."

"When I saw you enter the stadium, I thought to myself: 'They've sent him to command the whole operation. That's a logical assignment for someone like him.' But seeing you serve under someone else's command, well, that's not something I understand."

"Well, you won't get any answers from me, so let's turn the page."

"Unless it's a disciplinary measure."

"Do you like marijuana, poet?"

"To reduce stress."

"Well, it looks like you smoked some serious weed last night. Your shooting hand will be shaky, and your aim will be off."

"No smoke dreams for me, commissioner. If they're punishing your mother, the fact that they're punishing you as well isn't strange at all. Whether the punishment is just or unjust is another matter."

"Now you're really stepping over the line, poet. You don't know my mother. Don't get involved with her."

"There's nobody who doesn't know her by name. The truth is that her manservant is my nephew."

"Paquito?" Tongolele asked, the shock beginning to thicken in his stomach like some dark oil.

The poet Lira nodded a grave yes.

"He stays at my house when he's not working, and last night he showed up at three in the morning, deeply alarmed," he answered.

"The famous Paquito, so sentimental and melodramatic," Tongolele responded, trying to appear indifferent. "Always ready to turn anything into a scandal and pile stories on top of the stories he tells. When he's not simply making things up."

"In this case there's nothing to make up. A motorized ASP unit kicked her out of her house at one o'clock this morning: they threw her out on the street in her nightgown; they stationed an armed guard at her door to make sure she couldn't go back inside; and they left."

"If all that's a lie, I'll castrate you without anesthetic, poet."

The poet Lira smiled with the hint of a cackle that never quite broke through.

"Paquito stayed behind with her, and she asked him to make some phone calls. The first was to Lázaro, her son-in-law."

"Lázaro left the country."

"The next call was for you, but you never answered. They finally managed to track down that Señora Miranda, the businesswoman."

Tongolele sensed that the poet Lira was poking at him, pawing him. The old man knew very well who the woman was that he called "that Señora Miranda," and he also knew about her relationship with Tongolele.

"Her name is Fabiola."

"Yes, that's the one. She showed up at your mother's place immediately and took her to her own house. Once Paquito saw that your mother was in good hands, he came to my home."

Tongolele studied his cell phone under the poet Lira's curious eye. After talking with Fabiola about delivering the t-shirts and face-coverings, he had left his phone in silent mode. The call log showed the incoming call from his mother. Several hours later, multiple calls from Fabiola appeared, calls she undoubtedly made when the two women were together.

"My mother isn't guilty of anything. There must be some misunderstanding."

"How big must the misunderstanding be when they threw her out of the very same house they had given her, and then wouldn't even allow her to go back inside to find something to wear?" said the poet Lira, who seemed to be laughing, albeit silently.

"The only thing she did was advise them not to plant so many Trees of Life, because there was a limit that they shouldn't exceed," said Tongolele, his voice barely a whisper as his revelation of that secret actually frightened him.

"Don't get lost in the twists and turns of magical thinking, commissioner. The guns we're holding aren't meant to stop people from tearing down the Trees of Life, which are nothing but decorations. No, the guns are meant to defend the revolution's conquests."

"If only the issue were that easy. If only the trees were just decorations."

"Let's go back to the issue of Señora Fabiola Miranda, commissioner. People say that you two have a relationship."

"So Paquito continues to be your source."

"Paquito is more reserved than you think. I've told you about the woman because I study the Internet every morning for my job as a reporter. And the tweet about the Smurfs' attack is having a huge impact."

"So, you use anonymous sources like that one to report the news?"

The poet Lira's eyes grew larger behind his glasses, to the point where they practically popped out of their sockets.

"I write my news reports according to the guidance I receive. But I entertain myself by creating a background based on everything circulating around the country, even if I can't use that background in my reporting."

"It sounds entertaining," said Tongolele, standing up and slinging his rifle across his back. "We've arrived."

The buses parked together in a hilly vacant lot at the back of the land belonging to El Mercado del Mayoreo, where an abandoned warehouse stood. To one side of the warehouse sat four front-loaders from STREETS FOR THE PEOPLE, a public-works program sponsored by Managua's mayoral office; the front-loaders' operators were sitting in their cabs.

The market's administrator, a fat man who had difficulty breathing, was waiting for them. His shirt tails hung loose as he straddled a motorcycle, which looked like a mini-bike between his legs. Tongolele approached him in order to unlock the warehouse's gate.

The warehouse was a metal building that had had its electric lighting disconnected, with its interior stifling as an oven despite the early hour, and the only visibility came from the rays of light that pierced the numerous holes in the tin roof's panels, which the wind rustled in waves. But the light was enough to reveal two long rows of grey Hilux pick-ups, none with license plates, all of them parked along the side walls, their grills facing forward, their bodies protected by the protective layer of paraffin wax used on transport ships, and their seats still covered with transparent plastic.

Every truck had keys in the ignition, and Tongolele's lieutenants assigned drivers among those who knew how to drive.

The team was divided into four columns. The first, under Tongolele's command, would clear out the north highway from La Subasta to the airport, and from there to the Zona Franca. The second column, under Sergeant Mendiola's command, would take responsibility for the same north highway, but they would move from La Subasta to the junction with the Juan Pablo II Highway, in Plásticos Robles. The third column, under the poet Lira, would handle the Larreynega Road. And the fourth, under Sergeant Juárez, would be a flying column, a unit that could attack rapidly in any situation. The snipers would be positioned in high places wherever their column leaders ordered.

Before the columns climbed into the Hiluxes, Tongolele ordered them to form up in the warehouse for inspection.

"What about the victory parade?" asked the poet Lira when Tongolele stood before him.

"We're not here to waste time with parades," Tongolele answered.

The poet Lira stepped forward and moved close to Tongolele's ear.

"You need to be careful, commissioner," he said. "Imagine a scene on stage. Imagine some spotlights. Imagine yourself as part of that scene under the spotlights. They're watching you; they're watching every step you take."

Tongolele furrowed his brow.

"Why don't you go with your column to that parade, then come back here to fulfill your mission?"

"That sounds wise. That way we don't make the gap visible."

One of the men in the poet Lira's column was examining his gun carefully. He caught Tongolele's attention.

"I know you," Tongolele said. "Where have I seen you before?"

"Somewhere out there, somewhere on some road in this world," answered Rambo, and he tied the bandana over his nose.

CHAPTER ELEVEN

The Bicycle Messenger Surprised from Behind

FROM THE TIME THAT her topographer husband had abandoned her to run off with a waitress, Fanny had rented a house on La Carlanca Street in the La Colonia Centroamérica neighborhood. And because she did not own a car, she had converted the garage into a room by using plywood sheets to cover the dungeon-like iron bars enclosing the space, and she had adorned the door with a bedsheet for a curtain.

Doña Sofía had occupied this garage-room for the past several days so that she could take care of her friend while she was battling cancer. Aside from the folding bed that could be doubled-up during the day, the room contained a wicker rocking chair and an embroidering machine covered with canvas. At some point long before Fanny began working as a long-distance telephone operator, she had an embroidery workshop in the Altamira barrio, where she sewed monograms on towels, sheets, and pillowcases for bridal wares and linens, but the business had failed and Fanny had never found someone to buy the machine.

Whenever Doña Sofía arranged her bed at night, a strange image in a picture frame consistently confronted her as it hung on the plywood alongside the headboard. The image depicted Santa Lucía de Siracusa, a martyr from Christianity's earliest times, patron saint of blind people and eye doctors, along with dressmakers, tailors, and embroiderers.

Doña Sofía could not avoid feeling a vague sense of unease in the presence of that image, which Fanny had rescued from the workshop's shipwreck and placed under Doña Sofía's care. In one hand the saint carried a martyr's palm branch, while in the other she held a plate that displayed her eyeballs, which Sicily's proconsul to the Emperor Diocletian had ordered be gouged from their sockets, according to the inscription at the foot of the image. Simultaneously, however, Santa Lucía's eyes appeared in her face, and they looked upon Doña Sofía beatifically.

Unsettled, Doña Sofía had approached Fanny's own bed to better understand the mysterious image in the garage, and the first thing she learned was that the explanation printed on the image's inscription was mistaken. Proconsul Pascasio had not ordered that Santa Lucía's eyes be gouged out; rather, he had ordered her burned alive in a bonfire. She had torn her eyes out herself because a pagan admirer insisted on praising them constantly—what beautiful eyes you have, how seductive they are, how gorgeous, how lovely. So, she sent her eyes to him as a gift inside a beautiful crystal urn: If he liked them so much, he could stare at them right there, but she wanted nothing to do with idolatrous lovers. She was blinded by her own hand, but she could still see with the eyes of her soul, which explained why the image depicted her eyes on the plate and on her face at the same time.

Fanny, motivated by the uncertainties and pain of her disease, had grown increasingly fervent about her Catholicism, while Doña Sofía, who had previously been deeply inflexible in defending her own Evangelical Christianity, made no effort at all to criticize Fanny's belief. In fact, at Fanny's request, Doña Sofía herself had taken a taxi to the San Pablo Bookstore near La Universidad Centroamericana to purchase a handbook about the saints' lives. Fanny consistently kept that book on her nightstand, and it provided the new information Doña Sofía had learned about Santa Lucía.

About noon on that Wednesday, Doña Sofía was sitting on the folding bed and studying her cell phone to gauge the reactions to the tweet denouncing Monseñor Ortez's exile. Numerous people had reacted initially, but those numbers had multiplied copiously at mid-morning after the apostolic nuncio, Monseñor Gaetano Ambrosio, found himself obligated to confirm the tweet's content. The nuncio explained that Monseñor Ortez's "transfer was a routine part of Vatican management, a decision made long ago without the influence of any local circumstances," and that the new bishop would be assigned to the Congregation for Divine Worship and the Discipline of the Sacraments. These curt bits of information, made by telephone and published in La Prensa's electronic main page under the headline "ATTACKED, THEN KICKED OUT

TO BOOT," had created an avalanche of social-media protests from both secular and core Catholic sources.

An archive photo of Monseñor Ambrosio accompanied the newspaper story: the man had dull eyes underlined with dark bags, but he had bright lips and thick red-apple cheeks like those of the piggish friars depicted on the religious cards attached to the labels of digestive liqueurs. As Doña Sofía examined the monseñor's photo on her cell screen, she noticed the arrival of a figure riding a bicycle projected in deep contrast behind the sheet covering the garage door. The figure's head and tires stretched across the top of the sheet. The screech of the bike's chain stopped, then the figure propped the bike against the garage bars and disappeared from the sheet as the rider undoubtedly went toward the house's door, and Doña Sofía awaited the sound of the doorbell.

But the doorbell made no sound, so Doña Sofía hurriedly went to one of the bars and put her eye to one of the sheet's cracks. The bicyclist was moving toward the mouth of the side street, the bike rattling along with him. Doña Sofía had a sudden idea, and after stuffing her phone and a leather purse carrying money and keys into a handbag, she ran to the door. An envelope lay underneath it. She grabbed the envelope quickly, stuck it into the handbag as well, and left to pursue the bike messenger.

The messenger made no effort to hurry, as if fulfilling his task had left him with nothing more to do, and he had reached the avenue and was walking along one of the sidewalks, the bike alongside him as he gripped the handlebars. The messenger likewise made no effort to pay attention to the cacophony of engines and horns as drivers found themselves blocked by people beginning to squeeze together at the heights of the Jean Paul Genie roundabout to join the Mother of All Protest Marches. The drivers, trying to enter Managua from the highway to Masaya, sought passage through the streets of Colonia Centroamérica so that they could exit toward Solidaridad Road.

Doña Sofía used the handbag to shield her eyes from the sun's rays so that she didn't lose sight of the messenger, who traveled in the direction of the Managua Mall and was already arriving at the Church de Nuestra Señora de Fátima. Practically racing along the street, with the agility that her green phosphorescent running shoes provided, Doña Sofía caught up to the messenger at the corner of a restaurant, The Curly-haired Tortoise, then grabbed him firmly by his shirt collar.

The boy turned around in surprise, and Doña Sofía's surprise was no less than his. Before her stood SpongeBob, aide de camp for Dr. Pedro Celestino Carmona, alias Vademécum, back in the days when her old friend had owned a debt-collection business in which he used a squad of children dressed as elves trained to harass debtors into paying their obligations.

SpongeBob had grown taller since she had last seen him; at that time, he hadn't looked as if he would grow anymore. A slight bit of peach fuzz graced his upper lip, and his Adam's apple stuck out prominently from his neck.

"Don't tell me that Dr. Carmona is mixed up in this business of sending messages," Doña Sofía said without loosening her grip.

As always, words choked together in SpongeBob's throat, and he battled them as if he were suffocating before he could manage to say a single thing.

"He's been arrested," he finally said, with a deep voice that suddenly became high-pitched.

Doña Sofía imagined the worst. Perhaps the alcoholic haze that had enveloped Dr. Carmona for quite some time had led him to rob a liquor store, or perhaps his DTs had compelled him to gravely injure a patron in some trashy cantina.

"Why is he under arrest?" Doña Sofía asked, letting go.

"They arrested him during a protest march against the Trees of Life on Camino de Oriente, where he kept shouting 'Death to the dictatorship!' over and over. They've locked him up in El Chipote."

"And was the doctor drunk when they captured him?"

"As shit-faced as always. But that makes no difference. Happy and healthy or absolutely plastered, he's always willing to have a dick-measuring contest with the government."

What a mouth. Good Lord, such language, said Lord Dixon. But ignore the vulgarity, Doña Sofía. The important thing is to find out who's sending the messages.

"I hope to God that they don't torture the poor doctor, but if they have him in prison, at least he can't be drinking."

"For an alcoholic like him, the most likely thing is that the desperation of being locked up without any drink will kill him. Are you familiar with the blue demons?"

"I've heard about them. I've had a drink or two in my life."

"They're a horrible thing. They're a pack of demons that chase you down and corner you, and they make a racket so ear-splitting that you end up pounding your head against the wall."

Look at the education this kid's had, said Lord Dixon. What can we possibly hope for him in the future?

"What could you possibly know about delirious states like that? You're just a boy."

"I had an uncle who was absolutely crazy about whiskey. They had to tie him up because the pack of demons wouldn't stop chasing him, and he kept running around naked with his balls hanging out in the middle of the street. So, they tied him up and took him to the madhouse on kilometer five on the Highway Sur. Do you know it?"

"I've never even gone by it," Doña Sofía scoffed. "What would I ever have to do with places like insane asylums?"

I must insist that you not allow this boy's coarse language to distract you from your principal goal, Doña Sofía, said Lord Dixon.

She grabbed SpongeBob's shirt collar again.

"So, who sent you to leave this envelope?"

"My mother is the one they pay for delivering these letters. And when she can't do it, she sends me in her place. This is the second time I've done it for her, because she's been really sick with a high fever."

"So, did you drop off one of these letters at the Divine Mercy Church yesterday? I can already see that you're the one who went right in and rode a bike into the church."

"I gave the letter to that woman who looks like a giant, the one who's your friend. Do you remember that she left an envelope for you in the Guanacaste shopping center, and I was the one who accepted it for you? She didn't recognize me yesterday."

"Who gives the letters to your mother?"

"A woman she's known for a long time, because my mother used to be one of her servants."

"Don't use that ugly word," Doña Sofía reprimanded him. "The proper term is *domestic assistant*."

"Whatever. My mother worked in her house as part of the help," SpongeBob said with a shrug of his shoulders. "She was taking care of a bastard child that the woman had simply had, an unwed mother. No marriage or anything like that."

"The proper term is *child of a single woman*," Doña Sofía corrected, scolding him once more.

You go right ahead, Doña Sofía. Keep educating this troglodyte about proper gender language. All the old terms he uses are the legacy of a patriarchal society, said Lord Dixon.

"May I talk with your mother?"

"Yes, if we go to my house. The problem is that Magdalena has gone to shit with this terrible fever, so she doesn't go outside."

"You shouldn't refer to your mother that way. You need to be more respectful. How can you call her 'Magdalena'?"

And how dare he use the expression 'gone to shit'? said Lord Dixon. The proper expression is 'she's in poor health.'

"One day I called her 'Mami' like they do on TV, and she threatened to break a wooden pole on my back if I ever used a cute little queer-bait word like that around her again."

"Do we need to take a taxi?"

"It's close by here, in the La Fuente barrio, around the corner from the grounds of the Soldados de la Cruz School. We can walk there."

Doña Sofía had numerous issues to address. She had pursued SpongeBob without telling Fanny, who most certainly was worried about her absence. She also needed to read V's latest message, which she could not do on a public street. And she had to tell Inspector Morales immediately about the new letter left under Fanny's door.

"Did you already have lunch?" she asked SpongeBob.

"When I go back home, I'll buy a boli ice-pop and some bread at the corner store, and that will be enough," he answered.

"How would you feel if I took you to lunch and we went to your house afterward?"

"I'd feel great!"

They entered The Curly-haired Tortoise, SpongeBob leading the way and carrying his bike. Doña Sofía looked for the most isolated table in the dining area, and she found one in a corner among fern-filled flowerpots hanging from the ceiling. And while SpongeBob studied the laminated menu's color photos of the food, Doña Sofía went searching for the women's restroom.

She locked herself inside a stall, sat down on the toilet lid, called Fanny to reassure her, and opened the envelope:

The corrupt assassin Tongolole, chief of spies and hitmen, ordered the murder of his own brother-in-law,
Lázaro Chicas, a Salvadoran who once served as a guerrilla for the FMLN. The murder was the result of a fi-
nancial dispute between the two men, who worked together as partners in several lucrative businesses. Lázaro
Chicas was driving his wine-red Toyota Corolla from
his home in Bosques de Jiloá when killers crashed into
the car with a truck that buried it in the crater of the
Asososca Lagoon. The killers later made sure that Lázaro's body was identified in the morgue as a John Doe
and buried secretly in an unmarked grave. This crime
is one of only many that can be attributed to Tongolele,
a man capable of murdering his own sister's husband to
keep his share of the dirty businesses they ran as partners. The man is truly a snake, because aside from these
businesses with his brother-in-law, he runs other such
businesses with his lover, Fabiola Miranda, who is the
queen of contraband in El Mercado Oriental. May all of
these things be made known to Lázaro Chicas' family
and friends, along with Lázaro's mother-in-law, Professor Zoraida, so that she at least can order that a cross
be placed on the anonymous grave—plot 234—in the
last row against the south wall of the Milagro de Dios
Cemetery.

Once again, the envelope contained photos: one was a page
from Chicas' passport, displaying his face and the particulars of
his identity; the other photo showed his face as well, but from the
drawer of the morgue. In addition, the envelope contained an Ex-
cel spreadsheet listing Tongolele's companies, including those that
Chicas managed for him and those that Tongolele ran with Fabiola Miranda, and every entry displayed the company's name, its
business-license number, and its place of business.

Feeling rushed because someone outside the bathroom stall knocked on the door at first and then began pushing it, Doña Sofía arranged the pages and pictures on her knees to photograph them, then used WhatsApp to send everything to Inspector Morales, along with a message asking for instructions. She also told the inspector that she was traveling with the courier—none other than Dr. Carmona's number-one elf—on the way to learn who had sent the letter and thereby discover The Mask's identity.

As the pounding and pushing on the stall door came again, Doña Sofía flushed the toilet and opened the door. Upon doing so, she encountered a woman dressed in mourning clothes and wearing glasses shaped like butterfly wings. The woman, who was holding the hand of a little girl with a red bow in her hair, glared angrily at Doña Sofía due to her delay in leaving the stall.

When Doña Sofía returned to SpongeBob's side, the server was waiting to take their order.

"I'll have the steak on horseback, with the two fried eggs on top and the fried bacon that they put on top too," SpongeBob said, pointing at the menu. "I also want the pancakes with honey and a strawberry milkshake in a big glass, the kind that looks like a flower vase."

"You're going to get sick," Doña Sofía scolded discreetly.

"Magdalena says I'm like a bottomless barrel. But I've never had a tummy ache or the runs."

He continues to prove that he's a true disciple of Dr. Carmona, said Lord Dixon, sitting down at the table as well. Doña Sofía, have you checked the money purse to see whether you have enough to pay for this feast?

"Just coffee with milk for me," said Doña Sofía.

"They've put a pool hall where your detective agency in Bolonia used to be, but they left the picture of Dick Tracy painted outside," SpongeBob told her.

"I can see that you're allowed to ride your bike freely all over Managua."

"There's a massage parlor in Ovidio and Apolonio's old barbershop, but I think the masseuses are whores."

Don't let him talk like that, Doña Sofía, said Lord Dixon. The proper term is 'sex workers.'

"Does your mother know what the letters say?" Doña Sofía asked the boy.

He swirled the straw in the milkshake he had been given—a milkshake that was indeed the size of a flower vase.

"She doesn't know, and I don't think she wants to know. What interests her are the 200 bills that the woman she used to work for pays for each letter."

A sickly mother in need and a wayward youth with nothing to do but roam the streets, Doña Sofía thought to herself. Two innocent agents caught in a plot easy to unstitch because it was so poorly put together in the first place. On the other hand, perhaps the plan was well-thought-out and the agents in place acted blindly: they knew nothing beyond their own small role and therefore could not possibly reveal any valuable information.

Regardless, if SpongeBob's mother had some kind of relationship with the person sending the letters, that person was about to be identified—unless that person also acted blindly, a situation that would create yet another dead-end street.

Doña Sofía's phone received a WhatsApp message from Inspector Morales, a message filled with typing mistakes. The man was obviously never going to learn how to use his thumbs. His message gave her the green light to post The Mask's new message. He also provided a brief report about how a paramilitary unit had kidnapped the sacristan's niece, Eneida Robleto, a 23-year-old woman in her sixth year of medical school at the Universidad Americana. The commandos had masked their faces and wore yellow t-shirts.

Do you remember those bones in the sacristy at the Divine Mercy Church, Doña Sofía? Lord Dixon said. That girl used to go there to do her homework.

And while SpongeBob brandished his knife and fork because his steak on horseback had just been placed before him, Doña Sofía concentrated on posting a thread of tweets reporting the murder of Lázaro Chicas, including the dead man's photos and the details about Tongolele's business dealings.

At that moment, the thought occurred to her that she should also post the report about the kidnapping of the medical student, a thought that probably saved her life. She sent another WhatsApp message to ask Inspector Morales, who answered her quickly and set off a heated exchange:

Negative. The niece is a totally different issue.

I disagree, Comrade Artemio. It's worth it to expose these killers with yellow t-shirts.

You can be sure that paramilitary groups wearing t-shirts of many different colors will show up today. The shirts are a question of logistics.

They can torture that girl. They can make her disappear.

Padre Pancho already told her aunt to file a complaint with Doña Vilma Núñez's human rights office.

But we have a moral obligation, Comrade Artemio.

It's going to be a hot day. There will be more kidnappings. Stay calm.

May I ask you something, Comrade Artemio?

Make it short.

Who's taking revenge against Tongolele? You, or The Mask?

(connected / typing / connected / typing)
I don't understand the question.

The Mask is trying to get even with this horrible man for reasons that are probably personal. That's fine. I'm happy to help him take the monster down. Are you also acting out of revenge? Because I've noticed that you don't take much interest in any information that doesn't have anything to do with him.

(connected / typing / connected / typing)
Follow instructions as given.

Inspector Morales seems to think that he's writing telegrams in Morse Code, back when people had to pay by the word, said Lord Dixon.

"The older that man gets, the nastier he becomes," Doña Sofía complained.

He doesn't like having people dig deep into his most personal thoughts, not even you, said Lord Dixon.

"But isn't it true that what he wants is revenge on Tongolele?"

And what's wrong with that? Lord Dixon said. And let's not call it revenge. Let's call it justice.

"Let's say that this boy's mother gives me the necessary information and I find out who's behind The Mask. What does that get us? Why should we be concerned about squabbles between thugs?"

Ask yourself that question after you've got the information. For now, though, don't waste time, said Lord Dixon.

Wistful and saying nothing, SpongeBob had remained staring at the empty plates before him.

"I don't know what's got me so wrapped-up," he sighed, massaging his stomach with both hands.

Doña Sofía's going to feel even more wrapped-up after hearing something like that, said Lord Dixon.

"You're going to guide me to your house, and I'll follow," said Doña Sofía, taking bills from her money purse and smoothing them onto the table.

They crossed the Managua Mall's parking lot, and as they reached Solidaridad Road, long lines of Hilux pick-ups made their way toward the west. The trucks overflowed with paramilitary soldiers wearing face coverings and t-shirts of diverse colors as they waved their weapons high in the air. Comrade Artemio had been right. The soldiers shouted no chants and made no verbal threats to anyone. It was a soundless demonstration, and therefore more sinister.

SpongeBob and Doña Sofía crossed the La Fuente barrio under a scorching sun that seemed to bring everything to a slow boil, which sapped Doña Sofía's energy more than she had anticipated, and she sometimes lost patience with the boy as she was forced to repeatedly ask him to stop because he tended to suddenly mount the bike and race ahead.

The parish of Nuestra Señora de Lourdes was the only Catholic church in the entire neighborhood, and every half block or so and on every corner stood some kind of evangelical church, a fact that would have overjoyed Doña Sofía in the past. But just as her tolerance for Fanny's superstitious beliefs demonstrated, her revolutionary fervor was continually diminishing. Her feet rarely entered a protestant meeting nowadays.

All of the churches and nearby businesses had sacred names: next to a bulk used-clothing store called The Shulammite stood the chapel of arabesque windows that housed the Church de Profecías Libres en Cristo; alongside the Hebrón Billiards Hall appeared The Church of Jesus Christ of Latter-Day Saints, with its needle-shaped spire, a small building that seemed armed with wooden studs; in front of the Judith Piñata Workshop, where paper maché figures of Buzz Lightyear and Woody Price were swinging from the doorway, rose the building for the members of the Fourth Apostolic Church de la Fe en Cristo Jesús; meanwhile, the door to El Samaritano funeral home stood next to that of the Oración Fuerte al Espíritu Santo Church. And even the Ríos de Agua Viva Church, Doña Sofía's own evangelical congregation, had a branch adjacent to a rotisserie chicken outlet known as el Pollo de Emaús.

Near the neighborhood's borders, SpongeBob and Doña Sofía left aside the back fence of the Soldados de la Cruz School, walked through a children's baseball field where the outfield grass had burned over long stretches and grown knee-high over others, then traversed a pedestrian bridge that crossed a canal that served simultaneously as a garbage dump and a refuge for impoverished drunks who guzzled the lowest-quality liquor: *bazooka*. Eventually, the two arrived at a set of dwellings in a structure made of planks and corrugated roofs, which sprouted the inevitable red circles of satellite dishes. The structure contained ten domiciles, all of which opened onto a neighboring yard where two items of clothing were airing out as they hung from a cord and appeared on the verge of flying away: a green cassock and a priest's vestments, the long sleeves attached by clothespins.

SpongeBob leaned the bike against the last doorpost on the left, and with a gesture of his head he pointed out his mother inside, who was some distance away and had not sensed their arrival; she was bent over an ironing board in the shadows. She was sunburned but sinewy, like a troublesome teenager. When she set the metal iron down on the item she held in her hands, a tablecloth embroidered with liturgical motifs, her hardened arm muscles stood out.

As Doña Sofía moved toward the door, the thought occurred to her that the boy's mother washed and ironed all these things for the parish of Nuestra Señora de Lourdes, the neighborhood Catholic church surrounded by protestant churches.

Once Señora Magdalena noticed Doña Sofía standing backlit at the doorstep, she shot her visitor a hostile look, her eyes irritated with fever, and she didn't even ask Doña Sofía why she was there or what she wanted. And when she spotted SpongeBob sneaking furtively into the room, she unleashed a storm of insults berating him for how late he had returned, her masculine voice thundering louder than the vehement arguments of the litigants on the *Closed Case* show, who appeared before Dr. Polo as she decided cases on the TV that sat on a chair missing its seat.

In the room near Magdalena stood a half-empty bottle of Plata rum, with half a lime serving as a bottlecap.

Now I see the reason for Señora Magdalena's offensive behavior, said Lord Dixon. Walk carefully, Doña Sofía. You don't want her to sink her teeth into you.

The woman squatted down to take a sip from the bottle; she then sucked on the lime, stood up, and began calmly ironing the tablecloth. She seemed to have forgotten the boy, who had curled into a ball on the floor against the dividing screen that led to the bedroom. The screen was covered with advertisements for Yoplait, Toña beer, and Movistar offers for reloading cell phones. The woman also seemed to have forgotten about Doña Sofía, who stood vainly in place at the door without daring to cross the threshold.

Señora Magdalena appraised the iron, which had gone cold, and when she went to the charcoal burner for another, she drew her deeply ebony face close to blow on the fire, a movement that inflamed her facial lines with a red glow that made her eyes appear even more feverish.

"What do you want?" she finally asked, returning with the iron in hand.

"I've known your son for a long time," answered Doña Sofía, testing the waters.

"I don't think there's anybody who doesn't know that fucking little tramp who wanders all over Managua like some dog without an owner," responded Señora Magdalena, whose voice rang out like some public announcement.

"Your son was very kind to deliver a letter to the house where I live, a letter for a friend of mine," said Doña Sofía, maintaining her pleasant tone.

"Letters come. Letters go. They come here but they don't stay," answered Señora Magdalena, moistening the tablecloth with a spray of water before ironing one of the edges.

"My friend has not seen the person who sends the letters for a long time, and he would like to know where the person is living," Doña Sofía continued, and she tried to smile.

"How am I supposed to know anything about that?" said Señora Magdalena, squatting again to drink from the bottle. "That sneaky kid has actually wandered the streets dressed like an elf. I'm better off not getting involved with whatever he does. If he collects debts or plays cards, that's his choice."

Don't allow her to change the subject, Doña Sofía. All the boy does is deliver the letters in her place, said Lord Dixon.

"Please forgive me, Señora Magdalena, but you yourself actually took one of those letters to the Divine Mercy Church," Doña Sofía said, taking a step inside.

"I don't have to explain anything I do. And no one is going to come to my house and tell me what to do. That's for damn sure."

"I'm not telling you to do anything. I just came to ask you a favor," answered Doña Sofía, approaching the ironing woman.

There are no free favors, said Lord Dixon. Offer her an incentive.

"I've got a hundred-degree fever, but I have to get out of bed to iron these rags for the priests. Because if I don't do it, I don't eat."

See what I mean? Lord Dixon said. Give her everything you've got in the money purse.

"Can I help you somehow?" Doña Sofía asked.

"I can't put up with the varicose veins that cover my feet from having to stand all day long ironing. And then on top of that, some woman from the street comes to badger me and doesn't even ask if I need something for my pain," Señora Magdalena continued.

"Just tell me what medications you need, and I'll go to the pharmacy to buy them."

Doña Sofía, you don't have any gift at all for getting information out of people, said Lord Dixon. When she says she needs something for her pain, she means Plata rum.

"And to make things worse, you show up here and don't trust me either, as if you think I would take the medication money and buy something else."

"How much money do you need?" Doña Sofía, feeling timid more than anything else.

"If I could even have a nice TV, not this piece of junk that refuses to work no matter how hard I hit it," said Señora Magdalena as she began folding the tablecloth.

Now we're in the realm of big words, said Lord Dixon. Your money purse doesn't even have enough for a new TV. And she'll want a flat-screen, one of the smart ones.

"The soap operas are so beautiful on those big screens where the actors come close enough to look like they're in a mirror," sighed Señora Magdalena.

Then Doña Sofía noticed SpongeBob stand up in his corner, his eyes never leaving the door.

We have a visitor, said Lord Dixon.

Doña Sofía turned around.

The backlit figure of La Chaparra stood out in the doorway. She was wearing her short-sleeved guayabera with its tails tucked in and carrying a black-and-gray Swiss Army backpack on her back.

CHAPTER TWELVE

Worries in the Command Post

B Y THE TIME Tongolele climbed into his Hilux pick-up at the head of the column that would clear its assigned section of the Highway Norte, he had already decided to lead the operation in the open. For that reason, he had not masked his face with the red-and-black bandana he had taken from one of the cardboard boxes in the ballpark's entryway. In addition, Tongolele did not sit in the cabin; instead, he clambered into the bed along with the other troops and stood in front so that he could be seen.

He understood very well that he was imitating Leónidas, and he was doing so to ensure that his face would appear in some social-media video that would catch fire. Go viral, as La Chaparra said. More than enough people would use their phones to film the convoy from some balcony or window or vehicle, and all those people would be the revolution's secretive enemies, the kind who would crawl out from under the rocks. For that reason, Tongolele's image would be monitored, and it would be posted where it needed to go, sent to the eyes of whoever needed to see it. Whoever *he* needed to see it. And things would go best if those eyes saw him dealing death.

Earn points. The phrase danced around inside his head. He had tried to thrust it out, but it kept coming back, restless and stubborn before his eyes, so he let it be. His good-points account had fallen to zero because of misunderstandings, baseless attacks, and jealousies, and he had to fill it up again. He had to clear the path for the aide who carried the Chinese box. And if he had to do that work with his own hands, plug up the holes, and tear out the poisonous weeds and burn them, he would do so. He would work on his hands and knees if necessary. What if his tongue was necessary?

The route to the Sandino International Airport was a strategic objective, and it offered Tongolele the greatest opportunity to shine, which explained why he had chosen to personally lead the effort to clear that route, barricade by barricade. But in less than an hour he learned that the resistance had nothing like the power that the police described in their operational report, which stated that the coup's participants had numerous firearms.

The first of the four barricades consisted of bags of fertilizer, a refrigerator carcass, a single tractor's tires, construction stones, and plywood sheets dragged from a sawmill. The barricade stood in front of La Subasta itself, an ancient slaughterhouse that had been converted into a shopping center.

Two skinny young men had used their own shirts to cover their heads, leaving only their eyes visible and looking like the old Palestinian Fedayeen as they stood atop the barricade, where they were waving the Nicaraguan flag and bravely making themselves easy to see, until Tongolele himself gave the signal for the shooting to begin, and the first burst of gunfire took one of the boys down while the other leaped to the pavement like a marionette and began to run away, but he was wounded and fell to his knees upon reaching the curb; meanwhile, under a heavy hail of bullets, some of the people hidden behind the barricade ran to the left to take refuge in the sawmill yard, as others rushed to the right, picking up the wounded boy and carrying him on their shoulders to La Subasta's parking lot; simultaneously, people waiting at the bus stops fled in every direction along with the street vendors.

Yet another of the Fedayeen look-alikes remained in the middle of the street, and he walked forward with his arms raised in surrender, like people do in the movies, but he fell after one shot fired by a gun in single-shot mode. Incredulously, the boy placed his hand on his stomach and walked a few steps in reverse, then dropped on his back against the pile of fertilizer bags.

None of the other barricades fared any better against the fiery barrage of bullets unleashed by the artillerymen walking alongside the moving pick-ups. The area's last barricade had been constructed in the middle of the highway across from the cupola of Pharoahs Casino: protesters had piled beds and cots together along with a chiffonier's mirror, which blinded the gunmen and required them to blast it apart with bullets multiple times, and a daring young man fell dead while trying to light a homemade mortar launcher.

Yet another young man died while holding a small .22 rifle made for hunting iguanas; he never pulled the trigger.

By 10:00 a.m., Tongolele was ready to report to Leónidas that the airport route was free of subversives and clear of obstacles because the mayoral office's front loaders, which were following Tongolele and his men, had nearly finished cleaning the debris from the barricades. Tongolele's greatest challenge, if such a term could be considered appropriate, was a group of students from the Agricultural University that neighbored the Free Zone, but the soldiers had used their enormous firepower to eliminate the threat, and the little guerrilla hopefuls had been forced to take cover inside the buildings. Tongolele's men had followed the rebels inside and obligated them to vacate the classrooms and auditoriums. Tongolele was now turning control of the highway over to the riot squads.

Tongolele organized part of his troops to patrol the theater of operations because he knew that the rebels would undoubtedly attempt to build back the barricades; nevertheless, he decided to take most of his forces to the base of operations in the Mercado de Mayoreo so that he could collect the other units' reports and be ready to provide reinforcements wherever they might be necessary.

The first report from the walkie-talkie network came from the poet Lira. One of his force's pick-ups had abandoned the convoy traveling along Solidaridad Road near the National Lottery building. No one knew where the truck had ended up, but soldiers were on its trail:

"That's a serious problem, a serious problem. Who is the commander of that truck? Over."

"Cara de Culo: 'Asshole Face.' Cara de Culo. Over."

"I don't understand. Over."

"That's what they call the jackass: Cara de Culo. Over."

"Do you know the man? Over."

"Negative, negative, Delta One. Who knows anybody here? They assigned our troops to us in a rush. Over."

"Could they have switched sides? That would truly cause a shitstorm. Over."

"I don't think so. They either took matters into their own hands or they're out drinking whiskey, but I don't think they deserted. Over."

"You'll answer to me for those guns, which will cost you plenty if they don't show up. The last thing we need is for those men to commit some kind of crime. Over."

"Copy that, Delta One. But remember that I'm nothing but a soldier under your command. Over and out."

The pitiless heat broiled inside the abandoned warehouse, and whenever Tongolele went outside the sun would simply roast his eyes. Even worse, vegetables lay rotting under the overheated roofs of the market stalls. These vegetables had arrived during the early-morning darkness of previous days, and they produced a stench that would overtake him in waves of red-hot vapor. The troops wandered around freely, their rifles hanging on their backs, as the canary yellow of their t-shirts offended the scene under the sun's dazzling brilliance. They talked loudly to each other, held animated debates, discussed the people killed, mocked the students they had forced to flee, and whooped and cackled as they praised some obscenity or another. One of them walked over to a fig tree to empty his bladder on its trunk, and the bright sunlight made his urine sparkle.

From time to time, Tongolele climbed into the Hilux's cab and turned on the engine to make the air conditioning work. He eventually returned to the warehouse. Voices talked over each other on the walkie-talkie he had attached to his waist. Like bursts of gunfire, the words exploded and then disappeared.

Pedrón drove up. Tongolele watched him step down and saw a colorful image of Bob Marley with all of his dreadlocks covering the chest of the man's black t-shirt. The engine's purr told Tongolele that Pedrón had left the vehicle running, which meant that he had passengers who needed air conditioning. Could Fabiola herself be there? From a distance, Tongolele gestured for Pedrón to approach him.

In the first place, Tongolele wondered how Pedrón had found him. How did you find me? I haven't forgotten my duty to find things out, commissioner, and I haven't stopped doing so, although to be honest, and in all seriousness, they haven't given me much work to do in the office: the jolly fat man from Military Intelligence has never come back, and the major he left in charge doesn't care what we do or don't do. I assume he uses the reports we give him to wipe his ass. When I asked permission to leave, he said "Granted" without even looking up. He didn't even ask me if I wanted written permission or if I needed to be gone all day. What I'm trying to say, commissioner, is that they don't give a damn where I go, and the only reason I asked for permission is because Doña Fabiola had an urgent need to talk with you, and she begged me to bring her to see you. She said it's a delicate matter that can't be discussed over the phone. Things are problematic because she took Professor Zoraida to live with her. I don't know if you've heard what happened last night and early this morning at your mother's house: she was kicked out, and she wanted to come to see you as well; she's sitting right there in the back seat of the car, and I'm sorry if you're upset that I've brought her, but there was nothing I could do to avoid it because not even Doña Fabiola could convince her that it was unwise to come here when the situation on the streets is what it is.

"Too many words, Pedrito. You're making me dizzy, and this sun makes things even worse because it's overcooking my head."

"I'm sorry to bother you, commissioner, but such a huge number of incidents requires a huge number of words."

"So what does my mother want? What's her problem? I already know that they threw her out of her house. But what the hell am I supposed to do?"

"Commissioner, her problem is mainly Chicas, your brother-in-law. She's dressed in mourning, and she's coming in mourning to see you."

"Mourning? Why would she be mourning?"

"The problem is The Mask's tweets, one of many that The Mask has used to smear you. I assume you already know all about his tweets."

"Fabiola told me something about them. They blame me for the priest's nephew and even the pipe attack on the priest. What about now?"

"Now the tweets claim that the man who died in the Asososca accident is Chicas, and that his death wasn't an accident but murder. And there are photos of Chicas when he was alive, plus others showing his body in the morgue."

"And I'm guilty of that too, I'll bet."

"Do you see what I'm saying? They're claiming that you're responsible, commissioner. They've also posted the list of businesses that you and your brother-in-law owned together."

"I never owned any business with him. I hired him to run my businesses just to keep my mother happy."

"You don't have to explain that to me, because I know it's true, but that's what they're accusing you of in those tweets, along with all the little details of each business."

"I'd give up one of my balls and half of the other to find out who's behind this plot to bury me."

"Your enemies, no doubt."

"But now that every single dog is lifting its leg to piss on me, how can I know who is my enemy and who is my friend?"

"You don't have many friends. And heaven knows you've got more than your fair share of enemies."

"The dwarf Manzano, for example."

"He wouldn't be so stupid as to burn his own agent. They even included Baldomero's photo in that tweet about the attack on the priest."

"Or maybe the enemy's right here at home, Pedrito."

"Do you mean people from your inner circle? Someone like La Chaparra, or even me? Your lack of faith offends me, commissioner."

"Listen, *pendejo*. Do you think that you two are the only people who work with me? There are at least two-dozen people in the customs agency."

"But they're just case managers. They only know what's relevant to their cases."

"So, then, where do we go from here? If the enemy isn't an outsider or an insider, the only person left who wants to fuck me over is the Holy Ghost."

"Or the two Divine Personages. It's entirely possible that whoever's arranging these attacks is obeying orders from the celestial heights."

"Don't think I haven't considered that. Knock me down and kick me while I'm on the ground. Full service."

"If they ordered you to be locked up in this warehouse, you can't assume much else."

"But I'm not locked up. I let my dick hang out for all to see today, removing barricades from the highways and showing my face, but nobody is paying any attention to that."

"They'll pay attention later."

"Well, they should be paying attention now. More than one person must have taken some video of me and posted it. You haven't heard any news about such a thing, Pedrito? Some accusation against me for doing what I was doing?"

"I don't think there's been any news like that. La Chaparra is in charge of all the online stuff, and she would have told me. And anyway, you need to keep in mind that you yourself have taken great care to ensure that your face isn't known."

"And they're not finished. They're taking me apart fingernail by fingernail."

"In fact, it's as if they wanted to skin you alive. Those tweets also begin with a list of your businesses with Doña Fabiola, and they say that you and she share everything half and half."

"You see? I can't defend myself against an operation that runs so quickly."

"Quickly? As far as quickness goes, I don't see much moving quickly around here, commissioner," Pedrón laughed.

Tongolele gave him an exasperated look, then his face turned angry.

"Just what do you think a command post is? Can't you see that I'm always running from one side to the other making sure that our plans are working?"

"Don't be so sensitive, commissioner. We're used to a bit of joking."

"I'm still driving, Pedrito, and I can still drag you on the ground behind me if I choose. You're much better off being afraid of me."

"You're the one who raised me up; you continue to keep me where I am; and you have the power to toss me to the ground. I've never been out of your hands."

"At least with you I can be as unclear as I choose," said Tongolele, giving Pedrito a mock punch in the stomach.

"So, what should I tell Doña Fabiola?"

"Tell her to come to this warehouse, and she and I can talk here. As for my mother, tell her to wait."

There was nowhere to sit in the warehouse, which reeked of burnt diesel fuel. The sun sneaked in as tremulous drops of lava through the roof's holes, and gushing water followed the same path during heavy rainstorms, proof of which could be seen in the cement floor's bright oily puddles, which created gleaming reflections. One of the puddles contained a dying bird, a flycatcher that had gone off-course after fluttering blindly into the building and hitting one of the walls.

Fabiola entered under the furious flapping of the zinc roofing sheets shaken by blasts of hot wind, and Tongolele sensed that her normal jaunty step atop cork platform soles seemed unsure, even dejected. The bunions on her upper feet stood out like stumps; the roots of her wilted hair, which she had dyed blond, were visible from far away; the Ferragamo purse looked more counterfeit than ever; and the piercing that hung from her exposed navel looked more ridiculous than ever.

"I have only five minutes," Tongolele said, tapping the face of his watch.

She bowed her head, studied her own exposed feet on the platform shoes, and rubbed them against the legs of her jeans, as if she felt disgusted by the filth on the ground where she was standing. And when she raised her head, she bit her lips to restrain herself from sobbing.

"What more do you need, my love?" she asked, with fury and desperation in her voice.

What more did he need after the savage 3:00 a.m. raid in La Primavera against the three Pitufos, those Smurfs: Josiel, Gamaliel, and Joel. All of them had been captured and taken outside, tied-up in their underwear, and the police had stuck those numbered yellow packets in the sidewalk to signal the presence of drugs that the narcotics investigators themselves had planted inside the house without any attempt to hide what they were doing, and the three unlucky men were kneeling on the ground among hooded agents who held them fast while a uniformed cameraman filmed them, and without realizing that their words were making things worse, the Pitufos kept clamoring that the police should call me, that they should tell you what was happening. My heartsick aunt told me all of this because she's the one who gave them a place to hide after you told me they would be better off in Managua lying low, and if the police knew where they were hiding it's because someone close to you tipped them off, my love. I told my aunt we'd find them a lawyer, just to comfort her, but it's not much comfort when you yourself know better than anyone that the hand holding the stick is so powerful, which means the Pitufos are imprisoned and humiliated for the crime of providing an official favor, because the idea of the attack was certainly not theirs. I just wish that was all.

Because now this same Mask has made a post claiming that you ordered your brother-in-law to be pushed into the crater at Asososca Lagoon over a business dispute and that that's the reason your mother is with me now, and she also wants to tell you that she was thrown out into the street without a single change of clothes, but I can see in your face that you already knew that very well, although you shouldn't think that I'm finished yet, Papito. Stretch your five minutes out right now because I'm coming out to dance. *Throw Fabiola into the bull ring* must be the current order, because the new tweet contains a list of everything my sweat has gathered together: the distributors throughout the country, one by one; the networks of sector heads, including their names and cell numbers; the quality and detail needed to have every store properly stocked, whether it imported school backpacks, sold bulk used clothing at wholesale, or specialized in videos and video games; and the storehouses where we found the t-shirts for your sport team.

And now, what more? There is nothing more, you'll say, but your calculations are so wrong when it comes to me, señor, because the prosecutors from the General Directorate of Revenue have that list in their hands and they're digging into all my businesses: they're taking accounting records; they're kicking my employees into the streets and sticking crime-scene announcements on the doors; and I can't touch a single cent of the money in my bank accounts. Lawyers? And even more lawyers? It would be wonderful if I could escape this mess by paying lawyers, but just as the lawyers couldn't save the Pitufos from thirty years in the Modelo Prison for drug trafficking, I won't be saved from having everything taken from me, thrown practically naked to the street like your mother for the simple crime of being associated with you, because it looks like you've got leprosy and you've given it to me. I don't know how many people you'll have to kill today to be forgiven by those up above and be returned to your old position, but if you're not forgiven and you end up battered and bruised, wallowing in the depths, there's nothing we can do about it. I certainly can't say that Fabiola will somehow be free of this rancid man and leave him as the buzzards eat his entrails. No, my love, your fate will be my fate even if they abandon me naked, because just as I was born naked from my mother's womb, the soil will cover my naked body. And besides, I can begin again from down below, kicking along the roads with my sack of goods over my shoulder the same as I did when I was so young that I hadn't even begun my period.

She swallowed the splinters in her voice, which ended up breaking, and looked down at her feet again, exhausted as if she had just finished a marathon, lines of perspiration flowing down from her mouth to the collar of her table-server blouse and shining on her arms and exposed waist. Tongolele stood undaunted as he faced her: he wasn't going to turn sentimental at this point, and as far as this woman went, what was she even doing here? She should return to her home; after all, at least she hadn't been kicked out of it. For now. How many shots were truly necessary today to buy the Pitufos' freedom? How many to ensure that the prosecutors leave Fabiola in peace? How many to allow his mother to go back to the house she had been given? The question of his mother returning to her position as an enlightened and infallible official advisor probably meant asking a lot; furthermore, Tongolele would be asking far too much if he requested that the white-gloved aide with the white gaiters who bore the Chinese box stand at attention before him. No, Tongolele's first priority had to be silencing The Mask once and for all.

A drill bored into his skull, the fine bit penetrating the space between his eyes. If he closed them both he could see the sparks in the partial darkness, and if he took a single step forward, the dizziness all around him would take over.

"We have to wait," Tongolele said, stretching his arms wide as if he wanted to start flapping them to take flight.

"What do we have to wait for, my love?"

"We have to wait for this problem of the coup to be resolved."

"Who's going to resolve it? You?"

"Among others. The volunteer troops, the historical combatants, the police."

"Oh, really? So then, once they've cleared the streets, everything will be fine. You return to your old position; they return everything they've taken from me; and Merry Christmas and Happy New Year."

"We can't guess what the next step will be until we've taken the first step of clearing the streets."

"And as to the step after that, will it be a step forward or backward?"

"Your negative attitude won't get us anywhere," said Tongolele, lowering his arms as if had become convinced that he couldn't fly away.

"Ah, very good. Just fine. I should be shouting for joy because Fabiola is so lucky. See how they've rewarded her."

"We're not in this for rewards."

"Fabiola won the grand prize simply by adding the name of some campesino from Yolaina to the list of traitors, all because a historical combatant—one of yours—wanted to take the campesino's tiny bit of land to increase the size of his plantation."

"Don't talk so loud. Shouting doesn't get us anywhere."

"Or that other unfortunate soul, who lost his small pasture to some party boss from Palacagüina. The river passed through the pasture and the grass was always tender."

"No one ever forced you to do anything. You and I had an agreement."

"Well, then, the flower dies here, and its aroma dies as well. We'll see how Fabiola eats while you're here waiting in this warehouse when a new day dawns."

"You're nervous. You need to rest. So it's best if you go back home."

"Assuming they'll let me in."

"You've come at a bad time. I'm in a hurry, and you need to calm down. We can talk later."

"I'm asking a mango tree to give me avocadoes, so I won't bother you anymore. I don't know what kind of story you're going to tell your mother, and I don't think you can convince her to come to this warehouse. Go over to the car, please."

"Talking with her will only make things worse."

Fabiola looked him over up and down, taking his measure in shock.

"You're going to refuse to talk with your own mother?"

"We wouldn't gain anything from it. She won't believe me when I tell her the truth about my brother-in-law."

"And what truth is that?"

"That I had nothing to do with his death. That it was an accident. He was stone drunk."

"Drunk? At 7:00 in the morning?"

"He was a drunk; there was nothing we could do about it."

"You were exactly right when you said that your mother wouldn't believe a word you say."

"I've got a headache that's killing me," Tongolele said, pushing his fingers between his eyebrows. "I'll call you later."

"A Mejoral pill for children. That will make you feel better," said Fabiola, and she turned away.

He watched her walk away toward the car where Pedrón waited alongside the driver's door and where Professor Zoraida waited inside, dressed in mourning. Fabiola came to a halt halfway to the car as if she was about to retrace her steps, but she did not come back. He watched her sobbing shake her shoulders and her blonde-dyed mass of hair, and he continued watching as she eventually continued forward, tripping and bending over.

From afar he saw her speak briefly with Pedrón, after which the two of them climbed into the Passat. The car drove off, grinding the rocks and leaving a cloud of dust that remained floating in the air until it was dispersed by a gust of wind, which carried dirt and garbage, small branches and twigs, bits of plants, and dry crinkled leaves to the warehouse.

Before the gust of wind died down, a Hilux came speeding in and turned to park before him. The poet Lira, with his eyeglasses fogged over, smiled at him through the windshield and got out.

He took off his glasses and rubbed them with all the calm in the world on the sleeve of his pearl-gray shirt.

"I've come for a consultation," he said.

"That's what the walkie-talkies are for. Nobody authorized you to leave your troops behind."

"I don't trust those *chunche* walkie-talkies because anyone can listen to us on them," said the poet Lira, stroking his goatee. "Besides, I left a fine aide de camp in my place."

"You're just as disciplined as Cara de Culo."

"That's what I've come to tell you. Cara de Culo and the others who disappeared have shown up again."

"What a great military leader. He takes a little walk with his soldiers and then comes back as if nothing happened."

"Remember that we're talking about a man who's nothing but an animal gone wild, commissioner. He's a deliveryman from the Mercado Oriental."

"I assume that rather than a deliveryman you would have preferred a poet of poets like you."

"The fact is that my command post is at the Nicolás Maduro School, around the corner from the Virgin roundabout. The principal had just kindly allowed us to use the school when Cara de Culo and his soldiers came in, and I realized that they had brought a young female student after capturing her at the gate to the National University."

"Turn her over to the police. We haven't lost anything. And send those shitheads to go balls-out in the street."

"The problem is that they didn't just capture her. One of Cara de Culo's soldiers took me aside and confessed that they had raped her."

"They raped her? All of them?"

"Cara de Culo ordered them to take her to some overgrown area beneath a bridge near the road to San Isidro de Bolas. He raped her first, and then he turned her over to the other men, according to Rambo, the man who told me."

"Wait a second," said Tongolele. "Rambo?"

"Rambo and Cara de Culo belong to the Mercado Oriental's shock troops."

"So it is him. I already said that I knew his face. I exiled him to Honduras, and he sneaked back in."

"Exiled as a political enemy?"

"Not exactly. But there's a dangerous crippled man, his companion in arms, who could have ordered him to infiltrate our soldiers."

"Rambo is a first-class talker who never shuts up, but I don't think he has the brains to be an infiltrator."

"He might not have the brains, but the cripple certainly does. As soon as you go back to your post, you take Rambo's weapon away and send him to me."

"I left him guarding the student in one of the classrooms."

"The cat guarding the milk."

"He was the only man who refused to jump on top of her the way the others did."

"All the more reason not to trust him. I want to talk with him."

"So tell me now what I should do with Cara de Culo and the girl they raped. I have him under guard."

"Free Cara de Culo and return him to his command. You don't have enough soldiers to be wasting them—one man a prisoner, the other a guard. As for the girl, get rid of her."

"Freeing her would be a disaster, commissioner. She'll run around with a drum and a horn proclaiming that they abused her."

"Who said anything about freeing her? No one is going to pay attention to one more death among so many others today."

"If those are your orders, they'll be obeyed," sighed the poet Lira.

"I don't like those subtle little sighs. And if you need to find a way to console yourself, write her a requiem or an elegy. What do you poets call those verses used for mourning?"

"Odes, commissioner. They're called Pindaric odes."

Their voices became lost because a delivery van from El Pollo Ciudadano entered the vacant lot, and armed with loudspeakers on the roof, the van stridently blared "El Komandante Zekeda," a cumbia song performed by the mariachi band Azucena that the official radio stations had been playing since early that morning:

> *Although it might hurt you, although it might hurt you,*
> *The comandante will stay right here…*

Two workers—dressed in yellow chicken costumes, with tails, feet, beaks, and crests—emerged from the van's back doors and began to remove box lunches and cans of beer, dancing all the while and shaking their tails, and within a din of yells and shots fired into the air, the paramilitary troops grabbed their food and joined the dance.

CHAPTER THIRTEEN

Rambo Makes a Long and Detailed Confession

Doña Sofía couldn't attend the Mother of All Protest Marches that Wednesday despite the fact that she had her Nicaraguan flag ready, which she had bought in an alley section where people sold blue-and-white baseball hats and headbands. From 2:00 p.m. onward, the 100% News Channel managed to broadcast drone images of the column of soldiers that stretched along four kilometers from the Jean Paul Genie roundabout up to the metropolitan cathedral's grounds. But everything came to a stop in the Mother of All Massacres.

You missed the march, Doña Sofía, said Padre Pancho, but you probably saved your life too, given the fact that knowing you as I do, you are one of those people who insists on being at the front of the line, and the front of the line is exactly where most people were killed. The death toll is now at twenty, mostly young people and teenagers: The snipers targeted them from the roof of the national baseball park, and it's utterly shameful to think that they would turn a modern sports stadium that still smells of fresh paint into a paramilitary base. At least Dennis Martínez has denounced what the killers did from Miami, and he doesn't want his name on the stadium anymore.

Even now during nightfall, as everyone sat in the parish house's living room with the blinds shut and all candles unlit, they could hear the distant siren of some ambulance, the far-off echo of some explosion that dissipated among other even farther-off echoes. So many stories in such a short number of hours that I can't believe it, Madre mía, Padre Pancho said as he covered his face with his hairy hands: Dragunov rifle shots straight through the head, young people's brain matter splattered on the pavement, the bodies of other people punctured through the neck or the chest. You know the monstrous impact of rifles like those, inspector. But Inspector Morales' face looked bored. These stories of deaths and the dead left him in a state of limbo, as if the world's noises disappeared around him and the emptiness of his own head reigned from outside of him as well, which is the same way he had responded in the southern front's trenches among the four-barreled anti-aircraft batteries known as "four mouths." These weapons, a Stalin-era design manufactured by the Argentine army, which the Argentine dictator Videla gave as a gift to Somoza to defend himself against communism, repeatedly launched broadsides of rockets, and the smoke from the craters they left behind smelled like stink bombs.

Padre Pancho continued to recite his report about that afternoon's events as if his listeners had only recently landed from foreign countries and knew nothing about what had happened: the emergency rooms at public hospitals had refused to admit beardless youths with collapsed lungs, while any doctors or nurses who attempted to help the boys were fired; the police had united with the paramilitary groups on the street to repress the protests, firing tear-gas bombs into shopping centers, and beating and groping women after pursuing them into the cathedral itself; troops had occupied the studios at 100% News, where they confiscated cameras, consoles, and drones, and they had taken the station's manager and all the reporters captive; they had even arrested the people selling hats and flags, so the Nicaraguan flag itself has been banned, the most ridiculous thing possible; and here, right beside my own church, they're still laying siege against the students who took over the university: they've cut off the electricity and the water; they don't allow the students to receive any food or carry out the wounded; and here I sit; here I fucking sit locked in like a prisoner, good for nothing and doing nothing, as they say.

Padre Pancho lowered his head in a dejected position as he held onto his knees, his thick gray tonsure barely visible, and tried to calm down. Thanks to Padre Pupiro, who remained at the Metropolino Hospital to keep abreast of Monseñor Ortez's condition, Padre Pancho had found a female gynecologist, who had a horrific time making it all the way here. We now have a medical report about the university student's condition. She has no long-term physical injuries despite the savage abuse those monsters inflicted upon her body. And monsters are exactly what they are: demons who escaped from Hell, which was emptied out today. The gash in the girl's scalp doesn't need stitches. Her most serious injury is psychological—deep trauma—and we'll find a way to treat that later, but for the moment the doctor has ordered a dose of Clonazepam so the girl can sleep. Fortunately, we had a small bottle in the church's dispensary. The girl's aunt is staying beside her in my room, taking care of her, and she could probably use a dose of Clonazepam herself, but she absolutely refuses to take anything. Dona Sofía, would you please go and see whether the girl is asleep yet? And Doña Sofía tied the laces of her running shoes as if she were beginning a race and tiptoed toward the partially open door: The girl's finally gone to sleep, she reported.

"Let's see if we can understand things in order," Inspector Morales said. "Doña Sofía, begin slowly and carefully from the time everything started."

"It would be better if I stopped weeping and wailing," said Padre Pancho, and he made a gesture as if closing his lips with a zipper.

"Why should you be quiet, padre?" Doña Sofía sighed. "Especially not around me. I gave birth to a martyr, and with so many dead boys my wounds have been torn open again."

"We can't bring back the dead by talking," said Inspector Morales. "Let's concentrate on tracing the end of the thread that leads to The Mask, which is the only thing we have in our hands."

"I would remind you that this is the third time I've told this story."

"It's your own fault that you have to repeat things, because you tend to go off on tangents."

"With all the terrible things happening around us, Comrade Artemio, it's hard not to get distracted from the thread I'm trying to follow. And I haven't even told you about the anxious moments I experienced when I had to get by the police and paramilitary squads to come here."

Obey the inspector and stay on point, Doña Sofía, said Lord Dixon. Your biblical wisdom tells you very clearly that he who gathereth not scattereth abroad.

Doña Sofía moved to the center of the room, her back to the door, and Señora Magdalena's ironing board remained standing in the dining room.

"So then, when I turned around, I saw this woman, somewhat

short and stout, wearing a man's guayabera and a backpack," she said, slowly turning. "And I heard her say, with absolute calm, that she had come to pick up the tablecloth because there was a wedding in the Church of Lourdes, and the padre needed it to cover the altar."

"Hell, what a fantastic imagination: a wedding at 1:00 in the afternoon," said Padre Pancho, moving a lighter to the Ducados cigarette between his lips. "That's lie number one, verified by the phone conversation I had earlier with Padre Casimiro, the parish priest at that church."

"But I kept my eye on SpongeBob, and I could see from his expression that it was all an act. And I also realized that Señora Magdalena had a malicious look on her face as she folded the tablecloth."

"The woman could easily have put the new message in the backpack and delivered it directly, Doña Sofía. That would have saved you from having to work through so much deception and so many obstacles," joked Padre Pancho.

"You're right, reverend. The backpack contained another envelope with a new revelation," Inspector Morales interrupted. "But that unexpected discovery put an end to The Mask's messages."

"Everything was going great as long as it was a simple case of throwing a rock and hiding the hand that threw it," Padre Pancho agreed. "But once the hand was discovered, the game was over."

So tell them now, Doña Sofía, how you began to identify the woman you've been talking about, said Lord Dixon.

"Señora Magdalena put the tablecloth in a plastic bag; the stout woman put it in her backpack; and even as she was leaving the woman asked when the priest's vestments would be ready, which she must have seen hanging from the wire."

"Padre Casimiro told me that Señora Magdalena brought the tablecloth to the church that same afternoon, which means that the backpack woman returned it sometime later."

Father Brown here is sharp, inspector. He's not even a step behind Doña Sofía, said Lord Dixon.

"So, I told Señora Magdalena that I was leaving too, and I asked SpongeBob if he would walk me home so that I didn't get lost," and Doña Sofía began to move forward as if she were moving toward the door.

"But what Doña Sofía really wanted was to have SpongeBob confess, because she already suspected that he hadn't told her the entire truth," said Padre Pancho, raising the Ducados to his lips once again.

"SpongeBob was walking with me in silence, pushing his bike alongside, and I said: 'I can find my way from here, but you owe me because you lied to me.' 'Yes,' he said, 'you're right. I did lie to you. Magdalena isn't sick with a fever; she just drinks a lot.'"

"That's a problem that Doña Sofía can't cure," Padre Pancho lamented. "So that's why the only advice she gave him was to avoid copying his mother's example and to go to school rather than roaming up and down the streets and risking the chance of making bad choices."

Look how well these two work together, comrade. They're truly a musical duet, said Lord Dixon.

"But that's not the lie I'm talking about," I told him. "I'm talking about you not telling me the identity of the woman with the backpack."

"Well done, Doña Sofía. No beating around the bush!" exclaimed Padre Pancho.

"And SpongeBob said: 'She works in an office in Las Colinas where they spy on people.'"

"Oh, for the love of God, there's more to it than that!" said Padre Pancho, leaping to his feet in a single bound as his cigarette ashes fell all over his pants. "We're finally getting close to some answers!"

"And then SpongeBob said that his mother wasn't just part of the help at the fat woman's house. In fact, the woman had actually recommended his mother as a cleaning lady at the spy offices."

"Tongolele's kingdom!" said Padre Pancho, contemplating the cigarette butt as it burned down between his fingers.

"He also said that he had told me all this to thank me for lunch because he had only seen the menu's color pictures from a distance as he passed by."

"And now we're coming to the most important part: We're coming to the name," said Padre Pancho, barely managing to put the cigarette butt into the ashtray.

"And so I took a very kind approach: I buttoned the top button of his shirt and asked him the woman's name. I thought this would be the most difficult part."

"But it wasn't difficult at all. He didn't even hesitate. He just said 'Her name is Yasica.'"

Shakira and Juanes, today's most popular musical duet, said Lord Dixon.

"Even so, all the way back home I kept asking myself whether everything that young vagabond had told me was just lies designed to keep me satisfied."

"But this is where our friend Don Serafín comes in to complete the picture, inspector."

Another wrong key for the padre to play on the piano, said Lord Dixon.

"Don't talk to me about Serafín. If he had run off and left me a letter like that when we were guerrillas, I'd have shot him."

"That would make two men who want to kill him," Doña Sofía said, eying the inspector severely. "Because Tongolele must also be trying to find him so that he can skewer him for high treason."

"Inspector, I insist that you're wrong to refuse to read your friend's confession. All the rest of us have read it."

"Reverend, let me make my own decisions about what's right and what's wrong as far as Serafín is concerned."

"Comrade Artemio, Serafín rescued that girl after she was kidnapped; he risked his life to bring her here. And I believe he didn't participate in that horrible gang rape, just as he says in his confession."

"As for me, inspector, I can't keep using the sacristy as a jail cell."

"Serafín decided to join those people on his own. Let him leave whenever he wants and re-join the paramilitary units. He's not a prisoner."

At least you're right about that, inspector, said Lord Dixon. When have we ever seen someone turn themselves in and declare themselves a prisoner on their own?

"He says he won't leave until you talk to him, inspector," pleaded Padre Pancho. "Then he'll disappear and never bother you again."

"To me, Serafín's word is worth less than the spit I need to say his name."

"Will you at least let me tell you about the conversation we had when I went to see him in his cell? It concerns what we need to do next."

"What cell, Doña Sofía? This is all an act: Serafín is very crafty. But go ahead and tell me. That way no one can say that I've dragged my feet."

"Was Serafín just acting when Tongolele took him as a prisoner to El Chipote and tortured him during that case with Soto, the millionaire?" Doña Sofía asked.

"No. That was real," Inspector Morales acknowledged. "But what does that have to do with anything?"

"Well, in the sacristy, the thought occurred to me to ask him about the time those two swine, Tuco and Tico, were waterboarding him in the sink. So, I asked him if the only people entering and leaving the torture chamber were men."

"Holy shit, now that's what they call female intuition."

The confessional is a fantastic place to gain great wisdom about female intuition, said Lord Dixon.

"And Serafín told me that everyone was a man except for a particular woman who dressed like a man. She came in as if she was perfectly at home and delivered some office papers to Tongolele."

"Serafín got a close look at her when they were dragging him through the corridor back to his cell, with his lungs still full of water," Padre Pancho added.

"They drag him along, naked and bloody, with his face beaten to a pulp. They nearly drown him but don't complete the job. And despite those things he gets a good look at the woman who dresses like a man. Serafín was probably out of his mind at that point."

"I believe everything he says, inspector. He also remembers that subordinates stood at attention for the woman and saluted her, calling her 'lieutenant.' Just wait and see."

"Based on what the padre said, I was able to link two things: SpongeBob asserts that her name is Yasica, and Serafín asserts that she is a lieutenant. So, I sat down to consult the oracle."

"Yasica has to be the right name, Doña Sofía! The oracle at Delphi is known today as the Internet."

"After I searched and searched through many secret lairs and devious trails, the oracle finally showed me the caption of a photo from *El 19 Digital*, where Lieutenant Yasica Benavides was receiving a medal at the Casa de Pueblos three years ago. And I have the photo right here if Comrade Artemio deigns to look at it."

Inspector Morales reluctantly examined the picture.

"What an ugly woman."

"We're not judging contestants at a beauty pageant," Padre Pancho scolded him. "That photo is a piece of evidence, nothing more."

"Doña Sofía, if everything you're saying turns out to be true, you would be wise not to go back to Fanny, because you're in grave danger of being captured."

"I've been in danger for a long time—ever since I began working with you, Comrade Artemio. And I'm willing to keep taking any risks that might be necessary."

"Save your speeches. They're wasted on me. I'm referring to the fact that this lieutenant from Intelligence, if we accept that that's what she is, won't like the fact that you've seen her, because she knows that you're capable of tracking her to the end."

"That's true," Padre Pancho agreed. "The Mask never believed that we'd be able to unmask him."

"We haven't unmasked him yet," Doña Sofía reminded him. "The thread doesn't end with this woman."

"Regardless, we need to keep in mind that The Mask's game is over. There won't be any more messages."

"If there aren't any more messages, padre, we can create some. Reactions to The Mask's tweets remain strong: He has thousands of followers. Why should we squander them?"

"You're definitely a daring woman, Doña Sofía. Ballsy."

Inspector Morales, you can either throw yourself into the ring right now or stay in the stands watching the bulls from afar, said Lord Dixon.

"How would your plan work, Doña Sofía?" Inspector Morales asked.

"The paramilitary groups are running around committing atrocities, and Serafín is a first-hand source that we're not using. We'll post his entire written confession as tweets from The Mask."

"Think this through before rejecting it, inspector. Settle your differences with your friend when he leaves the sacristy, but let's take advantage of his testimony."

"Comrade Artemio, Serafín knows how many people the government has, how many forces have been deployed for certain tasks, who the commanders are, and what kinds of weapons they have."

"He provides all those details in his confession?"

"Read it yourself first. Then we'll see what's missing and you can ask him about it."

"I'm going to make myself a cup of coffee, and I'll read the papers in the kitchen while the water is boiling. Give them to me, Doña Sofía."

"Take them. Here they are. And just stay calm and read them right where you're sitting. I'll go make your coffee."

"Can you make some for me too while you're at it, if it's not too much bother?" Padre Pancho asked.

Doña Sofía turned her head back as she was entering the kitchen.

"I'm warning you that Serafín uses some strong language in his confession, as Padre Pancho can attest. Don't be shocked."

"You're like my Grandmother Catalina. Whenever I used strong language, what she called vulgarity, she used to threaten to burn my mouth with hot coals."

Padre Pancho had given Serafín a stack of extra papers from the program for the festivities commemorating Padre Pío de Pietrelcina's feast day. The padre also loaned Serafín his Esterbrook pen, the same one he had used in seminary, which Serafín used to write his confession on the back of the program papers.

The handwritten words on the paper became lopsided as they moved along, collapsing toward the right:

Most Excellent Sir colon

You don't know Cara de Culo but you do know his girlfriend, Milonga, the woman wrapped in a tiger-print bedspread that we bumped into as we walked through the Mercado Oriental alley on the night we were looking for the King of the Vultures. Well Cara de Culo, whose real name is Marcial Duarte, has never been a trustworthy man because he's violent and sly and like I said he's Milonga's boyfriend, and she has a little eatery in the market near the meat section so he gets to eat as much as he wants for free and he makes her happy in bed and he eats a ton because he works as one of the market's strongest and meanest deliverymen so he's just as hungry for food as Milonga is for what she wants. He can whistle while carrying two 100-kilo bags of corn on his back and when it comes to bar fights he can spin a man and crush him against a wall and break his bones as if he was nothing but a soft little pigeon which is why I'm warning you to never lay a hand on Cara de Culo because if you do he'll probably beat you until there's nothing but a stain.

And you remember that midnight when I left here that I wrote a message to you saying that I couldn't take living locked up because I need the fresh air of the streets but of course I had a twist of bad luck when I went into the market and wouldn't you know that the person I run into is none other than Cara de Culo himself, and you're going to ask me why I went there in the first place and I'll answer in all honesty that I have no idea because the truth is that I have nobody in my life but regardless that's what happened and Cara de Culo gives me a big hug and says it's been a long time since I've seen you brother.

You must be wondering why this man has such a disgusting nickname and I'll give you two reasons first because he's always has his brow furrowed in a furious way as if he's bearing down to force something out of his body and I mean like he's taking a shit and also because no matter how happy he may be he always has the same tortured grimace on his face and anyway he invites me for some beef and crab soup at Milonga's place and I say that it's two in the morning and there won't be any fire and he says what's the point in being in charge at Milonga's if they don't light the fire whenever he asks and my big mistake was eating that soup along with drinking half a bottle of Plata rum and then another half a bottle and I have to confess to you Jefe that everything that happened to me later was because I had been so hungry.

Concerning how I first got to know Cara de Culo, you should know that I met him in the King of the Vultures' shock troops, where Cara de Culo was my squad leader. So once the two of us were sitting at Milonga's eating soup, she kept serving him as if he was Rubén Darío's Prince of Golconda and treating me as if I was a street beggar and you could have seen yourself how stubborn and nasty she acted toward me because she's never liked me much and I have no idea what I did long ago to offend her but then Cara de Culo comes over and moves my head toward him and says look, Serafín, plans for a big fiesta are being made to put down the right-wing rebels who are trying to carry out a coup and in light of the fact that the holy child's grace and will have helped me find you I want you to know that I had been searching for you anyway because the party trusts you and we're counting on your support and help in the operation.

So I tried to play dumb like some pendejo and I told him that all that stuff with the famous shock troops had come to an end because the King of the Vultures was no more and I asked Cara de Culo whether he knew that they had dethroned the King of the Vultures and beat the shit out of him and then threw him into Honduras. And he laughed at me with that scrunched-up face of his as if he was in the middle of a trance on the toilet and that's when I remembered that some people liked to make fun of him in an elegant way by calling him Rectum Rictus rather than Cara de Culo but even though that memory made me want to laugh at that moment I understood very well that that wasn't the time for jokes and he says to me you're being an idiot because you believe that the world came to an end with Hermógenes but that's not true at all because they've reorganized everything and we now have a man who coordinates everything we do and he is none other than Leónidas and his dick reaches way up high and although Hermógenes might have been king of El Mercado Oriental, Leónidas now has supreme command over a lot more that.

So I turn to him and say that Leónidas is completely dickless and that he's nothing but a traitor and that we already knew during the war against Somoza that he would betray us and then we watched the CIA shower him with money when he returned as the leader of the contras but Cara de Culo says that's not true, brother, and you're obviously badly mistaken because it looks like you don't know that Leónidas was just playing a role in a scheme to infiltrate the imperialists and learn all their plans. I told him that that was just a story. And regardless I told him that I wasn't interested because I do believe that Leónidas is a traitor and I would never serve under the command of a traitor so then Cara de Culo got furious and started raging at me and saying that's fine brother but you're going to be the loser here because they're paying us fifty dollars per day so do the math and tell me that someone like you who I can see has two bare toes sticking out of his torn shoes is going to be so stupid and insane as to look down on money like that.

So I sat there quietly thinking while eating my soup and looking for the best way to open the crab shell and chewing the fat on a piece of brisket and sucking the marrow from a bone cut just below the ankle and sinking my teeth into a corn cob and chewing and drinking and talking to myself inside and telling myself Serafín here's your chance to get into the guts of this bloodthirsty scheme and learn from within how this huge effort to repress the protests is going to work so I can tell my jefe and that's the reason I told Cara de Culo okay let's go and he gets all happy and then he says let's drink the other half of the rum until 4:00 in the morning which is the time that everyone is supposed to be at the Uno gas station on the Gancho de Camino because that's where they're going to send transportation for us and then with a commanding voice he orders Milonga to serve us the "fighting rum" and as she was carrying the plates away from the table she obviously lost her patience because she dropped them back down so hard that they nearly broke but even though she was furious she still obeyed him and he acted as if nothing had happened and told her to get another half-bottle ready so that he wouldn't get thirsty on the road and she did that too as she held back her anger and ultimately gave in.

It was still dark when we arrived at the national stadium and there we saw Leónidas standing proud wearing his baseball jersey and camouflage pants and showing how happy he was with life because he had been given such high command and from the pitcher's mound he began speaking to the troops and saying to begin my report I want you to know that there are more than a thousand of us involved in this operation called Abate which was the name Leónidas himself had given it because as he explained we needed to understand that the operation was about exterminating vermin and not with pesticides but with lead and then they divided us into task forces assigned to particular zones and then they handed out weapons and that's when they gave every savage that you can imagine free rein as Leónidas told us to take whatever guns we wanted and there were loads of bullets and they had already given us bandanas to cover our faces and also t-shirts and my shirt was yellow because that was the color assigned to my zone and it was the zone that covered the eastern neighborhoods and just so you know that the risk I took to infiltrate was worth it I want you to know that my commanding officer was none other than Tongolele and even though you may be shocked I'm not lying when I tell you that it was Tongolele in the flesh.

They loaded us onto some buses bound for El Mercado de Mayoreo which was our headquarters and they assigned me to a column led by a scrawny and boney poet named Lira who has a little beard like you'd expect on a sick man and who doesn't have the kind of presence you'd expect for a military operation and he explains that our orders are to go to the Larreynaga Road to remove the barricades and once we're in formation in front of the warehouse where the Hiluxes we'll be using are kept and once I have my AK-47 in hand Tongolele notices me and walks directly toward me with movements that say where have I seen that face before so I kicked myself because if he recognizes me I might as well start reciting my own rest in peace amen but he studies me carefully and asks if perhaps we've met each other before and I just act like a dumb-ass and nothing else happens because he's in a rush and it's at this point where I think I have to express my concern jefe which is that I wonder how you can explain the fact that Tongolele is working under Leónidas' command given how much authority and pride Tongolele has but you will probably understand the situation better than I do.

They then tell us that before the operation begins we're going to do a victory parade to display our weapons and thereby convince the enemy that we're not playing games and so we get into the pick-ups and Cara de Culo gets in the cab because he's our squad leader but at the Lotería Nacional building we break off from the parade and take a different road and I'm thinking no way and that maybe Cara de Culo gave the wrong order or perhaps he's plastered from having started to drink so early because he's addicted to the hard stuff and while I'm asking myself these questions I hear Cara de Culo order the driver to stop near the Invercasa building and then he gets out and tells us that before we start fighting we're going to have a little fun wherever we want and if we grab some bourgeoise subversives we're going to teach them that the revolution is nobody's plaything so following his instructions we go searching in the direction of the university rotunda ready for a fight with our fingers on the trigger and we see some university students at the rotunda with some Nicaraguan flags so the truck stops and we start shooting as we're getting out and the kids begin running to the National University's grounds looking for cover but several end up scattered around because they'd been hit and two female students were wearing lab coats but one of them had a shoe come loose while she was running so she tripped and fell down and that's when the men caught her and cracked her head open with a gun butt and while she was bleeding Cara de Culo ordered them to throw her in the truck bed and I have to confess jefe that I said and did nothing to help her at that time but it made no sense to disobey a drunk man who can't even recognize his own mother when he's wasted, much less recognize a friend.

The truck then went along the side of the suburban street and soon turned onto San Isidro de Bolas Road, and there in a hidden spot of vegetation they forced the girl out of the truck and Cara de Culo brutally grabbed her and enjoyed himself with her while two other men held her down and the fact that she was covered with blood from her cracked head didn't bother them at all as they helped themselves to her and had their little fiesta along with everyone else who actually formed a line and waited with their zippers open and once they were all finished Cara de Culo says it's your turn brother so go ahead and give her a poke too. But I stepped away despite his insistence and then I made up a story about having a bad case of gonorrhea on my privates that I'd picked up at a brothel in Danlí and Cara de Culo laughed and said maybe I got it from my girlfriend or my wife and that a man didn't get a chance every day to use a newly minted whore and it's at this point jefe where although I know you must be furious with me I have to say that I'm willing to take anything you want to punish me except what for what happened in that disgusting moment because I had nothing to do with it and if you don't believe me you can talk to her and ask whether I ever touched her.

I went on and told Cara de Culo that enough was enough and

that it would be better to throw her under the bridge and leave her there and that would we should get back because we hadn't reported in and that our superiors would notice that we and our pick-up were missing and I said all that to stop the men from raping the girl because some of them wanted a second go-round and Cara de Culo answered in a snotty way that there was no way we could leave her behind because most likely everyone else would want a shot at her too and that's why we left her as a prisoner at the headquarters near the rotunda of the Virgin at the Nicolás Maduro School. Once we were there I made my sneaky way over to the poet Lira and told him what had happened just as I've told you and he was furious with Cara de Culo and said that we can't tolerate such things because the revolution has given us a mission and how can we possibly allow such horrible things and then he ordered me to take Cara de Culo's gun away and lock him up as a prisoner in a room before the eyes of the indignant men from the pick-up as some watched with rebellion in their faces and others with ferocity but I took a rather nonchalant approach so that they wouldn't realize that I was the one who had told their secret.

And the poet Lira told the squad that he was going to ask his commanding officer who is Tongolele for orders regarding the case and he chose me to guard the room where they had shut the girl inside even though she couldn't even walk because they had abused her so much and he also chose me to guard Cara de Culo in the other room under strict instructions that I should not allow anyone near the door and after the poet Lira left I went to the girl's room and told her to get ready because we were leaving and my plan was that she should pretend that she had asked permission to use the bathroom at the end of the corridor but she refused and said no sir no I can't because they've crushed my soul and I said all you have to do is pretend because the plan is to get out of this

building and you can do that by going into the bathroom and taking advantage of the chance to wash your face and get rid of that
blood-stained lab coat and when you come out I'll wait for you at
the door and we'll go down the stairs that lead to the courtyard
and you'll walk ahead until we reach the swings near the chain-
link fence because that part of the fence is broken which I know
because I checked it out earlier and all we have to do is lift it up and
we will be on the street.

The girl didn't say yes or no because her mind was so confused
so I just picked her up from the school desk where she was sitting
and carried her to the bathroom and she obeyed me by throwing
her lab coat away and washing her face and doing everything else
I'd asked her to do which means that we crossed the courtyard and
walked over to the fence and I took advantage of the chance to
toss my military gear into some bushes along with the yellow t-
shirt I'd been wearing over my regular shirt and I threw the bandana away too and then we escaped through the broken fence and
once we reached the street we were able to walk along without any
problems because anyone who saw us would think that she was my
daughter and I was her father and as we moved closer to the rotunda of the Virgin I asked her where she would like me to take her
and she stayed mute for some time until she finally started repeating my aunt my aunt like a broken record and so I kept asking her
where her aunt was and the girl kept saying the church the church
over and over again so I asked her which church and she mentioned Padre Pancho's name and then I became the person who
stayed mute and felt all confused because if the church was Padre
Pancho's then it had to be the Divine Mercy Church and the aunt
had to be the enormous woman whose footsteps make no sound
but regardless I was afraid to bring the girl here because I knew
that nothing good would happen to me when you found out that I

had left to join the paramilitary units to go around killing people and I could already imagine the insults you would hurl at me such as saying that that scumbag Serafín is so low he's not worth hitting even with a broom which is actually true and I deserve it but despite my fear about showing up in front of you I couldn't abandon that girl in the middle of the street where they might grab her again and that's why I stopped a taxi even though my pockets didn't have a single cent because I assumed that either the aunt or Padre Pancho himself would find some way to pay the driver.

Now Tongolele has three reasons for hunting me down because I snuck back into Nicaragua without permission, I deserted my post, and I deprived his soldiers of that juicy little morsel of a girl but because I don't want to add to the dangers already piled on top of you and I don't want to cause more problems or screw-ups or misery I've decided to disappear from here in a puff of smoke right after you've read this confession and right before you have the chance to have words with me because only after getting this burden off my shoulders can I find the strength to go back to the filthy street and try my luck at hiding from Cara de Culo who I can't believe they'll leave locked up but instead they'll most likely give him back his gun and his command and I'll have to try my luck at hiding from Tongolele too but that's how life will be so long as you say hit the road Serafín you fucking jackass although I officially pardon you because you did the right thing by not raping that girl and by bringing her back to her aunt and there's no trouble between the two of us and on that note

I say farewell as your true and faithful servant

"Everything Serafín wrote here is just a bunch of meaningless words," said Inspector Morales after he finished reading.

"Comrade Artemio, are you serious about 'meaningless words' when he says how he refused to abuse that poor girl and risked his life to bring her here through pure hell?"

"I'll take it back if that makes you feel better, Doña Sofía. Let's concentrate on Tongolele."

"The most surprising thing about Tongolele is that yesterday he held the power of life or death in his hands, but today he's under the command of someone else," commented Padre Pancho.

"That means he's being punished for something we don't know about, reverend."

"Couldn't The Mask's tweets be the reason?"

"Punish Tongolele for murder, scams, and robbery? Don't make me laugh, reverend."

"Except that the shenanigans related to his businesses may have gone too far," Doña Sofía interrupted. "Maybe he was running them all secretly and not paying the quotas on his earnings."

"The tithes and prime cuts," Padre Pancho chimed in.

"What we have here is a power struggle," Inspector Morales declared. "Behind this lieutenant passing information along stands a hidden figure who wants to ruin Tongolele and take his place. Who that person is remains to be seen."

"Regardless, Comrade Artemio, we need to throw more logs on the fire even as we keep investigating."

"Keep posting your tweets then, Doña Sofía. You always win."

"And what about Serafín, inspector? I need him: My plants here are dying because nobody's been watering them."

"If you want to keep him here under your protection, I'm not so heartless as to throw him back out on the street. He wouldn't even reach the first corner before they shot him."

I'm always moved by compassionate people, said Lord Dixon.

CHAPTER FOURTEEN

The Jolly Fat Man's Investigative Process

D URING UNEXPECTED MOMENTS, a puff of cold air would blow over their heads through the ceiling vent's slats. The puff would dissipate and seem like it would never blow again until it would gather strength once more and make itself heard from afar, as if arising from the very darkness of the night itself.

The two people seated elbow-to-elbow on the narrow vinyl sofa had neither spoken nor looked at each other for more than an hour, sitting together within the waiting room's brilliant light-green walls, where both acted as if they were in a hospital, silent and keeping their heads lowered as if awaiting news about a seriously ill patient. A table standing before them displayed numerous old issues of the army's official magazine, *Homeland and Liberty*, which contained photos upon photos on glossy paper: a successful drill for a high-seas rescue known as ALWAYS READY; a civic-improvement effort called CAMPESINO, GIVE ME YOUR HAND; an anti-drug operation labeled IRON FIST. Meanwhile, the TV's Channel 4 showed silent and shaky images from an ancient documentary depicting the revolution's day of triumph as guerrillas entered the plaza, their weapons held high as they rode on tanks captured from the dictatorship's National Guard, making their way slowly through the crowd.

The two people sat there until the jolly fat man poked his head through his office door and made a conspiratorial gesture inviting them to come in.

After visiting Tongolele in El Mercado de Mayoreo that past Wednesday at noon, Pedrón had stayed to talk with Doña Fabiola at her Bello Horizonte home and tried to console her, accepting first one beer and then a second, and he had simultaneously attempted to comfort Professor Zoraida, who remained nailed to her rocker, not responding with a single word or showing interest in anything other than using her feet to swing endlessly back-and-forth. Her own son had refused to speak to her after all she had suffered: she had lost her position as an advisor and been thrown out of her own house. On top of all that, the fact that her son had refused to explain the death of her son-in-law was a very heavy burden, an opinion that Doña Fabiola shared. No heart could possibly withstand the weight of such woes.

And when Pedrón had returned to the customs agency, the major had been pissed off and kept shouting at him about where he'd been and what he'd been doing, but the major's complaints were completely unjustified because he was the one who had given Pedrón permission to leave in the first place. A UAZ SUV from military intelligence had been waiting for Pedrón for quite some time, the major had said, shouting again, and the SUV was in fact sitting there, with a soldier at the wheel and another alongside him. La Chaparra occupied the back seat, and from a distance Pedrón gestured with his head to ask her what was happening, and she put her wrists together and raised them to his view, as if she were wearing handcuffs.

The jolly fat man awaited them at his office, which the two people entered meekly and quietly. The same brilliant yet soft light-green paint covered the walls, but the office seemed more like a classroom because it featured an acrylic blackboard on one wall; student desks with folding chairs arranged around the other walls; a metallic desk at the front; another smaller desk standing alongside the metallic desk, with a laptop and a printer sitting on top; two additional student desks standing before the big desk; and a camera screwed onto a tripod.

The jolly fat man asked them to sit down at the student desks, then took a short, graceful leap to ensconce himself in the big desk and begin to playfully swing his black moccasins, which were so lustrously polished that Pedrón thought he could see himself in them.

The fat man appeared to have arrived recently from a barbershop, with his cheeks and jowls fresh and smooth. He had begun to lose the hair in the middle of his head, and the blubbery folds of his ample gut oozed from beneath the greenish cloth of his everyday uniform: proof that he obviously did little physical exercise. This man had nothing to do with the old guard, the group of historical combatants who were destined for extinction, so skinny and slovenly during those days of triumph, reduced to skeletons from lack of food and reeking from lack of bathwater, the very kind of men who had pointed their guns at Pedrón as he hid in the kitchen pantry at Somoza's Campo de Marte military base. Yes, the jolly fat man belonged to the new crop of army officers who had graduated from the José Dolores Estrada Military Academy, men who received scholarships to study high command not at Havana's Military Command School but either in Saint Cyr, France, or in Mexico's War College. And aside from having been named as a colonel without any intermediate steps or delays, the jolly fat man was a lawyer with a degree in forensic investigation, which he obtained from Brazil's Federal University of Santa Caterina.

He removed a file from the desk and then removed a sheet of paper from the file, which he reviewed. He used a pen to write corrections on the paper. Nothing more than a few questions, that's all, and he'd written them down to ensure that he didn't forget them, especially given how a person's head could become distracted with so much to do, but if some question occurred to him, he'd ask it at the appropriate time. You two don't mind if we make a video recording of you, do you?

Captain Tapia, a stenographer, will transcribe the conversation—and let's not call it an interrogation. As the jolly fat man was speaking, Captain Tapia entered the room, wearing a military uniform and cap along with frameless eyeglasses that were almost invisible, her lips painted in pastel pink. She sat down in front of the computer screen and was followed by a cameraman and a soundman, likewise dressed in military uniforms and caps. The first took his place behind the camera, while the second carried a case filled with lapel microphones and moved closer to the two declarants: he attached one microphone to the mouth on Pedrón's Bob Marley t-shirt; and he affixed another to La Chaparra's guayabera collar. He then gave the jolly fat man a hand-held microphone with a foam-rubber cover.

"We're ready," said the jolly fat man, pointing the microphone at Pedrón and La Chaparra. "I want you to talk carefully and in great detail. Please don't spare any words. Either of you may answer the questions, and you should feel free to expand upon or complete any answer given by the other if you believe that answer to be insufficient. Captain Tapia is experienced, and she will provide an accurate transcription. As I've already explained to you, this meeting is a conversation, not an interrogation, and you are not here as accused criminals, so I'm counting on your full and honest cooperation."

Throughout this speech, sweat formed on Pedrón's groin and pooled between his butt cheeks, and he wanted to move around because the sweat made him itch, but the back of the student desk was too high. Witnesses cloistered and forced to testify were no different than accused criminals. So, was the army now sitting in judgment? And as for the jolly fat man, was he a judge or a prosecutor? But Pedrón was there to answer questions, not ask them.

"Each of you will now identify yourselves, please, stating your first name, last name, age, marital status, military rank, and current assignment," the jolly fat man commanded.

Pedro Claver Salvatierra Moreno, age 63, single, captain in the National Police Force, assigned to the General Directorate of State Security. His voice was practically a whisper, like a broken clay whistle, and the sound barely escaped his parched throat, which was dry from the lack of saliva. The jolly fat man then made a gesture, and people brought small bottles of water for everyone present.

In contrast, La Chaparra's voice was smooth, articulate, almost melodious: Yasica del Socorro Benavides Mairena, age 38, single, first lieutenant in the National Police Force, assigned as personal assistant to Commissioner Anastasio Prado in the General Directorate of State Security.

"Well done!" exclaimed the jolly fat man, as if praising a rehearsal for a children's theater production. "Except that from now on we'll refer to Prado as Ex-Commissioner Prado, and his name will appear as such throughout the transcription."

The declarants expressed their acceptance of the foregoing statement.

"And now, given that we're all alone here and we're free to speak in confidence," the jolly fat man continued, "how would you describe the relationship between you and Captain Salvatierra, Lieutenant Benavides? You may remain silent if you choose."

Lieutenant Benavides stated that she had no reservations about answering the question asked, and she continued by declaring that she and Captain Salvatierra had had a romantic relationship for many years, the result of which was a son named Daniel del Rosario, but she added that due to mutual agreement she and the captain did not cohabitate under the same roof, which statement Captain Salvatierra confirmed.

"Now tell me, lieutenant: By whose order or decision did you two carry out your plan to divulge information from the agency where you work, given that such information was classified?"

Lieutenant Benavides answered that she and Captain Salvatierra conceived and executed the plan together without anyone else's participation and that their access to the agency's files facilitated the plan's implementation, aided by the flow of information that necessarily passed through each other's hands.

COLONEL PASTRANA: I want each of you to tell me what motivated you to join together in creating the plan that is the subject of this investigation.

LIEUTENANT BENAVIDES: The declarant answered that despite having worked so many years alongside Ex-Commissioner Prado and having always given her best effort without ever giving a thought to her schedule, including placing her work responsibilities above the family duties related to caring for her own son, her supervisor never showed any support for or inclination toward helping the declarant's career development, to such a degree that she was never promoted beyond the rank of first lieutenant that she received upon beginning her government service. She added that the presidency had granted her the Medal of Fidelity despite the fact that her supervisor never answered the official request for particulars about why she had earned the medal.

CAPTAIN SALVATIERRA: The declarant stated that he was hurt most deeply by how Ex-Commissioner Prado treated him with gross contempt, repeatedly subjecting the declarant to constant humiliation by making him the butt of the most degrading jokes. The declarant further noted that another reason behind his frustration and outrage was that that the ex-commissioner used him to conduct personal affairs and private business, essentially converting the declarant into a personal servant, obligating him to fulfill the whims and demands of the ex-commissioner's lover,

Fabiola Miranda, as well as those of his mother, the so-called Professor Zoraida.

COLONEL PASTRANA: I want you two to explain why you chose the drawing of the mask used by the character known as Vengeance to create anonymity for what you did: leak secret documents.

LIEUTENANT BENAVIDES: The declarant stated that she initiated the scheme because her work necessarily required her to become familiar with digital information. As a result, she had closely followed the hacker network that has conducted massive cyber-attacks in different parts of the world, a network that has protected its identity by using the mask of the character to whom Colonel Pastrana referred.

COLONEL PASTRANA: After reviewing the leaks to which you yourselves have confessed, I found that they address highly varied subjects. I'll ask about them one by one.

You two claim that Ex-Commissioner Prado bears responsibility for the attack in which the parish priest of Ocotal, Monseñor Bienvenido Ortez, suffered a head injury, and yet you made this claim knowing that the attack wasn't ordered by the agency under the ex-commissioner's command at the time, but rather by other agencies assigned to intelligence matters. Furthermore, upon revealing the attacker's identity and residence, you put him at risk, along with two high officials in the National Police Force who are publicly known as employers of said attacker.

LIEUTENANT BENAVIDES: The declarant answered that while it is true that the attack had nothing to do with Ex-Commissioner Prado, the impetus behind the accusation was to create the impression that he was in fact responsible, for the same reasons that both she and Captain Salvatierra had already explained. As for the man who carried out the attack, she stated that both she and Captain Salvatierra were confident that his employers would take all immediate steps necessary to remove him permanently from the residence that had been posted online.

COLONEL PASTRANA: The next case, which occurred before the previous one, concerns a deterrent operation ordered by the agency under Ex-Commissioner Prado's command. That operation, carried out against a person very close to Monseñor Ortez, was meant to discourage the monseñor's hostile activities. Both of you compromised the agency in that case.

LIEUTENANT BENAVIDES: The declarant responded that the objective was to expose Ex-Commissioner Prado's lack of control over information concerning his agency's operations and thereby demonstrate the unreliability of a person who cannot prevent leaks of such information to the public. Such leaks obviously represented a risk to the agency itself, but because the leaks would free the agency from obsolete and corrupt leadership, the declarant and Captain Salvatierra considered their posts a strategic move to preserve the agency in the long run.

COLONEL PASTRANA: Now we have the exposure of the Vatican's decision to transfer Monseñor Ortez to Rome. This case is especially delicate because it involves leaking government decisions at the highest political levels. Papal authorities could have used that leak to modify or annul those decisions to the detriment of the revolutionary government's interests.

LIEUTENANT BENAVIDES: The declarant answered that the decision to make that leak came about by chance, given that she received the leak's content through personal channels. In other words, she did not learn about the Monseñor Ortez transfer through classified documents. The declarant added that if the leak had any purpose at all, that purpose was to mislead the intermediaries who posted the messages to the public. That is, the declarant hoped that the intermediaries would incorrectly believe that the leaker actually represented a large gamut of sources that were not necessarily connected to the government's intelligence apparatus, a mistaken belief that would lead the intermediaries to depend upon diplomatic resources and agencies. Regardless, that information was going to go public very soon.

COLONEL PASTRANA: We'll move on to the fourth message. The objectives behind that leak are clearer to me because you both had the ultimate goal of having Ex-Commissioner Prado terminated from his position. Accusing him of homicide for personal reasons and exposing the range of his private businesses fall within your objectives. But Captain Salvatierra, you yourself were the person in charge of arranging the deceased Lázaro Chicas' neutralization, and you can't avoid responsibility for that.

CAPTAIN SALVATIERRA: As the declarant had done before, he re-iterated his statement that he felt obligated to follow Ex-Commissioner Prado's orders regardless of their official or private character. He further noted that the colonel should remember that he was a subordinate prohibited from questioning his commanding officer's orders, regardless of the official or unofficial nature of those orders.

COLONEL PASTRANA: The scanned photos and documents that accompanied the packages of written materials and posted on the Twitter account known as The Mask were taken from the intelligence agency to which you both belong. However, such is not the case for the photo of the dead Lázaro Chicas' corpse. That photo was taken at the morgue of the Medical Examiner's Institute. I require an explanation from each of you.

CAPTAIN SALVATIERRA: The declarant stated that he himself had used his cell phone to take the photo in question after giving the morgue's duty attendant 1000 córdobas to convince him to open the correct drawer. He had also warned the attendant not to record anything about his actions in the corresponding registry.

COLONEL PASTRANA: Concerning the affair that this authority is investigating, the most difficult part to understand concerns your decision to use intermediaries to promulgate the information. That decision alone seems odd, if not poorly thought-out. But the fact that those intermediaries created a Twitter account for that very purpose, acting exactly as you hoped they would, compels me to assume that they had had prior contact and an agreement with you.

LIEUTENANT BENAVIDES: The declarant avowed that the intermediaries were chosen for the reasons that Captain Salvatierra would soon describe. She added that for her part, she had no prior communication with the intermediaries, which is why there was no certainty that the intermediaries would actually post the information at issue.

As a result, if the intermediaries had not paid attention to the first messages, the declarant and Captain Salvatierra would not have sent them the succeeding messages. If such had been the case, the back-up plan was that the declarant would nevertheless have used a disguised online site to publish the messages, although she understood that doing so would have necessarily increased the risk of discovery.

At this point, the investigating authority gave the floor to Captain Salvatierra.

CAPTAIN SALVATIERRA: The declarant intervened to state that Ex-Commissioner Prado had ordered that Inspector Dolores Morales, whom the National Police Force had discharged some time ago, be exiled from our nation's territory to the neighboring republic of Honduras, along with an individual named Serafín Manzanares, alias "Rambo." The two men had therefore been taken overland to the border town of Las Manos. A third man, Hermógenes Galeano, also known as the "King of the Vultures," had been transported in the same vehicle as the other two men, although Galeano was exiled for different reasons.

Furthermore, because standard operating procedure required surveillance of the exiled men, observers determined that while Galeano took the road to Tegucigalpa, the other two men stayed at the border and procured the services of an individual named Genaro Ortez, who guided them secretly back to Nicaragua. By pure coincidence, this individual was already under special surveillance so that watchers could learn when he would return to his home in Dipilto Viejo, which he normally did via the road through the village of San Roque, where the neutralization operation previously described today was planned to take place.

Moreover, after the operation was completed, the two exiles remained under constant watch throughout their journey, so the intelligence agency always knew their location: the place in Dipilto Verde where they stayed with the neutralized man's sister, Edelmira Ortez, and asked for transportation; and the parish house for the church within this city where the men took refuge under the priest Bienvenido Ortez's protection, this fact having been confirmed by a source for the intelligence agency who infiltrated the aforementioned priest Ortez's circle long ago.

The declarant continued by stating that this same source allowed investigators to determine the exact date and time that the two previously mentioned exiles began their return to Managua. The source also provided the exiles' final destination. This last bit of knowledge was essential to executing the declarants' plan, because by the time Ex-Inspector Morales reached his journey's end, the first message was already there waiting for him, and he wasted no time giving it to his collaborator of many years, Señora Sofía Smith.

The declarant explained that the exiles were kept under watch throughout their trip to Managua and that a priest, Octavio Pupiro, accompanied them the entire way. They passed some time in Sébaco due to the disturbances caused by coup-leading vandals protesting efforts to erect the Trees of Life. When police officers used tear gas to end the disturbances, all three men took refuge in the house of Señora Jaqueline Arauz, the owner of a women's clothing store called Modas Jaqueline.

The declarant pointed out that from this moment forward, Ex-Commissioner Prado stopped paying attention to the activities and location of the exiled men, and he paid them no further attention except as an afterthought and in incidental ways.

COLONEL PASTRANA: Then explain to me your reasons for choosing Ex-Inspector Morales and his assistant, Señora Sofía Smith, as intermediaries.

CAPTAIN SALVATIERRA: The declarant responded that the choice flowed from a meticulous analysis, which revealed that the first person mentioned, Ex-Inspector Morales, had sufficient motives to participate in a campaign that would damage Ex-Commissioner Prado, given that the latter had exiled him from the country, said exile arranged to benefit the patriotic businessman Miguel Soto as a result of the ex-inspector's involvement in a case that the declarant assumed was already known to the investigating authority. As for Señora Sofía Smith, Ex-Inspector Morales' faithful assistant, she was chosen because she is a woman of acute intelligence with great curiosity about social media networks, and the declarants anticipated that the ex-inspector would seek her help to disseminate the leaks. To encourage her to do so, the second message was sent directly to her.

COLONEL PASTRANA: Given that both declarants are professional intelligence officers, there is another issue in this case that seems strange, if not downright confusing. That issue is the selection of the courier to deliver the messages into the intermediaries' hands.

LIEUTENANT BENAVIDES: The declarant answered that circumstances required the plan to be executed while it was in progress, which demanded a certain degree of improvisation, but all such improvisation had to be employed without compromising the plan's confidentiality limits or the degree to which the person selected needed to be trusted. That was the reason for choosing Comrade Magdalena Castilla, whose loyalty and discretion the declarant could guarantee.

COLONEL PASTRANA: The person you describe was your own domestic helper, and according to the intelligence agency's personnel records and notes, she was hired as a cleaning lady in the main office upon your recommendation and received the rank of corporal, but after some time she was fired due to her penchant for alcoholic beverages. On top of that, this woman delegated the delivery of some of the messages at issue here to her son, a minor who does not attend school and has been arrested for several misdemeanors, according to police records. But let's move on to another topic.

The online leaks of classified information that appeared during the past few days attracted the attention of the military-intelligence branch, which is why we began the investigation that led us to the two of you. But that is not why I was ordered to go to the offices under Ex-Commissioner Prado's responsibility; instead, I was sent to replace him for reasons unrelated to that investigation.

So tell me, why didn't you stop your campaign when you learned that Ex-Commissioner Prado had been relieved of his duties? Didn't his loss of command satisfy both of your wishes, thereby making further leaks and their attendant risks to national security unnecessary?

LIEUTENANT BENAVIDES: The declarant answered that the message in question, which was sent after Ex-Commissioner Prado was relieved of his duties, accomplished two goals. First, the message denounced his use of agency means and logistics to consummate the liquidation of personal accounts. Second, the message exposed the ex-commissioner's personal business activities, which he created using corrupt methods contrary to the revolution's creed.

The declarants concluded that for the foregoing reasons, the above-referenced information needed to come to light. For despite the fact that Ex-Commissioner Prado had lost his command, they did not know whether that loss was temporary or permanent, and their hope was that it be permanent.

COLONEL PASTRANA: I'm not referring to the fourth message, which nevertheless raises deep concerns. Here in my file I have another message, which was published at 7:00 p.m. today as part of a tweet, listed as number five in this file. I will read it to you now:

As our citizens have seen with their own eyes today, they now know that hordes of paramilitary soldiers are walking the streets freely and killing innocent people in an operation code-named Abate. The paramilitary commander is a man that the government raised up from infamy, and sadly he is none other than the famous Leónidas, a man the government originally called a traitor and is now using to commit crimes, for today alone his hosts of assassins have murdered at least twenty young people, according to human-rights commissions' lists of first and last names, and many of those killed were the victims of snipers, who shot them this afternoon from atop Dennis Martínez National Stadium. These soldiers have been divided into six squads known as "task forces," who gathered together at that same stadium very early this morning. Squad members wear face-coverings and t-shirts, and the shirts' color identifies each squad's zone of operations.

Also, the government has placed Tongolele under Leónidas' command. This is a strange thing because Tongolele used to be the head of all the government's killers, and now he's second-class. But he's not happy about this situation at all and he believes the government has demoted him by making him subordinate to a traitor. He has been given command of one of the "task forces," and his thugs can be identified by their yellow t-shirts. Tongolele is in command of 120 men, who were recruited from among the most fanatical and depraved classes, and he has divided his glorious "task force" into four groups so that they can spread blood and fire in the eastern section of El Mercado de Mayoreo. A vacant supply warehouse serves as his command post, located at the rear of El Mercado de Mayoreo. The government has given him cute new Hilux pick-ups, AK-47s, and Dragunov rifles for his snipers.

But Tongolele's soldiers haven't limited themselves to committing murder, no. They have also kidnapped and raped women, such as happened today about 9:00 this morning, when the yellow-clad men went to the university rotunda and kidnapped a female medical student whose case we are passing along to the human-rights commissions. The group who committed this crime are under the direct command of a despicable swine named Marcial Duarte and more commonly known by the horrible nickname C — a de C — o. And they didn't just kidnap the young woman, no. In addition to the kidnapping, every single one of those savages raped her after taking her to a secluded place on the road to the San Isidro de Bolas region, exactly 2.5 kilometers off the main highway.

More to come in future messages.

LIEUTENANT BENAVIDES: Having just had the foregoing message read to her, the declarant voiced her surprise at its contents for two reasons. In the first place, she knew nothing about the activities reported in the message because she knew nothing about where Ex-Commissioner Prado had gone after he was relieved of his command. Second, she knew nothing about the character or the logistics of the operation designed to restore public order as the message described.

COLONEL PASTRANA: Captain Salvatierra, according to the reports I've received, I understand that at noon today you visited Ex-Commissioner Prado in his command post in El Mercado de Mayoreo. Two people accompanied you on that visit: the ex-commissioner's widowed mother, an individual known as Josefa Viuda de Prado; and an individual known as Fabiola Miranda, the ex-commissioner's lover and business partner.

CAPTAIN SALVATIERRA: The declarant, who had also read the aforementioned message, acknowledged that he had in fact visited Ex-Commissioner Prado after orally requesting permission to leave the agency's offices from the appropriate officer, which permission was granted.

COLONEL PASTRANA: As a result, you were in a position to observe how Ex-Commissioner Prado deployed the soldiers under his command as well as the weapons, means of transportation, and the soldiers' clothing and emblems, all as described in the leak posted online.

CAPTAIN SALVATIERRA: The declarant stated that while he did visit the place described and observed a few dozen soldiers at ease, the only things he could actually verify as true were as follows: the soldiers were indeed armed with automatic weapons and dressed in yellow t-shirts. Beyond these observations, however, he could not calculate how many soldiers were under Ex-Commissioner Prado's command, particularly given that the remaining soldiers were away from the command post at the time. Furthermore, the declarant had even fewer means to learn exactly how many soldiers were dispersed across the city or that those soldiers served under Comandante Leónidas. Finally, the declarant noted that he had no means at all to hear about isolated events such as the rape of the female student described in the message.

COLONEL PASTRANA: I understand that you have a personal, intimate, and permanent relationship with Ex-Commissioner Prado. Therefore, I ask you to state whether it is true that during your noonday conversation with him in the aforementioned place, the ex-commissioner told you about the following things: the number and composition of the forces under his command; the initial gathering of all forces within the national stadium; the high-command structure for the operation known under the code-name Abate; the division of troops organized into six task forces assigned to different regions of Managua; and the task forces' weapons, equipment, emblems, logistics, and combat resources.

CAPTAIN SALVATIERRA: The declarant responded that Ex-Commissioner Prado never told him anything about military plans or their implementation. The declarant further avowed that regardless, the noonday visit essentially consisted of only a very brief conversation between the ex-commissioner and Señora Fabiola Miranda, who had a genuine and urgent desire to talk with her business partner and lover. The declarant stated that one could say that the ex-commissioner's mother had a desire similar to that of Señora Miranda, but he noted parenthetically that the ex-commissioner refused to speak with his mother.

COLONEL PASTRANA: In addition, state whether it is true that during that same conversation, Ex-Commissioner Prado provided you details about a case involving a lack of discipline among members of a task force under his command, who decided on their own to kidnap a female medical student and, allegedly, subject her to sexual abuse.

CAPTAIN SALVATIERRA: The declarant denied that the foregoing was true and stated that he was willing to have a face-to-face confrontation to ensure that Ex-Commissioner Prado fully corroborate the fact that he never told the declarant anything about the case nor anything concerning the prior allegation.

COLONEL PASTRANA: State that it is true, as in fact it is, that during the aforementioned conversation, Ex-Commissioner Prado complained in your presence that he opposed his assignment to serve under Comandante Silverio Pérez, known by his war pseudonym of "Leónidas," because he felt disrespected and humiliated, a fact maliciously revealed in the document that I've given you to read and that this investigative authority believes you two wrote together, absent evidence to the contrary.

CAPTAIN SALVATIERRA: The declarant stated that while he readily acknowledged that Ex-Commissioner Prado voiced these complaints, he did so earlier—yesterday, to be exact, last Tuesday night, when the investigative authority questioning him here, acting on behalf of the General Directorate of State Security, ordered the declarant to drive the ex-commissioner to a new location, a plantation in the Chiquilistagua region known as the Quinceañera, where Comandante Leónidas himself awaited their arrival.

COLONEL PASTRANA: The declarant acknowledges, then, and the fact is therefore proved, that he knew about Ex-Commissioner Prado's complaints, exactly as they appear in the aforementioned message posted on social media.

CAPTAIN SALVATIERRA: The declarant stated that he acknowledged that he knew about Ex-Commissioner Prado's complaints, but he also stated that he never revealed the content of that conversation to anyone, and he reiterated that he had nothing to do with the aforementioned tweet.

COLONEL PASTRANA: Lieutenant Benavides must affirm that it is true, as in fact it is, that she is the person who sent the intermediaries the aforementioned information, which intermediaries proceeded to post on social media, following the pattern of prior occasions.

LIEUTENANT BENAVIDES: The declarant avowed that she never sent anyone the aforementioned information. She further declared that she never managed to send the final message she wrote to the person who acted as her courier. She added that she had a USB drive on her person that contained all the prior messages she had sent, and as a show of good faith she proceeded to hand the drive over, stating that an examination of the drive would prove that it did not contain the message described by the investigative authority.

As additional proof of her good faith, the declarant hastened to explain that the final message she had mentioned sought to reveal that Ex-Commissioner Prado's mother, who calls herself Professor Zoraida, was nothing but a charlatan who—contrary to her claims—had no education in the area of spiritual and esoteric arts, and that she had never been a disciple of Sai Baba, with whom she feigned to communicate through encounters in the astral planes. Professor Zoraida's claims that the Trees of Life had magnetic protective powers were likewise false—as the coup leaders' attacks on the streets proved. In fact, Professor Zoraida's actions indicated that the enemy had used her to infiltrate the government and thereby damage and disparage the revolution.

COLONEL PASTRANA: Let the record show that the device provided by the declarant has been added to the file, and at this point the declarant herself will explain the circumstances that prevented her from delivering the above-referenced message to the person who acted as courier.

LIEUTENANT BENAVIDES: As requested, the declarant explained that when she went to the home of Comrade Castilla in this city's La Fuente neighborhood, she was surprised to find that the intermediary, Señora Sofía Smith, was already there. The declarant later discovered that Comrade Castilla's minor son had guided the intermediary to the house.

COLONEL PASTRANA: Based upon your explanation, I must conclude that Señora Sofía Smith had followed the trail of your messages and identified the couriers. Accordingly, she was in a position to recognize you upon catching you in the act of trying to deliver a new message.

LIEUTENANT BENAVIDES: The declarant avowed that she had never had any personal interaction with Señora Sofía Smith and therefore did not consider the woman capable of recognizing her.

COLONEL PASTRANA: The fact should be obvious to you that you are facing a person of proven shrewdness, "a woman of acute intelligence" in the words of Captain Salvatierra, your accomplice in this scheme. As a consequence, you can be certain that this woman has clearly identified you by now and that she has likewise identified the agency for whom you and your life partner have been working until this time, compromising our national security yet again.

At this point the investigative authority stated that he had no more questions concerning the present case and proceeded to have his preliminary conclusions written down, said conclusions impeding in no way the possibility that others could be added later, once the file had been studied in greater detail:

> *First:* Sufficient proof exists to charge both witnesses as primary suspects in leaking classified information they were obligated to keep confidential, making them accomplices in a conspiracy that has compromised the security of the agency provisionally assigned to my command.
>
> *Second:* The General Directorate of State Security no longer requires the services of the two suspects because they lack the suitability and trustworthiness necessary to retain the positions they have filled to this time.
>
> *Third:* An expedited recommendation will be sent to higher authorities to the effect that the two suspects be discharged and forced to retire.
>
> *Fourth:* Both suspects shall remain available to this investigative authority, and they will therefore appear before this authority whenever requested for any later investigations. For these reasons, the suspects are prohibited from moving from their residences and leaving the city limits.

The jolly fat man ordered the video recording to stop. The cameraman left in silence. The participants' lapel microphones were removed, and the soundman disappeared with his case. Captain Tapia, without removing her cap, watched the printer work as it spit out the transcript's papers.

Once the transcript was ready, the jolly fat man placed the stacked papers on the desktop before La Chaparra.

"Just one simple signature here, on the last page, and we'll be done," he said. "Captain Tapia is an artist when it comes to transcripts like these, and I don't even bother to read them because I already know that what they say is precisely correct."

La Chaparra signed the page, and Pedrón did so afterward, dwarfing the pen in his bulky hand, which resembled that of a retired boxer. The jolly fat man was the last to sign his name, bending over the desk as he remained on his feet.

"Can you drop us off somewhere?" Pedrón asked. "It's very late, and given the conditions in the streets…"

The jolly fat man raised his head, enjoying the act of signing each page, and he gave Pedrón a very serious look, although his face appeared to be at the point of bursting into laughter.

"You can hail a taxi at the corner," he said, continuing to sign pages. "There's nothing to fear. Order on the streets has been completely restored."

CHAPTER FIFTEEN

The Divine Mercy Church under Fire

T HE TIME WAS MIDNIGHT on Saturday, the third day after the attacks against the Jesus of Divine Mercy Church, and Padre Pancho, after returning from the kitchen carrying a new cup of coffee, sat down once again before the cathode-tube monitor of the ancient computer, which took forever to boot up. The priest's pig-headed fingers continually mis-spelled words because they hit the wrong keys, some of which—to make things worse—stuck in place after each stroke. Furthermore, because the priest wrote rapidly and used only his index fingers to type, he grew more and more furious with himself for the number of errors littering the page.

At the request of the vicar general of the Presbyteral Council of the Managua Diocese, Padre Pancho was preparing a draft report in the name of the archbishop, and he was struggling to separate the facts he needed to include in the official report from the private reflections that he would keep to himself, reflections that for now he was leaving in parentheses:

Your Most Reverend Eminence:
Per my role as priest for the Jesus of Divine Mercy Church, which responsibility I received from the archdiocese under the authority of Your Eminence, pursuant to the accord signed with the provincial superior for the Society of Jesus, I am writing to fulfill the command to provide a report about the events that occurred in my church, which report describes those events from the time they began until they ended at sunrise on Thursday of this week:
At approximately 11:00 on Wednesday night, paramilitary forces began an armed attack on the National University's grounds, located but a stone's throw from my church. Through blood and

fire, the attack sought to disperse students who had taken over the university buildings as part of a protest.

Aware of the intense gunfire, I observed the attack from the parish house's living room along with my gardener, hereafter known as Don Artemio; and my gardener's assistant, hereafter known as Don Serafín. Our party also included a visitor, Señora Sofía Smith, who could not possibly return to her home given the dangerous circumstances. Two other people forced to be my guests were also present in the house: Señorita Lastenia Robleto, leader of the guild that manages the altar and devotional activities for Padre Pío de Pietrelcina; and the señorita's niece, a student named Eneida Robleta, who is completing her last year of study in medicine, a diligent and exemplary young woman for whom I have long felt great affection and provided support in her studies. A gang of paramilitary soldiers had kidnapped and viciously raped Eneida early that same day, and I gave her my own bedroom so that she could rest, thanks to a powerful dose of tranquilizers prescribed by a physician.

We found ourselves together that way, stretched out on the floor and careful to stay in the dark, filled with worry as we listened to the intensifying gunfire without being able to do more, while Don Artemio, who has some experience with weapons in his past and lost a leg in combat, tried to explain to me what he called firepower and cadence of fire, subjects I understand very little; but at that moment, if I managed to perceive anything at all, I heard almost constant shooting with almost no answering shots, except for the sporadic sound of some low-caliber hunting rifle or some revolver, to the degree that Don Artemio was able to identify the weapons.

The explosions detonated so close to us that their echoes shook the house's window glass, and the offensive was obviously designed to progress through the campus's various entry gates, along the front of which students had erected barricades using cobblestones from the pavement, having done the same across the adjacent side streets. My greatest fear was that the attackers had already broken through those barricades, destroying any resistance that could have been nothing but weak and ineffective against the attacking forces' superior and vastly more numerous weapons, according to Don Artemio's experienced judgment.

Due to the noise and confusion from the detonations, which lasted for a very long time, we did not immediately realize that someone was furiously and insistently knocking on the door. When Doña Sofía asked who was there, a voice answered that he was a student, and after Doña Sofía opened the door, we saw a young man on the threshold, whom I will hereafter call Tigrillo to protect his life, and he had come to see me. I stood up to welcome him and met an extremely skinny boy wearing tattered clothes, who told me that one of his friends was lying in the far-west section of the church-yard, adjacent to the university grounds. The boy had been shot in the head by a sniper round, and Tigrillo and some of the other boys had carried him there on the detached door of a bathroom stall, because they didn't have a stretcher.

I urged the student to have his friends bring the wounded boy inside, and then I went to turn on the lights and look for the first-aid kit; meanwhile, Doña Sofía began to start some water boiling in the kitchen, and next we all moved the furniture out of the way to create a space on the floor for the door on which the young man—a boy who could not have been twenty years old—was ly-ing, his torso uncovered and his head pillowed on his shirt, which was stained with the same dark blood that also soaked his head. One of the female students in the group was a nursing student, and she held up a saline bag that had been connected to the wounded boy's arm, because the students had taken some medical supplies to create a place to provide an aid station. At that point I gestured for Don Serafín to go to my bedroom and look for my old clothes rack, and we hung the saline bag on one of its hooks.

But perhaps because Encida, the abused student, had been awak-ened from sleep when Don Serafín went searching for the clothes rack, thereby enabling her to discover what was happening; or per-haps because Eneida had already been awakened by the gunshots and had therefore heard the cacophony of voices inside the house, the fact of the matter is that she suddenly appeared in the living room, not sleepy at all, and approached the wounded boy directly to examine him, after which she pulled me aside and told me that the boy's condition was desperate because the bullet had fractured his skull, exposing his brain matter, and the only thing we could do was to add some tramadol—a medication the nursing student had with her—to the saline bag to make the boy's death somewhat less painful. I therefore put on my stole and knelt beside the boy to administer his last rites.

(The boy's name was Allan, according to what Tigrillo told me after I finished the ritual kiss of the stole, and I felt as if his voice and the other voices were coming from a far-off place that I wasn't familiar with, or perhaps I wasn't the person listening but rather someone foreign and distant from me, and I wondered who this listener was, this other person who heard the repeated pounding of the muffled blasts that had begun one after the other again, each one hungry for the other as if they were biting into each other with every bark; or maybe I was the one who heard the question from the nursing student, who continued watching over Allan, when she asked if we could still operate on him because his pulse felt fine to her and his breathing was calm. But Eneida subtly nodded no, as if she feared that the dying boy would notice her hopeless gesture.

(According to Tigrillo, his eyes burning with fury, Allan had remained prostrate on the sidewalk for thirty minutes after his friends removed his wounded body from the barricade, waiting for an ambulance that never arrived because no one would allow it to pass no matter how much the driver made the siren wail. And Tigrillo seemed to blame Allan when he said that despite every warning, Allan insisted on sticking his head out from behind the parapet because he was anxious to see whether the paramilitary troops had already taken the nearby barricade, and Tigrillo added that Allan was studying construction methods and paying his expenses by selling smoothies under the campus's pedestrian bridge, where he had a stand with plastic cups, a blender, a block of ice, a punch to chip the ice, and a supply of fresh strawberries, mangos, bananas, and papayas; furthermore, Allan was an incorrigible folk-dancer, and there was no one who could perform the marimba-driven black dance better than he; and when Tigrillo realized that he was talking about Allan in the past tense he wiped away the tears that he had not noticed until that moment, and then his face became as enraged as before, and that's when I spotted a pistol in the belt under his shirt tail because he moved to adjust the gun, which tended to slip down off his waist due to his boney frame.

(This Tigrillo—who spouts torrents of words, harsh expletives, and insults filled with unlimited creativity against those he calls the Tutankhamens of the revolution, male and female mummies whom we must send back to their corresponding sarcaphogus via express mail or special delivery, he says—is a nervous type, and I was not surprised that he quickly used up the pack of Ducados that I offered him. And on one occasion among many, as if probing an issue first and then resolving it, he asked me if I feared death. I answered—not without a bit of petulance, I confess—that I would respond by quoting the infamously profane Quevedo, who was not a father of the Church: "[D]eath has a better entourage than birth, for death follows life, and resurrection follows death." Tigrillo paid no attention to my answer at all, and instead showed me the sutures in his cranium, the place where a sniper's bullet had grazed the nape of his neck, and he then told me he did not fear death but rather having his life cut short before he could put an end to all the Tutankhamens.)

I was surprised to hear that a sniper could hit a person's head so accurately in the middle of the night, as in Allan's case, but Don Artemio explained to me that Dragunov rifles, along with their Venezulan-made twins, the Catatumbos, were high-precision weapons equipped with night-vision scopes that allowed them to hit their targets over long distances; and I wish to emphasize this point among the many things I am telling Your Eminence so that they can be denounced as contrary to all humanity before the nations of the world.

We were in a difficult situation as numerous people walked in and out of the living room's narrow space, creating disarray. Then, Don Serafín asked me to accompany him outside to show me that the yard was filling up as large groups of people emerged from many different areas among the shadows by climbing over the fence and breaking through the gates. Leading the way were students—some of them gunshot victims—who were approaching the house, helped and supported by their friends; other students came coughing and vomiting, exhibiting the effects of tear-gas grenades, while yet others arrived sobbing, holding each other as they experienced nervous breakdowns. The truth is that all these students' desire to fight had been broken, and they were now withdrawing from the hunt that had been announced campus-wide, a hunt that progressed as paramilitary groups shot into buildings to make the remaining students abandon their hiding places, the flames visible from above the trees.

A large variety of people were mixed among the escaping students. These people had been trapped for hours in neighboring streets under the hailstorm of bullets, and they included pedestrians and street vendors, vehicle drivers and passengers, along with reporters dispatched to cover the events, and there were still other people—neighbors and my parishioners—who claimed that they felt safer in the church than in their homes, particularly given that snipers had taken position on several of these visitors' roofs. And there was yet another group of visitors in a similar situation: paramedics who had answered students' social-media pleas for first aid; these first responders were at the church because the paramilitary groups had kicked them out of their improvised care stations.

I then took the urgent measure of ordering the church doors to be opened, which the guild leader, Señorita Lastenia, did along with Doña Sofía's help, and we brought the wounded people inside, and then we allowed the refugees to go in as well, although many chose to camp outside in the yard.

We put the wounded on the pews, the chancel steps, and the bare floor, and we placed the most seriously injured in the sacristy. From the beginning, our problem was a lack of medications and treatment supplies because the paramedics had so little, even after adding what we had from the church's first-aid kit. This limitation severely hindered our efforts to stitch and bandage wounds, although we got creative and used common thread and torn bedsheets, plus altar coverings and packing boxes for splints.

Suddenly, a motorcycle burst in, having obviously avoided the lookouts by following a path that crossed the center of the university's borders. The cycle was carrying three riders—two young men supporting a wounded one between them. I later learned that like me, the victim's name was Francisco. Immediately upon braking to a halt, the driver told me that his friend's situation was serious, because like Allan, he had been shot in the head while running away from the barricade he had been defending. That barricade had been the last to fall.

I told the driver to take the boy to the parish house, where Doña

Sofía quickly cleared the dining-room table to lay him there, although the table wasn't big enough because the boy was so tall that his legs extended beyond the edges. Eneida went over to examine him, but after doing so she said that he likewise had no chance to survive because according to her observations, he had lost too much blood. And sure enough, the boy died thereafter, so I had no time to administer the last rites, while Allan survived a little bit longer.

After these events, I was walking back to the church when the electricity abruptly cut out, and we found ourselves in darkness. This blackout served as an attack signal: countless bullets began hitting all around us, and the people who had been in the yard ran for refuge within the nave, which provided poor protection from the storm of projectiles that shattered the stained-glass windows. In addition, bursts of gunfire smashed into the main altar's painting of Jesus of Divine Mercy, which became a sieve, as Your Eminence must already have seen in the photos and videos that have been made public, along with the numerous bullet holes in the outside walls.

Gunfire came from the nearby streets, and gunshots targeted the parish house as well, according to the report that Doña Sofía gave me at the church. Doña Sofía demonstrated great bravery by acting as a messenger between the two buildings in the darkness. She came to tell me that Allan had just died. He passed shortly after people had moved him to my bedroom because nothing remained of the living room's blinds, leaving the house's entire interior open to snipers.

This moment was when I decided to call Your Eminence for aid, because the only way to prevent more deaths and injuries was for that attack to cease. If the paramilitary units had already used despicable means to accomplish their objective to force students to abandon their hiding places at the university, the attack on the church was even more despicable and sacrilegious as well.

(Hiding on the floor next to the great altar, with Doña Sofía protected by my side, I dialed the cardinal's personal number while watching the burning sparks ricochet as bullets crashed into the altar slab and bounced off the floor's pavers. But no one picked up the phone, and the answering machine sent me to voicemail, and the mailbox said that it was full. I kept trying to call at intervals that seemed to become eternal. I wondered if perhaps the cardinal had his phone on silent. I wondered if perhaps he was asleep, but then I thought that there was no way in hell that he could possibly be asleep.

(Then the gunfire came to a halt. In the dark, all I could see were glowing cell screens, like lanterns in a shadowy forest. And now, Your Eminence, at this point I beg your forgiveness for waxing poetic, given that we live in a country where destiny has left us exposed to the muse's contagion, but I wanted to tell the cardinal to answer my phone call right then, and I would have said you can't sleep under these circumstances, and you have no right to sleep.

(Beside me was a young female law student, probably around 18 years old, her face half-illuminated by her cell screen, which she did not hold to her ear but rather before her face as she spoke. She was talking intensely with someone—her mother or her boyfriend, for all I know—and vowing that she would not be taken alive when the paramilitary soldiers entered the church. And when she finished, I didn't apologize for my bad manners in listening to her phone conversation; instead, I told her to please have faith, that all would be well with us because the Lord would not abandon us, and I asked for her to pray together with us.

(Where was the Lord yesterday, she asked me, when the paramilitary soldiers kidnapped her and took her to a torture chamber, where they tore out her toenails with pliers? Where was the Lord when they stuck a lamp attached to a wooden block in her vagina and then her rectum, while all of her stupid torturers demanded that she tell them who was financing the coup? Where was the Lord when the soldiers threw her nude into a garbage dump along the shore of the lake near the Acahualinca area? A wagon driver and his son had discovered her among the mounds of garbage, where they customarily searched for things they considered valuable by ripping open the black-plastic bags and taking rotten items that the buzzards regularly flew over. The son gave her his shirt as a covering, and then father and son put her in the wagon to take her where she could find a taxi, and she simply went home for a bath to clean up the blood from the gashes—her vagina red and raw, her rectum burned—and purge the stench of dead animals that clung to her from the garbage dump. After that she returned to the university to rejoin her friends, even though walking was excruciating because every step felt as if one razor after the other was slashing between her legs, with sharp pain shooting down to her heels. And to ensure that such a thing never happened again, to make certain that no one every tortured her again, she was determined that she wouldn't be taken alive. And using her cell phone like a flashlight, she showed me a sharpened piece of glass in her other hand, which she planned to use to slice her wrists.

(Cowardice overcame me and prevented me from replying to her at all. I didn't dare tell her that the wagon driver who searched through the garbage was the Lord and that the wagon driver's son, the one who gave her his own tattered shirt as a covering, was the Lord as well. But Doña Sofía, who belongs to an Evangelical faith, the name of which I can't remember because it's one of the countless Protestant churches here, enlightened the girl with the kind of wisdom I wish I had when preaching to my own parishioners. Doña Sofía described her own experience as the mother of a rebel soldier who had been captured and murdered, his dead body left on El Plomo Hill. And she told the girl that because she felt her heart was completely broken at that moment, she had wished she was dead, but she drove that thought away after recognizing that her son's lost life had granted life to everyone else, because Christianity is life. The girl, obstinate in her hopelessness, responded that she admired the sacrifice of Doña Sofía's son, but she then asked what use his death had served when it only empowered killers who now committed murder just like the dictatorship they had fought against. Without hesitation, Doña Sofía answered that her son's death had made her an orphaned mother, and for that very reason she was at the church that day, surrounded by young people she viewed as her own children. And the girl responded that she wouldn't get in the way, and then she asked me if I wanted to pray with her: Let us pray. Let us pray together, padre.)

Our prayer—a prayer I began aloud during a break in the gun-fire, and one that other voices in the darkness joined—came to an end, and after numerous failures I finally made successful contact with Your Eminence, and the first thing I wish I could have told you is that there, seated beside me on the chancel floor, was a girl who had lost all hope in salvation through Our Savior's redeeming blood, a girl who instead had decided to shed her own blood, a situation that made me feel absolutely powerless in my ministry. But I had no time to indulge myself in telling you such things, but rather, as you'll recall, I informed you about the two dead boys, the dozens of wounded people, and the savage assault being waged against us, and I told you that I didn't know if we would survive the onslaught.

Forgive me, Your Eminence, for having said at that time that I was not asking but demanding that you intercede with those in authority over the animals who were trying to murder us with bul-lets and order them to stop. I also beg you to forgive me for my angry tone. I am rather coarse at times, perhaps because I come from a campesino family in Spain's impoverished Alavés region, and my grandfather, who raised me, had no manners at all and did not even own an animal to help with the farm work: He was just an old man filled with sorrows and adversity whose only happiness was a bowl of potatoes with chorizo on Sundays.

Your Eminence told me that you were aware of the crisis and that everything was in the hands of the apostolic nuncio, Monseñor Gaetano Ambrosio, and that he was struggling to make a petition to the government authorities, whose repeated response was that the attacking forces had no relationship to the police and that the authorities could therefore not order a cease-fire. I did not take this news very humbly because—and I beg your forgiveness once again—such a hopeless answer from those in power revealed depravity and cynicism. Furthermore, I insisted—inappropri-ately, yet again—that Monseñor Ambrosio would never bring the same energy to his petition as he did when engorging himself at elite government banquets.

Your Eminence ignored my impertinence and then asked me a question, which I likewise did not take well. The question was whether the students I was protecting in the church had guns that they were shooting from inside the building, as the police claimed, and whether those gunshots were the reason that the people outside felt they were under attack and simply defending their own. I answered this question with yet more unfortunate outrage.

But now, at this point in time, with the spirit of serenity and discretion that I should always have, I reiterate that apart from the completely empty pistol that the student Tigrillo was carrying, I did see a couple of other firearms, including a pair of hunting rifles, but I have no idea whether anyone fired them, and regardless, Don Artemio stated that the guns were equally useless whether someone was shooting them or not because they were small-caliber rifles with limited range. As for other weapons, if someone could even seriously use that label, aside from Coca-Cola bottles converted into Molotov cocktails, there were some mortar launchers like the ones used to shoot charges into the air at religious festivals; construction pickaxes and mattocks, digging bars, and slingshots for throwing pebbles—the kind children use when hunting; and finally, sticks and some rather heavy rocks.

I emphasize this lack of weapons not only to contradict police allegations, but also to respond to the National University's leaders, whose blind acquiescence to government dictates is very well-known and who have stated that they found large numbers of weapons in classrooms, thereby denouncing their own students as terrorists. If that allegation was true, the students would have brought their weapons here and not left them behind. With similar unfairness, university leaders have blamed their students for burning some offices and laboratories, but as I have said before, I have no doubt that the paramilitary groups pursuing the students started the fires.

If I seem biased in my conclusions, I am not ashamed to confess that I am indeed biased, because my ministry obligates me to favor the oppressed who groan under a brutal Pharoah who keeps a club on every neck to force obedience. And I am also biased to favor the Scriptures as well, which promote the same bias I've just described and command me to gird my loins so that every person who needs justice can find support from me and rise up with me.

(The bullets had stopped once more, and Doña Sofía was now approaching me on all fours to provide a sad new report about the parish house: Don Serafín, the assistant gardener, had taken advantage of the prior lull in the shooting to empty his bladder in the yard because the bathroom was occupied, but a single shot had hit him in the neck.

SERGIO RAMÍREZ

(The pause in shooting gave me time to cross the yard
and reach Don Serafín's side. I found him stretched out on a
mat on the porch, where other people had hurriedly carried
him. Eneida was there on her knees, using a towel as she
tried to staunch the blood flowing from the wound under
the glow of a hand lamp held by Inspector Morales, who
was sitting on the bench where parishioners usually wait to
see me for help. Don Serafín's body lay before the inspector.
Because the flashlight's halo was pointed toward the floor,
the gleam illuminated only the bottom part of the inspector's
face, which allowed me to glimpse his lower jaw trembling
as he struggled to hold the lamp steady.)

I had the impudence to call Your Eminence again because we
had a new person who was seriously wounded: The assistant gardener, Don Serafín, had been shot in the neck by a sniper, and the
young medical student had warned me that we urgently needed to
take the man to the hospital because he faced a serious risk of death
without surgery, and there was no other way to stop his bleeding,
which was why the people besieging us needed to allow an ambulance to come through. And you told me that the Red Cross would
soon be able to enter the area to pick up the wounded and the dead
because the apostolic nuncio had just finished negotiating that very
issue with the government, as the nuncio himself had just told you.

(We heard orders outside via megaphone commanding
that the police barriers be raised to allow ambulances to pass
through. We then heard the sirens. A convoy of ambulances
entered the eastern gate while the police remained on the
street. There were no paramilitary groups visible because
they had been withdrawn. The red flashes of the ambulances' revolving lights illuminated the ruin of the stained-glass
window and the hundreds of holes in the church's walls. Tigrillo was in charge of evacuating the wounded. I went over
to him and asked that he give preference to Don Serafín,
whom I accompanied to the ambulance door along with Inspector Morales, who remained closed to the stretcher and
held the hand lamp to keep the light shining on the wounded man. Don Serafín smiled at me despite how the terrible
wound impeded his breathing and despite his blood loss.
The Red Cross supervisor vehemently opposed the idea of

Inspector Morales getting into the ambulance, but I intervened to explain that the two men were inseparable friends, and I added that the inspector was disabled and deserved the chance due to his age. The supervisor's entire answer was to walk away and attend to something else. Then, after several assistants situated the stretcher inside the ambulance, one of them helped Inspector Morales climb in as well.)

The police did not allow any evacuation until the day began to lighten. That was also when they permitted the bodies of the two dead boys to be taken to the morgue, which permission resulted from the second agreement between the nuncio and the government, according to what Your Eminence told me. This second agreement stated that all refugees would be taken to the Church's holy cathedral, where Your Eminence would welcome them along with the nuncio, so that all could return to their homes with a guarantee that they would arrive alive and unharmed. I hope to God that that guarantee is honored despite my fears, which are many, and with which I will burden you no further.

If Your Eminence requires additional information on my part, I await your request, and meanwhile I beg your paternal blessing.

PADRE FRANCISCO XABIER ARAMBURU, SOCIETY OF JESUS
PARISH PRIEST FOR THE JESUS OF DIVINE MERCY CHURCH
ARCHDIOCESE OF MANAGUA

(To supervise the evacuation, a police squad entered the church's grounds under the command of a commissioner. The paramilitary groups had disappeared. The snipers had vanished from the roofs. I asked the commissioner if they were going to inspect the church to verify the damage it had suffered during the attack, but he looked at me as if he didn't know what attack I was talking about.

(Doña Sofía decided to go to the cathedral on one of the buses, and I approached her to say good-bye. The female law student stepped into the bus as well, and Doña Sofía took advantage of that moment to tell the young woman that she should return something to me that she was carrying. Understanding completely, the student extended me the sharpened piece of glass she still held in her hand.)

CHAPTER SIXTEEN

A Corona of Fire

THEIR DINNER had been delivered to them early, once again in the same boxes but without the cumbia music and dancing chickens, although each box contained a surprise of some kind: a pair of balloons, a plastic whistle, Power Rangers stickers. And now that the time was nearly 4:00 in the morning and Thursday was dawning, Tongolele's head was resting on his backpack. He felt a ferocious rumbling in his gut, and he was surprised to note that he could feel such hunger and yearn so deeply for even an unripe mango, particularly given the fact that lack of sleep tormented him because so many thoughts were rattling around his mind that he couldn't rest, and every time he lost consciousness he would awaken with a start.

Leónidas, surrounded by a large retinue like some Roman emperor, had been looking for Tongolele and had found him at that moment. The dazzling headlights of the Jeep Wranglers, filled with bodyguards, forced Tongolele to cover his eyes with his arm. The Wranglers signaled a mark of distinction because they were used only in presidential corteges, and the entire group entered the warehouse, the armed escorts encircling Tongolele like a wolfpack. He stood up unseeing, and still unseeing he walked toward the Porsche where Leónidas awaited him at the wheel without turning off the engine, just as none of his entourage had turned off their engines. Tongolele had to pay close attention to understand what Leónidas had come to tell him in such a hurry and surrounded by so much equipment.

"He told me I was fucking things up," Tongolele reported to the poet Lira, who had made himself quite comfortable in the principal's office of Nicolás Maduro School, where he had his own coffeemaker and had served Tongolele a plastic cup filled to the brim, which spilled when the highly courteous host stirred the sugar he had added himself.

You're fucking things up, brother, Leónidas had told him while looking towards the warehouse ceiling as if somewhere up there lay some mystery—hidden in the darkness where the wind blasts through and the vehicle lights fail to reach—that demanded all his concentration to be resolved. Just imagine! They've asked Leónidas to dress you down because a large stretch of the road to the Mercado de Mayoreo remains in rebel hands, and they want to know why Leónidas hasn't done anything to kick the rebels out.

But Leónidas was determined; he promised to find out immediately, and not just find out but fix the problem immediately, because this anomaly is discrediting our victory: All of Managua is under control. All the other cities throughout the country are under control. The remaining problem at the university is being rooted out: the terrorists have stampeded away and abandoned their cache of weapons; they've run off like the crybabies and mama's boys they are and have sought refuge under the skirts of the priests at the Divine Mercy Church, but we'll force them out of that hiding place, kicking and screaming.

And what does Leónidas discover when he asks about this shitty road that remains out of control? He learns that it's under your jurisdiction, brother dear, and the rebels have no reason to face justice for their sins. Leónidas will not allow himself to be blamed for the dead man, and that's why he's come to see you personally, and he hasn't wasted time with shit like saying over-and-out on walkie-talkies. Yes, Leónidas is here in person so that you can tell him what's been happening, whether you can or whether you can't.

"What's happening here is that that things have been more difficult than anticipated," the poet Lira explained, lowering his head toward the coffee cup without moving it from the saucer, then blowing on the liquid before sipping it.

"Now is not the time to be talking about things being difficult. That's nothing but excuses," Tongolele scolded. "Things are either resolved or they get resolved."

The poet Lira took a careful sip and licked his whiskers.

"It's not easy to fight with the kinds of people you've given me.

Consider that Rambo fellow who ran off with the captured girl after I left to talk with you."

"You already reported that to me—a serious mistake on your part. I warned you that that man could be an infiltrator, and all we need now is for that girl to use social media to denounce the men in your squad as child rapists."

"I'll take care of Rambo. I already told Cara de Culo—who knows Rambo's favorite places—to hunt him down and bring him to me."

"Forget about Rambo. I put you in command of those troops because you argued that you have combat experience. I gave you enough men. And as for weapons, I gave you more than enough. And you're not providing good results."

"The results have been very good. We now control many neighborhoods: Karl Marx, Larreynega, Rubén Darío, and Rafaela Herrera. And we forced the students at the Polytechnical University to run away in every direction."

"What I want is for that road to be cleared without any more delays or fuck-ups."

"Talk to me more respectfully, commissioner, because the higher-ups are blaming you, and your attempts to criticize me seem unjust," said the poet Lira, smiling as he eyed Tongolele from head to foot.

"This is a military organization. We're not holding poetry contests with flowers for prizes like the Floral Games. And anyone who disobeys orders has to be reined in."

"It's not the same thing as giving instructions at the stadium from an air-conditioned office like Leónidas, commissioner. Out here we're trying to chew through logs."

"You have nothing to do with Leónidas. I'm your commander here, and I'm a long way from any air conditioning. I'd love to see you suffocating and sweating like a pig in this warehouse."

Your fuck-ups are your fuck-ups, a steaming pile of shit, and I don't take responsibility for so much as even the stink, Leónidas had told Tongolele without removing his gaze from the darkness of the warehouse ceiling, stroking his thick beard in the same way he had seen Fidel Castro do on stages, slowly and reflexively. So, before this morning has even begun to heat up, you are going to personally take charge at the front of this operation, because nothing gets resolved from long distance, and if you tell me that you have something that makes it impossible for you to either act or have the will to do so, or if your balls have ascended to your uvula and ended up hanging from your throat like a necktie, which is what fear does to people, believe me when I say that Leónidas understands, but here and now you'll return your command to me, and from then on whatever happens is a question of fate, because I'll have to report you, and you know very well that during the last few days you haven't been very popular."

"Forgive me for insisting, commissioner, but don't be fooled by Leónidas' little show. You know how much he enjoys theatrics. He's just trying to steal the scene from you, taking credit for all you've done."

"I'm not even on-screen. The movie's over. And that was the final scene."

"That's what he wants, but don't throw in the towel. That's my advice as a friend."

"A friend? I've never thought that the dignity of that word applied to you."

"I'm offering my friendship with complete sincerity," said the poet Lira, solemnly extending his hand.

Surprised by this gesture, Tongolele had no option but to offer his own hand in return. The poet's hand was cold and sweaty.

"Now let's do what we came here for. What's the true operational situation?"

"There's just a short stretch of road that we still don't control, from the corner of the Luz y Sombra Tavern to the Las Primas eatery."

"Just how short a stretch?"

"Seven blocks, more or less. Four barricades or so."

"So what's the trouble with that area? Why has it been so tough for you? Do you need reinforcements?"

"The barricades are very well made—the rebels have even dug ditches in the pavement. And they're armed. They may be former revolutionary combatants who've switched sides."

"Things won't go well for them because there's no forgiveness for traitors. What kinds of weapons?"

"You can hear bursts from automatic rifles, perhaps AK-47s," said the poet Lira. "But usually handguns."

"So you've stopped advancing because of a few pistols? You're making a lot of excuses. We'll send more troops."

"It's not a question of troops. What I need are some snipers who can make heads explode from above."

"You've got snipers. I gave you two of them."

"I have a different kind of problem. The only available high spot is the rooftop of a three-story house with a mattress factory on the first floor."

"So what's the problem with the roof? Just take it. Why haven't you taken it over already?"

"The owner, Don Abraham, has shut himself and his family inside and ordered them not to open the doors."

"Don't come to me with childish stuff like that. Break the doors down and enter by force. Why have you waited so long?"

"The problem is that Don Abraham is the pastor of El Aposento Alto Church, which is affiliated with a mega-church called El Ministerio Apostolar de la Palabra. We'll find ourselves fighting all the eastside neighborhoods if we use force to enter the church. They have thousands of members."

"How many people do you think we've fought since this operation began? Thinking about it just slows us down."

"In addition, Don Abraham has a big family: children, nieces, and nephews, and all of them work in the factory. They live together on the second floor. Don Abraham uses the third floor for church meetings."

"Whether there are lots of people or only a few, that doesn't change what we have to do. So, reverend, you don't want to open your door? Well, I'm terribly sorry, but we need your roof."

"If he resists and we have to shoot, people could get injured. There are many young children there as well, Don Abraham's grandchildren."

"As for this pastor who worries you so much, which way does he lean? Is he for us or against us?"

"It's odd that you of all people would ask me for information like that, commissioner. You're the one who knows what people eat simply by examining their turds."

"Thank you. No one has ever flattered me that way before. As for evangelical pastors, they're generally easy to manage, unlike Catholic priests. It would be unusual if this one opposed the party."

"As far as I've been able to find out, he's not known to have any animosity toward the revolution."

"If that's true, why the hell won't he open the door to us?"

"The families have people of all kinds," responded the poet Lira, showing Tongolele his cell phone. "Watch this Facebook video posted by one of Don Abraham's sons, who is married and also the oldest. He made the video early this morning from the rooftop."

On the road a police patrol car approached at high speed, its siren blaring as it opened the way for two Hilux pick-ups filled with armed men shooting into the air. Meanwhile, terrified people ran to take refuge in their homes. Then, the man making the video began narrating what he was watching:

> "…the masked men have gotten down from the pick-ups. Watch them there. They're wearing yellow t-shirts. And now they're surrounding the beauty salon. They're pounding on the door with their gun butts. The people inside don't open the door. Now the men are pointing a rifle at the door lock. Listen to the shot. They've forced the door open and poured in, out of control. Listen to the shouts. Listen to the threats. Listen to the shattering of mirrors. They're smashing everything in the hair salon, and now they're taking the people out. They're taking them outside. And that woman they've brought out there, the one they're grabbing by the hair and pushing, the one with the pink jeans, the one whose sandals are coming off. That woman is Lady Di, the salon's owner, and the man they're dragging behind her, the one with the checked shirt, is her husband, Frank. He's a taxi driver.
>
> "Now watch that policeman who gets out of the patrol car. He's carrying two sets of cuffs in his hand. We can see him give the handcuffs to the paramilitary soldiers. Now the soldiers have handcuffed the couple and put hoods on them. Now they're putting the hooded couple into the bed of the second truck, taking them as prisoners to some unknown location. Special alert, Nicaraguan Center for Human Rights! Don't allow the government to claim later that the police weren't involved. Those people were taken alive, and we want them back alive! God alone names and removes kings! Lord Jehovah, confound the enemies of thy people! Thou art my refuge in the day of evil! Bring upon them the day of evil, and destroy them with double destruction."

"The men taking those people prisoner are our men," said Tongolele.

"And the man leading them is Cara de Culo," the poet Lira agreed. "He's stayed under control since the time I took him back after you told me to do so."

"Why did Cara de Culo take that couple away?"

"The idiot known as Lady Di is a transvestite who believes he's the Princess of Wales. And Frank, the taxi driver, is another degenerate who plays the role of Lady Di's husband."

"But you didn't order that those two be taken away in handcuffs."

"We're not that unoccupied here. Lady Di was leading a network to provide food for the subversives at the barricades, an effort aided by her *pendejo* husband."

"And this pastor's son isn't satisfied with making videos. He has to narrate everything too, a true *cabrón*."

"You've already seen that they won't open the door for us."

"Regardless, the barricades can't stay where they are."

"How are we going to remove them, commissioner?" asked the poet Lira, moving the coffee cup close to his mouth and stretching his lips. "I've already told you that without the snipers, we're going to have a battle on our hands, and that will give the false impression that we don't have things under control."

"I'll talk to the pastor myself," Tongolele answered.

"A good idea," laughed the poet Lira. "All that's needed is for you to appear at the front door, and Don Abraham will shit his pants from fright."

"And if he doesn't listen to me, because he thinks just like his son, it doesn't matter. The snipers will climb up to the roof regardless, and we'll move forward to sweep the barricades away."

"Are you taking command, commissioner?"

"You failed me. I have no other choice," answered Tongolele. Before standing up, he pushed his own untasted coffee away. Filled as the cup was to the brim, the coffee spilled over again.

"I'm charmed to be your aide de camp."

Tongolele commanded his available forces to gather at the Virgin roundabout, and at 4:45 a.m. he commanded them to begin their advance eastward on the road, two columns of masked men marching in single file alongside the sidewalks and carefully approaching each corner, then speeding up as they hunched down to cross the side streets. Meanwhile, the Hiluxes now overflowed with more masked men and slowly patrolled the downtown area with their headlights on.

The Luz y Sombra Bar, where the first remaining barricade stood, was located seven blocks east of the roundabout, while the mattress factory was halfway along the road, per the poet Lira, who was sandwiched next to Tongolele in the cab of the lead pick-up. Cara de Culo was standing in the pick-up's bed, flanked by two snipers who were dressed in black and masked by balaclavas, their Dragunovs strapped on with rifle belts and their ammo in bandoliers across their chests.

One block before the mattress factory, the poet Lira said that it would be wise to stop the convoy so that Tongolele could continue alone and find a way to talk with the pastor. Such a conversation could avoid provoking hostile reactions such as people inside again refusing to open the door when the multitude of weapons arrived. The poet Lira, Cara de Culo, and the snipers stayed behind while Tongolele advanced along the sidewalk on the road's right-hand margin. He stopped at the front of the mattress factory's metal access gate—the only possible entrance to the entire house.

The pastor had designed the house with no guidance beyond his own tastes, adding adornments and details to the degree that the mattress-factory's profits allowed. The dwelling's upper floors had green-painted pilasters forming a balustrade, and a spiral staircase wound from the third floor's extreme right to the rooftop, where another balustrade appeared. The picture windows on every floor were arched, and the second floor's façade displayed a double door shaped like an arch as well. And in front of the door, a narrow walkway led to a bulging Neapolitan balcony that protruded toward the street.

As Tongolele looked through the windows' ironwork, he saw that the entire first floor was dedicated to the factory: sewing machines, rolls of striped and printed fabrics for upholstery, mounds of foam pads, piles of waste cotton, and stacks of finished products.

Tongolele next contemplated the empty street. He recognized the salon he had seen on the video. According to what remained of the sign on the broken store window, the salon was named after its transvestite owner: Lady Di Hair Cuts. He could still see the figure of the Princess of Wales, wearing her diamond diadem on her head and displaying her emblematic pixie razor-cut hair. Among the shards of glass on the sidewalk lay the shell of a hair dryer, half-burned nylon hairnets, shampoo bottles spreading their contents all over, and beauty magazines with their pages torn out by the wind.

Lightbulbs still glowed on porches and under the eaves of houses during this early morning hour, and the silence of the closed doors was broken only for an instant by a child's cry, which was quickly muffled. A great-tailed grackle used its beak to gather scraps from the pavement. Suddenly, it fixed its round eye upon him. Distrustful, the bird flew away to perch upon an eave. Tongolele had no doubt that certain shadows moving behind window curtains and blinds were spying on him. Most likely someone was filming him when he raised his finger toward the doorbell, which resounded throughout the entire block with the arpeggios of a xylophone.

From the second floor he heard faint noises, muted voices, and urgent footsteps, but no one came down to open the door. He had practiced a speech, and the words he would use when he met the pastor kept returning to his head like a walkie-talkie conversation: A thousand pardons for bothering you, reverend, over; we are here to request a bit of cooperation with you, over; the terrorists, as you know, over; a threat to every good Christian, and we all need to do our duty, over; guarantee our citizens' right to move freely, over; the serenity of your own congregation, over; peace and public order, over; our urgent mission is to clear the streets and put things back to normal, over; I'm grateful for your understanding and support. Over and out.

The murmurs and whispered voices from above came to a stop. The great-tailed grackle flew low by him, the brief shine of its blue-black plumage absorbing the sun's first rays. The bird left behind only the mocking vestige of its harsh call.

Tongolele called out a second time, and this time he kept his fingertip on the doorbell. The xylophone played again, insistently now, and he recognized that it was playing the chords of "La Cucaracha":

> *La cucaracha, la cucaracha*
> *ya no puede caminar*

This song was the catchy tune to which his father had always danced after drinking too much, during his birthday parties in León among his drinking buddies, stomping around as he either slapped his palms on his back or raised the backs of his hands toward his eyes as if he wanted to study them, always moving back and forth, back and forth, heavy, clunky...

> *porque le faltan porque le faltan*
> *cuatro patas para andar.*

Tongolele turned his head for a moment. From behind him, the poet Lira had made his approach—rifle loaded and ready to shoot—and scornfully observed Tongolele's powerlessness before a closed door. Cara de Culo, crouched behind him, held a bottle filled with gasoline, ready to light the rag with a lighter. Tongolele had not given an order for any such thing. Where had that Molotov cocktail come from? The poet Lira turned his face away when Tongolele tried to look at him. Homemade weapons weren't included among the task forces' equipment because the troops already had the best weapons—the most modern and efficient ones.

The snipers' eyes were fixed upon him, watching through the balaclavas' round holes just as the grackle had done. He took his finger off the doorbell. The xylophone's last arpeggios continued echoing on their own until they disappeared. And Tongolele, as if obeying a voice that could not be heard but seemed to be speaking to him from within the Chinese box, took one step aside so that the poet Lira could move forward and loose a short burst against one of the picture windows, which shattered in a storm of pieces, while Cara de Culo lit the rag and threw the bottle through the hole.

Tongolele watched the cocktail explode over the piles of waste cotton, and the stench of burning gasoline enveloped him as a lazy wisp of blue smoke did not linger much before it violently disintegrated and hungrily climbed the wall, and then the poet Lira shot another short gunburst and Cara de Culo tossed another burning bottle inside. When Tongolele felt the fire's scorching heat on his face he backed away into the middle of the street, as the thick dark smoke obscured the machines, the tables, and the mattress covers. Meanwhile, smoke poured through the broken windows and wild flames climbed the stairway leading to the second floor, where shouts and the coughs of choking people emanated from

SERGIO RAMÍREZ

the bedrooms, along with the heartbroken cries of a small boy, as the highest windows came alight with the fire's violent glare and then rained ashes onto the pavement, at which point the poet Lira grabbed Tongolele's shirtsleeve and pulled him along. Let's go, commissioner; there's nothing more for us to do here. And after Tongolele's heavy, clunky feet dragged slowly along the uneven pavement, he climbed into the pick-up, which then drove away.

These things happen because they happen, commissioner. This whole unfortunate episode would have happened regardless of whether it was in our hands or not, the poet Lira explained. I had already warned you that the pastor was a stubborn man—and he didn't even deign to answer us, much less open the door, and the worst part is that a lot of people living in that house are going to get hurt because those insolent flames will burn all that flammable material so fast that the firefighters won't be able to come anywhere close, a consequence of how foolish the pastor was to store those things there. But truth be told, we never went to that place anyway, a fact I will make perfectly clear in my report. And after all, everybody knows that that area of the city is boiling with terrorists, and they're the ones most likely at fault for this attack, which is just one more of the vicious things they do. Everywhere they go, the coup leaders leave proof of what they truly are: arsonists and killers. And as for those last two, the father and son, at the end of the day it's impossible to know which of them was the most obstinate: the son was a mulish fool, his mind fixated—as he said in his video—on the idea that Jehovah fought by his side, a condition known in scientific theory as primary religious extremism. He's the kind of man who wants to die by being buried standing up. And now, regardless of how the military operation works out, we're leaving without the support of the Dragunovs, but we'll find a way to get rid of the barricades some way or another. Isn't that right, commissioner? We're arriving now, and I'll walk behind you because you're in command.

Varnished bamboo poles decorated the façade of the Luz y Sombra Bar, and the sidewalk had been closed off by a corral, also constructed of bamboo, while the plastic tables and chairs were chained together to prevent them from being stolen.

The barricade, made of zinc roofing sheets and tree branches that were beginning to wilt, extended from the corral to the other side of the street, where from behind wrought-iron bars a store window displayed a figure: a recently re-touched plaster statue of Jesus' Sacred Heart, the heart encircled by thorns and standing out in bright red against the folds of a sky-blue tunic.

All the doors along the block were closed. Three tires were burning in front of the barricade, the flames close to dying: one of the tires remained practically intact while the other two had been consumed so much as to reveal their fiber-cable skeletons.

"There's no one at the barricade," Tongolele said after turning off his rifle's safety.

"They must have run off when they saw us coming," said the poet Lira from behind him.

"And those tires have been there for a long time," said Tongolele, taking a step forward.

A great-tailed grackle left its perch on an eave of the Luz y Sombra Bar and landed rather presumptuously near his feet. It pecked at the pavement with nervous movements, then gazed at Tongolele from the side, its eye unmoving. The bird must have been the same one as before.

Tongolele sensed heavy breathing blow across his nape. He tried to turn around, but Cara de Culo grabbed his neck and forced him to bend down to his knees. Cara de Culo then pushed him forward with a boot to the back. Once Cara de Culo had him down on the ground, he took the Jericho pistol that the poet Lira handed him and shot Tongolele three times through the head.

Tongolele's body left a bloody stain on the asphalt as the two other men dragged him by the feet to the barricade. And while the poet Lira held the body in a sitting position, Cara de Culo hung one of the nearly burnt-out tires—the most nearly whole—around the body's neck and stoked the flames with a burning gas filter. Then the two men left the body leaning against one of the rusty zinc sheets, the flaming tire ringing his neck like a corona of fire.

CHAPTER SEVENTEEN

A Burro Yoked to a Millstone

INSPECTOR MORALES SAT on the dressing-table stool in Fanny's bedroom, already dressed for the ceremony. Although he was still wearing the same faded jeans, which hung loosely from his rear, and a pair of braided-leather sandals for walking in the house, he had donned a new long-sleeved white shirt with a stiff collar, which Doña Sofía had raced to buy for him at the Managua Mall's Mil Colores store, a purchase she had made so recently that the shirt's fold marks easily stood out. He had put the shirt on in front of the chiffonier's oval mirror, nervous as any groom and inserting the buttons in the wrong holes. He had managed to secure the last button—the one covering his stomach—only after a mighty struggle.

Fanny rested on the bed as the time drew closer. Having applied her make-up carefully, she had put on the emerald-green Caribbean blouse that would go well with her turban, one that effectively hid her baldness. Inspector Morales could see her reflection in the chiffonier mirror, the soles of her beaded high heels close-up. Along with the blouse and the turban, Doña Sofía had taken upon herself the task of buying the shoes at a boutique near the La Tortuga Murruca restaurant.

Padre Pancho would perform the marriage upon returning from the airport, after he had said farewell to Monseñor Ortez. The monseñor was still recovering from his injuries, but he was following the Church's order to leave for Rome that day and present himself before the Congregation for the Causes of Saints.

The altar had been prepared in the living room much earlier—by Doña Sofía, of course—according to the instructions Fanny had continually given her from the bed: a tablecloth, originally part of the dowry for her first marriage, with embroidered violets cross-stitched along the edge; the lithograph of Santa Lucía of Siracusa, placed on the tablecloth; and next to that a vase filled with asters taken from the backyard garden.

In addition, every chair in the house had been placed before the altar to accommodate the guests: one of Fanny's sisters, who was coming from Ciudad Sandino with her husband; and several neighbors from La Carlanca, a dead-end street.

But convincing Inspector Morales to get married had not been such an easy task for Doña Sofía. Proof of that difficulty was the conversation that took place two days earlier in Fanny's garage, where Doña Sofía lived. The conversation addressed several topics, but the wedding was always the principal concern.

"If it were my choice, Comrade Artemio, Reverend Wallace, the pastor of my church, would perform the wedding ceremony," said Doña Sofía while standing upright, having calculated that doing so would put her in a stronger position to enter the impending battle.

Seated in the rocking chair, Inspector Morales leaned forward, resting his cheek on his hands as they gripped the handle of his cane.

"I don't know what wedding you're talking about, Doña Sofía."

"Fanny wants it. The only one dragging their feet is you."

"Isn't Pastor Wallace the same man who gambled away the donations to the El Edén evangelical church, all in a single night at the Pharaohs Casino black-jack table?"

"The congregation kicked Pastor Wallace out because of that. And I defended him, because if he was gambling he was doing so to increase the church's funds. But he just had bad luck that night."

"And what about the new pastor? Does he gamble the alms?" Inspector Morales asked, now resting his chin on his hands, but always using the cane for support.

"Stop going off on tangents. You know that I have nothing against Padre Pancho performing the ceremony."

"I haven't decided to get married yet, and I'm begging you not to make the decision for me. Besides, a civil divorce doesn't count for the Catholic church."

"The Roman church didn't perform her marriage. I already got a copy of her single-status certificate from the Episcopal Curia. She's as free as every bird that wants to make a nest."

"This thing about birds making nests sounds like something from the selected readings of a children's storybook, Doña Sofía."

"And besides, you need to remember her dangerous health condition."

"But she's better," Inspector Morales responded, and immediately felt weak. "Doctor Catina said that the metastasis in her bones has stopped and that the radiation, along with the chemo, is having a positive effect."

"So should I understand that you're saying you'd marry her only if she were dying? Aren't you interested in growing old alongside a woman who loves and respects you?"

Our comrade got old years ago, said Lord Dixon. But he doesn't want to understand that an old man alone is like a kite without a tail.

"You twist everything around and misinterpret it, Doña Sofía," said Inspector Morales, brandishing his cane as if defending himself. "You know very well that if I took so many risks to get back here from Honduras, I took those risks to be by her side."

You're falling into your own trap, inspector, said Lord Dixon. If you don't measure your words carefully, the trap will snap shut. You'd be better off taking the conversation another direction.

"So, then, why are you afraid to stand in front of an altar, Comrade Artemio?"

"It's not fear. It's respect. We buried Serafín less than a week ago, and here I am about to have a party."

Come up with better excuses, inspector, said Lord Dixon. How many days did you mourn for me before you went back to your habitual carousing?

Still in the ambulance on the way to Monte España Hospital, the closest hospital to the Divine Mercy Church, Serafín had raised his head from the gurney and asked Inspector Morales to move closer, as if he wanted to tell the inspector a secret. The EMT had used strips of tape to affix a bandage to the injured man's neck, and the bandage was quickly turning a shade of scarlet that seemed unrecognizable to Inspector Morales, as if he had never seen the color of blood. Serafín's voice, which kept breaking down into a rasping whisper, likewise seemed unrecognizable to him: *Jefe*, I never could have imagined that a sniper would catch me unaware with my dick in my hands, and I'll bet he laughed his head off when he saw me make that same stupid *pendejo* face that we all do when

we're taking a leak. Serafín tried to keep talking, but a fit of coughing choked off his voice, and now his lips were wet with blood as it
bubbled through them.

Could it be that Serafín never said anything at all? Did the
whole incident take place only in the inspector's imagination?
Later, Padre Pancho had explained to him: Inspector, under those
conditions, with a ruptured larynx, he couldn't have said a word to
you, but if you heard him joking about his own death throes, such
a thing would have been perfectly in character for him, and you
shouldn't try to correct your own memory about what happened.

The surgeon had arrived at the small waiting room and discreetly gestured for Inspector Morales to follow him. After walking along a corridor dimly lit by fluorescent bulbs that buzzed like
hornets, they arrived at a small room used for piling dirty sheets
and gowns. There are spies everywhere here, the doctor said, raising his finger every now and then to steady his glasses as they
danced on his nose. That's why this will be the last time we talk,
and what I'm about to tell you won't appear in the medical report
because we're forbidden to mention wounds caused by weapons of
war, much less say that we had the success of taking a patient into
the emergency room or into the operating room for surgery, an
even greater success. Do we understand each other?

Inspector Morales had nodded his agreement. Was this patient,
Serafín Manzanares, his brother? Yes, he was his brother, and the
patient had taken a high-caliber bullet through the neck. Like him,
we've received other patients with head, neck, and chest wounds,
but this patient is the first older man we've seen: All of the others have been youngsters who could be either his grandchildren or
yours. The shot hit the older man's larynx and trachea at the level
of the fourth vertebrae, and we've inserted a thin tracheostomy
tube. We'll take him to surgery and stitch a vascular muscle graft
that we'll have to create from another part of his neck to repair
the wounds. You're speaking gibberish to me, doctor, the inspector
had replied with a melancholy smile.

And the doctor, adjusting his glasses once again, had looked at
him with distracted pity, the pity of someone in a hurry who can't
waste time on incurable sorrow: And if that operation goes well,
we'll perform another operation to insert a tube through his ab-
dominal wall to feed and medicate him; of course, both surgeries

SERGIO RAMÍREZ

are high-risk, particularly due to his age and creating the possibility of heart failure, and I'm telling you all this now so that you can
see that if I were in your shoes, I wouldn't keep my hopes high.

"We're not talking about a party here. We'll have a more-or-
less intimate ceremony," said Doña Sofía, returning to form again.
"You've done enough for Serafín. Didn't you stay in the hospital
at the head of the bed, risking the possibility that they would see
you and arrest you?

"That's nothing to brag about. I was only there for two days,
because things worked out just as the doctor feared: poor Serafín
died of a heart attack. Besides, with Tongolele dead there was no
danger in my being there."

"Nobody can know that. The only thing that changes is the
leader of the pack. They probably replaced him with someone
even more brutal."

"You can see for yourself that they haven't sent anyone looking
for me. Of course, that doesn't mean I'm not on their to-do list."

"Well, as for me, I've been terrified about seeing one of those
pick-ups without license plates show up at the door since the time
we left the cathedral early during the morning that the buses took
us there."

"Two errands in one trip. What a pleasant surprise for them
when they catch us together. That way, they won't have to keep
searching and searching."

"And I'll bet Lieutenant Yasica will be leading them, because
she knows very well where to find us."

"You're right about that. Just as she showed up at Señora Magdalena's door pretending to come for the priest's clothes, she can
certainly make a sudden appearance at the door of this house."

"There was no news of her until the notice I told you about, the
one from the paper in El Mercado Oriental. I have it here, just as
I promised"

She went to a shelf beside the bed and searched for a copy of
El Marchante, a tabloid where women bared their breasts or bot-
toms for the camera, along with photos of market-stall owners and
those who owned portions of the market, and pictures of the same
people's children and grandchildren getting christened or taking
their first communion, all of these images accompanied by articles
reporting stabbings, public disturbances, thefts, arson, and other

[258]

events that occurred within the market's boundaries, plus the latest news about international showbusiness and European royalty.

Beneath an article headlined in red letters that said LINDSAY LOHAN SLEPT WITH 150 MEN, the notice Doña Sofía had mentioned appeared, set apart by a thick border:

> Notice to all customers, suppliers, debtors, and creditors of the direct-to-home business Abonos Suaves and the stores known as Paca Paca, El Trapo Contento, Todo para Todos, and El Videíto Feliz: Without exception, all commercial and financial affairs of the aforementioned businesses shall hereafter be conducted by the new owner and general manager, Señora Yasica Benavides, who will attend to these issues in the companies' head offices, located on the main street of Ciudad Jardín

"Those were the businesses owned by Tongolele's lover, the one who went down with him," said Inspector Morales, folding the paper. "Someone gave them to the fortunate Yasica as a reward."

"That means she's higher up than ever before. We need to fear her even more."

"Doesn't it seem more likely that by rewarding her, they've removed her from her old position? She's got a lot of businesses to run, and she can't do two things at once."

"I hope that's true and that all those businesses keep her from remembering us, so hopefully she never picks up the phone and says something to Tongolele's replacement like: 'Hey, what happened with that old woman? Why hasn't she been arrested?'"

"She was all part of the plot against Tongolele. And once she'd played her role, everybody said 'Adiós, sweetheart. Move on. Get down to business. Enjoy your little reward.'"

"You're right about that, Comrade Artemio. The messages they sent us were obviously designed to pull the rug out from under Tongolele's feet before they liquidated him."

"And we actually helped them do it as ignorant collaborators with our little scheme."

"While they may have used us, they still put a high-caliber weapon in our hands. And our posts provided a good outlet for our exposés."

We would be foolish not to recognize Doña Sofía's leading role in all of this, regardless of the origins or motivations behind the information she received, said Lord Dixon. She transformed some very short messages into genuine newspaper and magazine articles.

"Don't pay any attention to me. The truth is that regardless of whether they tried to use us to promote their agenda, you counteracted them with your exposés, Doña Sofía."

"You're exactly right to use the term *them*," responded Doña Sofía, filled with pride and unable to restrain herself. "Because this Lieutenant Yasica was backed by a bunch of people who have climbed to the highest levels of power."

The Mask's tweets were quoted in the mission report submitted by the European Parliament, said Lord Dixon. And by the Inter-American Commission of Human Rights for the Organization of American States.

"Now we have to decide the fate of this Mask that you created."

"What are you proposing? Do you want him to disappear? As for me, I'm not keeping my mouth shout until they make me."

"Nobody's saying that we should keep our mouths shut, Doña Sofía. But we have to understand that everything we do draws us into a tighter and tighter circle. Eventually we'll have nowhere to hide."

It's a good thing that Doña Fanny has a little money saved and that they're paying her pension for retirement, said Lord Dixon. The three of you can live on that under this roof, so long as you're not taken prisoner.

"As long as they keep throwing me pitches across the middle of the plate, as they say in baseball, I'll be happy as can be. Like that announcement from the police, where they claimed that terrorist coup plotters set a mattress factory on fire, even though a video proved that wasn't true."

"Six people died in that fire. The pastor and his wife, their eldest son and their daughter-in-law, and their two youngest children: a one-and-a-half-year-old girl and her five-month-old sister."

"I took advantage of the fact that a neighbor filmed the paramilitary soldiers as they threw Molotov cocktails into the factory. And Tongolele shows up in the video."

"Those same paramilitary soldiers executed Tongolele in front of a barricade. And the same savages left a burning tire around his neck."

"That's what the second video shows, which another neighbor made. I posted both videos on The Mask's account."

"Think about how they killed Tongolele. If that's what they're willing to do to one of their own, imagine what they'll do to the opposition."

Congratulations, Doña Sofía, said Lord Dixon. Both scenes, one after the other, linked together like a sequence from a movie. You did an outstanding editing job with those videos.

"Lie after lie unmasked," crowed Doña Sofía, rubbing her hands together enthusiastically. "The sequence already has more than 50,000 'Likes' and 10,000 re-posts."

"The fact that Tongolele just happened to be walking nearby supports the police report," Inspector Morales laughed. "Some retired official was just walking by or running an errand, and the terrorists at the barricade grabbed and murdered him."

"People who saw the videos identified the two paramilitary soldiers immediately: one is the poet Lira, a reporter for Radio Comrade; the other is that man with the horrible nickname who belongs to El Mercado Oriental's shock troops."

I respect your choice not to say the man's nickname, Doña Sofía, said Lord Dixon. Not to mention its variants: Anus Grimace and Rectum Rictus.

"In his report, Serafín says that the man with the nasty nickname led the gang-rape of the medical student, the niece of your sacristan friend."

"The confession that you stubbornly refused to read, Comrade Artemio. And now that the girl has escaped to Costa Rica, my Mask has been able to post everything about it."

"Tongolele must have done something seriously wrong. They kick him out of his position, demote him, send him to clear out the barricades, and take advantage of the chaos to blow his head off."

"And the losses don't stop there: His lover, the queen of El Mercado Oriental, has had everything confiscated; his mother, the great official sage, has been thrown out of her house. The Mask has posted all of that as well."

"Tongolele had too much power in his hands, and that's what led to his end."

He who casts a shadow loses his body and his shadow, said Lord Dixon. Write that saying down, comrade, which I made up myself.

"There's nothing for us to do but continue posting exposés," Doña Sofía sighed. "Because for now at least, this rebellion seems to have been in vain. Government soldiers killed young people left and right, but the government remains in power, strong and secure."

"My Grandmother Catalina had a burro that spent his entire life going around in circles, yoked to a millstone that ground coyol fruit to produce palm oil. Could it be, Doña Sofía, that our country is like that burro, yoked to a stone and doomed to go round and round?"

I'm willing to bet that you use this Catalina of yours for whatever suits your needs, inspector, said Lord Dixon.

"The saddest part about that story is that the burro manages to break the rope from time to time and believe he's free," Doña Sofía responded, sighing once again. "But what he doesn't know is that the same people who tie him to the millstone again are the same ones who helped him get loose."

If you're going to talk about nothing but anguish and sorrows, I'm better off going back to where I usually am, where my ears hear much better things, said Lord Dixon.

"We're going to end up with depression, Doña Sofía, and flagellating ourselves does us no good."

"You're feeling this way because you're battling the topic of marriage. Your rebellion against marriage is what we were talking about, and you made me go on a tangent."

"The truth is that I just don't know. I've never been married, and I've gotten used to being alone."

"Don't tell lies. Lies don't become you. You told me yourself that during the war, Padre Gaspar performed a marriage ceremony for you and a Panamanian woman named Eterna Viciosa."

"That marriage was pure hell, and don't try to tell me otherwise. Besides, it wasn't valid. It was performed under guerrilla law, in a guerrilla camp, and we never had a marriage certificate or anything like that."

For a man like Dolores Morales, who should marry a woman named Carnal Pleasures, Eterna Viciosa is the perfect wife, said Lord Dixon.

"People get old in the other world too," Inspector Morales said between his teeth. "Your habit of repeating the same stupid things from long ago means that you're getting senile."

"Well, then, if your first marriage isn't valid, there's nothing to prevent you from getting married now, just as nothing prevents her. So, it's time for you to drop the subject."

"I've been listening to everything from behind the door for some time," Fanny announced as she suddenly entered the garage, supporting herself with her walker. "And there's nothing to worry about. I'm not going to tie any man up and force him to the altar."

"Fanny, it's wonderful to have you join our conversation," said Doña Sofía, completely unfazed. "That way we can clarify everything and know what's best for everybody."

Inspector, I have a deep suspicion that the two women arranged this untimely entrance beforehand, Lord Dixon declared.

"I'm not offended," said Fanny, whose nose was red because she was about to burst into tears. "I'm not going to kick him out of my house or out of my life, whether or not I die tomorrow. If he wants us to continue living as we are, that's fine."

"How can you two misunderstand me so badly?" asked Inspector Morales, as his cane fell from his hands and he had to squat down to look for it. "I was simply wondering when the most appropriate time for the ceremony would be."

What an embarrassing way to sound a retreat, said Lord Dixon.

"Well, Padre Pancho is simply waiting for us to let him know, and then he'll come right over," said Doña Sofía, picking up the cane and returning it to the inspector. "He doesn't even have to bother with going to the church because it's been under repair since all those bullets hit it."

"For the record, he should acknowledge that he's marrying me by his own free will and choice," said Fanny, and her tear-filled eyes looked at Inspector Morales.

"And we would be wise to set a date that's near at hand, Comrade Artemio, because the government can kick Padre Pancho out of the country at any moment as an undesirable foreigner."

"You're right," said Fanny, drying her eyes. "Radio Comrade is always making some kind of wild accusation against him, and they never stop calling him anything less than a demonic priest in favor of a coup."

"It's that poet Lira, who laid his rifle down and went back to pick up his microphone," Doña Sofía added.

Comrade, I don't understand why you would try so hard to kick up-

ward while drowning when you were never going to be able to get your head above water, said Lord Dixon.

Doña Sofía was busy finishing her food preparations in the kitchen, which included some sangría drinks she had made herself and a pair of typical dishes: fried plantains with cheese and tortilla triangles smothered in refried beans. She had covered the food with plastic wrap. Meanwhile, Inspector Morales noticed that Fanny had fallen asleep, so he sat down on the living-room sofa in front of the marriage altar and searched his phone for the streaming transmission of Monseñor Ortez's departure, which had been announced on social media.

The TV reporters, whose stations had been blocked or removed from the cable services, used their phones to make live reports through Facebook Live or YouTube, and they took the risk of entering closely surveilled places like the airport, where at least one reporter, from News 66, had managed to make a place for himself.

The camera focused on the monseñor while he stood in line at the Copa Airlines check-in desk, just one man among many passengers who either didn't know him or stayed quiet from fear because they actually did know him. Skinnier and more stooped than Inspector Morales remembered him, the monseñor was wearing a heavy, dark clergyman's suit, as if he were already dressed to confront the cold that awaited him in Rome. He also wore a fedora like Humphrey Bogart. And when he turned to face the camera, which zoomed in so closely that it deformed his face, he was smiling with an exhausted smile, and tangled wisps of white stood out on his face: Evidently, he had not shaved for several days.

The camera moved along in front of him as he walked down the corridor toward the immigration registration windows. He was pulling a wheeled suitcase and carrying his passport and plane ticket, and Inspector Morales recognized Edelmira, the monseñor's niece from Dipilto Viejo, walking beside him, attached to his arm is if she meant to protect him. Rita Boniche, the parish house's housekeeper, walked on his other side with solemn but hesitant steps because she normally went barefoot and street shoes appeared to make her uncomfortable. She was keeping a tight grip on a handkerchief, prepared to dry her tears.

At that moment, an obese woman suddenly appeared from the grotto filled with cheap memorabilia and all the other crap sold in the airport corridor's many souvenir stores. The woman wore a short skirt and a starched white apron, and she had squeezed into a t-shirt emblazoned with a Tree of Life that glowed in phosphorescent colors. She planted herself firmly in front of the monseñor and displayed a cardstock sign with a message written in felt-tip marker:

DEMONIC PRIEST AND COUP SYMPATHIZER
MAY YOU NEVER RETURN

And while the monseñor smiled with the same exhaustion as before, the woman unleashed a series of insults at him, words that could not be understood through the phone that Inspector Morales held before his eyes. The monseñor's niece attempted to move him away by keeping close to his body, at which point Rita Boniche sprang at the obese woman and tore the sign from her. The surrounding crowd became noisier and noisier, and then a pair of female police officers arrived with the intent of taking Rita Boniche prisoner, because the obese woman kept shouting that Rita had punched her in the face and scratched her with her nails. At that moment, however, Padre Pancho and Padre Pupiro entered the scene and took hold of the monseñor, supporting him together. Meanwhile, the niece argued with the police officers, who eventually let Rita Boniche go free. As Rita walked away, she kept screaming at the police officers that she knew they were there to protect *sicarios*—hitmen—and persecute the righteous. Inspector Morales had not known that this woman, who was always looking for a fight, even knew the word *sicarios*.

Inspector Morales walked away half-dazed, with the phone still in his hand.

CHAPTER EIGHTEEN

A Diverse Collection of Stuffed Frogs

IT WAS 7:00 A.M. when a taxi dropped them off on one of the corners of Del Campo Avenue, three blocks away from the old house disguised as a customs agency, a precautionary habit that dated back to the time when they worked at the place. As usual, the electronic bolt on the pedestrian door in the surrounding wall slid open with a squeak, and they crossed the yard where the platinum-gray Kia Morning taxi sat parked in a corner. Upon entering the building's deserted living room, they could not rid themselves of the feeling that everything there felt strange to them now.

This visit marked their first return to the place since they had been fired, and none of their former colleagues seemed to notice the presence of another person as they approached Tongolele's old office, which the dwarf Manzano now occupied. The agency's workers were either leaning over their typewriters or transcribing recordings of telephone conversations from their headphones. They were the same people who had always worked there, although the visitors no longer belonged to the clandestine world in which the workers had spent so many years.

A crowd of workers wearing deep-blue overalls moved back-and-forth through the living room and the hallway. They were lugging boxes of electronic equipment, hanging cables, and installing circuits in metallic cabinets, all their efforts indicating that every officer would soon be working in front of a computer screen. The Skorpion digital system was finally being adopted, and the office had its own server, linked to the Chaika satellite ground station in Nejapa Lagoon's crater.

Pedrón recognized the overalled workers' foreman, a half-bald man with a prominent jaw, light-blue eyes, and practically invisible eyebrows. His name was Vladimir, from Russia's FSB mission, and he had once given Pedrón a decanter of Stolichnaya vodka along with a minuscule dollop of caviar. But Pedrón had to stop trying to greet Vladimir from a distance when the man responded with an expressionless look.

The dwarf Manzano was wearing his everyday uniform. Having recently showered, he smelled of Jean Naté Unisex lotion—a fragrance so powerful that a person could sense its hair-salon perfume a mile away—and offered the visitors his most crafty smile as he invited them in, the wrinkles in the corners of his eyes and mouth standing out on his clean-shaven face.

The office furniture had been changed since the dwarf Manzano took over, and the new Romanesque seating was uncomfortable. The chairs, like their straight narrow backs, were made of tooled rawhide with armrests that stood too high. The dwarf Manzano made no move to sit in his own armchair on the other side of the desk, where his military cap rested atop a pile of folders. Instead, making a great show of deference, he sat down with his visitors in one of the Romanesque chairs, as if he were joining a social gathering. But before beginning, he picked up the phone, ordered coffee for the three of them, and smiled at his visitors once again: If now was the time for making a toast we would do so, but the morning has barely begun, and drinking so early is reserved for unrepentant alcoholics.

During the revolution, the dwarf Manzano had led the security detail for Comandante Cipriano, the first chief of the National Police, and Manzano had inherited from Cipriano a complete collection of stuffed frogs, examples of the taxidermists' art that had accompanied Manzano from office to office, and which Manzano had brought from his last office to the Agency for Special Protection.

The frogs were arranged in a glass display case, their skin varnished and their bodies stuffed with sawdust, and a person could admire them in many different poses: one had a carbine on its shoulder and was wearing fatigues as it reviewed military plans; another was wearing a Scottish tie with a detachable collar, smoking a curved pipe like that of Sherlock Holmes; yet another sported a tight-fitting Lycra suit as it was riding a bicycle; two others were getting married—the groom wearing a tuxedo, the bride displaying a veil and a tiara—while a third frog stood before them wearing a mitre and a chasuble; and finally, a band occupied an entire section of the case: all the musicians were made of cotton, each sporting a palm sombrero and wearing a bandana around its neck, and the group was playing all kinds of instruments, including a marimba with a bow, a guitar, a violin, and some maracas, while a pair of female dancers in traditional dress gracefully tapped their feet. But several of the frogs had resided in the case for so long that they had lost some of their varnish, and the stuffing was poking through the feet of others where the thread had come undone.

The dwarf Manzano's round belly stood out under his uniform's combat jacket, and seated as he was in that strange chair as if he were in a scene from a play, his feet—sheathed in boots of brown crocodile skin—struggled to find support on the floor. His mid-calf boots had high heels and a zipper on the side, and they belonged to an extensive collection. The collection was large because the dwarf Manzano had the same passion for boots as he did for frogs, and all his boots—with high heels, hidden wedges, and double-thick soles—were designed to increase his height up to four inches. The collection included embroidered Texas boots made of Cordoba leather; John Wayne calfskin boots, decorated with tassels or harness straps; country-type boots made with vintage natural-tan pigskin; Elvis Presley boots of white suede; and high-shaft snakeskin Madonna-type boots, for late-night parties. Of course, the collection also included his black patent-leather boots, which he wore as part of his dress uniform.

The group's coffee came in miniature Dutch-porcelain cups on cobalt saucers, all part of a set—very few pieces of which remained—that had been lost in one of the house's cupboards when the family of Somoza's Minister of Agriculture had fled for Miami. The dwarf Manzano grasped his cup's handle with inevitable delicacy and moved his lips closer to sip the coffee that had been prepared Cuban style—thick and loaded with sugar. As he did so, he watched La Chaparra with a sympathetic twinkle in his eye, signaling to her that everything had been arranged in a satisfactory way.

Doña Fabiola had resisted him a little at first, claiming that they were treating her unjustly, accusing them of stealing what was rightfully hers, and she had even pretended to cry. There is no injustice here, Doña Fabiola, no stealing. You should consider yourself fortunate that you're not in jail. And after blowing her nose and drying her tears, she eventually accepted the deal: she willingly turned her companies over in exchange for keeping the house where she lived. And as for the dwarf Manzano, he had even allowed her to keep her car: *"Implacable in battle, generous in victory,"* as the old revolutionary saying went. Chaparrita, at 11:00 this very morning you can stop by the lawyer's office to sign the legal papers, and the only thing remaining will be recording the transfer documents in the public registry, but that's just a formality at this point. All the accounting records are in order, and the auditors from the General Directorate of Revenue will be waiting for you this afternoon at Ciudad Jardín in your offices—and I mean *your* offices because they are unquestionably yours. I told them to be there at three so that I would have time to give you every last sheet of paper along with all inventory records, bank statements, customs permissions, receipts, invoices, and checkbooks.

"There's just one other thing: the next step will be merging all these companies, which are involved in so many diverse areas, into one corporation. The lawyer has already been told about that."

"So this new corporation is the one you said you'd be taking over with me. All I can say is a thousand thanks, commissioner," La Chaparra smiled.

"I'll just be there to provide support so you don't feel alone," said the dwarf Manzano, returning the smile. "And to ensure that no one tries to go above your head or get you kicked out."

"I would love to have Pedro help me with the corporation as well, because we're getting married."

"Well, I'm very happy for you. What percentage do you want for Pedro? Since the two of us are splitting everything fifty-fifty, you and Pedro can divide your half however you wish. But I do expect a gift from the both of you, Chaparra."

"What gift can we possibly offer you? I'm embarrassed even to hear the words."

"Something trivial. It's nothing, really. One-percent of your shares for my last grandson, who's named after me."

"It will be as you say, commissioner. You arrange things as they suit you best, and that will be the best for us as well."

"You should understand that the lawyer will issue my shares in your name, including the small one for my grandson. You'll just endorse them to me. We'll avoid gossip that way."

"There's no such thing as a useless precaution," Pedrón interrupted.

"Congratulations to you both on the wedding. The time has long since passed when you should have given the boy your family name, Pedrito."

"Commissioner, can you do me a favor? Please don't call me Pedrito anymore. I don't want you to misunderstand me, but that's what the dead man used to call me, and I hated it every time he used it."

"I understand completely, of course. I'm not going to try to give you reasons to remind you how badly he treated you personally, nor how badly he treated you both."

"Shall we send you the company's monthly accounting report, or will you have an auditor in our office?" asked La Chaparra.

"I have absolutely faith in you, my dear, absolute faith," the dwarf Mangano assured her. "Just send me the quarterly reports, and that will be enough."

"Commissioner, I'd like to move on to another subject. I want you to know that Paquito came to see us at the house. He's the one from the ASP who had been assigned to Professor Zoraida."

"If he wants to come back, there's no chance. He embraces the life of a fairy more and more every day. She let him paint his toenails and fingernails, and she even let him get a mole on his cheek."

"He knows very well that there's no coming back. Mono Ponciano already hired him as a waiter at his gay bar."

"So what did Paquito want from you?"

"He actually came with a message from Professor Zoraida. She begged the government not to treat her so ungratefully, and she said that she is one thing while her son is another, and she wondered why she should pay for someone else's sins when she was always so faithful."

"How shameless can she be? She's still talking about faithfulness after her own shitstorm of a betrayal."

"She said that she used her learning and esoteric knowledge to neutralize every enemy plot and all evils."

"A wild old woman, an old fraud. She dares to say such things even after she and her son hatched a conspiracy to destabilize the government. And they almost did it: You both saw the trouble they stirred up and the cost of putting it down."

"The question that Paquito brought to us was whether the old woman could at least have her house back. How can you leave her homeless on the street, she asks, and thereby force her to live with her son's harpy of a lover?"

"They can go ahead and kill each other. I'd be more than happy to bury them both. Which brings me to something else. How did you even come to meet Paquito?"

"He's the poet Lira's nephew," Pedrón intervened. "The poet is my friend, the one we recruited for the corona-of-fire operation."

"Your friend is irresponsible. His face appears uncovered in the videos that are showing all over social media. The only thing missing is that he never shouted out his name and address."

"I warned him and Cara de Culo a thousand times that they should never take off their bandanas. But the poet is a poet, and he says that a revolutionary's duty is to perform his role in broad daylight for all to see."

"And to top things off, Cara de Culo wanders out-of-control from cantina to cantina," the dwarf Manzano complained.

"He went a bit crazy with so much money in his hands. His mill doesn't stop grinding until he has nothing left to drink."

"I'll have to hold him captive for a bit until the people have forgotten him, after he sobers up and the scandal dies down. As for the poet Lira, we'll have to send him to Cuba to cool off as an attaché to the embassy press for at least a year."

"He can't complain that you're sending him on vacation as a punishment. He can lie down on the white sands of Varadero Beach. Maybe the time off will give him a chance to finish his book."

"Are you saying that he really is a poet? I thought people just called him a poet because people around here will call almost anyone a poet."

"Guinea pigs would be jealous of how fertile he is. He's compiling a series of poems to honor the Trees of Life. That's his next book."

"Tell him to avoid that subject. A book like that would probably be seen as unwise."

"But aren't the Trees of Life sacred and therefore deserving of praise and reverence?" La Chaparra asked, confused.

"Not anymore. Don't you understand that they were recommended by Professor Zoraida, a traitor?"

"So the Trees of Life are a betrayal, commissioner?" Pedrón said, even more confused.

"Exactly, my young friends. Professor Zoraida and Tongolele worked together to convert the trees into a dangerous weapon for the counter-revolution."

"Commissioner, do you mean that all those trees the rebels pulled down are going to be left on the ground?" asked La Chaparra.

"The answer to that question lies with *You Know Who*, according to the pronouncement of the new spiritual advisor."

"Has the new advisor already been chosen? And announced?"

"I've been given the green light, Chaparra. After a highly selective search, I've recommended Professor Kaibil."

"I've never heard of him."

"That's because I'm bringing him from a foreign country. He works in Guatemala, but he studied in India. He was the great guru Asaram Bapu's favorite disciple."

"Then I'm assuming that this Professor Kaibil wears a turban and a robe," said Pedrón. "And he'll have his own cobra. And a flute."

"This man is not some street magician going around making snakes dance at local fairs," responded the dwarf Manzano, reprimanding Pedrón with a look. "He's a man of science. I like his proposal to create a web of celestial antennas to absorb the waves of ether and transform them into protective energy."

"Across the entire country?" Pedrón responded in shock. "How many antennas would there be?"

"He's going to give me a proposal in writing. These aren't everyday antennas. They have flexible solar panels that look like wings."

"I'll bet all that energy could generate lots of electricity and power," Pedrón noted.

"The energy that these celestial antennas create can't be used for such things; the energy produces spiritual power."

"This Professor Kaibil is obviously a true modern sage," La Chaparra said admiringly.

"I used a magnifying glass to investigate him because I don't want to have the bitter experience of dealing with any more frauds. Professor Kaibil has served as the advisor to none other than President Jimmy Morales."

"The president of Guatemala hired him and brought him from India?"

"No, Chaparra. Professor Kaibil has lived in Guatemala for years. He met President Morales in a TV studio."

"Did the President own the TV channel?" Pedrón asked.

"No. The two of them worked there. Professor Kaibil presented horoscopes, and the president had a comedy show. Of course, he wasn't the president at the time."

"So the president acted like a clown?" La Chaparra asked.

"He was a comedian, which is different from a clown. His show was called Nito y Neto, and he ran it along with his brother. The show was about two small-time farmers—rancheros—who are quite likeable and filled with self-confidence. The President played Neto, while his brother played Nito. And the President always ended the show by saying: 'I'm Neto. I'm not a he-man; I'm a she-man. The ladies love me.' The audience died from laughter."

"I imagine that the laughter is what won the presidency for him," Pedrón agreed. "People love comedy shows."

"There's no denying that his popularity came from that program."

"Professor Kaibil is truly a tremendous acquisition. Congratulations, commissioner."

"He'll arrive tomorrow, and I'm going to let him live in the house that the impostor Zoraida left free. But even though this guru is trustworthy and comes highly recommended, I'll keep him under tight control, right down to every time he cuts a fart."

"You're absolutely right. We can't allow any more missteps or betrayals."

"That's why I'm here. And once again, I want to say that I'm especially grateful for your help in unmasking the traitor."

"We're the ones who can't express how grateful we are that you brought that colonel's investigation about us to such a sudden stop," La Chaparra smiled.

"Our dear little Colonel Pastrana loves the formalities. He didn't want to give up the investigation," answered the dwarf Manzano with disdain. "He's quite the believer in official reports and interrogations and red tape."

"We began the interrogation with confidence because we knew we had you behind our backs," said Pedrón. "But we eventually became nervous because the colonel adopted such a threatening attitude toward us."

"Officers like him are mass-produced in classrooms. They've never been tested in combat. They've never heard any bullets other than blanks in their entire life."

"Commissioner, don't you think that the colonel was trying to follow your trail? Because the shit could have hit the fan if he had ever asked us who was the brains behind the plan, the person who ordered us to carry it out."

"He might have caught a whiff of something, but people who sniff around too much risk losing their noses."

"We both sang him the same song: the old resentments we felt toward our superior officer drove us to come up with the entire plan ourselves. And no one made us budge from that story. Right, Pedro?"

"Your story actually contained plenty of truth, Chaparra," the dwarf Manzano agreed.

"Well, the truth is that like people say, we certainly weren't living fat and happy with him."

"The fact that he forced me to act like a lackey for his mother and his lover is true. That's not a lie I had to make up at all," Pedrón added.

"And the fact that he never tried to get me promoted or do the paperwork to get my service medal isn't a lie either. If you hadn't intervened on my behalf, commissioner, they never would have given me that medal."

"Chaparra, I began that process as soon as you told me about it, although I had to act carefully so that he wouldn't find out. Unfortunately, no one could process the paperwork for your promotion without his signature."

"Commissioner, we would be greatly relieved if that paperwork was just burned up," La Chaparra pleaded. "You never know."

"The two of you should just forget about that: the paperwork is dead and buried. I talked about it with Colonel Pastrana's superior, General Potosme, and we've taken care of the problem together."

"We still haven't been officially notified that the case is over," La Chaparra persisted.

The dwarf Manzano raised his feet to examine his boots, as if he were looking for something on them.

"General Potosme agreed to give me the paperwork, and I have it locked safely away in the bathroom archive."

"General Potosme's a smart man who knows which way the wind blows," noted Pedrón.

"There's no one who doesn't fear the person who receives the Chinese box every day," said the dwarf Manzano, preening. "So, then, enjoy your reward in peace: You've more than earned it."

"Commissioner, without meaning to pry into affairs that are none of our business, please excuse me for asking a question."

"Go ahead, my esteemed colleague. I welcome anything you'd like to know or any advice you'd like to give. You two should consider yourselves my special advisors."

"Since you've given me permission to ask, what's going to happen with Inspector Morales and Doña Sofía? She saw my face, and she discovered everything else on her own. So she knows where the information we leaked was coming from."

"We're still in a state of emergency. There are many things to worry about, many priorities," answered the dwarf Manzano.

"The problem is that The Mask keeps tweeting. And the tweets are very aggressive. Inspector Morales and Doña Sofía are taking advantage of their followers to spread falsehoods."

"I know, but they're not the only ones. We have a lot of anti-propaganda work ahead."

"The rebels keep repeating on social media that more than 100 people have died," Pedrón interrupted.

"That's the first thing I have to neutralize, and we have to make thorough use of friendly countries' technology to do so."

"I already noticed that you're modernizing everything. I saw Vladimir. The Russian project is finally underway."

The dwarf Manzano smoothed out his combat jacket, checking to ensure that the fabric had no wrinkles.

"It's an area that had been completely ignored. Your leader was none other than Fred Flintstone."

"That ignorant man was certainly born before the Great Flood," La Chaparra agreed. "He was afraid of everything related to cyberspace."

"The first thing we're going to do is create a professional team of trolls to attack enemy propaganda. I've already named the task force 'The Gadflies,' like the Spanish TV and streaming show."

"Well, we have to use all these new resources against The Mask," La Chaparra said enthusiastically. "Those videos you mentioned before, the ones where the poet Lira and Cara de Culo show their faces, have been the most viral."

"I've already studied that case. And I've been asking myself whether those videos are hurting us or helping us."

"I'd say that they're hurting us," responded La Chaparra, shrugging her shoulders. "It's obvious."

"I disagree. If we're talking about Tongolele, I want people to know that there's no forgiveness for traitors. If we're talking about the factory fire, the message is the same: those who refuse to cooperate will face the consequences."

"So, you don't even plan to troll those tweets?"

"Why should we get involved with them? Why should we interrupt their little game? The more 'likes' that people give those images, the more fear they cause."

"Regardless, Inspector Morales can't be ignored," Pedrón said. "If I were you, I wouldn't take my eye off him."

"I don't take my eye off anyone. But I don't waste the ammo in my backpack on every gecko I see."

"And don't take your eye off Doña Sofía either," La Chaparra requested. "She has everything in her head: She knows everything related to operating systems, software, apps, trolls, fake news, hacking, cracking, and smart mirrors."

Once again, a smile began to paint its way around the dwarf Manzano's eyes and mouth, a smile that seemed to be drawn with a moderately fine brush.

"Well, I'm going to use Doña Sofía in the future. I'll send her false information so she can have some fun with her tweets. I'm going to help us by doing what everybody calls planting alternative facts."

"And as for Inspector Morales, are you going to let him open his detective agency again?" Pedrón asked.

"As long as I have him under surveillance, he can do whatever he wants. The truth is that I don't understand why you're making such a fuss over him."

"Because he's a dangerous S.O.B., as I've already warned you. He proved that in the case of the industrialist Soto's stepdaughter."

"I was studying that file. I didn't see anything professional there, just Tongolele using his power to do personal favors and expecting a millionaire to reward him."

"The orders to help Soto were delivered in the Chinese box," Pedrón insisted.

"I'm not convinced about that. At this point, we can't be sure how much of what Tongolele did was what he chose to do on his own and for his personal benefit. Exiling an old man—and a cripple to boot—was an abuse of power."

"But crippled or not, Inspector Morales came back to the country illegally. That's why he was put under surveillance."

"A pair of agents followed him from El Espino to San Roque, then from there to Dipilto Viejo, and afterward a new pair trailed him to Ocotal. Next, two new men followed him from Ocotal to Sébaco, then from Sébaco to the Divine Mercy Church. Men, travel allowances, fuel. A waste of resources."

"You need to remember that all those things happened because he was the person we chose to receive and spread the messages," intervened La Chaparra. "If things had been done another way and we hadn't known his final destination, we couldn't have gotten the messages to him."

"And what would have happened if he had decided to stay in Honduras? My plan to pressure Tongolele and bring him down wouldn't have worked."

"We knew that Inspector Morales would come back whenever the opportunity presented itself. We heard his conversation with Doña Sofía when she told him that his lover's cancer had come back."

"And we knew where Monseñor Ortez had sent him to hide in Managua," Pedrón added. "The monseñor sent him along with a recommendation to Padre Pancho, the priest at the Divine Mercy Church. The monseñor's sacristan, who also worked as his driver, told us all that, so we had the monseñor's operation infiltrated."

"And that was the same day that the monseñor was punished, for having a filthy mouth," laughed the dwarf Manzano. "The only problem was that Abigail has a heavy hand, and he hit the monseñor much harder than necessary."

"I've never seen anyone so confused as our dead man when I told him about the pipe attack," said La Chaparra, laughing too. "And it was hilarious when he ordered me to investigate every single thing I already knew."

"We had to hurry the nuncio along with the monseñor's transfer to Rome," said the dwarf Manzano. "And the blessed Mask helped us do that too."

"As you see, commissioner, everything turned out as planned. So, there's no reason for you to complain," La Chaparra continued laughing.

"And to be precise, Tongolele didn't know anything about Inspector Morales' return from Honduras," said Pedrón. "We made the surveillance arrangements behind his back, pretending that the orders were his."

"Regardless, it would have been much easier to go directly through Doña Sofía. Didn't you have her handy, knowing exactly where she was? And haven't you two said that she was the real brains behind everything?"

"She never lifts a finger without Inspector Morales' authorization," La Chaparra declared.

"Fine, fine. We gain nothing by talking about what might have been but didn't happen. Even though she did all that work for free, you got her to do it, and things worked out well. We were able to get our horses across the river."

"And now that we've made it across the river, we have to dismount," La Chaparra sighed.

"There's no way around that," said the dwarf Manzano, and the smile painted itself across his face once more, although with a higher-quality brush. "Sometimes we have to sacrifice the best riders to win the race."

"I've already trotted around for more than forty years. Now I'll find out how things go for me as a Turk, walking along the streets selling bloomers and brassieres," lamented Pedrón.

"Those are the things that interest you most," La Chaparra scolded him. "Your mind is always filled with morbid imagination."

"Well, please don't imagine fannies and boobies, but rather the respective articles of clothing used to cover those body parts," said the dwarf Manzano, reaffirming his pleasure by waving his feet, which didn't touch the floor, as if he had just been jolted by an electric shock.

"I'm old enough to walk around entangled in bad thoughts, Chaparrita, as you well know."

Having eventually calmed down from laughter, the dwarf

Manzano stood up and stretched to yawn, putting the interview to an end.

"The famous Inspector Morales and the not-famous-at-all Tongolele," he said. "Do you know what both of them are?"

"No, commissioner," answered Pedrón, paying exaggerated attention.

"Losers. That's what they are. Losers from the day they were born."

At that moment, three powerful knocks sounded at the door, which opened immediately. The aide stood at the threshold wearing all his adornments and carrying the Chinese box in his gloved hands, and the dwarf Manzano moved forward quickly to receive the box with all solemnity. He offered the aide a military salute, and the aide then handed him the box, snapped his heels, and turned back.

With the box in his hands, the dwarf Manzano stood contemplating the lacquered black top, where the female phoenix with extended wings used the talon of her right foot to attack the open-jawed serpent. The commissioner remained so lost in thought that he did not even wish his visitors farewell.

When La Chaparra and Pedrón went out to the hallway, the Russian brigade's workers were already inside the agency offices, removing computers from boxes and installing them as intelligence officrs stood against the walls and observed the work in progress.

As the couple arrived at the deserted anteroom and looked for the exit, darkness began to fall outside as if night were coming, even though it was still daytime. Outside, a far-off thunderclap resounded. A stiff wind whipped through the yard's Indian laurel trees, and their swirling leaves fell into the empty pool. Suddenly, enormous raindrops began to double their strength, landing wildly as they pounded the roof's zinc sheets.

"Look at this, it's raining in the middle of summer and at this time of the day," said the sergeant of the guard as he caught up to them at the door to give Pedrón the keys to the Kia Morning taxi.

"I'm not the owner of that taxi," said Pedrón, stuffing his hands in his pockets as if the keys were embers capable of burning his palms.

"Commissioner Manzano's orders," declared the sergeant. "He says the car is yours, but you need to remove the taxi insignias from it."

"Take the keys. What are you waiting for?" La Chaparra urged Pedrón.

They ran to the Kia and Pedrón started it up. It had enough gas. He turned on the windshield wipers, even though the rain had begun to stop, and the sun, suddenly resplendent, made the fine drizzle sparkle as it fell.

The lawyer's office was in Managua's Bolonia neighborhood, close to the Japanese embassy, so they could shorten their drive by taking Jean Paul Genie Avenue until they arrived at the university roundabout.

"You saw it. That slippery dwarf kept the case file for security."

"A message sent via signals, Chaparrita. That's how he warns us that he has us by the throat if anything goes wrong."

"And he does all that after the risks we took to recommend him. If not for us he'd still be where he was before: becoming an old man."

"And I believe he loves his new job. He does everything; he controls everything; he orders everything. At least Tongolele's gone."

"The higher they leap, the harder they fall."

"And you really believe these astral kites will work and bring protective cosmic energy to Nicaragua?"

"They'll work as well as the Trees of Life."

"As far as I'm concerned, Professor Kaibil's days are numbered."

"Whose days are most numbered? Professor Kaibil's or the dwarf Manzano's?"

"You're better off setting some money aside from our new companies. But be careful about it. You never know when we'll be in for a sudden surprise."

"I'll start as soon as I set foot in the offices at Ciudad Jardín. After all, the ocean carries off the sleeping shrimp."

"That's the way it's always been, and that's the way it'll be for century after century," said Pedrón.

"Amen," La Chaparra agreed.

EPILOGUE

And they worshipped the dragon which gave power unto the beast: and they worshipped the beast, saying, Who is like unto the beast? Who is able to make war with him?

Revelation 13:4

A God Who Feeds on Cadavers

INSPECTOR MORALES AWOKE when he heard the phone hit the floor after it had slipped from his hand. He crouched down to pick it up, then grabbed his cane, ready to stand. But before he got to his feet, he took a moment to examine the cane's handle, which had been carved to resemble a jackal's head, with pointed ears and snout, as if the head were interrogating him.

When Chuck Norris, Managua's DEA station chief, had been transferred to Kabul, he had left the cane—bought in Cairo—as a gift for the inspector. The jackal's head represented the Egyptian god Anubis, one of the oldest gods in the world. He was known as a carrion eater, for Anubis fed on cadavers.

Everything with Chuck Norris had taken place more than twenty years ago, and the Taliban had killed him during an ambush along the Pakistani border, an event Inspector Morales learned about only years later. He could not understand why he was thinking about the ancient god of death at that precise moment, but he felt burdened by depression, as if taking his next step would be a task that demanded too much from his body. Lord Dixon reprimanded him for his melancholy sentimentality. After all, today was his wedding day.

He approached the bedroom door. Fanny was still asleep, snoring softly with her mouth half-open. Perspiration had made her make-up run down her face, and the black of her painted-on eyebrows—her real ones having fallen out, like her hair—had become smeared across her eyelids.

A walker stood beside the bed, while bottles and boxes of medication crowded the nightstand. Everybody in the world, neighbors and acquaintances, prescribed Fanny different remedies for killing cancer, along with vitamins and tonics to strengthen her defenses and create antibodies, and she added all these products to those she found by herself on the Internet.

Inspector Morales then walked toward the small backyard, which was jammed with plants in clay pots and served as the area for hanging clean clothes to dry on zinc or tin roofing sheets. The yard was a rectangle enclosed from above by iron bars, like a roof, to deter thieves. A common green iguana—a garrobo lapo—was calmly sunning itself on the wall's edge.

Inspector Morales raised his face to look at the bit of 3:00 p.m. sky that the bars separated into squares, but the light dazzled and hurt his eyes. He shut them tight, and like a lightning bolt he saw Chuck Norris wearing fatigues, doubled over in the back seat of a burning SUV on the shoulder of a rocky roadway, alongside a poppy field that stretched out until it was lost in the distance, a soft red wave combed by the wind. Then with another lightning bolt he saw Tongolele lying against a barricade in a street lined with closed doors, the corona of fire burning around his neck, and even the inspector's nostrils could sense the scorching heat.

He was making his way back to the house when he stopped, his attention drawn by some music. A neighborhood radio was playing an old Colombian vallenato song, dance music that awakened his oldest memories, the accordion's bellows folding and unfolding provocatively and insistently, opening the way for festive rhythms to enter his ears:

When I crawl drunk from bar to bar I do not think of death.
I'd like to grab death close and file a formal true complaint.
For death ne'er stops its hunt for me: I fear it in my heart.

He heard Padre Pancho's deep voice at the front door, followed by the voice of Doña Sofía, who had opened the door to welcome in the priest.

Don't forget that I'm right here beside you, said Lord Dixon, and the inspector felt the affectionate weight of his friend's hand on his shoulder.

San Isidro de la Cruz Verde,
June 2019—December 2020